THE WO[...]
IN SAN CARLOS

A Novel

MARTIN WILSON

Copyright © 2023 by Martin Wilson

All rights reserved. This book may not be reproduced or stored in whole or in part by any means without the written permission of the author except for brief quotations for the purpose of review.

This is a work of fiction. Names, characters, places, and incidents either are the product of the author's imagination or are used fictitiously. Any resemblance to actual persons, living or dead, events, or locales is entirely coincidental.

ISBN: 978-1-960146-11-3 (hard cover)
978-1-960146-12-0 (soft cover)

Edited by: Karli Jackson

Warren publishing

Published by WARREN Publishing
Charlotte, NC
www.warrenpublishing.net
Printed in the United States

*For my best friend, Peter McGill, recently deceased.
Peter shaped my life and my sense of humor.
Also for his son, Owen, who predeceased his father.*

CHAPTER 1

Donald Has an Idea

IN APPEARANCE, DONALD PLUM was an unremarkable, slightly lumpy man of average height with a pasty face and a shock of curly black hair. He smiled a lot, smiles that were forced and insincere. At the same time, he crinkled his eyes in an attempt to charm. It would have pained him to know that almost everyone on first meeting thought him untrustworthy. He talked all the time about himself, about what he liked, and about what had happened to him. In sum, his personality was bland and self-centered.

He was forty-four years old and strove to keep his age secret. The only people who had really known him were his parents, and they had both died when he was in his late twenties. Donald had been their only child. Donald was now a cosmologist and mathematician who had, when he was a boy, imagined himself to be the reincarnation of Einstein. He even had the hair! He had, in fact, been an extraordinarily clever child. But he was no Einstein. What Donald could do was follow Einstein's math. And that was rare enough.

He became a professor at a local university and began to establish himself as a teacher and researcher. In his day-to-day interactions with the world, he enjoyed showing off. He liked to present people with facts that were commonplace in his field of study. "Imagine traveling at three hundred million meters a second. A second!" he'd bark at anyone who would listen. "That's the speed of light, you know. Nothing can go faster. No one can imagine this. But neither can we imagine the very slow. How can anyone imagine a million years? We can't, of course, but this is the world I and my colleagues live in."

He was, however, not prepared to allow others to express wonder at the universe. And if people were particularly annoying, suggesting their feelings were inspired by some personal insight, he would throw out a couple of equations. The ensuing bafflement quickly snuffed out their imaginings. Oh, how he enjoyed the awe and respect that followed the equations. This was a private language only he and very few others understood.

"Solid, pedestrian, and uninspiring" was the verdict of his department's chairman, who had never taken an interest in any of Donald's equations. If Donald was the real deal, it would be brought to his attention soon enough. So Donald was tolerated and his research ignored. After a couple of years of this indifference, the ambitious Donald decided to concentrate on teaching.

It was a decision welcomed by the other members of the department. Teaching was the millstone around all their necks. Donald made tenure easily and quickly assumed a leading role in the affairs of the department. His youth and energy made his rise inevitable. Then he became active in a number of associated academic societies. He wrote a few short books on broad topics such as the big bang, general relativity, and time travel. None of his colleagues read them nor even knew he'd written them, but the books didn't disgrace the department and sold reasonably well before fading from public awareness.

Researchers in the field of cosmology simply ignored him. They were an exclusive bunch. They just didn't have the time to spend popularizing their work. And since insights tended to present themselves mainly to the young, it meant that the majority of established researchers spent most of their time exhaustively re-evaluating their past contributions, seeking their place in the cosmology canon. Older cosmologists tended to be resigned and philosophical about their lack of continuing importance to the field. "Priest" wasn't an altogether fanciful epithet for people like these. They made a religion of science.

So few people these days did any serious reading. Yet, somehow, everyone just seemed to know more about everything. The internet rendered internalization of knowledge irrelevant. The general public had become, over the last couple of decades, all-knowing, smartphone-clutching ignoramuses. This trend suited Donald. And the equations were an effective gatekeeper that kept out even the most determined of the know-nothings.

* * *

Donald lived in California. He had lived there most of his life. He had been there when the tech industry blossomed in Silicon Valley. He'd watched enviously as college kids with a few very ordinary ideas became fabulously wealthy. These kids weren't scientists—hell, some of them didn't even have an undergraduate degree. They were, for the most part, emerging adults who had made out like bandits.

And now the complexity of the internet had grown enormously, far outstripping expectations. It had outgrown its early origins and spread into almost all activities. Yesterday simply vanished. It became unimaginable, even for those who had just lived through it. In a few short years, the world had morphed into a digital universe of staggering depth and richness. Young people, of course, never having known anything different, were oblivious to life before the internet, and Donald couldn't help but be envious.

As part of Donald's busy life, he attended Rotary Club meetings in San Mateo, where he lived. One evening, after a fairly dull session during which the members discussed earthquake preparedness, he'd fallen into conversation with a corpulent, energetic, seemingly ageless businessman. This was a man who shared Donald's envy of the techies with their newfound wealth. His name was Bob Levy. He was, he told Donald, recently retired from the pharmaceuticals industry and was now pursuing a career as an entrepreneur. Donald looked him over, noting the tightness of his collar and his nearly bald, slightly sweating head, and asked, with the inevitable sly smile, what being an entrepreneur actually entailed.

"Oh, I'm always trying to put together good ideas with money. If someone has a good idea and can sell me on it, I take it to my investor friends and offer them the chance to bankroll it."

"Well, how long does that normally take?" Donald wanted to know.

His quizzical expression and slightly impatient manner implied he already knew the answer: Bob's participation would be minimal, and he would be paid handsomely for his brief involvement.

"It could take a lifetime," he told Donald seriously. "If the idea is truly great, I might want to take on running the business myself. The guys with the ideas always lose sight of the business objectives, and the enterprise invariably goes belly up. I've seen it time and time again." He laughed and grinned wolfishly. "In fact, so far I've never seen any other outcome."

Donald didn't say much after this. He recognized in Bob the same oily, superficial charm he himself exuded and wondered briefly about the man. He decided he quite liked him. He and Bob parted as friends that evening, and Donald went home wondering if he could come up with an idea for a business.

"This should be easy for me," he told himself. "I have ideas all the time."

**

They met again at the next Rotary Club meeting. This time Donald sought Bob out and invited him to a nearby bar for a chat. He noted with approval Bob's inviting and encouraging demeanor. Bob, for his part, seemed to find Donald's interest in establishing a friendship with him unremarkable.

"I've been thinking about what you do," he told Bob, smiling his slippery smile. "I have to say I find it fascinating."

"So what's your idea, Donald?"

Donald looked startled. "I haven't said I've got one yet," he protested.

"Only people with ideas find what I do fascinating," laughed Bob. "Come on, Donald, don't be bashful. I can see you've got something. What is it?"

"If I've had a great idea, you could get money for us to explore it?"

Bob accepted a business partnership with Donald without comment. "I'd have to convince the investors they were going to make money out of it. It can be as wild as you like. The best investors to snag are rich guys who are big risk-takers. The guys who can afford to gamble. Then, when the idea looks like it could work, we sell up and make millions. We are rich, the investors have the chance to make fabulous money, and everyone is happy."

Donald looked taken aback by Bob's ebullience. "I thought you said it could take a lifetime. This sounds as if it's only going to take a couple of weeks."

Bob, who was a big bear of a man, laughed and put his arm around Donald's shoulders. "For some entrepreneurs, it can take a lifetime. Five years is long enough for me. What's the idea?"

Donald, looking decidedly uncomfortable in the casual intimacy of Bob's embrace, shrank back and freed himself. Bob didn't seem to notice his skittishness.

"Well, Bob," he began, after he'd composed himself, "I'm a cosmologist, as you know. In recent years, black holes have been discovered and appear to be at the center of every galaxy. And now, along with black holes, wormholes are coming into the picture. These are singularities that allow travel at speeds greater than that of light, and that, in turn, allows time travel. If you're interested, I can rough out the math for you. Anyway, my idea is to target items of technological, medical, and scientific interest from the future of a parallel universe. We can have these items delivered through a wormhole to us in the here and now. Ultimately, I suppose we could travel to the future through these wormholes, but that technology is not quite in place yet. For the time being, we will just have to settle for objects to come our way. Wormhole creation is not well understood, and the fact I can produce one will put our company at the very cutting edge of progress. Just think about the benefits of seeing the future. The payoffs will be enormous."

Bob looked at him, perplexed. "Are you joking? Connections to another universe? I know I said 'wild' and 'far-out,' but it can't be actually crazy."

"No, seriously Bob, the math is there. I'm certain I can do it."

Bob's face settled into near immobility. He looked Donald over with a kind expression. "Okay, Donald, this is the plain truth. For something like this, you have to have unimpeachable proof. Is this wormhole something you can look at?"

"It's got a portal. I've calculated its position. You know what a portal is, Bob, don't you?"

"A door?" answered Bob faintly and uncertainly. He entered the new and fantastic world Donald was describing with reluctance. He wasn't ready yet to abandon common sense no matter how brilliant Donald was.

"Exactly, Bob. It's a door. A door to interuniverse communication. And the universe I'm communicating with is practically identical to ours. There is almost an infinity of parallel universes. But notice the word 'almost,' Bob. That's a very important word. What, after all, is infinity? Can anyone imagine it?"

"Something that goes on forever?" asked Bob more confidently.

"Exactly. But can you imagine it?"

Bob looked back at Donald, his fat, unlined face a testament to a life spent avoiding perplexity. "I can't, Donald. I can think of going round and round in a circle, and that can seem like forever. But the fact we're mortal puts forever out of reach, doesn't it?"

"You've got a brain, Bob. There's no doubt about it."

Bob looked pleased at the news. "You think so?" he asked hopefully.

"Of course you have. Most people on being asked to imagine forever would be struck dumb. But not you. You thought of your own mortality. You thought of a circle, a profound insight. And there's math behind that as well. Let's get back to 'almost.' I'm calling the company Almost Infinity because that is something we can imagine. What do you think about when you hear those words?"

"Something very large or something going on for a very long time?" ventured Bob, uncertain once again.

"Exactly. A googolplex to the power of a googolplex. But at the end of all the fancy descriptors, you can always say: plus one. So none of this is infinity. That's what makes my math different, Bob. I'm excluding infinity. It's a bogus concept anyway—imaginary, like heaven and hell. With my new math I've constructed a wormhole portal. The technology, of course, is still in its infancy. The universe I am in communication with is very much like ours. Time, or should I say time travel, is the exciting point here. Forward to the future or backward to the past. Obviously for the company to make money, we'll have to go forward. Let me see what I can bring you."

He suddenly stood up. Bob looked up at him, surprised at his apparent intention to leave. He didn't think the conversation was anywhere close to a conclusion. Donald's body language radiated decisiveness and impatience. "Okay. So we've got a name—Almost Infinity—and you want proof of the portal, so I've got to fish something out from our almost identical parallel universe, from its future, of course."

He shook Bob's hand and walked quickly away.

Bob watched him go. He smiled to himself. That was one queer bird! He had to admit though, he'd been impressive in his decisiveness, and he'd left Bob with the impression he'd just made, or was on the verge of making, some tremendous breakthrough. And he'd agreed to provide material proof! That was going to be very interesting. He wondered if he'd show up with anything the next time they met. On balance, he thought, probably not. It had been an interesting evening anyway, and Bob didn't have to do anything but wait.

***

A great future had been predicted for Donald when he was a child; his parents spoiled him and made a great fuss over all his small accomplishments. When he was eighteen, he made his parents very proud when he gained a place at Harvard, which, of course, was no small accomplishment. Donald went, in their eyes, from being a bright kid to, potentially, being a world leader in mathematics.

At Harvard, Donald rubbed shoulders with some of the leading mathematical minds in the country. His abilities were ruthlessly assessed. They decided he was rather ordinary. Good enough for teaching at some institution of higher learning, just not at Harvard. He was awarded a bachelor's degree and encouraged to pursue a career somewhere else.

Research was all he claimed to be interested in, and he enrolled in a PhD program at San Francisco State University because, as he told his few Harvard acquaintances, he had to be near his parents in order to look after them. He concealed from them the fact that Harvard had no interest in retaining him as a graduate student. The arc of his life as a prodigy had been brief and narrow. Donald was awarded a PhD from San Francisco State and then became one of the university's youngest faculty members. Shortly after he'd joined the faculty, his mother had died of cancer. A year later, his father had a heart attack and died while walking on one of the trails around his neighborhood.

Donald was plunged into clinical depression by these developments. His life became increasingly lonely. He had told flagrant and obvious lies all his life; this was his incipient *pseudologia fantastica*. But his parents had helped him, and it had never gotten out of control. They thought of it as the price to be paid for a brain that was always throwing out new ideas. With their deaths his condition had morphed into the full-blown disease. Now lies just poured out of him. No one, of course, had the faintest idea of what was wrong. Everyone assumed the lying was volitional, which for individual lies it was. But the pathology lay in the outpouring. Initially the lies propelled him to the center of everyone's attention, and that pleased him. But as time went on, the lying became tedious, and people stopped paying attention.

He was aware he was ill. But he had no idea what was wrong. He didn't look for help; he thought he could live with it. One fortunate effect of his resulting ostracism was that he gained a measure of control over his malady. Now the volume of lies diminished, and the lies he did tell were usually associated with self-promotion. He developed his sly, insincere smile as a reflexive shield for his constant mendacity. Strangers found him impossible to read. So this was the man Bob had chosen to cultivate in his quest for exciting business ventures to promote; this was the man Bob was going to introduce to entrepreneurship. It was, by any measure, a very interesting choice.

* * *

Bob invited Donald to meet him on his boat in Sausalito. Donald turned up at the harbor. The sunshine touched the little waves with tiny sparkles, and a cool, light breeze wafted over the water. The air was fragrant, redolent of the sea and of all the flowers festooning the harbor. It was absolutely jam-packed with boats, but there didn't seem to be many people about. Bob welcomed Donald with a glass of white wine and invited him to sit on the comfortable chair he'd placed on the deck in anticipation of his arrival. It was late afternoon. Donald sat down and sipped at his wine. The sun played gently over his face.

"This is heaven, Don, right?" asked Bob, grinning at him.

The pseudologia fantastica flared into life. Donald smiled his smile.

"Practically used to live like this when my parents were alive. My dad used to sail an eighty-footer. We spent months going up and down this coast."

"Eighty-footer," repeated Bob respectfully. "How old were you then?"

"Teenager."

"What about school?"

"Didn't worry about school."

"Your mom go with you?"

Donald nodded. "Neither Dad nor I could cook." He laughed. "We really needed her."

"Wow! Eighty-footer! How did your dad make his money?"

"Stocks. Made killing after killing."

"And I'm guessing your mom was a looker. Those guys always get the best."

"I liked how she looked, Bob. But she was my mom. All kids like how their moms look."

"I expect you're loaded, Donald. You must have inherited your dad's wealth."

Donald shook his head. "He gave it all away. Left enough for me to keep the wolf from the door. But my dad believed in standing on your own two feet. So no, no eighty-footer for me."

Bob gazed respectfully at him, and Donald bathed in the fantasy he'd created. His dad had been a high school chemistry teacher and his mom a stay-at-home wife. The most time the little family had spent on the water was when they had taken the ferry to Alcatraz one Labor Day weekend. The Plums had lived a respectable, somewhat frugal existence. They had been, for the most part, happy.

Bob resumed his low-key inquisition. "So where did you go to college?"

Donald returned to reality effortlessly. For once, truth trumped fantasy. "Harvard." His knowing, superior smile faded and he regarded Bob seriously.

Bob, who had wanted to go to one of the top schools himself, looked Donald over with fresh envy.

"Harvard," he repeated, nodding as if he'd been expecting nothing less.

"Then I came back here to look after my parents. At the same time, I did a PhD at San Francisco State. Now I'm on the faculty there."

"Well, Donald, you're quite a guy. I really hope this idea of yours flies. Investors love Harvard."

Donald looked around casually, content at having established ascendancy over Bob. He took another sip of his wine and said: "Of course it will fly. Once I've got a vacuum chamber, I can create the portal. Then we can start pulling things through from the future. I need to get just a bit further along with the math first, though."

Bob sat there with a calculating expression on his face. He felt a frisson of excitement at the casual, assured way with which Donald had described pulling things from the future.

"Will you show me something you pull through? Can we show whatever you get to investors? Hell, this could be worth billions! Is anyone else trying this?"

Donald nodded slowly. "They might be. I tell you what I'll do, Bob. I'll do more than show you wormhole production—I'll show you the wormhole in action."

Bob stared at him. Donald was growing in stature by the minute! This was real escalation. This was daring! The wormhole in action, and he was going to see it!

"It's not dangerous, is it? I mean we won't get sucked out into the future or something scary like that?"

Donald laughed, pleased that Bob's imagination was engaged.

"We are too big to fit through the wormholes I'm making. No worries there."

"Well, Donald, if you want to go ahead with this, I would be pleased to be your partner. The first thing we should do is incorporate. You will be the CEO, and I will be the president and head of operations. We will each own fifty percent of the company. We've got a name. The only thing we need right now is a business plan for the investors, and I'll put that together over the next few weeks. I wouldn't recommend you give up your day job, though. Can you manage the both of them?"

Donald smiled at him, an impenetrable, foxy smile signaling acceptance of Bob's proposal and hinting at great forces stirring, world-shaping events in the offing. He could manage anything. He said nothing.

CHAPTER 2

A Company is Born

NIGEL AND HIS PROFESSOR were not on the best of terms. Kutti was Indian and Nigel was British. And here they were, sitting in a lab eating lunch together with their colleagues in mind-numbingly hot central Florida. Kutti held all the advantages in this environment. Nigel would never have admitted it to anyone in America, but, like many of his fellow countrymen, he looked down on most Indian scientists. After all, there were countless millions of them. He had been to a proper university in England, not some ragtag institution in sweltering Bangalore. Really, what could Kutti tell him about science? Still, in terms of the weather, he had to admit his boss was more at home here than he could ever be.

He'd been in the US for just less than a year. He'd come to Florida in January, and the weather had been chilly. There were even frost alerts for the orange growers. People joked with him about having brought the weather along when he'd arrived. The state of emergency had lasted for six days, and since then it had been brutally, unrelentingly hot. During those first few days, he'd acquired a bicycle and ridden it to work every morning. The exercise had been protection against the cold. Now though, in the searing heat, he always arrived at the lab dripping with sweat.

He had a visa for a year and was going to have to renew it soon. He wondered what he'd do if Kutti, his sponsor, washed his hands of him. And he was beginning to think, from his recent interactions, that was a real possibility. He always kept his eye on the want ads in the magazines subscribed to by the department, and so, after lunch one day, he went along to the departmental library and looked through the ads in the latest issue of *Science*. There was one that looked interesting: "Opportunity for go-ahead young scientists. Please, exceptional candidates only. Chance to work with elite professionals in exploring a new initiative. Interested in scientists of all disciplines but especially biologists, chemists, and cosmologists. Work in San Carlos in sunny California. The Bay Area offers you the chance to live the life of your dreams. Apply to Bob Levy, President, Almost Infinity Corp."

Nigel deconstructed the ad and decided he wasn't impressed. "Exceptional candidates only"? This he read as "Riffraff, please apply here." And cosmologists? What on Earth did that mean? He copied down the address, intending to prepare an application later that day. But he wasn't holding out much hope.

***

Nigel had a dinner date with Charlene that evening. She was a tall, bespectacled, good-looking brunette who worked as a research assistant in Kutti's lab. She was also serious, kind-hearted, and athletic, a recent graduate of the university that employed Kutti and where they were all now working. Over pre-dinner drinks he told her he suspected Kutti was going to fire him. Charlene, who hadn't noticed anything threatening in her boss's behavior toward Nigel, was disbelieving. "Come on, Nigel—has he actually said anything to you? You're imagining things."

But as it turned out, Nigel wasn't imagining things. The next week Kutti called him into his office and told him: "We like to give people a month to find new employment."

"You're ... you're giving me a month?" he faltered.

"Yes, we think it's only fair."

He would say "we." Who did Kutti think he was? The Queen? This was an Indian in America talking to an Englishman, for God's sake!

"Hell, I haven't even been looking for a job," Nigel said heatedly, forgetting his application to Almost Infinity. But that hadn't been a serious application in any case.

Kutti was unmoved. "Your replacement will be here in January. He will be taking over your stipend. You can use me for a reference."

He smiled, inviting Nigel to appreciate his magnanimity.

"Why are you doing this? Because you're afraid I'm going to show you up for the fraud we both know you are?"

Kutti's face grew grave. He wasn't used to such brazen hostility from his lab personnel. He considered himself an established senior figure in his field. But he knew Nigel was different from the people who normally passed through his lab. Nigel had a PhD from Cambridge. Kutti knew his PhD supervisor had died recently, and everyone knew about him. He was a famous man. If he'd still been alive, Kutti wouldn't have dared to fire Nigel. But without his protection, Nigel was vulnerable. Kutti stared hard at his enraged subordinate. Who was this pathetic nobody daring to show hostile feelings to a man of his stature? He drew himself up.

"We stand by our results," he said heavily.

Nigel sneered at him and stormed out. Kutti sat and thought about what had just happened. He wondered if he'd done the right thing.

Later that evening, when Nigel was alone with Charlene, he told her he'd been fired. The full weight of his predicament now settled on him. He was going to have to leave the lab and find another job—and he was going to have to do it quickly because, without a sponsor, he couldn't stay in the country. Charlene sympathized with him.

"If you're strapped for cash, you can always stay with me for a while," she told him.

He looked back at her, gratitude softening his face.

"I can't stay with you Charlene. I'll have to leave the country. My visa is expiring in just over a month, and without a sponsor I can't get another one. It's the end for me in this country, and it's what Kutti wants. I really despise that man."

Nigel expected Kutti to be vindictive, and he was. Kutti had a thin, rodent-like face, and Nigel was always put in mind of the vermin when contemplating the Indian.

"Crawled out of a rat hole," he'd told Charlene, the first time he'd slept with her.

Now Charlene offered to marry him.

"You can stay here, then. You'll be the husband of a US citizen."

Nigel was tempted. He knew he liked Charlene, but was she the love of his life? And was he the love of hers? He just didn't know. On the Monday of the last week before the start of his months' notice, he received a letter from Almost Infinity inviting him to San Carlos for an interview.

***

Bob Levy had been busy since meeting with Donald on his boat. He'd talked to two young lions of the IT world who'd dreamed up and then sold investors on the idea of using software to keep track of the bowel movements of babies and infants. They had even filed a patent application. Parents needed to know everything about their kids, didn't they? Especially when they were babies. Mothers wanted to know how their small charges were managing in the strange, new, and complex world of defecation, the poor things. The new software allowed them to easily record, characterize, and quantify excretion. Odds were presented on the likelihood of baby contracting various maladies. The software could be used to chart the daily, weekly, monthly, and yearly outputs of the little darlings.

"With our software, no trend can escape your attention. And is baby's diet okay? Our software can tell you. It's a fact that has to be faced: many serious diseases make their presence known by causing minor alterations in the pattern, quantity, and quality of defecation. And our software is now being used by top researchers! So please, try it. It will help you protect your precious offspring."

How could anyone with small children say no to that? They had raised an initial $5 million from venture capital and then, almost immediately, sold their company to Optifit, a health and fitness giant based in Palo Alto. Optifit had paid $100 million for the company, which the two founders had named Real Excretions Inc. As they had joked to the executives from Optifit, "Everything about us is crap!" They'd all laughed long and heartily over that.

So when Bob met the two young excrement pioneers, he'd had no difficulty selling them on the notion of a functioning wormhole.

"Our lives seem to be dedicated to things that come out of holes!" they'd exclaimed jubilantly. "This is a really good fit for our business model."

Bob jollied them along. They ended up investing nearly $5 million in Almost Infinity. Privately, they told themselves: "We've been lucky once. Who's to say it won't happen again?"

Bob then rented a large warehouse in San Carlos. Bob explained to Donald how things were going to proceed.

"We want a business filled with young, bright, creative scientists. You are going to be bringing artifacts from the future. I don't think this will be an easy sell for the bright young minds we want to attract. So first, we have to hire a couple of big shots. We want a couple of guys the young people admire. We'll set aside one percent of company stock as an ownership incentive, pay them a salary as good as or even a bit better than the one they are making currently, and generally treat them like royalty."

Donald looked dubious. "But will our investors be able to understand wormholes? I'm nervous about that."

Bob laughed. "Of course not. But that won't matter. We'll have world-famous scientists working here. They and the people they recruit will make discoveries, maybe in conjunction with the wormhole, maybe not. Who knows? Anyway, it won't matter. But first we have to get our research leaders."

"How are we going to find them?"

"I've got a buddy at Berkeley who can help us there. We just want a biologist, a chemist, and maybe a cosmologist."

In the event, they found their biologist and chemist quite easily. The biologist had recently moved to the Bay Area from his home country, Canada, where he had been retired from the Canadian Scientific Civil Service. He had done his PhD while in its employ and was now a couple of years shy of turning sixty. He enjoyed a worldwide reputation and was considered by many to be the world leader in plant cell biology. He was a good organizer and had an eye for work that was exciting and new. Bob asked him if he was interested in creating another research empire south of the border, and he said he was. The money made the offer irresistible to him. He was married with adult children living away from home. He expressed polite interest in Donald's wormhole and was not put off by Donald's strangeness. The fact that Donald had been to Harvard reassured him.

The man's name was Nils Jensen. His current means of support was the handsome pension he was being paid by the Canadian government. He and his wife had emerged from the frozen wastes of northern Canada after his compulsory retirement and had settled delightedly in the balmy brilliance of the Bay Area. It was an area he'd visited several times in the course of his career, and he already knew it slightly. He'd even lived here for three months while participating in an exchange visit with a professor from Berkeley. The professor had gone to his lab in Saskatoon to learn techniques Nils had pioneered, while Nils had come to Berkeley to write a review of plant biotechnology progress for one of the leading journals in the field. And now he was being offered the chance to work in this earthly paradise. Life had been kind!

Nils and his wife were Canadian with a Danish pedigree. The married couple had arrived in Canada when they were in their midtwenties. Nils was a brilliant and charismatic man, and when he took up his position at Almost Infinity, plant biologists around the world took notice. But very few people realized he'd been compelled to retire. They simply thought he'd gone on to a better opportunity.

It was a major coup for Almost Infinity to have attracted Jensen to its employ. Now, suddenly, many plant biologists were interested in working for the company. Jensen himself hadn't focused too much on Bob and Donald when he'd been recruited. He was a man confident in his own abilities. He knew, of course, that he was no cosmologist—but then he didn't need to be. He just accepted what he was told about Donald's idea at face value. With what they were going to pay him and with his pension from Canada, he and his wife Trudy would have more money than they had ever had in their entire lives. And now here they were, living in sunny California after so many years of long, brutal winters (cheerfully endured, admittedly). To Nils it seemed like a fair reward for all the years of unremitting scientific effort spent in a frozen wilderness. He really did deserve this.

The appointment of the chemist was less obviously a smashing success. The man Bob's Berkeley friend found for him was Japanese. He was living in Pittsburgh at the time of his recruitment. His name was Arthur Nanomura. Arthur had been educated in Japan and America and for the last twenty years had been working for a giant German chemical company in Pittsburgh. He didn't have the worldwide reputation of Nils, but among the small group of chemists working in his field, he was well-respected. He was conversant with many of the emerging trends in chemistry and the life sciences. He was very interested in molecular biology and was considered an expert in the chemistry of this field.

Arthur Nanomura knew two things about Donald Plum: Donald knew much more math than he did, and Donald had gone to Harvard. Arthur was forty-five years old and, unlike Nils, did have something to lose by joining Almost Infinity. By leaving his present employer now, he was forfeiting a substantial part of his pension, and he was also running the risk of being unemployed if Almost Infinity collapsed. But he loved California.

With the appointments of biologist and chemist settled, Bob turned his attention to that of the cosmologist. This was a trickier appointment. Donald would have to be heavily involved in this recruitment. Candidates were likely to ask many questions about wormholes, and they were not likely to be so easily bamboozled by Donald and his questionable math. They'd held interviews with a couple of local men not from Donald's university—interviews that hadn't gone well. The reactions of the candidates to the wormhole had shaken Bob's confidence in Donald.

Bob took himself off to the public library and skimmed a couple of books on wormholes. Several of the books had been written by a professor at a second-rate southern university. Bob mentioned these books to Donald and asked about their author. Donald was dismissive. "The man's not a researcher. He can't do the math."

Bob convinced him that the author was good enough for them. "He's written books. He'll be good with the investors. And anyway, we don't need another expert in wormholes. We've already got you!"

Bob contacted the professor from the southern university and invited him for an interview. Marshall Hunt came and quickly realized he would be the only one at Almost Infinity to have any real idea of what Donald was proposing to do. He was, of course, intimidated by the Harvard graduate. In the course of his interview, Donald had written out a few equations that he couldn't follow, a fact he was too embarrassed to admit. In a couple of the conversations he'd had with Bob and Donald, he'd allowed his incredulity to show. The two of them had just ignored him. It was as if they didn't care what he thought.

Bob was proposing to pay him almost twice his current salary. A lifetime of much greater wealth stretched out invitingly before him. So, in deference to the money and to the inferiority complex he'd developed regarding Donald, he'd suppressed his reservations, accepted his prospective employers' reality, and accepted the job. And the environment was just so seductive! Maybe he was brighter than he'd realized. He began to think of his own modest contributions to cosmology with more respect.

Marshall spoke to everyone knowledgeably about black holes, relativity, wormholes, the speed of light, Einstein's cosmological constant, quantum mechanics, and dark matter. He made it all seem so plausible. Everyone was very impressed with him. He was greatly preferred to Donald. The attractive women who popped up everywhere became a factor in how he thought about his new life since his recent divorce. No children, so it wasn't so bad—and at fifty-four years of age, he was definitely on the lookout for a new love interest.

Initially, a blonde named Connie had caught his eye. She had been hired to run human resources at the company. Everyone liked her.

Marshall thought of her as the quintessential California girl. And, in fact, Connie was a local. Connie had gone out to dinner several times with Marshall in the course of his move, and he had felt the first stirrings of a romantic interest. But Connie was a busy woman and, once Marshall was settled, had moved on from attending to him. With Bob, she had hired a financial manager to control budgets and also an IT consultant to help them put together their infrastructure. Finally, Marshall was forced to move on himself.

After two months in existence, Almost Infinity had acquired forty-two employees—twenty-seven with PhDs, including Nigel, who'd beaten Kutti's deadline for departure by two weeks. Bob spent a lot of time around the warehouse in San Carlos, supervising the build-out of their labs. Nils provided professional input. He had supervised construction of new labs several times in the course of his career. Thus, the labs were designed mostly with the cell and molecular biology of plants in mind. Arthur commandeered a small area in one corner of the warehouse specifically for his chemistry work. Donald rarely put in an appearance at the warehouse, feeling a bit shy about his exalted status in the company, and he especially wanted to stay out of Marshall's way. Also, of course, he still had to attend to his duties at the university, and so extended absences from Almost Infinity were to be expected.

He enjoyed the majority of his interactions with the younger staff, however, and he always turned up for the meetings of the scientific steering committee. This was composed of the three scientific directors, himself, and Bob. Occasionally, depending on the business to be discussed, the committee expanded to include Connie and the chief financial officer. Maria, Bob's executive secretary, made sure the committee meetings were appropriately attended.

With Bob leading them, these meetings were always enjoyable for Donald. Bob flattered him and treated his every utterance with great respect. Donald felt like the sultan of sultans with Bob as his pasha. Donald liked the word "pasha" and thought it accommodated Bob's corpulence. Bob the pasha. The word winked out at him through his pseudologia fantastica, encrusted with fabulous gems and the mysteries of the East. It was Donald's secret pleasure, his Turkish delight.

CHAPTER 3

Look What Came Out of Donald's Wormhole!

WITHIN ONE WEEK OF NIGEL taking up his position at Almost Infinity, the company received an application from Charlene for the position of research assistant. She had put down Kutti and Nigel as references. On receipt of the application, Connie had handed her résumé to Nils. Nils came around to see Nigel.

"Got an application from a friend of yours," he announced.

Charlene had told Nigel she was applying, and so he was ready to discuss her application.

"She *is* a friend, Nils," he told him frankly. "I want her to work with me."

Nils laughed. "A friend? That's nepotism, Nigel. And I was going to tell you, I also got a letter from Kutti warning me against hiring you. He said you were extremely mediocre, rude, and aggressive."

"I suppose it's true," said Nigel. "In his company I was all of those things. It was hard not to be, actually. But now, thanks to you and

Almost Infinity, I'm free of him. Charlene won't let us down. And it's cronyism, Nils, not nepotism. I mean, we aren't related."

Nils looked at him blankly and then gave him the thumbs-up sign. "You've got your wish," he smiled.

He left Nigel sitting there in his office. Alone, Nigel felt tears coming to his eyes. Some people are just so kind, he thought. He went home and called Charlene with the good news.

Of the three senior men at Almost Infinity, only Nils Jensen had sufficient stature to attract bright young scientists. Nils was first and foremost a plant scientist, as were all his recruits. Bob welcomed this bias and thought it boded well for the company. The goals of the company now shifted to feeding the world and providing sustenance for future generations.

One day Donald made a rare appearance in the lab. He was looking for Nils. He was carefully carrying a small white reference card, holding it in a horizontal position. On close inspection, minute white grains could be seen scattered over its upper surface. On further examination by Nils and then by Arthur, the two men determined that these minute grains were, in fact, grains of salt. Donald then told them this was the first item to come forth from the wormhole. Nils counted the grains. There were eighty-six in all. They held a meeting to discuss the significance of this first wormhole product. Present were Bob, Donald, Nils, Arthur, and Marshall.

"Eighty-six grains of salt, gentlemen," announced Donald, beaming around at them all. "What the hell does it mean?"

"How did you find it, Donald? I mean, what was the process like?" asked Marshall.

"I set up a pattern, a vibrational pattern of closed strings, and then when I'd got it just right, I pulled the vacuum. Then I was into a whole world of extra dimensions. I adjusted for the cosmological constant, and suddenly there they were, just sitting in the vacuum chamber. I didn't see them materialize, more's the pity. It was fantastic, almost unbelievable. I mean the math was calling for this outcome, but to see it validated before my eyes was very satisfying."

"I'd love to have seen that," said Marshall sincerely.

"Next time you can join me," said Donald expansively.

Marshall nodded and looked pleased. Clues from the wormhole! It was just so exciting. And it didn't seem so unbelievable. After all, it was just salt. Bob was wildly excited. This was the artifact Donald had promised him, and now he'd produced it. Bob watched the others at the meeting closely. Were they disbelieving and disparaging or accepting and welcoming? There was no doubt. Donald had won them over with his quiet, unassuming artifact. Salt! Who would have thought it? Now Bob believed in Donald again. The worrying skepticism from the cosmology candidates before they'd gotten Marshall was forgotten.

The news from the wormhole was transmitted to the rest of the employees by their directors.

"Someone from the future is leaving us messages?" asked Jeff, a molecular biologist. "We should get whoever it is to send us messages about gel technology."

Nils laughed. Gel technology? Typical of a molecular biologist to have such a specific, technical wish.

"We've got to meet it head-on," he told them all now. "Are we being asked to develop salt or drought-resistant plants? People in the future will know who we are and what we are trying to achieve."

"How thoroughly has the deposit been analyzed?" asked Arvik Roy, a plant pathologist from the University of Wisconsin at Madison. "We should make sure there's nothing there other than sodium chloride, shouldn't we?"

Nils looked appraisingly at him. "Right, Arvik. I'll get Arthur to check it out. I don't think any of us at the director's meeting thought about that."

They all laughed.

"Good catch, Arvik!" called out Jeff.

And everyone looked at Arvik reverentially, even Nigel, who was thinking: *Arvik's an Indian just like Kutti, but he's okay.* And in the sunshine of California, equality was in the air and a lifetime of learned prejudice was forgotten and Nigel was happy about that.

***

Nigel had hired two lab assistants. One was a small, pretty young woman with a wide mouth and bright eyes named Judy. She had a bachelor's degree in biology from a local college. The other, of course, was Charlene, who'd joined the company a week ago. Judy was a native Californian. She'd lived in the local area all her life.

One night, a couple of weeks after the first wormhole manifestation, Nigel, Charlene, and Judy went to a party at the home of Stan Lippowitz, a hard-charging molecular biologist who was widely recognized as a coming force in his field. Stan was only at Almost Infinity because Al Steptoe had recently joined and he knew Al and respected his work. For his part, Al had joined because Nils Jensen was there and he, like every scientist working with plants, admired the charismatic Canadian. He thought the two of them would be an exciting new force in the field of molecular plant pathology, which was Al's field. Al had given up a tenured faculty position at a major Midwestern university to join Almost Infinity. He had truly taken a leap into the unknown.

Al himself had a big reputation. He had attracted a bevy of young, up-and-coming molecular biologists, as well as several traditional plant pathologists like Arvik. Al was director of his own department. In Almost Infinity's hierarchy, he was Nils's equivalent, and he appeared that way in the official organizational charts Bob released from time to time. Nils and Al would have been a very considerable force if they had both been at the peak of their powers. Unfortunately, the Dane's star was on the wane. He was eighteen years older than Al, and his best years were definitely behind him. Al had recognized this reality shortly after joining Almost Infinity. Donald and Bob, however, continued to regard Nils as their most important scientist, which, from their perspective, he was. Nils's reputation in the world of plant biology was simply bigger than Al's. His was still the brightest star in Almost Infinity's firmament even if it was on the wane.

***

Nigel, Charlene, and Judy arrived at Stan's in Judy's little car. They arrived at eight thirty. The party was already roaring along at full tilt when they gained entry into Stan's apartment. Stan was nowhere to be seen.

"Where's Stan?" Judy screamed at a girl she recognized from the warehouse.

"In the back. He's in the hot tub," she yelled back.

"Oh wow! A hot tub!" And Judy took off immediately in search of the warm water.

Nigel and Charlene followed more slowly, negotiating their way carefully through the dancing bodies. They passed through the french windows at the back of Stan's living room and emerged onto the patio on which sat the hot tub. Stan and a couple of men, along with three women, were already in the water. Nigel stared at them, shocked. They were all stark naked. Judy stood at the side of the tub, slipping off her clothes. She climbed over the edge of the tub and into the water.

"Wow!" she yelled. "Come in, you two. The water's lovely!"

Nigel waved weakly at her, declining the invitation.

"Maybe later," he called. "It looks pretty full to me."

He and Charlene backed away cautiously. They passed back into the throng and stood for a moment looking at each other. Nigel had recognized all the hot tub participants as employees of Almost Infinity.

"What did you make of that?" he asked Charlene.

Charlene shrugged. "To each his own, I guess. I could never do that. I just wasn't brought up that way."

"Not even after you've had a few drinks?" Nigel asked hopefully.

"If I was drunk, then maybe I could do it. But I'm definitely not like Judy."

A couple of hours later Judy reappeared, toweled up and looking wonderfully refreshed.

"That was great," she told them. "Stan is such a hoot. And very important to the company," she added to Nigel. "He's really going places."

Nigel registered the information as a provocation. Was Stan really so important? He smiled back and said nothing.

Judy took them both home. She dropped Charlene off at the hotel the company was putting her up in while she looked for an apartment and then drove Nigel to his apartment. She brought the car to a stop outside his front door and turned off the engine.

"Jim and I have an open marriage," she told him seriously.

She watched him and waited. Nigel knew she was married to Jim, a much older man who was also an employee at Almost Infinity. Jim was a builder by trade and, it was rumored, a bit of an architect. He supervised all the small jobs that needed doing, such as installing equipment and providing office comforts to the scientists. He was also an autodidact and proud of it. He was, in Nigel's opinion, a lewd, half-educated loudmouth who was married to a woman young enough to be his daughter. He thought of him with a distaste that unfortunately spilled over to Judy. Nigel didn't know what Judy meant by an open marriage. He just nodded thoughtfully, wished her goodnight, and climbed out of the car. He took his leave hesitantly, noticing an air of expectancy about her.

He mentioned the exchange to Charlene when he saw her the next day. She knew what an open marriage was but, out of consideration for her brash new colleague, chose not to enlighten Nigel.

***

Bob told Donald they had already run through $2 million of the almost five invested by the founders of Real Excretions Inc. The burn rate at Almost Infinity was already approaching three quarters of a million a month. This meant they had to get more investors—and soon. Bob decided, in light of the way recruitment had gone, to focus on making his pitch to major agribusiness enterprises. And Donald had pulled grains of salt out of the wormhole, hadn't he? Nils had suggested salt and drought-tolerant plants could be indicated.

He was going to sell the wormhole to agribusiness executives. These men were like sheep, he thought. Snag one of them and the rest would follow. Two hundred million was the figure that floated into his mind. Hell, they'd actually be making money in ten years. He knew it was risky, but what worthwhile business venture was free of risk? He reviewed his contacts and decided to set up a meeting with All Grains, a major food and commodities supplier based in the Midwest. He persuaded them to receive him and Donald. They would fly out to Minneapolis and make a presentation in which they would describe the wormhole and all the brilliant scientists at Almost Infinity. He was going to introduce Donald to the All Grains executives and play up his Harvard pedigree. Then he, Bob, would promise them fantastic riches from the secrets revealed by the wormhole.

He would mention the Manhattan Project from the Second World War. He knew there were a couple of Germans in the All Grains leadership, but he didn't think they'd be offended. The Manhattan Project had, after all, saved the world. He imagined them sitting around their boardroom table, glancing furtively at each other. Patriots! That was what they all were, even the Germans! Men lucky enough to have control of money they could use to serve their country. He got a couple of American flag lapel pins and gave one to Donald. They would wear them to their meeting with All Grains. It was a small detail, but one Bob knew all the men around that table would remember.

Bob and Donald flew out to Minneapolis on a Monday morning. The most senior of the All Grains executives, the CEO of the company, was a spare middle-aged man named Tex Schumer. Bob knew him from his days in the pharmaceuticals business.

"Tex," he said familiarly and reached out his hand.

The other All Grains executives, on noting Bob and Tex knew each other, apparently as equals, instantly assumed postures of subservience. Bob introduced Donald to Tex and then shook the hand of every man present. This concluded, he turned and introduced Donald to them all.

"This is Dr. Donald Plum, the founder of our company and the sole inventor of the Almost Infinity wormhole."

Donald attempted a modest smile but failed to suppress the superiority always turning up at the edges of his mouth.

"Donald is a full professor at San Francisco State, by way of Harvard. He came back to the Bay Area to take care of his elderly parents, both, sadly, now passed away."

The Midwesterners looked with sympathy at the curly-haired genius in their midst. Donald looked back and didn't say anything.

Bob turned the presentation over to Donald, who began by talking about Einstein. Of course, he hadn't actually met him. Einstein had died before he was born. But Donald had met professors at Harvard who'd known him personally. And so the torch was passed. Donald gave the impression that had their lives occupied the same time period, then a meeting would have been inevitable.

"Particle fields in an oscillating, vibrating vacuum—this is what creates the wormhole. I have put together a device that creates wormholes routinely. The math is calling for a connection between the portal of a wormhole in the here and now with a portal some fifty years in the future in a parallel universe."

There was a quiet moment. Donald stopped talking, and the executives regarded him in mute wonder. Bob, looking at them all, felt a little uneasy.

Then, Helmuth Kuckuk, a senior man and German board member, asked: "So is this fifty years in our future or fifty years in the future of the parallel universe?"

"It's almost the same thing," said Donald, nodding appreciatively at him. He looked at him silently for a moment as if willing him on to a deeper understanding. "I can tell you today I've received the first tangible output from the portal. I got it a few days ago—the product of an experiment I conducted."

Only Helmuth understood what Donald was saying. He kept his eyes locked on the shaft of understanding shining out of Donald's eyes.

"So you've received something from the future?"

"I have!" Donald clapped his hands delightedly. "It's so cool. I brought it with me to show you."

"What is it?" asked Tex, speaking for all of them.

Bob looked uncertainly at Donald. He was going much further than they'd agreed back in San Carlos. He was actually going to show them something! He waited for Donald's next words in an agony of fearful expectation. He was going to tell them about the salt, wasn't he? He hadn't received anything else, surely?

"The math calls for fifty years into the future. But you have to remember this is fifty years on in a parallel universe." Again, he offered Helmuth an appreciative nod. "This is not exactly our universe. It is, however, a universe very close to ours, close enough for all practical purposes to be the same. As a matter of fact, gentlemen, there are a very large number of universes parallel to ours, but not, significantly, an infinity. And that's why we call our company Almost Infinity."

"So the stuff you got came from the parallel universe?" persisted Helmuth, sounding as if he could hardly believe he was asking such a question in the company of his colleagues.

"Exactly," said Donald, giving Helmuth the impression, with the forcefulness of his utterance, that the executive had just demonstrated a profound insight in theoretical physics.

"Now gentlemen, I'm going to show you what came out of the wormhole. You are the first people outside Almost Infinity to see this, and for obvious reasons we have to insist on absolute confidentiality. I know Bob sent you all confidentiality agreements in advance of this meeting, and I'm asking you now to hand me the signed documents."

Everyone passed their signed agreements to Donald. He made a show of doing a head count and then counted the agreements to make sure the numbers matched. He nodded and looked up.

"Okay. I think we're ready."

"Are you sure this is quite safe?" asked a thin, lank-haired individual with rimless glasses. "What if there's some infectious agent present? We have to worry about this all the time with grain shipments," he added apologetically to his CEO.

Donald looked back at him, seeing in the officious-looking spectacles and the man's thin, bloodless face the first faint outlines of the inevitable tidal wave of government regulations and howls of protest from outraged environmentalists heading in their direction.

"You raise an interesting point," he said smoothly. "Obviously, I can't swear to its safety. You have to decide whether or not you stay and want me to proceed."

Donald grinned and waited. The All Grains men, looking uncomfortable, remained. Donald reached down into his bag and carefully took out a small cardboard box. He placed the box in front of him, maintaining its horizontal status, and he removed its lid. They all stood to peer into the box. Inside, they could see a small white card. They stared, perplexed.

"There are eighty-six grains of salt on that card, gentlemen. Dr. Arthur Nanomura, our lead chemist at Almost Infinity, confirmed the chemical composition yesterday. I hadn't even told Bob about that." He laughed, thoroughly enjoying the general bewilderment. "Think about it, gentlemen. What does it mean? Well, we know there's a portal to fifty years in the future. Someone from that universe must have recognized it. Maybe, in the future, detection of these portals will be a trivial business. I'm actually working on this myself as a matter of fact. Anyway, the presence of the salt means someone has delivered this message to us."

"Why don't they just send us the documents, then?" asked Helmuth, belligerently. "That would be a lot clearer."

Donald nodded. "I've given this some thought myself, er ... Helmuth. You see, I think they could send us documents or a memory stick. The math, of course, is there fifty years in the future; I'm certain of that. It's practically here now, isn't it? So maybe they've placed an embargo on the transmission of detailed information. Maybe the preservation of free will is important to our ultimate fate. Maybe the math only works in a universe in which free will exists. So through the portal they can drop hints, but they can't instruct us because that would be denying free will its role in our present. That would be ripping apart the fabric of space-time. They've sent us grains of salt instead of something unambiguous. Now it's up to us to decide what to do about the message. Well, we've got Nils Jensen, and we're going to put him to work on this. He was the one who came up with our interpretation of the message. He's going to develop salt tolerance and drought resistance in crops. We will work with the confidence of the wormhole, which can be yours too, if you invest in us."

Tex looked at him sharply and then turned to Bob. "How can we be sure this is right? You're telling us salt and drought, but that's just your interpretation, isn't it? Or Jensen's? Why bring plants into it?"

Bob nodded his understanding of Tex's reservations and then turned back to Donald. Donald appeared unconcerned.

"This is just the first message, Tex. There will be more, and we will be able to put together a clearer picture."

Tex looked back at Bob and then nodded. It was the decisive moment of the meeting. Tex had given his tentative approval. He turned to his fellow All Grains employees.

"Sounds interesting boys, doesn't it? Salt from the future. One more thing, Bob. We'll be wanting to see this wormhole in action before we can commit to anything. We'll put together a team and send them out to you next week. I have to go now—I've got a meeting with the governor. Pleased to meet you, Donald. Later, Bob."

And he was gone.

The meeting finished shortly after Tex's departure. Bob realized the All Grains men were totally subservient to Tex and didn't want to do or say anything in his absence for fear of making a mistake. Light hearted levity was safe, and that was how they passed the remaining time. There were no more questions about the wormhole.

In the plane on the way back to San Francisco, Bob told Donald he didn't think it could have gone much better.

"We're going to get the money, Donald. I don't know how much, but I do know Tex. When he nodded, we were home free. But what about the demonstration, Donald? Are you going to be able to do that? We have to impress the hell out of them."

"Will Tex come with their delegation next week?" asked Donald.

Bob shook his head. "We probably won't see Tex again. Tex is at a level higher than us. I was quite surprised he came to our meeting today, actually. Something must have piqued his interest."

"You don't have to worry about the demonstration, Bob. It will go well. So you think we've got a chance with All Grains? How much? One hundred million?"

"Good times are ahead," said Bob firmly.

CHAPTER 4

The Wormhole Portal

NIGEL'S OFFICE, WHICH HE SHARED with five other employees, was directly off the cavernous lab in the warehouse. As he stood at his desk, he was immediately engaged in conversation by the garrulous Peter Blakely, a recent doctoral graduate in horticulture from the University of Wisconsin at Madison. Nigel's desk sat back to back with Peter's, so they faced each other when they were sitting and whenever he made eye contact, even for the most fleeting of moments, Peter would immediately start talking. This meant when Peter was in the office, Nigel spent every minute at work at his lab bench. Other employees, mainly lab techs, noticed his frequent presence in the lab and were impressed by it.

He went out into the lab now to escape Peter. He decided to make up a couple of liters of Hoagland's solution. In the large open lab someone had placed a boom box on the top shelf of a lab bench, and it poured out daily an unending blast of thudding bass and howling guitars accompanying dirges about murderers, suicides and bitches. Thankfully, the "music "was only one of the sources of noise in the lab and was, in fact, almost inaudible from where Nigel worked. It was largely drowned out by the background roar of laminar flow hoods and centrifuges. Judy's significant other, Jim, the elderly facilities director, had suspended a raft of sound-absorbing boards from the high ceiling of the warehouse. They didn't really do much, but Jim would tell everybody that life in there would be unbearable without them.

Nigel believed him. Nigel liked quiet labs. For him it was hell with or without the sound-absorbing boards, but at least the boards made it a manageable hell. What was unmanageable for Nigel was Peter's chatter. Just a few minutes in Peter's company was enough to guarantee him a headache. Now he saw Peter emerge from the office and head off purposefully, carrying a notepad. Some unfortunate soul was about to be deluged. Nigel slipped back into the office and sat down thankfully at his desk. Nigel was growing *Spartina townsendii* in the Almost Infinity greenhouse facility, which was up in Belmont a couple of miles from San Carlos and where he had just been. The company's "greenhouses" were a ramshackle group of old structures of glass and rotting wooden frames that Bob had rented from a local businessman. He was paying $20,000 a month to rent what they were calling, euphemistically, their greenhouse facility. Nigel had gone there to view the collection of scrawny shoots he was growing. He took out his company-supplied lab notebook now, an item that all scientific employees had assigned to them and in which they were supposed to keep a daily record of data in support of patents. He wrote today's date on the next empty page and then wrote below: "Spartina townsendii. Looks okay." He sat back and closed his eyes. It had been a busy day.

***

It was four thirty and Charlene was looking forward to going home. She was putting away the few pieces of glassware she'd been using that afternoon, having just washed them, when Stan Lippowitz appeared at the end of her bench. She knew Stan was a senior scientist at the company and knew him by sight but had never spoken to him. She was intrigued to see him at her bench, apparently intent on talking to her. He was not one to stand around gossiping. He fixed her in his gaze. She noticed his small, intense eyes.

"Fancy a beer?" he asked. "We're all going to O'Malley's. I'll take you in my car and then bring you back afterwards."

Charlene looked him over. He had a flat, expressionless face with a grayish tinge to his complexion—from all that work, she supposed. He definitely wasn't what anyone would call handsome. But he was charismatic. He just swept people along with his energy. It was only when you got to know him a little better that you realized he rarely socialized unless he wanted something. The last time Charlene could remember seeing Stan up close was at his party when he was in his hot tub. If he was aware of her having seen his naked body, he gave no sign now. She blushed slightly as these thoughts passed through her mind.

"Okay. Give me a minute and I'll be right there."

"In the parking lot," he said and immediately vanished.

Charlene thought about what she had just agreed to. She was going to go to a bar with him, probably spend a couple of hours in his company, and then negotiate a conclusion to the evening. She remembered how a couple of the girls in the admin offices had nodded and smiled when his name was mentioned. No one had said anything outright, but she had formed the definite impression that Stan was a philanderer. She thought briefly about Nigel. They'd slept together a couple of times when she'd first arrived in California, but he hadn't pressed himself on her. She wondered just how serious he was about her. Maybe he wanted an open relationship. Maybe he knew what that was now.

At O'Malley's, Stan was attentive to her. There was a smattering of the more senior scientists from Almost Infinity in attendance, and Stan introduced her to all of them. She felt, without quite knowing why, as if she were being promoted. Stan's passion for his work shone through brightly. There was much laughter and many derogatory remarks about absent colleagues. And some of it was really funny. She decided she was enjoying herself. Seven thirty arrived and people began to drift off home. None of the remaining people at O'Malley's seemed surprised that she and Stan had become a couple. Nothing was said, and she found herself being driven to his house.

In the car he suggested a session in the hot tub. He noticed her uncertainty.

"Come on, you'll enjoy it! It's really relaxing. We deserve it after working in that shithole all day. Why not? Don't you want to enjoy life? And afterwards, I'll cook you dinner. How about that?"

His insistence was unrelenting. She realized that if she refused, he would be angry with her. She hadn't read Stan very well, however, probably because she didn't like him. If she wanted to spend more time with him, she would have to refuse. But thoughts of a long relationship with Stan never entered her head. Finally, she acquiesced with a mute nod and wondered what the sex would be like. It turned out to be brief, rough, and for her, wholly unsatisfying. When it was over, there was no question of him cooking dinner for her. He took her back to her car in the parking lot and wished her a curt farewell.

She went to bed that evening feeling used and unloved. It was, she thought, probably how Stan made everyone feel. She wished she'd stayed true to her quietly positive feelings for Nigel. But the next day, the sun shone as usual, and the foliage outside her apartment looked green and fresh. A cool breeze wafted over her face as she sat by the open window looking out. The world, at least, looked bright and happy. She cheered up. One thing she decided immediately: she wouldn't be spending any more time with Stan.

Whenever they bumped into each other at work now, he gave her a conspiratorial grin as if to say: "I had you, didn't I?" She began to watch him and realized he grinned that way at quite a few of the girls at work. Charlene smiled back at him, grudgingly acknowledging his triumph. Privately, she hated him. He was just so unbearably arrogant.

For his part, Stan had been a little surprised she'd shown no interest in pursuing a relationship with him. But Charlene was unlike his usual conquests. She carried on as if nothing had happened between them. She smiled back at him, but that was all. Stan couldn't really understand it, but he didn't dwell on her aloofness.

***

Bob and Donald returned from Minneapolis like conquering heroes. They assembled Nils, Al, Marshall, and Arthur and began to plan for the visit of All Grains. All the scientific directors had hired supernumerary personal assistants, whom they brought with them to meetings.

Bob told his assembled team of directors and their personal assistants that a visit from a team of executives and scientists from All Grains was expected next week.

"This will be a crucial visit for the future of our company," he told them. "We will have to do our best to make their visit memorable. Even the smallest of details can be important."

He outlined the activities he had in mind. On day one, Donald would demonstrate the wormhole portal and retrieve something from the future. Then, in the afternoon, they would tour the labs and have meetings with all four directors. He was open to suggestions as to what they might do in the evening.

"These are Midwesterners," he told them. "They'll want to eat dinner by six, so we'll have to entertain them for the rest of the evening."

On the second day, he thought they could just relax and meet with a few of their brightest scientists: "We want to give them a feel for all the progress we are making."

They would have to leave for the airport by four to catch their flight back to Minneapolis. He went on: "These men have it in their power to ensure the success of our company for the next ten years. We simply have to make a good impression."

There was a collective moment of concentration while they thought about an evening entertaining the Midwesterners. It was Nils's assistant, Lynne, who had the best idea. She suggested taking them to the circus.

"It starts at eight p.m.," she told Bob. "I'm going to take my nephew. It's the Ringling Brothers and Barnum & Bailey Circus. They say it's the greatest show on Earth."

They all laughed upon hearing Lynne repeat the familiar slogan, mercifully obscuring the fact that she appeared perfectly serious.

"Well," said Bob, "why not? These hicks are from Minnesota, and the circus winters in Wisconsin, I believe. It'll make them feel right at home."

Again, general laughter. Lynne, however, was nodding seriously. Susan, Marshall's assistant, patted her hand and nodded affectionately at her.

"Great idea, Lynne," she told the older woman.

Susan's encouraging words sobered them all up. One or two faint smiles lingered, but the mood of the meeting grew serious again.

"George will organize this visit," Bob told them now. "He'll draw up and circulate their itinerary and make sure everyone we nominate is available for meetings."

George was George Nipper, a young executive Bob had hired who regularly came to work in a three-piece suit. He was physically small but possessed quite a large head. He looked old beyond his years. He was, in fact, in his late twenties. George had done an MBA at Yale, this after completing a chemistry degree at the Ohio State University. Before coming to Almost Infinity, George had been working for Bishop Inc., a large pharmaceutical company, in business development. At Bishop, he kept himself and his colleagues up to date with all the latest scientific and technological advances as well as maintaining a watching brief on all relevant business alignments. Now he was doing the same job at Almost Infinity. There was very little in the pharmaceutical, chemical, and agribusiness areas that got past George. He was an invaluable resource for Bob.

George was married and the father of three small children. The temptation to refer to George's children as "little nippers" was too great for almost everyone to resist. His wife, Victoria, however, didn't like it, a point she made by simply not laughing at all the cracks. Away from his wife, George made similar cracks himself, and his colleagues appreciated him not taking himself too seriously. George, everyone knew, was a bright guy. He and his family had been living in a suburb of Chicago before moving out to the Bay Area. They, like all the other employees who had been brought in from other parts of the country, were slightly disoriented by the constant stream of perfect, bright days parading past them, days that lit up the vibrant green foliage surrounding every home in the sun-kissed suburb in which they found themselves.

Victoria, a neat and personable woman just a little shorter than George, struggled to keep her feet on the ground in this new and highly seductive environment. She was a devout Christian and wasn't about to lose sight of what was important to her. She was also somewhat disturbed by George's new job. He'd told her about Donald and his portal to the future. Victoria thought it sounded sacrilegious.

"Man playing at God, George," she'd told him warningly. "It's never turned out well."

***

Donald got busy preparing the wormhole portal for his visitors. He got the workshop at the university to put together a large (two-foot square) heavy metal chamber with a thick plexiglass door. The chamber was completely airtight. He borrowed a heavy-duty vacuum pump and connected it to the chamber with a rubber tube thick enough to withstand the force of air pressure when under vacuum. Then he bought a car-racing game from Radio Shack. The game had a colored light display that played through a starting sequence—yellow, blue, green, and then four red lights. This he would place on top of the vacuum chamber and tell everyone that the display was providing the needed oscillations in the vicinity of the vacuum chamber to create a portal.

He decided to hold the vacuum for exactly five minutes, which he'd time with a lab timer. This would go off with a loud "ping!" when the five minutes were up. If anyone questioned the colored lights or the vacuum pump, he would simply blow them away with a few equations. He was going to conceal the items to be revealed under a flimsy cloth, which would be removed along with the air by the vacuum pump, and he was going to leave the interior of the vacuum chamber unlit to aid him in this subterfuge. Light, he was going to tell his visitors, would disturb the oscillations necessary for the entrainment of the portal.

Donald didn't dwell on the ethics of what he was doing. Arranging the demonstration provided its own reality.

* * *

Nigel was wondering what would emerge from the wormhole next. Eighty-six grains of salt—didn't anyone else feel that this result was unsatisfying? It was an ambiguous message and dangerous for a company like Almost Infinity. They could easily go down the wrong path. He'd tried to discuss it with several of his colleagues, but everyone seemed strangely incurious.

"But it's the basis for our entire company," he'd tell anyone he could get to listen.

Judy had pointed out the company was now comprised of a group of very bright, young, and energetic scientists who were certainly capable of finding ways to make money.

"We don't really need the wormhole," she'd told him.

He had to admit: she had a point.

The pace at which the company had grown was astonishing. More people were arriving every day. It was difficult even to keep up with all the new arrivals. The wormhole, under direction from upper management, remained top secret. People knew how sensitive knowledge of its existence was, and most of the new hires knew nothing about it nor its presence at the heart of their new company. When the old-timers (people who had been at the company for a couple of months) realized Bob and Donald were no longer talking openly about it, they also stopped.

"It's all perfectly logical," Judy had told Nigel. "They just don't want anyone else to know about our edge."

Nigel agreed. He'd read books about wormholes where authors wrote about them as if they were real, but he'd never heard of anyone actually creating one. That didn't mean it wasn't possible, though. Nigel was intelligent and well-educated like nearly all of Almost Infinity's employees. For them, wormholes were encountered only in science fiction. This was a field of science underpinned by advanced mathematics that very few people understood. It's the math that binds them all, decided Nigel. The math that exists in pristine isolation from everyday reality, separate from any physical phenomena.

Nigel, as he thought more about this, realized the mathematicians and cosmologists who dealt in the purely theoretical could get away with practically anything. It could all be, Nigel decided, one massive swindle. He reviewed his reservations now and set them aside. Wormholes were possible—that, after all, was what educated people thought—and Donald had proved their reality by creating a portal to one. They really were taking advantage of the future, which, he admitted, was genius. They would be able to avoid all the blind alleys that previously everyone had stumbled down. He knew the future could only be dimly and imprecisely perceived at present and took comfort from this fact, believing these ongoing difficulties lent veracity to the wormhole and, in some indefinable way, to the math.

Stan Lippowitz went barreling ahead with his project to clone disease-resistant genes in plants. The area was, of course, Al Steptoe's main scientific interest, and Stan knew that with Al behind him, he would have the freedom to do what he liked. He was now indirectly leading all company research. Stan was an abrasive character. He was rough and crude, and people were afraid of him. He'd called Nigel "a dumb asshole" in front of everyone when Nigel was delivering an update on his group's progress. Nigel nurtured the insult.

"He's an animal," he would tell people when the talk turned to Stan.

Many people had heard about Stan's contemptuous dismissal of Nigel and found themselves attracted to him when he listened quietly and with apparent admiration to an accounting of their own efforts. They, like him, were definitely superior to the Nigels of the world. Stan's vibrant, charismatic character quickly attracted a whole host of hangers-on. Nigel, more reserved and honest, had fewer allies and was, in any case, a less impressive scientist than Stan.

This conflict between scientists was watched over and adjudicated by Nils and Al. It was tolerated and regarded as the inevitable consequence of throwing together so many bright young people so quickly. And anyway, friction often generated the best science, didn't it? Nils and Al had seen this many times already. It had won for them the mantle of impartiality that set them apart from their younger colleagues.

CHAPTER 5

A Couple of Clowns

CHARLENE NEVER TOLD ANYONE she'd had intercourse with Stan. Stan, of course, wasn't so discreet. And so it was inevitable that one day, as Peter Blakely was pouring forth his usual incessant stream of verbiage, Nigel heard the words: "And Stan has had Charlene. Said she couldn't get enough of it."

He raised his eyes, and for one of the few times since they'd shared the same office, Nigel made eye contact.

"What?"

"Stan and Charlene. They've slept together."

Nigel concealed his disappointment by wringing a small smile from his lips.

"When?"

"He didn't say. Said it was in his hot tub. I said I hoped they weren't underwater. That could be putting lives at risk. He got a good deal of ribbing about that. But really, that wouldn't surprise me with Stan. He's so crude. And I know you don't like him, Nigel."

"He's an animal," said Nigel. "I'm just surprised at Charlene for letting him, really."

Peter gazed at Nigel, a half-smile lingering on his face. This was really the first time Nigel had engaged him in conversation since they'd introduced themselves to each other. Now, recognizing Nigel's obvious misery, he forgot himself and allowed a silence to develop. Nigel spoke into it.

"He's disgusting, isn't he? Crude, as you say, and arrogant. Always putting people down. I hate people like him."

Peter, who behind all his bluster was a kind soul, said: "Well, I don't think Charlene is still with him. I was behind her walking into the seminar, and she just ignored him."

They'd been at Jeff Daniels's seminar earlier that morning. Jeff was one of the senior molecular biologists employed by Almost Infinity. He was a very bright and witty individual with good manners, a sense of humor, and a lot of confidence. He was also quite good-looking and popular with the opposite sex. Everybody liked Jeff. He'd given a talk about genetic engineering and how they might use it to create drought-resistant crops. Nigel had actually learned something from it. All of that new knowledge was forgotten now, though, as his mind concentrated itself on Charlene and her fall from grace.

Speaking largely to himself, he said: "I really like Charlene."

The fascinated horticulturalist watched him closely, unable to believe he was actually participating in a meaningful conversation.

"She and I were at the University of Florida together, you know. We know each other really well." He asked him to keep this closeness in confidence. "It might upset Judy if she knew Charlene and I are old friends. You know, make her doubt my fairness in how I was treating the two of them."

Peter was transported. Not only a conversation but also a shared confidence! In just a few minutes Nigel had become his only close personal friend.

As Peter sat in uncommon silence, Nigel found himself thinking again about the wormhole. It was a portal to the future, he'd been told. "Portal" was a word that made everyone who used it sound educated.

"But what does it mean?" he'd asked his fellow employees. No one had risen to the challenge. One or two of them had affected to understand the theory behind wormhole construction. A few innocent questions had exposed these affectations as total bullshit. Some had tried to support the unsupportable with incomprehensible mumbo jumbo.

"It's all to do with multiple dimensions, dimensions that are hidden. We can't see them now, but one day we will, and then we'll see the parallel universes."

"Why do you believe this?" Nigel had shot back. "You know what one of the most famous skeptics said, don't you? 'No phenomenon is real until it is observable.'"

The discussions always ended at this point, when Nigel's interlocutor would say: "But it is observable, Nigel. Donald has established that. He's done the math and produced a wormhole."

It all came back to Donald.

***

The great day finally arrived. The All Grains contingent appeared at the back door of the warehouse and was met by Bob and Donald, who had been waiting in the parking lot. They stepped out of the minibus that had brought them from the airport and blinked at the sun-washed white building.

"Sorry we don't have any snow for you," Bob told them cheerfully.

He was wearing a light blue shirt and chinos. His shirt was open at the collar. Donald, similarly tieless, was wearing a white shirt, also open at the neck, and dark pants.

"We'll come back to the main lab later," Bob told them all, as he led them across the parking lot to a nearby building complex, which Almost Infinity also rented and which housed their administrative functions and boardroom. "We have a serious enterprise underway here, gentlemen. As I told you in Minneapolis, we like to think of it as the new Manhattan Project. We've put together a collection of the brightest scientists in the world, and we're here to explore the most revolutionary technology since the splitting of the atom."

The Midwesterners were deeply impressed. *This is the new Manhattan Project!* Their company was being offered the chance to take part in the latest revolutionary advance to transform the world. These men, these latter-day Oppenheimers and Einsteins, they were just so cool. This was America! Here they were now, in sunny California, about to look literally into the future. They took their places around the boardroom table and sat waiting, attentive and polite. Coffee and Danish pastries appeared in front of them. Bottled water and coffee stood on the credenza at the side of the room. Bob cast a glance over the offerings and said: "There's also soda and other soft drinks if anybody wants them. Just let Maria or Anna know."

The men looked at the two smiling young women standing by the door.

"I'll take a soda," said Billy Woodruff, not because he particularly wanted one but because he wanted to prolong the time the girls were spending with them.

Billy had much longer hair than the other Midwesterners. He wore quite thick glasses that, with the hair, lent him the look of an intellectual from a bygone time. To someone less imaginative, he could also pass for a present-day yob.

"These farm boys love their fizzy drinks," chortled Bob.

The guests, none of whom had spent as much as an hour on a farm, dutifully smiled back. Maria delivered the soda to the admiring Billy and then, with a smile especially for him (or so he thought), left the men to their meeting.

Bob watched the door close behind her and then handed out nondisclosure agreements to them all.

"What you are about to hear and witness is, of course, highly confidential. This is not covered by our previous agreement."

The group, with the phrase "Manhattan Project" echoing in their heads, signed without comment and without reading the document. Bob duly witnessed all the agreements, and Donald signed them on behalf of Almost Infinity.

"Now," Bob began, "very shortly I'm going to hand it over to Donald, our cofounder and cosmologist."

"Is there life on Mars, Donald?" asked the irreverent Billy, drawing grins from his colleagues. "I thought you guys were going to tell us where to point our nukes," he went on, still caught in the spell of the Manhattan Project.

Bob looked at him, a serious expression on his face. The time for levity had passed.

"But where Donald differs from his cosmology colleagues is in being an entrepreneur. Cosmology and entrepreneurship is a very rare combination. Most guys like Donald don't even know how to talk to regular Joes like us. One or two of us might have done a bit of calculus in school, but Donald understood all that when he was in diapers."

The listening men, all carried along by the unusual content of Bob's words, looked Donald over, checking to make sure he wasn't still wearing them.

"Donald has been able to construct a device we can all touch and see, a device that can bring the future to us, a device that generates wormholes. Do any of you know what a wormhole is? I know I didn't until I met Donald."

"It's a hole in the ground made by a worm," grinned Billy, but to his discomfiture, no one grinned along with him.

"A wormhole is a portal. Remember that word. It'll put twenty points on your IQ," Bob bestowed a kind smile on Billy. "It's a door to a corridor connecting two realities. One of these realities is us in the here and now, and the other is a parallel universe in another dimension. I'm already out of my comfort zone. I'm going to turn it over to Donald now."

Donald stood up and walked to a door at the back of the room. The door opened into a small side room in which stood a cart. The cart had two shelves. On the top shelf was the vacuum chamber. On the shelf below sat the squat, heavy vacuum pump. Sitting on top of the vacuum chamber was the console with the colored lights from the game Donald had bought at Radio Shack. Donald wheeled the cart to a halt in front of them all. He took the lead from the vacuum pump and plugged it into a receptacle on the wall.

"Now you will observe that the chamber is empty, gentlemen," Donald began. In fact, it wasn't empty. On the platform inside the chamber lay a sheet of gossamer-thin dark gray cloth covering a white reference card with a sticky surface with ninety-eight grains of sodium chloride adhering to it. No one could see this from the outside. He'd affixed the card to the platform with minute drops of adhesive, a contact that would be easily and undetectably broken when he pulled out the card, and one that ensured the card stayed in place when Donald was drawing the vacuum.

Donald snapped on the vacuum pump, and they all watched as the needle on the pressure gauge climbed close to minus thirty pounds per square inch. He plugged in and turned on the Radio Shack console, and the colored lights blinked into action and ran through their unvarying sequence.

"Here, I'm initiating the vacuum fluctuations we need for the establishment of the portal," he told his admiring onlookers, who were staring agog at the blinking colored lights.

Donald held the vacuum for exactly five minutes, the end of which was announced by the ping of a lab timer he'd set running. In the interior of the chamber, they could now all see the white card sitting on the platform. The gauze had been sucked away. There were one or two hastily suppressed expressions of wonder from the onlookers. Donald turned off the pump and then opened the valve to let the air back in. It rushed in noisily, and the needle on the pressure gauge fell back to zero. Now Donald could open the door. Unnoticed by him, however, the small square of gray cloth had floated back into the chamber and settled in a crumpled heap in a corner of its interior. He opened the chamber door wide and invited them all to look inside. They all saw the white card and noticed the grains of salt that had been affixed to the card by Donald.

"What's that?" asked Billy Woodruff, pointing into the corner of the chamber. He had seen the small piece of crumpled gray cloth.

"Well," said Donald smoothly. "That's a first."

He removed the card and the piece of gray cloth and set them before the visitors.

"From my reading of the Calabi-Yau manifold, I would say in these conditions the portal is quite large, and these artifacts are coming to us from about fifty years into the future. Make of them what you will, gentlemen. You don't need to be a cosmologist or a mathematician to hazard a guess at their meaning. In fact, your guesses are likely to be more meaningful than any I can come up with. I'm no farmer. I'm going to count the salt grains. Last time there were eighty-six. It looks about the same this time, but we'll have to count to make sure."

He went to the door carrying the card carefully, maintaining it horizontal to the ground. The All Grains executives looked at each other. They were shell-shocked. They'd just witnessed the materialization of the card and the cloth in the empty vacuum chamber. They could all still see the flashing colored lights and hear the ping of the timer. Something from nothing! It was truly the stuff of fantasy. They struggled to accommodate what they'd just seen with the perception of reality they'd held since they were children.

"Can you do it again?" asked Pete Renquist softly. He was a marketing manager and would always be the first to ask for the seemingly impossible. "That was truly remarkable. The card seemed to materialize out of thin air."

"I need about two weeks to prepare these deliveries," demurred Donald. "I have to work out the pattern of the jittering vacuum fluctuations. Only then can I create another wormhole. This involves some pretty serious heavy-duty math. But the wonderful thing is, it works! But I must correct you, er ...."

"Pete," supplied Pete Renquist.

"I must correct you, Pete. These artifacts didn't come out of thin air; they came out of nothing in this time. Now, gentlemen, give me a moment to count these grains of salt."

He left the room.

Bob watched him go and then beamed around at the All Grains men.

"Pretty impressive, huh? That's the kind of thing the wormhole produces. Is it predicting the future? Well, I suppose it is, in broad brushstrokes. But that has value, doesn't it? The vacuum pump created the wormhole, and these items appeared. Out of thin air, as Pete said, notwithstanding Donald's correction. I've looked into your company, gentlemen. You spend five hundred million annually on research. The wormhole will help you focus your efforts. And even a broad focus, if it's on the right track, has to be of enormous value to you. It will save you billions in the long term. No one else can offer you this. While he's out of the room, I can tell you about him and spare him embarrassment. He is simply a genius. And with him directing the course of our work, we can't fail to become world leaders. Just imagine, you'll be able to position yourselves for all the hot areas years before your competitors have a clue about what is going on. You will always be ahead, always first to market, and I'm sure you don't need me to tell you how important that is."

"I wonder what the gray cloth is telling us," Pete said dreamily, almost as if he were talking to himself. Then, more firmly: "We really should take a good look at it—get it analyzed. You know, do the thing properly."

"We need to know what it's made of," said Billy Woodruff. "Cotton? Silk? We've got programs in both those materials."

"Salt and cloth," said Clive Nunn, another of the All Grains deputation, a chemist. He was speaking up now to justify his inclusion on the trip. "Should we be thinking of them together?"

"I've been trying to do that," said Billy. "I just can't get anything."

Donald swept back into the room. He was wearing a lab coat now. It was unbuttoned and flapped around behind him. It lent him a scientific, professorial air.

"Ninety-eight grains of salt," he announced briskly. "Twelve more than last time. And I've reviewed the math. We are a little farther into the future this time."

He went and stood at the whiteboard and then wrote down a string of incomprehensible symbols. The only recognizable writing was at the end of the string where he had written the words: "equals one hundred and seven." He wrote down another string of symbols and concluded with the words: "equals twelve." Then he put the number 107 over the number 12 and turned around to face the room.

"Makes about ten, doesn't it? This puts us about ten years farther on in the future."

"Less than nine actually," put in Clive Nunn.

Donald smiled pityingly at him.

"Whatever," he said airily. And then, "All right, eight point nine one six recurring; that is eight years and eleven months, almost exactly. Anyway, I definitely think it's calling for salt-tolerant crops. Maybe the oceans have risen—they are supposed to rise aren't they?—and have polluted large areas of crop land with salt water. And I was thinking about that gray cloth. It's going to be hotter in the future, isn't it? Maybe we start to shade our fields. That gray cloth could simply be a small piece of shade cloth."

The visitors all stared at him, transfixed by his words. They seemed shocked by how easily he had come up with such a compelling narrative for the artifacts. They were also deeply impressed by his facility for mental arithmetic. Billy checked it on the calculator he'd brought with him. He showed it excitedly to his colleagues. Donald was exactly right. They were now all certain he was right about the artifacts as well. It just felt right. Salty soils and a hotter climate—wasn't that what all the climate boys were predicting?

Pete said slowly: "The information we've acquired today—this is ours exclusively, right?"

Bob smiled. He looked at Donald and then back at the All Grains men.

"Become investors, gentlemen. We'll put cast-iron agreements in place. You can think of us as working for you. We'll be a Californian outpost of All Grains. Is it time to talk about money now?"

"You and I will talk about it, Bob," said Helmuth, and nothing more was said then.

***

Nigel met the All Grains group when they passed through the lab later that afternoon. Bob didn't introduce his visitors to any of Almost Infinity's scientists, but Al had told Stan and Jeff who they were, and so by the time they reached Nigel, their identity was an open secret. Nigel thought Bob was particularly ebullient that afternoon. Nigel started talking about salt tolerance and the adaptations that plants had evolved to meet the challenges of salinity. He showed them his little collection of *Spartina*, and rarely, if ever, had the untidy little group of weeds been regarded with such collective, concentrated fascination.

"How do you spell that?" asked Clive Nunn earnestly.

"Just how it sounds: s-p-a-r-t-i-n-a," Nigel obliged.

Clive wrote it down in the notebook he was carrying and nodded gratefully. The Minnesotans moved on. They finished their tour of the labs shortly after talking to Nigel and then departed for their hotel. They would relax for half an hour, have dinner, and then visit the circus. Donald, who wouldn't be joining them for the evening, took his leave of the guests.

"It's been a real privilege," their leader, Helmuth, told him, shaking his hand firmly. "I don't meet people like you every day."

Donald flashed him his oily, evasive smile.

"People?" he inquired.

And then, without waiting for an answer, he was gone. Helmuth looked after him, an uncertain smile lingering on his lips.

"What did he mean, Bob?" he asked his large Californian host.

"Who knows?" laughed Bob. "He's a genius."

And, dimly, Helmuth understood. Donald didn't want to be referred to as a mere person. It was insulting to someone extraordinary like him. He would remember next time.

***

After dinner Bob chauffeured Helmuth to the circus. Nils and Al took care of the other three All Grains men. They had very good seats at the circus. One of Bob's friends, Ted White, was the head trainer of the big cats at Marine World, Africa, USA, a theme park near the site of Almost Infinity's labs. Ted was always given complimentary tickets to the best seats in recognition of his role as supplier of big cats to the circus. This time he'd passed on his tickets to Bob. The Almost Infinity group took their places in the Cow Palace, all of them except Bob, initially oblivious to how privileged they were.

The night at the circus provided a satisfying conclusion to the first day of the All Grains visit. The men gawped at the fantastic scantily clad acrobats and contortionists, the loud and irreverent clowns, the jugglers, tightrope walkers, and trapeze artists. They watched, fascinated, as dogs, horses, and elephants picked their way through elaborate routines without making a false step, as the big cats were persuaded to attempt a more limited repertoire of movements, all the while snarling and flashing threatening glances at their trainers. The greatest show on Earth was a three-ring circus, each ring showing a different act, and all being put on at the same time. It was an unremitting assault on the sensibilities of the spectators packed into the enormous Cow Palace.

The show was hurtling along to its conclusion when one of the muscular young women sporting herself on the netless high wire suddenly slipped and fell straight down to the sawdust-covered floor. Of Bob's party, only Billy Woodruff witnessed the entire incident. He heard the soft thud as her body hit the ground. She lay there, still and alone, as all the mad activity whirled around her. Then, a shocked hush gradually crept over all the spectators as more and more of them noticed the still figure of the fallen girl. Two clowns raced up to her carrying a stretcher, loaded her onto it, and then raced off. There was an ear-splitting bang, and another clown was thrown high into the air from the barrel of a fake cannon. This provoked a smattering of uncertain applause, and then the show rolled on to its conclusion. The incident cast a pall over the Almost Infinity party.

"God, I hope she's okay," said Pete sincerely. "She must have fallen at least twenty feet."

The Almost Infinity party, now standing together outside in the parking lot, near their cars, had all moved closer to one another to share reaction to the fall. They nodded in sympathy with Pete's expressed wish. Bob decided they needed cheering up.

"Probably happens every show," he told them. "Do you think any respectable enterprise would have a couple of clowns like that working for it as stretcher bearers? No, gentlemen, if it had been a serious accident, we would have had the local emergency services involved. Those clowns were out there right away. They were probably waiting for her to fall. Don't worry! It was all part of the show."

"I wish we could have seen them waiting," said Pete. "Then I would have felt better about it."

"Her body made some thump when it hit the ground," pointed out Billy.

"Circuses are in the business of tricking people," protested Bob. "Sometimes you can't believe your own eyes."

Everyone reflected quietly on his words. They got into the cars and drove back to the hotel. The Midwesterners took their farewells of Bob, Al, and Nils in the hotel lobby.

"Let me know how that young girl is doing, Bob," instructed Helmuth.

Bob shook hands all around, fixing them with a warm smile.

"Have a safe trip home," he told them. "I won't be seeing you tomorrow."

"We'll be in touch," promised Helmuth.

"Sometimes you can't believe your own eyes," murmured Billy Woodruff to himself as he was getting into bed. Then he mumbled, "A couple of clowns like that," and he fell asleep.

CHAPTER 6

Let's Make a Deal

NIGEL ASKED CHARLENE out to lunch.

"I'm your boss and you can't say no," he told her.

She laughed, pleased at his interest in spending time with her.

"I'm sorry I've been a bit distant since we moved from Florida," he said, as they took their places in the restaurant. "You know I really like you, don't you, Charlene? To hell with cronyism. I just like being with you."

"I like you too, Nigel. I always enjoy myself when I'm with you."

"Always?" asked Nigel, raising his eyebrows.

"I think so," said Charlene, smiling back at him. "I can't remember when I didn't."

"All right, then," said Nigel seriously. "We should just live together. And it will be cheaper for the both of us. I know it's a big step, and if you're not sure, I'll understand. But one of us had to bring it up."

The thought of marriage and a life-long commitment to Nigel, of having his kids and bringing up a family, all appeared before her immediately on hearing him say this.

"Are you sure?" she asked disbelievingly. The intensity in her eyes unnerved him and his resolution faltered.

"Don't make a decision right now," he temporized. "Just think about it for a bit. We'd certainly save some money."

Money again! Perhaps she was jumping to conclusions. She decided not to explore the proposal further for the time being.

"I can't say I was surprised Kutti fired you. You were always making him look like an ignorant prick."

"I know I'm not the brightest bulb. I should have been a lot more diplomatic in my dealings with him. But he's really vindictive, Charlene. Nils told me he'd written to Almost Infinity urging them not to hire me. Would I ever do a thing like that? I don't think so."

Nigel asked her how she was enjoying sunny California.

"A lot nicer than the furnace that is central Florida, isn't it? And Kutti and his wife coming from Madurai are right at home there, aren't they? They probably think it's a bit on the cool side."

"I'm from Georgia, Nigel. The weather in Florida didn't bother me. Of course, it's beautiful here. It's almost too nice. It can make you forget yourself and do dumb things."

Nigel waited for more. He wondered if Charlene was girding herself to tell him about her fling with Stan. She let a silence build, and in it, Nigel thought he recognized an invitation to bring up the subject of the noxious Stan. He decided to let it pass. He liked her too much to embarrass her.

"When the weather is so beautiful every day, it makes it easier to forgive yourself for little lapses."

Charlene smiled at him, acknowledging his tact. She knew her fling with Stan was common knowledge. Several of the girls at work had sent little feelers out in her direction to encourage her to unburden herself. So she knew they knew. But she'd refused the invitation. She was really pleased Nigel had apparently taken the news of her lapse in such a mature and understanding way. And now he'd asked her to live with him!

"We should go out together more, Nigel. After all, we almost got married once, didn't we?"

Nigel smiled back at her.

"You're the most kind-hearted of girls, Charlene. I'll always be grateful to you for caring about me. No one else in the lab seemed to have the faintest idea of how desperate my situation was. Only you."

"Well, you've paid me back. You got me here. And this is a really exciting place to be, isn't it?"

***

Bob was talking to Donald.

"I told him we were looking for two hundred million. He didn't seem surprised by the number. He asked me for a time frame. I told him ten years. 'So,' he said, 'twenty million a year, then.'"

"For agriculture only," said Donald. "Helmuth can't expect to monopolize the wormhole for a mere twenty million a year. We have to be able to go after other customers."

"He understands, Donald. That won't be a problem. So as soon as we sign the agreement, we'll get our first tranche. And hey, we need it. We've only got enough on hand for another few weeks. This should make Real Excretions happy. Hell, we may even be able to squeeze a few more million out of them."

Donald looked at his heavyset, slightly sweating, coarse-faced business partner. Bob exuded energy; the prospect of acquiring large sums of money really seemed to animate him. He looked ready for anything.

"Let's try to get US Home Products as soon as we can, Bob. A couple of million won't do it for us now. Our burn rate is already about a million a month."

Bob concurred. He was impressed by the speed with which Donald had absorbed the realities of venture funding.

"How much of us does he want?" Donald asked now.

"Forty percent," said Bob. "I know it's high, and I'll try to beat him down to twenty, which was the most I was prepared to offer. He said for the amount of money All Grains was putting up, his board insisted on at least forty. We might have to settle for this if we can't get US Home Products on board right away. I know one thing: we can't afford to run out of money. We would never recover from that."

"What a bunch of ignorant assholes," proclaimed Donald. "Who do they think they are? This really is pearls before swine, isn't it?"

"Those guys," averred Bob, shaking his head in exasperation.

Donald nodded approvingly.

"Who is competition for All Grains?" he asked.

"US Home Products, Federated Chemical, Norton Holdings, Biolarge. These are the companies that come immediately to mind."

"Okay. Get George Nipper to set up visits with these companies as soon as possible. I can prep the necessary wormhole demonstrations. The All Grains demo went well, didn't it? More of the same?"

"Definitely, Donald. More of the same."

"We'll just keep Helmuth on a string. Get the first tranche and get the competition in place. Then we can talk tough about percentages. You're my pasha, Bob. You know that, don't you?"

Bob didn't. He looked the word up afterwards and was mystified. Donald was thinking of himself as the sultan or king of Almost Infinity? And he, Bob, was his subordinate? Well, it fit with the smile, didn't it? The smile proclaimed everyone was his subordinate.

***

In four days, Bob was going to fly out to Minneapolis to nail down the deal with All Grains. He was going to go alone. Bob let the figure of $200 million slip out to Al Steptoe, and within a day the whole company was buzzing with excitement at what this could mean. Orders were placed for all manner of expensive equipment by the electrified scientists.

"What's twenty thousand? We're getting two hundred million!"

Bob tried to keep a cap on spending, but it was hard work, and the volume of the orders ensured some simply slipped by him. The burn rate at Almost Infinity exploded, and the six weeks they thought they had quickly shrank to a month.

George Nipper scrambled to set up visits from other companies. Only US Home Products could be persuaded to come out quickly. They had heard of All Grains' interest and were intrigued. George had them arriving in California one month after Bob returned from

Minneapolis. All the other companies he contacted were either not interested or made vague commitments to visit at a later date.

So there was no position of strength from which Bob could conduct his negotiations with All Grains. He came back to San Francisco a chastened man. Helmuth had proved entirely intractable. He'd insisted on the 40 percent and would only commit All Grains to one year of funding. In October of that year, All Grains would review progress and decide whether or not they wanted to commit to a second year. He'd tried to be encouraging.

"If we make great progress, Bob, we can run through another twenty million. And if you can keep it, how you say, 'on the up' beyond that, well, there's every chance we'll make it through the ten years and the two hundred million. And you will be able to keep it on the up, won't you? After all, neither of us sees this as a short-term relationship, do we? We are definitely looking to a long-term. That's the way our company has to operate. We are just too big to do anything else. But we need to review the progress every year. Nothing else is going to fly with our board. These are very conservative people, Bob. If it was up to me, you'd get your two hundred million and you'd get it up the front. But they will never go for that. Believe me. I did well to get the twenty mill. The truth is they don't like the wormhole, Bob. I told them we are getting access to all the research produced by a very bright group of scientists. It's the win-win. Well, eventually they calmed down. And you know what really bugged them? It was the thought of looking into the future. 'It's ungodly,' they told me. 'Man shouldn't be doing this.' I told them about our trip to the circus, and sadly, they were all more interested in the young girl who'd fallen off the high wire than they were in grains of salt and the piece of shade cloth that had appeared in the vacuum chamber. She was all right, Bob, wasn't she?"

"I told you, Helmuth. It happens every show. She's never hurt."

"Well, thank God for that, anyway. I'm telling you it was really the close-run thing."

Bob looked at Helmuth and made his calculations, his eyes flickering nervously back and forth. US Home Products? A few weeks too late. Other companies? Months late. They needed help right now. They had just tried to run before they could walk, a very common mistake and one for which he took full responsibility.

"Take twenty percent Helmuth?" he asked hopefully. "Twenty percent for ten million?"

Helmuth shook his head. "I can't go back with the different deal, Bob. The board is just too, how you say, delicate?"

"You get the paperwork drawn up, Helmuth. I'm going to take it back to Donald and see how it flies. I'll give you a call in a couple of days."

Helmuth took him out to eat, an unremarkable steak dinner at a popular Minneapolis restaurant. Bob noted the farm memorabilia affixed to the walls of the dining room and wondered about the impact of the land on these simple folks. There was a hooker waiting for him in his room when he got back to his hotel, courtesy of All Grains. Bob flew back to California the next morning, thoroughly and satisfyingly knackered.

Donald was contemptuous of the deal he'd agreed to with Helmuth.

"Forty percent and basically for only twenty million. The two hundred million was a figment of our imagination. I'm sorry, Bob, but it's just not good enough. You've got to tell those assholes where to get off."

Bob counseled caution.

"Let's see how it goes with US Home Products," he said. "If we can get at least ten million from them, that will buy us some time."

Donald was skeptical. "How easy is that going to be, Bob? There's overlap between their interests and the interests of All Grains, isn't there? We won't be able to offer exclusivity to either of them. All Grains will go ballistic."

"Let's not get too far ahead of ourselves. Let's just see what we can get with Home Products."

Donald flashed his slippery smile. "Do the best you can, Bob. If we have to go with All Grains alone, we'll just redirect our in-house efforts to pharmaceuticals and leave all the agricultural research to them. We'll offer all our people to them. They can take over paying them, and our burn rate will drop through the floor. The twenty million should last a lot longer. We can still guide the efforts through wormhole output. That's what they are getting for their twenty million anyway—wormhole product, not a bunch of agricultural research."

Bob thought it was a possible solution to their problems. Helmuth, however, shot down the idea crisply and decisively over the phone. "The twenty million is for research you are going to do for us. That's how I sold it to our board. It never was for wormhole product. The board doesn't care about the wormhole product. They want Nils and Al to lead our research. That's what we are paying for."

"So we can sell the wormhole product to someone else?" asked Bob incredulously.

But at this Helmuth demurred: "Of course not, Bob. The trends are important."

"The bastards want it both ways," snarled Donald, on hearing this exchange from Bob.

Bob tried one last time with Helmuth, but he sensed he'd reached the end of Helmuth's tether. He summed it up: "All right then, Helmuth. We are looking forward to our first twenty million."

At the other end of the line, Helmuth nodded cautiously. He imagined Bob enjoying the hooker they'd provided for him. He'd seen their president up close and personal and reduced him to an All Grains scale. There would be no more grandiose talk about the Manhattan Project.

CHAPTER 7

Nils Sucks Dirt

LIFE AT ALMOST INFINITY settled into a routine. Stan became the de facto leader of the molecular biologists at the company. He impressed everyone with his volcanic energy and capacity for sustained hard work. Jeff provided the more acceptable face of molecular science. You could work with Jeff without becoming his vassal. Stan tolerated Jeff because he was clearly a very clever man and also because he was good-natured and disinclined to foster vendettas. Stan needed collaborators to further his grand designs for the company and enlisted them through his association with Jeff. He remained ostensibly reporting to Al, as did Jeff and all the other molecular biologists at the company.

Nils's star had begun to wane. He was less politically aware than Al and made no attempt to get close to Bob. Now he often appeared in the lab wearing a lab coat and began to spend extended periods of time actually working at the bench. Al also did this, but much less frequently than Nils.

Nigel settled into life at Almost Infinity. He turned out, to his own surprise, to be rather a good organizer. Al and Nils noticed, and he was moved into position for a serious promotion. The other plant scientists noticed as well and were envious, but Nigel never put a foot wrong. Whenever he was called on to make a presentation that included other people's work, he always made sure he gave full credit to the scientists he was representing. The good favor in which he was held by upper management was, as a consequence, broadly tolerated by his peers. He began talking with Oliver, a senior molecular biologist in Al's section, who was on good terms with Jeff and even with Stan. They started to plan work together, work centrally relevant to the company and its goals as they understood them.

He and Charlene grew closer. They spent more and more time together and eventually just began living together. They attempted to conceal their closeness from the others at the lab, but everyone knew they were an item.

Nigel hired a young male graduate, Kevin, so now three people were officially reporting to him. When he took part in discussions, he was listened to and knew his opinion mattered. Judy, Charlene, and Kevin all came to him frequently throughout the day to ask his advice on their tasks. Really, he had never been happier at work. Nils left him alone, and his day-to-day activities were essentially unsupervised. That was how it was supposed to be—after all, he did have a PhD.

Judy and her husband Jim continued to fascinate him. Judy, being a native Californian, had grown up in this sunshine-filled world. Jim was from New York City but had spent most of his adult life in California. They both took the perfect weather for granted. Nigel, coming from England, was used to daily discussions about the weather. But in the Bay Area, with its perfect blue skies and constant sunshine, there was just nothing to discuss. Every morning when he got up, he would draw back the curtains and say to Charlene: "Guess what? It's another perfect day!" And they would smile at each other.

Nigel thought Jim and Judy were leading a fascinating life. They lived together on a houseboat moored in a nearby harbor. Judy had told him this was saving thousands of dollars, and looking at his own costs for rent and utilities, he believed her. Also, he couldn't forget Judy had offered herself to him when he'd first met her (this had been explained to him finally by Charlene). But as he thought about his relationships with women, Charlene was front and center. He realized he was more deeply invested in bringing her happiness than he had ever been with any girl. He thought this might be true love, but still he doubted himself.

For her part, Charlene had started to dream about marriage. She decided she was in love with Nigel. She thought he was probably going to do well at the company, and he would be able to provide for her and their children out of his share of the two hundred million. The huge figure hovered over all of Almost Infinity's employees and lent a long-term perspective to their plans. Nigel, when he was thinking about Charlene, could see that she fit right in with all her fellow Americans. She shared with them a common upbringing. He was amazed at where he found himself. He listened to them talking together and recognized the unspoken shared experiences that bonded them together—experiences he had never had. Perhaps he would just have to marry an English girl. But at night, when he was lying with Charlene, he would look at her and feel his heart soften. Was she really so different?

"We are from different countries," Nigel told her one night in bed. "My father said he would never give up his birthright, his nationality, Charlene. I think I agree with him."

"But you don't have to, Nigel. You're English. You can become an American and keep your British citizenship."

Nigel wanted to know how she knew this. She told him she'd looked into it when she'd been thinking of marrying him to keep him in the country. Nigel teared up. He took her into his arms.

"You're such a sweet girl," he told her sincerely.

And suddenly the British bulldog and the American eagle seemed unimportant. Before the wonder that was Charlene, they both beat a hasty retreat.

***

George Nipper had once been a scientist and could still speak the lingo. He had turned to business to round out his career. He enjoyed talking to scientists in his new role as the voice of commercial acumen.

"Yes," he would say on being informed of some advance, "but have you filed a patent?" And then: "How are we going to make money out of this? Who are going to be our customers? What need does this invention meet?"

George developed a reputation in the company as a realist, a first hurdle to overcome on the road to commercial success.

George, in his job, supplied most of the written work that Bob's activities generated. Through this he became intimately familiar with the company and its finances. His position in the small inner circle at the head of the company became widely known and gave him standing with all employees. Stan was often seen in George's company.

George also attended senior management meetings, meetings that included Nils, Al, Marshall, Arthur, and Ben (the company's comptroller) as well as, of course, Bob and Donald. Stan made a beeline for George after these meetings. A couple of months into Almost Infinity's brief existence, Stan had picked up on Nils's passivity in these meetings. Of course, George said nothing directly, but he had blighted Nils by omission. He never reported any of Nils's comments because Nils never made any. And Stan had noticed. He began raising questions with Al, George, and Bob about the Dane's fitness for his position. He drew comparisons between the vigor of Al's section and the relative lack of quality in the people Nils had hired. His concerns were well directed.

Nils, on taking up his position at Almost Infinity, had begun recruiting immediately. It was the major function of his new job. Of course, there was lab equipment to purchase and set up, but he had done this many times before in his own field. Now he needed recruits to help him expand the activity to encompass areas less familiar to him. He had never had such a broad license to hire. He realized he needed help, and so his first major hire wasn't a youngster. It was Al Steptoe, a molecular plant pathologist who had already gained prominence in his field. Al was no longer young, but he wasn't old either. There could be as many as twenty good years still in him.

Al was familiar with Nils's work. He even knew him slightly. But Al, like everyone else, was not aware Nils had been compelled to retire. When Nils mentioned working in California, Al could see himself and Nils working there together in the pleasant sunshine. Al was a risk-taker and, unlike Nils, really did leave a solid position in academia for the excitement and uncertainty of Almost Infinity. Nils hooked him with the promise he'd be allowed immediately to hire up to fifteen scientists for his projects. For a man who was spending almost all his time writing grants, this sudden injection of talent and cash was irresistible. And his team would be so much bigger than the one he was laboring to produce at his university. There was also the beauty of the surroundings in the Bay Area to be considered. So for Al, it was a gamble but a calculated one.

***

On first meeting with Donald, Nils and then Al had immediately come to the conclusion he must be a genius. He was a genius, or else there was something wrong with him. But neither of the scientists had ever met anyone suffering from pseudologia fantastica. Very few people had or were aware that they had. The condition just didn't exist in the public consciousness. In fact, neither Nils nor Al was even aware such a condition existed.

Of all the people involved in the fledgling company, only Bob thoroughly understood its genesis. He had first seen it lurking in the crazed mind of Donald, and then Nils had really brought it to life. Nils had a personal agenda. He was going to show his old bosses they had retired him too soon. The people in Canada who knew Nils best had always suspected him of egotism. But they stopped short of labeling him a self-promoter. After all, he had brought Canada honor though his research, and no one could deny he was a hard worker. It was, however, noticeable that among all the scientists he'd recruited at Almost Infinity, there were no Canadians. Bob did wonder about that, and it made him cautious about extending trust to Nils.

Nils, for his part, sensed Bob's reservations. Of course, the situation was rife with reservations. Nils had reservations of his own about the foundations of his new company. He didn't believe in the wormhole, for example. He concealed this fact from others at the company behind a façade of naïve enthusiasm. In time, he came to believe in this façade himself.

He wanted a leader and found him in Donald. Here was a man with a fantastic vision, cloaked in impenetrable math and concepts beyond his comprehension. This man was promising them all a brilliant future, and he was making these promises with the authority of the money he'd helped raise.

*＊＊

Stan's signaling of Nils's lack of engagement in company business led Bob to begin to consider demoting Nils. Shortly before this change in Bob's thinking, however, Nils had managed to hire Forrest Pursuit, a plant breeder with a fine academic reputation and who, like him, had been eased out of his previous position for age-related reasons. Forrest was going to head up all plant-breeding-related activities at Almost Infinity and would be the link between the lab and the field. In a company that was expected to produce improved crop plants, it was an enormously important position.

Forrest was an urbane and civilized man who liked to dream of exciting new research initiatives. He was also old. In fact, on joining Almost Infinity, he became its oldest employee. So one of Nils's final contributions to the company in his role as research director had been the installation of a plant breeder who had seen it all at the center of its operations. To compound the disaster, Bob was going to appoint Forrest as the temporary head of Cell Biology, an area about which he knew absolutely nothing. Bob would appoint a permanent successor from among the young guns already at the company. He was going to watch them fight it out with interest. Bob also disappointed Marshall by transferring Susie from her role as his assistant to a new role as Forrest's assistant. Bob knew Marshall was never going to have any scientists reporting to him.

Nils realized he was coming under fresh scrutiny as research director. The Nils of old would have fought tenaciously against any suggestion of a reduction in rank. And if his resistance proved futile, he would have quit. But the new Nils was a markedly altered man. His conception of himself had been changed by his enforced retirement. He was no longer invulnerable, and he knew it. He was even failing a little physically. He'd fallen down recently when jogging and had scraped his face. "Sucking dirt," he'd explained cheerfully when people wondered about the marks.

Now, most of his life was behind him, and he was aware of his limitations. Finally, Bob had a quiet word with him and offered him the prestigious position of research fellow. He would be the only one at the company. Forrest, an older man, would take over his administrative duties as head of Cell Biology, and this would defuse age discrimination as an issue. Bob did worry about Nils suing, but Nils embraced his new position. His salary had been only slightly reduced, mainly by the withdrawal of incentives and bonuses. It was, he was told, the very top of the scale for a research fellow, and he was no longer expected to attend the senior managers' meetings. He told himself he wasn't interested in these anyway. He spent all his time in the lab now, working with his two bright young research assistants, Roy and Wayne. Everyone was impressed with his transition from office back to lab. He picked it up right where he'd left off twenty years ago when he'd been promoted to the position of director of his institute in Saskatoon. He enjoyed the work again now and took satisfaction in the performance of tasks others had performed for him over the years. His interests narrowed to soybean cell biology.

"It's like riding a bike," he told Al. "Once you learn it, you never forget."

Al wasn't sure he could do the same himself. There were many new techniques in molecular biology that he had never practiced. For him, the learning curve would simply be too steep. If he were demoted like Nils, he would just have to quit.

These creaks and groans in the upper echelons of the hierarchy at Almost Infinity remained largely invisible to the vast majority of its employees. Nils's demotion was, of course, fairly widely known, but no one knew for sure if it had been forced on him. He carried on, seemingly oblivious, and, as a consequence, so did everyone else. Stan let it be known that the company was better for the change, and whereas before he'd maintained a polite, nodding acquaintance with Nils, now he simply ignored him. Stan and the other young guns—Jeff, Oliver, George, and, to a lesser extent, Nigel, all began to assert themselves. At first only hesitantly, but then more confidently, and in so doing they created a second tier of management at the company. Only George occupied a place in both the first and second tiers. He was widely regarded as the second most important business person after Bob.

Nils settled quickly and easily into his new position at the company. People outside the senior management group thought he must be comfortable in his new position because he gave no indication of being aware his position had changed. And he remained the recruiter-in-chief. Nils's scientific reputation was still greater in the minds of plant scientists around the world than the reputation of Almost Infinity as a new center of research excellence. And in the minds of everyone, Nils and Almost Infinity remained inextricably linked.

CHAPTER 8

Hucksters, Amateur and Professional

THERE ARE HUCKSTERS, and then there are *hucksters*. Some people join the order by default—in Bob's case, through willful ignorance; in Donald's, through illness. Others take up and follow the calling knowingly. These people generally start out in research, often with the best of intentions, but quickly decide it's just too hard. They move away from science and become salesmen, but the only product on sale is themselves. The first thing to suffer is the integrity of their work, and they begin to fabricate results. Hucksters active in scientific research are easily recognized by their colleagues since their results are never reproducible.

Almost Infinity, as it was bound to by dint of the sheer number of hires rapidly made, had acquired a couple of these characters. Bernie Gabbard was first on board, followed a couple of months later by Bob Stone. Neither of the young men had a PhD. Bernie had a master's degree in horticulture from the University of Nebraska, while Bob had one in chemistry from a local private college. Bernie had been hired by Nils, who knew several of his references at the University of Nebraska. He hadn't bothered to ask for their opinions of Bernie. He'd just assumed the references would be good. They would not have been.

Bernie quickly recognized that the Dane's commitment to Donald's cause was less than total. Nils, after all, had been a practicing scientist all his life, and his habit of caution was ingrained. Bernie was a serious man, a born-again Christian, and he'd quickly latched on to Donald and begun sowing seeds of discontent over Nils's coolness. He found a way to meet privately with Donald (about which, more later) and began mentioning his reservations about the Dane, pointing out that he, Bernie, was far more committed to Donald's cause. He presented himself as a clean slate, on which Donald could write his dreams of the future. He would work with Donald to create a new science, one tailored to the development of wormhole product. He showed willingness in trying to understand the wormhole and flattered Donald and fed his ego. He always sided with him in disputes with the senior men Bob had hired. These were men who could never understand Donald. Only he could supply Almost Infinity's founder with what he needed.

For his part, Donald recognized kindred spirits in Bernie and Bob. These were young men who'd been passed over by their departments, not considered good enough for the PhD degree at their universities. Just as, all those years ago, Harvard had not wanted him. They had all been told that research was just not for them. Bernie and Bob had met at a local evangelical church. Bernie, who was already working at Almost Infinity at the time, had encouraged Bob to join him. Bernie put in a good word with Donald, and he was duly hired.

Bob found himself working with Bernie on the creation of new super crops that were both salt tolerant and drought resistant. Almost immediately Bernie and Bob began to ease themselves out from under Nils's supervision. With the collusion of Donald, they very quickly emerged as an independent force within the company. And this, mainly by chance, happened to coincide with the fall from grace of Nils. They hired half a dozen young men and women, all just with bachelor's degrees. Donald provided the necessary signatures required from upper management.

Al and Nils regarded all these busy, energetic, under-qualified, young people who had suddenly appeared at the heart of the company with frank distaste. There was no science here. Bob and Bernie had hired a bunch of naïve kids. The company was now wasting prodigious money on what Al was calling a cult. Al and Nils tried to talk to Bob about it, but he was unsympathetic.

"Look, if these guys are giving Donald what he wants, who are we to complain? Don't worry—Donald knows what he's doing."

But with the sudden materialization of the Bernie and Bob show at the very center of their personal fiefdoms, Al and Nils did begin to worry. In the everyday life of the company, it was impossible to ignore the strangeness of this group. After several months at Almost Infinity, Bernie and Bob were each asked to give a presentation detailing the progress they were making. Nils told them it was expected of all research groups. Of course, he reassured them, everyone realized neither had had time to do very much, but what the senior staff were looking for was evidence of planning, of application of the scientific method to the challenges they faced.

In the event, Bob talked about his master's dissertation. He made no mention of research at Almost Infinity. There were only a couple of chemists working there at the time, and the director of their little section, Arthur Nanomura, who'd played no role in Bob's hiring, didn't attend Bob's talk. Anyway, Arthur, like the couple of chemists who had attended, was a retiring character and would very likely have said nothing in any case. So Bob's talk passed by generally unremarked upon.

Bernie talked about the practical aspects of growing plants. He presented his work in its horticultural aspect. There was little experience at the company in horticulture, and no one took exception to any of his remarks. Al, Nils, and now Forrest realized there was nothing of substance in the Bernie and Bob show. As Al pointed out, Bernie's talk could have been given by any one of thousands of science graduates or even undergraduates. Members of the cult, however, saw Bob and Bernie standing in front of the company's senior scientists giving them talks that appeared to be acceptable. The senior scientists were, however, appalled. Stan, Jeff, Oliver, and Nigel all asked questions that exposed the lack of depth in the presentations. Stan practically asked Bob if he'd ever done research. Nigel asked Bernie to talk about hormone action in plants. Bernie fended him off with nods and winks, implying he knew exactly what Nigel wanted him to say. They could talk about it in private later, which, of course, they never did. Nigel subsided, looking baffled. Jeff and Oliver asked pertinent and pointed questions, but they were both essentially kind men and set the bar too low. Bernie and Bob stumbled over it.

When the presentations concluded, Donald looked pleased. His personal scientific crew had emerged from their grilling intact.

***

Bernie and Bob devised a code for identifying the reagents they were using, and without the code, no one could tell what it was they were actually doing. And besides the corrupt feel all this hiding engendered, there was also the flagrant flouting of good safety practices. Could anyone not in the know really be sure that "gladiator oil" and "mermaid's milk" were safe and harmless? What if they were strong acids or alkalis? What if they were poisons? The cult was assured care had been taken not to code anything dangerous. But this wasn't true. Gladiator oil was a one molar solution of sucrose. You could put it in your coffee, and unknown to anyone, Bernie and Bob did. Mermaid's milk, which sounded like you could drink it, was actually a concentrated solution of barium chloride—and you didn't want to drink that.

Oliver had been nosing around Bernie and Bob's lab benches and had found fifty solutions with deceptive labels. He asked Al to take it up with Donald.

"Really, Al, we can't be associated with work like this. We have no idea what it is they are actually doing. And Bernie's talk the other day was an absolute crock, wasn't it? The advantage of using peat pots? How many people and how much time do you need to investigate that? It's the kind of thing you give to a high school kid, isn't it? And here we are, a state-of-the-art lab, filled with brilliant people, allowing this to flourish in our midst. We've got to put a stop to it. All Grains must never find out we're spending their money like this."

Al agreed with Oliver. But he didn't talk to Donald. He wasn't comfortable talking to him. Instead, he took the matter up with Bob.

"You've got to make him see sense, Bob. Donald has got a group of young, inexperienced people—well, kids, really—running around in our labs doing God knows what. Bernie and Bob have got to go."

Bob wasn't as concerned as Al. Just a lot of scientists squabbling among themselves, as far as he could see. But when Al told him how much money Bernie and Bob were burning through, money that could be spent so much more wisely, he began to worry.

"Neither of them has a PhD," Al protested. "They don't know what they are doing, and thanks to Donald, neither do we. And with Nils out of the picture and Forrest not having a clue, what have we got? I'll tell you. We've got rot at the heart of the company. We just can't afford this, Bob. We can't present their work to potential investors. They'd laugh at us. And every dollar they spend is a dollar wasted. We've just got to get control of the money."

"I'll talk to Donald," promised Bob. "I'll let him know of your concerns. Let's see what he says."

Bob thought Donald would be content to let Al take care of things, and so, when he brought up the subject of firing Bernie and Bob, he was surprised when Donald pushed back.

"These are boys who are working ten times harder than anyone else," he exclaimed. "Hell, they're in the lab practically all the time. You can go to the lab at three a.m. and find them all working away. It makes me proud to see such dedication."

"What are you doing in the lab at three a.m.?" asked Bob, with wonder. "Don't you ever sleep?"

He was quite prepared to hear that Donald never did.

Instead, Donald said reasonably: "Oh, sometimes I just can't sleep. Not every night, of course, but definitely once in a while. I like to go to the lab then and just look over what we've created. And honestly, each time I've been there, there were Bob and Bernie and their crew working away. I've never seen anyone else in at that time."

Bob just looked back at him, unable to think of anything to say.

Donald went on: "And this is the kind of commitment that will bring us success, that will separate us from all the other companies out there."

Bob nodded, accepting Bernie's and Bob's selfless devotion to Almost Infinity's cause. But he was also skeptical.

"Did they know you liked to come into the lab in the middle of the night?"

"No," Donald shook his head. "They were as surprised to see me as I was to see them."

This, however, was a flagrant lie. Donald had told first Bernie and then Bob about his penchant for visiting labs in the middle of the night. He'd told them proudly, aware that people were always impressed by this evidence of a passion for work that transcended everyday human limitations. After all, only shift workers went to work in the middle of the night. Bob and Bernie had seen their opportunity and instantly grasped it. By coming in at night as well as the day, they were bound to impress the founder of the company and establish a unique line of communication with him. They could discuss the inner workings of the company and do it when everyone else was asleep. Their meetings would always be private. At the same time, they would be safe from the prying eyes of their colleagues, escaping the inevitable disparagement of their efforts. And these colleagues would, in spite of themselves, be forced to admire the sacrifice Bob and Bernie and their team were making for the success of the company.

Now, Bob and Bernie were always present at work between 7:00 p.m. and 8:00 a.m. In addition, they attended any meetings held in the mid to late afternoon. The impression this created was that they were working pretty much all the time. Nils and Al were very impressed by this dedication (if by nothing else) from Bob and Bernie. Stan and the rest of the Almost Infinity scientific staff less so. After all, they came in around eight thirty every morning and were often still at work at seven in the evening. And they were definitely working, unlike Bob and Bernie, who could be doing anything in the middle of the night. But anyway, everyone liked the fact that the company never slept—that it was always full of busy, industrious people 24/7. People in neighboring businesses noticed, as did the local tradespeople. Almost Infinity was definitely going places.

**

All Grains was pushing for more wormhole product. Donald explained that the most they were going to get with the present portal construction were random artifacts once every four weeks.

"How can we get more?" persisted Helmuth, as if he were asking for a mere increase in production of something fungible. Donald demurred. But a few days after receiving Helmuth's request, Donald got back to him. He'd talked it over with Bob (he hadn't), and they decided that Donald could construct a second portal and synchronize it with the first. The two portals would then produce something once every two weeks. Donald didn't think he could do any more than this.

"I don't think I can handle three portals, Helmuth. The math takes too much time and is, frankly, hard."

"Can you get something that is the commercial product already?" Helmuth wanted to know. "Something with new technology? We could really make the killing then."

Donald thought they would need a new contract before he could agree to something like that.

"You've got us for agriculture, Helmuth. Products in other areas are up for negotiation. You've got to be careful what you wish for. You can see how difficult it's all going to get, can't you?"

"So what if we paid for another portal? All products coming out of it would presumably belong exclusively to us."

"You mean with royalties for us, of course," said Donald.

"Oh, of course. About how much would another portal run us up?"

"I'd only be guessing. I'm going to have to talk to Bob."

Helmuth hung up and then sat at his desk thinking. What had they just been talking about? Wormholes? Time travel? Did he understand any of this? He didn't, of course. But then he didn't understand in any detail the million other things his company was busy using, making, and selling. *So what exactly*, he asked himself in a rare moment of introspection, *is it that I do?* He wasn't an expert on any of his company's activities. He had been a salesman in his native Germany in the early years of his company career. He'd been good at it and had progressed through the ranks, emerging as an executive first in Germany and then at the world headquarters of All Grains in Minneapolis. His title now was Executive Director for New Business Opportunities.

He decided that by any criterion the wormhole was an obvious opportunity. Of course, he didn't like being dependent on Bob and Donald and didn't really trust either of them. But he could see wormhole product, fuzzy though it currently was, was going to allow them to focus their research and steal a march on their competitors. Almost Infinity was literally selling the future. And, as he thought more, he realized that Donald's invention, if real, had the potential to be literally life changing.

Helmuth sat on in a daze. Myriad thoughts whirled around his head. He watched, passively, as they raced about. Donald had talked to them about multiple universes, hadn't he? He'd spoken as if multiple universes were an established fact. There were, in fact, many millions of them. Maybe, though, there was only one that accommodated an error-free, perfect existence. For everyone at one and the same time. That had to be a very special place. Maybe this was the universe to end all universes. And this was why Donald had called his company Almost Infinity. The perfect universe was the end, and of course, infinity had no end. But his mind rebelled at such a prospect. Why should such a place exist? Was this perfect universe what they had called, from time immemorial, heaven? If this was heaven, why should people die?

* * *

Helmuth decided to keep his thoughts to himself. He didn't want to be the first one to equate Donald Plum's wormhole to heaven. He thought others on the All Grains team would eventually reach the same conclusion without any prompting from him. He thought about Billy Woodruff. He was a down-to-earth kind of guy. He would reach the same conclusion, and he would speak freely about it. Billy could be relied upon. Billy was going to go far in the All Grains organization but not, Helmuth thought, to the very top. His fondness for speaking out would eventually be held against him. It was bound to upset those people who didn't reach the same conclusions as quickly as he did. He just didn't think Billy was enough of a diplomat.

"Aaach," Helmuth sighed aloud, alone in his office. Being a good company man was enough of a task in itself, without having to deal with all these profound questions. Almost Infinity! Wormholes! *Gott in Himmel!*

***

Bob had finally prevailed upon Donald to allow him to ask Bob and Bernie to present their progress to a company-wide audience. This time they'd be asked to focus on the progress they'd made in their research and to outline plans for collaboration with colleagues.

"They will enjoy the opportunity, Donald. They've had enough time to make some real progress now, haven't they? And it will settle all the other scientists, open up channels for communication, and foster team building. We just have to get them all working together, don't we?"

Donald forewarned his protégés, and so when Bob told them he was initiating an in-company seminar series in which all groups would get the opportunity to present their very latest research progress to their peers and he had chosen them for the honor of introducing this series, they were ready for him. They accepted the honor gracefully. And yes, they realized what an honor it was to be asked to be the first to present in what was sure to develop into a venerable company tradition. They did have something special to present now, and this would be the perfect opportunity.

Bob was relieved. This, he thought, was how it was supposed to be. This would get Al and Nils and all those other bastards (he thought here primarily of Stan and Jeff) off his back. If it went well, if Bernie and Bob did a good job, he could imagine handshakes and pleased smiles all round. If it went badly, if there was outrage and scorn, he would have to let Bob and Bernie go. Donald might not like that, but at least he would have seen his boys being treated fairly. And he'd have to see parting company was the only way to go if Bernie's and Bob's work was as egregious as Al and Stan were making it out to be. Keeping Donald happy, Bob realized, was the most important outcome. He was the star of their show. No one else had a Donald to front for them, with his unassailable math and magic wormhole.

Bob decided he didn't like to think about what Donald was doing. He had never believed in time travel. He suspected Donald of practicing deception. He thought the wormhole demonstration Donald had presented to the All Grains visitors was nothing more than a glorified magic trick, but, like all good magic tricks, it defied explanation. Maybe, somehow, Donald was concealing the fact of the deception from himself.

Finally, he adopted a pragmatic position. He was fairly sure he was taking part in a dishonest enterprise but decided he just didn't care. There was still the lingering possibility that Donald was for real. And then he thought about their funding. All Grains was their principal investor. But venture capital funding was often like this, wasn't it? The original ideas almost never worked out. If you were lucky, the original ideas invariably morphed into something different, something that had been invisible at first. He thought that with Nils and Al, Forrest and Arthur, George Nipper and the administrative staff, he had the core of a real company, one seated in reality. The wormhole was still useful to them though, if only as a fundraising device. Bob wondered how important constancy of purpose was to a new company. He and Donald, albeit fortuitously, had engineered the perfect test to answer the question. They were going to raise money with the promise of one future and then deliver and live in an altogether different one.

***

Bob thought with satisfaction about the money they'd raised. No one was disputing its reality. They were going to generate exciting research for the staid Midwestern company, research All Grains could never have undertaken on its own. The success of Almost Infinity would be recognized by further funding from All Grains. He was also going to get US Home Products on board. They would be visiting Almost

Infinity in the near future. So his task was simple. Keep Donald happy and keep everyone believing in him.

Bob had made inquiries about Donald from some of his friends of long-standing at San Francisco State. Donald, he was told, was known in his department as a pathological liar. His colleagues laughed about him and treated his behavior as a harmless eccentricity. Now, for Bob at least, any laughter had died away. Donald had raised $200 million. Hard to find much amusement in that. Suddenly, it was all so shockingly real.

Almost Infinity had not gotten off to a perfect start. They had hired plenty of ambitious and aggressive people who were focused on achievement at any cost. Stan was the leader. He was taking them all down a path to solid, respectable science and away from the fantasy of the wormhole. Bob realized, as he thought about this, that the resolution of the conflict between Donald and Stan would be the event that would make or break Almost Infinity. Depending on who triumphed, their future would either be one of relatively modest rewards in the here and now or one of unimaginable wealth and fame in the near future. Whatever happened, life was going to be interesting.

CHAPTER 9

The Visit

NIGEL SAW SEX LIKE A CLOUD enveloping Almost Infinity. It was all around him—Judy, glances exchanged with many of the young women at work, Charlene at home. When he thought about Charlene, though, he calmed down. Charlene was more than just sex. He sensed that with Charlene, commitment lay just around the corner. If you wanted that kind of commitment in your life (and not everyone did—he thought of Stan) you just had to be more in control of yourself. Maybe you couldn't have everything after all, but people around here definitely tried for it!

Nigel had a few more casual conversations with Oliver and then began to work collaboratively with him. Oliver, he realized, was a very bright guy, a bona fide molecular biologist. He needed this kind of collaborator to take part in the central preoccupation at Almost Infinity: the production of salt-tolerant and drought-resistant plants, a preoccupation Stan was doing his best to make exclusively his own. Together with Oliver and his group, Nigel had the chance to be a member of the first team to produce salt-tolerant crop plants at Almost Infinity or, in fact, anywhere. He knew a transgenic plant was one of Stan's principal goals, and if he and Oliver could beat him to it, it would be a serious black eye for the arrogant prick.

Nigel began to work harder, much harder, and to stay later. He became much more engaged in the company's objectives. Somehow, California's seductive sunshine seemed much more manageable when viewed through the filter of hard work, and he was content to go home and just be with Charlene. He was still at work at fifteen minutes past seven one evening, busy in the lab and by himself, when he heard the custodian's voice ringing out from a distant corner of the cavernous main space. In the cadence and rhythm of the speech, it sounded to him as if Emmanuel was preaching. *Maybe he's practicing for a Sunday sermon*, he told himself. Intrigued, he wandered over in the direction of the sound.

He approached cautiously and found himself looking into a partially walled-off area. This was the area of the lab where all the microscopes were kept. He froze as he realized there were about fifteen other people in the area, mostly women, all sitting with their attention focused on Emmanuel. This, at least, was what Nigel imagined since he couldn't actually see the custodian. None of the listening people noticed Nigel. He was taken by the completeness of their attention, their apparent immunity to distraction, as they listened to Emmanuel. He also noted most of the lab-coated audience were young technicians working for Bob and Bernie. He stood still, listening, as the custodian proclaimed in a ringing voice: "And you are the incorruptible seed. You are the chosen."

Heads bent as these words were recorded on notepads. Nigel withdrew quietly. No one had seen him, and he was embarrassed to have come upon such a scene. He stepped softly away and returned to his office. He sat down and thought about what he had just witnessed. He'd just come upon a dozen of his younger colleagues, employed like him at a research company engaged in developing cutting-edge technology in biology, and chemistry, attending faithfully to the words of a custodian (who was also a fundamentalist preacher, he reminded himself). What were these people doing? What did they hope to learn? Had they turned to Emmanuel in reaction to the world of sex and sunshine that surrounded them? Yes, he could imagine that. It was the contemporary rejection of Sodom and Gomorrah. As his mind played over these reflections, Donald floated mysteriously into view. Why was he thinking about Donald? There was no way he could blame Donald for this. His thoughts sank slowly to the prosaic. Emmanuel clearly didn't have enough to do in his custodial capacity. Perhaps he should mention it to Jim. With that thought uppermost, he went home to Charlene.

* * *

They ate dinner together. Nigel told her about Emmanuel preaching to the Almost Infinity employees.

"Mostly Bob and Bernie's crew as far as I could make out," he said. "They were taking notes! They all seemed very serious to me. And you know what, Charlene? I suddenly realized how alike Emmanuel and Donald are. They are both putting forward propositions that normal people have no right to be taking seriously."

"Normal people?" queried Charlene. "What do you mean by that? Lots of people take the Bible seriously."

"'Incorruptible seed'? Grains of salt out of the wormhole? What the hell have we got ourselves into here?"

Charlene laughed. "Put like that, I have to agree with you. But Bernie and Bob's lot are a cult, aren't they? That's what Dr. Steptoe is always telling us."

"Normal people," murmured Nigel, pursuing his theme. "Normal people who believe in time travel and normal people who are 'born again.' What do the born-again-ers believe, anyway?"

Charlene smiled at him. "Well, coming from rural Georgia, I can help you there. They believe in something called the Parousia, or the second coming of Christ, which announces the end of the world. Jesus arrives from the sky and collects all the faithful, at the same time consigning the rest of humanity to hell."

"They really believe that?" asked Nigel incredulously. "If you can believe that, time travel should pose no problems for you. Basically, you can believe anything. No wonder Donald gets on so well with Bernie and Bob. They are birds of a feather!"

Charlene stood up and came around the table and stood next to the sitting Nigel. He looked up wonderingly at her as she took his head and cuddled it against her body.

"How long can this last?" she asked him quietly. "Maybe we should be making plans to find something else. Together."

Nigel gave Charlene a quick squeeze and said: "It can last a long time, Charlene. We've got two hundred million from All Grains, and Nils, Al, and Forrest will keep us on the straight and narrow. There are a lot of very clever people here. I've never been anywhere like this."

Together. He realized that Charlene had declared her readiness to accept him as her permanent partner. He was flattered and at the same time felt a small rush of tenderness in response to her declaration.

He didn't want to just push her away, and so he finished the conversation by declaring ambiguously: "If we left now, we might regret it for the rest of our lives."

He didn't say "together," but at least he'd let her know she was in his thoughts for the long haul.

***

Now the money from All Grains began to flow into Almost Infinity. Its arrival signaled the start of furious activity. The pace of hiring dramatically accelerated, and soon Almost Infinity had almost one hundred employees. Crate loads of new equipment arrived at the warehouse practically every day. Bob and Jim began a number of building projects that would extend and customize their rented facilities. Al was the main driving force behind these initiatives. Nils and Forrest looked on, impressed by his ambition and enterprise. Bob wanted the building projects finished as quickly as possible so he could take potential investors on a tour of their new and improved facilities. He wanted everyone to see the depth of their commitment to success. Almost Infinity was definitely going places!

Bob now focused all his efforts and hopes on the visit of US Home Products. After his success with the All Grains visit, he was confident he could repeat it with another international behemoth. He was going to try for another two hundred million. Once they had US Home Products on board, they would have a stash of four hundred million at their disposal. With all that money, they were certain to be successful. They'd have no need of the wormhole then.

Donald had told Bob about the improvements he'd made in wormhole construction, about the display he was going to put on for its next materialization. He told Bob there'd be more colored lights and new sound effects. This had made Bob nervous. He wasn't sure gimmicks would work in the sale of the wormhole. He thought of warning Donald about using them. But in the end, he decided to do nothing. You could overthink these things. And Donald had done pretty well so far, hadn't he? A money infusion from US Home Products would put some distance between the wormhole and all the clever scientists at Almost Infinity producing real results their investors could understand. He, with the help of Nils, Al, and Stan, would have created a new company, a force in food production ready to meet the challenge of feeding the world! And it would emerge untainted by the dodgy wormhole.

Contractors began to appear at the warehouse. Building materials were delivered. The hubbub in the warehouse was increased by all the sawing, drilling, and hammering that accompanied the modifications of the working space. Cinder-block walls came up, and new enclosed spaces appeared. The massive cavernous lab became less cavernous. The researchers adapted their activities to the demands of the contractors. There was very little downtime. Jim had a right-hand man to supervise and coordinate the day-to-day activities of the contractors and the scientists. This was Don Klingel, a dour and unimaginative man who had spent many years in the US Navy. Don was a jack-of-all-trades. He performed all the little tasks the scientists required. He set up equipment, made sure all the necessary utilities were hooked up and safe, and operated the temperature controls in all the labs and offices. He made sure all the equipment was regularly serviced and that the emergency generator was working and available at all times.

Don had frequent spirited disagreements with Jim, who was his line manager. These disagreements always ended with Don carrying out Jim's instructions to the letter with an air of simmering resentment. Don knew his place and wanted to keep his job. The resentment, however, generally lingered. When each little project was completed, Don would take great pleasure in pointing out to everyone where he and Jim had had differences of opinion and how they'd been resolved. In Don's mind, his commonsense concerns were always vindicated in the project's resolution. But this, in fact, was usually not true. Jim knew his handyman well and didn't feel the need to justify what he'd instructed him to do. For Jim it was enough that Don followed direction. And Don always regarded the completed projects with a pleased, proprietorial air.

Bob set up a visit and a wormhole demonstration for US Home Products. And he was looking forward to showing off all the construction they'd undertaken. Donald told Bob he would get to work on the math needed for the construction of the wormhole, the completion of which would coincide with the visit of US Home Products. Bob let his visitors know how much work the team was carrying out to prepare for a successful visit. He told them also that there was great curiosity about what would emerge from the new and improved wormhole.

Most of the scientists were expecting more or less salt depending on how far into the future the wormhole reached. They were all praying their projects would be left intact after this next manifestation. Bob didn't share this information with US Home Products. And, as he thought more about it, he realized that wormhole manifestations would have to be regarded as proprietary events. The first vision of the future was now the property of All Grains. This next one would belong to US Home Products. All ensuing work would therefore have to be kept separate. Now he started thinking about their business model. He realized it was unsustainable in its present iteration. If wormhole product was very different from manifestation to manifestation, they couldn't keep hiring new teams, could they? No, the research would have to be done by the partner. This was by far the best solution. But then, taken to its logical conclusion, Almost Infinity only needed a research team of one: Donald.

He accepted they might have jumped the gun, hiring so many scientists with just the All Grains contract in hand. But without a lab turning out exciting research in the here and now, how could they attract new investors? Currently, almost the entire scientific staff at Almost Infinity was working on drought and salt tolerance in crop plants. Almost Infinity had morphed into a plant genetic engineering company.

***

Don Klingel looked over the cinder-block construction in the corner of the cavern with a warm and satisfied eye. It was finished on time and looked good. And he had played a big part in its success. The visitors from US Home Products would arrive later this morning, and now they could be walked safely through the new warren of labs and offices. He was expecting Bob and Donald to make a pre-tour inspection and was waiting for them.

They approached him walking quickly. They were both excited. This was it! Another two hundred million! It was so close. They flustered him, asking rapid-fire questions, nodding impatiently—Donald especially. They barely listened to his answers. Donald suddenly stretched out his neck and looked around a corner and down a short corridor inside the cinder-block warren. He barked out: "Where are the safety showers?"

Nobody had mentioned safety showers to Don, and he took offense at the question.

"What safety showers?" he asked querulously.

Bob understood his truculence. The man was expecting praise, but instead Donald had put his back up. So typical of Donald!

"Look," he said soothingly, "you've done a wonderful job here, Don. Just drill a few holes in the walls where the safety showers are to go, and I'll tell them this is one of the very few finishing touches we still need to make."

"Where are they supposed to go?" demanded Don. "We've had no discussions about this."

"Well, just drill some token holes then. Who knows what could come out of them?" Bob glanced at Donald as he said this, wondering if he would rise to the sly dig. Donald was oblivious.

"Whoever heard of a lab with no safety showers? Sheesh!"

Don's brow darkened. Bob ushered Donald away before he could say anything else.

"They'll notice straightaway, Bob," continued Donald as they stepped out into the parking lot. "These guys take part in safety inspections practically every day. They are all experts at it. Most of them don't have anything else to do. It's just as bad at the university."

Don went straight to his workshop and picked out a heavy drill. He selected a bit for masonry, and soon the entire warren area was shrouded in a thick cloud of brick dust. Nigel, who was wandering around his lab area, conducting a final check before the tour, caught sight of the billowing clouds of brick dust pouring out of the cinder-block warren. He was horrified.

"Good God!" he exclaimed. "We can't take anyone in there."

He spotted Don, addressing a wall with his drill. He watched as Don brought the bit of the drill into contact with the wall and began drilling furiously away. He was already covered completely in a coating of brick dust. No one had told him about the tour, obviously.

"Don! Don!" Nigel shouted, practically screaming to make himself heard above the din. Don shut off the drill and glared ferociously at him.

In the sudden relative silence, Nigel felt the naked force of Don's bottled-up rage.

"There's an important tour coming around this morning. Didn't anyone tell you?"

"I just do what I'm told," Don replied, fixing Nigel with a knowing, sardonic look, a look that also conveyed a cascade of hurt feelings.

Nigel went off to find Jim. Something would have to be done quickly or else the day would be a disaster. Quite fortuitously, Jim was in his office. Fortuitous because he rarely came in this early in the morning, but this morning he'd had a fight with Judy and was glad just to get off the boat. He was not in the best of moods.

Nigel asked Jim to accompany him back to the warren. He didn't try to explain the emergency. Instead, he asked after Judy.

"Is Judy in as well, Jim? It's early, isn't it?"

"The little hag is still on my boat," replied Jim, shocking Nigel into silence.

What a way to talk about your wife, he thought. *This wasn't an open marriage—this was more like open war.* They arrived together at the warehouse just as Don resumed drilling. Clouds of brick dust were again billowing out of the warren into the main lab. Jim went straight to the lead running to Don's drill and yanked the plug out of its socket. Don spun round, furious.

"What the fuck are you doing?" he roared at Jim.

"Have you gone mad?" Jim roared back. "Jesus Christ, we've got an important tour starting in an hour."

"I'm just following orders!" Don yelled.

"Who ordered you to fill the air with brick dust?" asked Jim, lowering his voice. "We've got to clean this up right away. Our futures may depend on it."

"All right, if that's what you want. I'll just blow it out of the construction."

"Blow it where?" asked Jim threateningly. "Out into the main lab? No, spray the air with water. It'll be messy, of course, but it will dry up and then you can brush it away. The dust should stay down for the tour. We might get away with it. You can clean it up later."

"As you wish," said Don shortly.

Nigel walked away, reflecting on the interaction between the two men. Jim was Don's boss, and he'd exercised his authority naturally and unselfconsciously in front of Nigel. Don should have been chastened, but he wasn't. He just seemed very angry. Nigel, after seeing the look on Don's face, was thinking he wouldn't be surprised one day to find Jim had been murdered. He would be found with a screwdriver sticking out of his eye, leaving everyone in no doubt who the killer was. He wondered how he would handle a man like Don. He certainly didn't have Jim's confidence.

After Don had finished spraying the dust out of the air, the floor of the cinder-block warren was a mess. Nigel ventured into the area and noticed how slippery the floor was.

"Put up some signs, Don?" he suggested deferentially.

Don snapped upright. He was still fuming.

"Great idea, you limey prick. I'll just go and get some and ram them up Jim's ass. I'll tell him it was your idea, though, don't worry."

And he stormed off.

***

The US Home Products group was standing in the lobby of Almost Infinity's business administration building. This was the stand-alone building that housed various offices including Bob's, the company library, the boardroom, and the auditorium used for seminars and company-wide meetings. It was about fifty yards from the warehouse. The visitors were excited. The group was headed by the chairman of the US Home Products board, Sir David Barnes. Bob was greatly encouraged by his participation in the visit. If two hundred million were to be discussed, he was the man you wanted along for the conversation. Sir David was a British Knight of the Realm, knighted for services to industry. He was quite a slim, sallow-faced individual, an unlikely survivor of many overindulgent, heavy, alcohol-charged meals suffered through in service to his American paymasters. He had a ready smile and an easygoing manner. But he was also aware of his rank at US Home Products and expected to be treated deferentially at all times. He was wearing a dark three-piece suit with a crisp white shirt and dark blue tie. He moved languidly and was the picture of calm and elegance.

He was accompanied on this trip by four senior executives and his vice-chairman, a dynamic American named Ernie Sikorsky, who actually ran the company. Sir David's foreignness was tolerated by the board of US Home Products because they needed his contacts in the world of high finance. He actually had no idea how to run a business in America beyond having read assorted magazine articles and one short book on the topic. He left Ernie to it. He liked to think of himself and Ernie as a team, and Ernie didn't mind. Ernie regarded Sir David's knighthood with typical good-natured American contempt. And everyone else at US Home Products took their lead from Ernie.

Sir David, of course, didn't take any of his American colleagues seriously. He thought of them all as crude and half-educated, barely able to speak English. But he made an exception for Ernie. Ernie had told him on the flight over in their private jet that Almost Infinity had been founded by a man who claimed to be able to tell the future. Normally, he wouldn't have wasted time on a matter like this, but his friend Helmuth, from All Grains, told him they were in for twenty million. With this in mind, he thought they had better check it out. Sir David agreed and was, in any case, very ready for a trip to California, particularly in the face of what would undoubtedly be an unpleasant winter in New Jersey.

And it was going to be exciting! They were going to see a real, honest-to-goodness time machine. Only in America! So now here they were, in sunny California, where all the people seemed indifferent to the glorious weather and the beautiful environment, and who smiled indulgently while their visitors praised it to its blue skies. Bob and Donald materialized in their midst. Donald patted Sir David on the arm and gave him his most oily smile. Sir David smiled back but thought Donald looked like a very slippery customer indeed. Bob, who knew Ernie Sikorsky was the real power at US Home Products, clapped him on the back.

"Nice to see you again, Ernie. How's the golf?"

"Middling, Bob," Ernie supplied. "Just middling."

"Well, let me introduce you to someone at the top of his game." He maneuvered Donald into a position directly in front of Ernie. "Ernie Sikorsky, meet Professor Donald Plum, internationally recognized cosmologist and founder of Almost Infinity."

The two men went to shake hands, but just at the moment of contact, the ring on Donald's pinkie touched the ring that Ernie wore on the third finger of his right hand. There was an audible crack, and the two men jerked their hands away in recoil from the unexpected discharge of static. Ernie looked startled. Donald grinned at him.

"Your presence is electrifying," he laughed. "I feel as if I've been struck by a bolt from the blue."

He had, in fact, been preparing surreptitiously for this handshake, rubbing his hand assiduously against his polyester shirt. Ernie smiled.

"Bob tells everyone you're a firecracker, Professor. Now, I guess, we all know it's true."

He reached out his hand again and shook Donald's warmly.

"Didn't happen that time," he observed.

Donald, the master magician, smiled back from beneath his halo of curly black hair.

Bob made a short welcome speech and finished by asking what they wanted to do first—tour the labs or see the wormhole demonstration. Sir David answered on behalf of the group. Bob realized then he was the only one who could answer. The others all looked submissively in his direction, even Ernie, as they waited for his decision. Bob thought it a revealing moment.

"Well, I think we should start with the tour first. I know I always think better after exercise, and we all want to be on our toes for the wormhole demonstration, don't we?"

The others nodded agreement in perfect unison, and Bob immediately led the way to the warehouse. He thought they could start the tour by inspecting the new labs that had just been constructed.

"The work is all finished now. We won't need hard hats," he called out as they walked into the cavernous main lab. He led them across the warehouse floor to the cinder-block warren in the corner.

"Of course, a lot of very specialized equipment is going to go in here," he announced. He noticed the wet floors and wondered what had been going on. "There's going to be a fluorescence-activated cell sorter and a microdensitometer for a start."

He looked down again at the floor with its thin layer of standing water and noticed the thick coating of dust floating on the surface. There was probably an eighth of an inch of water underfoot. Not enough, he thought, to bother his visitors, but he didn't want to dawdle around in it. He was definitely going to bring it up with Jim. He slid his foot experimentally along the ground and noted how slick it was. He didn't say anything though; he didn't want to draw attention to the mess. Just inside the warren, the floor sloped sharply. The slope was all that remained of a ramp leading down to a loading bay that had, at one time, occupied the front of the warehouse. Bob approached the ramp cautiously, but Sir David Barnes, striding out at the head of his group, hadn't noticed how slippery the floor was. There was a sudden, startled shout, and his legs went flying up into the air. He landed on his back in the shallow pools of dust-befouled water. He scrambled back to his feet with amazing agility, but the back of his once-immaculate suit was now caked with dirty, wet brick dust. He also had some in his hair.

The instant transformation of the dapper, elegant British businessman into this dirty, disheveled apparition rendered the entire party speechless. Ernie immediately moved to help Sir David out of his jacket. But Sir David didn't want to take it off. He was wearing a corset, the outline of which could be seen through his shirt, and he really didn't want anyone to see that. He fought off Ernie's sympathetic hands and hung on grimly to his dirty coat. Ernie was baffled by his behavior. Hell, he'd have to take the coat off sooner or later, wouldn't he?

Sir David fought tenaciously to keep his jacket. The sight of the two men struggling over the coat was simply too much for Donald. He roared with laughter. This was infectious, and several of the US Home Products men couldn't resist joining in. The sight of the chairman and vice-chairman reduced so quickly to such straitened circumstances was simply too much. None of them had expected this! Ernie, seeing how things were going, realized he had to get Sir David to see the funny side and he would have to do it quickly; otherwise it could all end very badly.

Sir David, however, was well beyond laughing at himself. He crouched over, his arms wrapped tightly around his body, still protecting his coat. Two of the US Home Products, men each grasping an arm, walked him out into the main lab and sat him down on a lab stool. Ernie approached the trembling figure and asked solicitously if he was all right. He told him they were bringing a car around to take him back to his hotel. Sir David shook his head violently from side to side, indicating he was not all right. His golden hair flew out at all angles from his shaking head, sending dirty water flying into the air. At the back of his head, where it had rested briefly on the floor, there was a kind of skullcap made up of a coating of brick dust slime. Several Almost Infinity employees came up from the depths of the lab to ask if an ambulance was needed. Sir David roused himself at this. All he wanted to do, he told them, was to go back to his hotel and then go back to New Jersey. The other members of the US Home Products party looked glumly at each other upon hearing these words. The visit was over before it had begun.

***

Bob, as might be expected, was incandescent with rage. He gave Jim a tongue-lashing. Why hadn't he checked the floors? The place was a goddamn death trap! Jim vented his mortification on Don. Don was told, not for the first time, that Jim was never the muggee. He was not a soft Californian. He was a tough guy from New York. If he was anything he was the *mugger*.

"What a load of fucking clowns," Don observed later, bitingly, to Nigel.

Nigel, having witnessed the transformed Sir David Barnes being whisked away, murmured: "If only we'd thought to put up some Caution: Wet Floor! signs."

Don glared at him but didn't say anything. It was not clear to Nigel he even remembered Nigel's gentle suggestion of half an hour ago. His angry eyes bored into the concerned, deferential face of his young colleague. Their unspoken message was, *Fucking clowns like you*, as Nigel understood it.

For Stan and his fellow gene jockeys, it was one of the funniest things that had ever happened.

"And Donald laughed his guts out, apparently," Oliver protested, holding on to Jeff for support.

"The best thing," gasped Stan, "the best thing is that Jim was at the bottom of it all. Jim and his brainless assistant, Don. What an asshole! I must have told Bob a hundred times that Jim and all who sail with him are assholes. And boy, has he proved it now. How many other two-hundred-million investors are we likely to get a shot at? Not too many, I think."

"They never even got to see the wormhole, did they?" asked Oliver. "And that can't be a good thing for us."

"They got the wormhole demonstration, all right," said Stan. "Jim ran it. He sent the chairman of their board out into the future and brought him back covered in shit. That'll be two hundred million, please."

They laughed on, but later, alone with their thoughts, they all realized the day had been an unmitigated disaster for Almost Infinity. To George Nipper, who had spent weeks setting up the visit, the events of the day were more than catastrophic. He wasn't sure Almost Infinity could recover. He realized now they were wholly dependent on All Grains. But the catastrophe had been brought about by incompetence on the part of the physical plant and facilities section. And this was incompetence from the bottom to the top. At the bottom, of course, was Don. But the top wasn't Jim. No! It was Bob. He was going to have to talk to Donald about it. Maybe he should ask for more responsibility. He should have been in charge. He would definitely have made a visit to the warren before the tour; he would have seen its state and would have removed it from the program. That was what Bob should have done. And now they were left at the mercy of All Grains.

CHAPTER 10

The Departure of the Hucksters

AFTER THE DEBACLE of the US Home Products visit, life at Almost Infinity began to settle down again. Hiring became less frenzied, and a rhythm established itself, driven by the demands of quarterly reports and weekly seminar presentations. They had the twenty million from All Grains in the bank, and that would be enough to keep them going for the rest of the year. Everyone was working hard, and the brightest people began to shine. It was only a matter of time before real scientific breakthroughs made an appearance.

Bob took it upon himself to make sure the work at Almost Infinity was exploited to the fullest. He contracted a firm of patent attorneys to make sure all their inventions were protected. This legal team didn't think they would be able to patent wormhole construction. They just thought it was outside the purview of patent protection.

"It has to be reproducible and understandable to those familiar with the art," they told Bob. "None of us can understand the concept. He keeps telling us it's driven by the math, but he won't share that. We really are stuck."

When pressed by Almost Infinity's legal team, Donald frankly admitted he wasn't prepared to give away his secrets. It was simply math, and he didn't think they could ever enforce such a patent. There was much to-and-fro-ing, but the outcome was never in doubt. There would be no patent application for the wormhole.

"So your famous wormhole is going to remain unprotected," Bob complained to Donald. But Donald was equal to this jibe.

"Like a black hole at the center of every galaxy," Donald had told him. "And as long as we don't approach the event horizon, we won't get sucked in. You can't patent a wormhole any more than you can patent a black hole. No one can patent the universe, Bob."

Bob was disappointed but understood Donald's reasoning. Man could never be, literally, master of the universe. And he thought it would be easy to maintain the wormhole as a trade secret. He still thought of the wormhole essentially as a fundraising device. As long as they could use it for that, they would be okay. And, over time, their company would mature and eventually emerge as an enterprise grounded in innovative, reproducible, and patentable science.

***

Bernie and Bob were getting ready for their next presentation to the company's scientists. They reviewed the results their team had obtained to date, and they had to admit there was nothing remarkable to be highlighted. This was very disappointing but hardly a surprise. Bernie tried a couple of off-the-wall experiments but only succeeded in demonstrating their off-the-wall-ness. He decided to include them in the presentation anyway. He would make up results, those he'd hoped for, and present these. Bob helped him in the creation of this fantasy. They said their prayers together and agreed they were merely acting for the greater good. What exactly this meant wasn't clear to anybody, least of all to them.

And if anyone could pull this off in front of an audience, it was Bernie. He would position all the members of his and Bob's group directly in front of him, and they would give him strength with their devoted, uncritical support. Bernie looked over his presentation. He knew where he was most likely to be challenged, but he thought these were primarily technical matters Bob and Donald wouldn't understand. The PhDs would look down on him and Bob, of course, but who cared about them? They were without any real entrepreneurial spirit.

It was a couple of weeks before their presentation, and Bernie was, as usual, at work sitting in his office at three o'clock in the morning. He'd been dozing, in between making efforts at trying to think of something truly inspiring for his upcoming talk, when Bob came in and invited him to join in a prayer before he went home. He was going home early that morning because he wanted to get some sleep before driving to Portland later that day to visit his parents. A forest fire was raging in an area he'd have to pass through, and he spoke about it as he was taking his leave of Bernie.

"It's all about regeneration, Bernie," he said. "Once it's burned itself out, all the living things that survived will make their way back into the world. There will be fresh new growth, saplings will spring up, it will all be green again in a couple of years."

After he'd gone, Bernie sat on thinking. His mind wandered to the forests and their regeneration after fire. New growth springing up as Bob had said, vigorous and fresh at the sites of the conflagrations. His mind considered the word "regeneration." That was a word they used all the time at work. Regenerating plants from callus cultures. Suddenly, a new thought popped into his head, pristine and unencumbered: callus and fire! *Oh, thank you, Bob. Thank you for helping. Callus and fire!* He doubted anyone had ever had such a daring thought. He experienced a rush of euphoria. This was why he loved research.

He was going to try fire to encourage growth of callus cultures. Hell, he could try it right now! He knew exactly what he wanted to do. He lit a spirit lamp—the flame of a Bunsen would be too intense—and began to transfer pieces of callus to fresh medium, passing each piece through the flickering flame for varying lengths of time. Too long and they sizzled. Some even caught fire. All these pieces he discarded. Those that showed little or no obvious damage he placed carefully onto the surface of fresh medium. Then he did this with one or two of the singed pieces. *After all, you never knew!* He created a control set that had never seen fire. This, of course, was growth he'd witnessed over and over, but the PhDs would want it. Those fussy know-it-alls.

Todd, one of his young and ignorant assistants, came up behind him and watched as Bernie passed a piece of callus through the flame.

"A different way of sterilizing, Bernie?" he asked respectfully, after a moment of silent contemplation.

Bernie, who was still lost in his own thoughts, was startled.

"What? Oh, it's you, Todd."

He decided it was too soon to share his flash of genius. Sharing would have to wait for the presentation.

"Yes, that's it. Got a pesky virus I just can't get rid of. I've even been considering antibiotics. That's how desperate I've become."

They both laughed at that. Antibiotics? For a virus? Oh, it was just too funny! Todd stood there shaking his head in admiration for Bernie's irreverence. He prepared to take his leave, but before he went, he told Bernie about a comic book he'd been reading.

"The Green Lantern was up against Fireman. Fireman was always setting people on fire. He called his superpower 'the delta factor.' It was really cool."

"The delta factor," repeated Bernie, when he was alone. "Yes, I really like that! That's what I'm going to call this. It's a general constant, one that can be considered for events taking place on a massive scale like forest fires as well as those that occur in a culture vessel. The delta factor. It even sounds scientific, doesn't it?"

And so it came to pass that the delta factor became the central message of Bernie and Bob's presentation. This was going to reduce their scientific colleagues to the status of gawping admirers. And it fit right in with wormholes, didn't it? Donald would definitely like it. No one else at Almost Infinity could have even dreamed of such a concept. Bernie and Bob's contribution would open the way to time travel through a flaming wormhole. *Life,* Bernie told himself portentously, *is, after all, a circus, isn't it?*

***

The scientific staff at Almost Infinity was definitely underwhelmed by Bernie and Bob's new presentation. There were shared glances of comic horror and a general feeling of excruciating embarrassment when Bernie brought up the concept of trial by fire. The members of the cult, however, were transported.

"Oh, it's so out of the box!" one of them, a pretty girl named Gloria, exclaimed.

Stan, Jeff, and Oliver remained stonily silent at the end of the presentation. Donald smiled and looked pleased. Bob turned his massive bulk around to face the audience.

"No questions?" he asked disbelievingly. "No questions from an audience of great minds? Impossible, surely."

Nigel felt guilty. Someone should ask a question, if only for form's sake.

"I've got a question, Bernie," he called out. "You haven't mentioned it in your talk, but I've just got to ask. What's mermaid's milk?"

Nigel was sitting near the front, and Bernie squinted down at him. "What?"

"'Mermaid's milk.' You have a bottle with that label in your lab area. Oliver told me about it. What is it?"

Bernie laughed. "I can't tell you that, Nigel. It's a trade secret."

Nigel smiled back, feeling, for reasons he didn't quite understand, slightly foolish. Bernie smiled around at them all and began to leave the front of the room. But before he could take more than a few steps, Stan opened up.

"You can't keep trade secrets from this audience. It's fucking insulting. How can we make any progress when we're keeping secrets from each other? How, Bob?"

Big Bob shifted his attention gratefully to Stan. He'd thought for a moment Bernie and Bob were going to get away with their laughable presentation. And where were Al and Nils? Why hadn't they spoken up? He turned to Bernie.

"He's got a point, Bernie, a good point. Everyone in this room has signed a confidentiality agreement. We are all sworn to secrecy."

"Just can't do it," said Bob, Bernie's sidekick. "These are the tricks of our trade. This is all Bernie and I have to offer another employer if, God forbid, that eventuality arises. We can't have someone going to another company and taking the secret of mermaid's milk with them. This is for the good of our company as well, you know."

Beneath his impassive exterior, Bob felt a flush of anger. Who was this scrawny, jumped-up sprat of a man? Who the hell did he think he was talking to? "Can't do it"? This wasn't his decision! He realized Bernie and Bob were setting a dangerous precedent. If they got away with this, the company would be fatally compromised. The company's intellectual property would be worthless.

He said, in an even voice: "There's no 'can't do it,' Bob. Who do you think is paying your salary? What are we paying you for?"

His voice began to rise and take on an angry edge.

"Can't do it? You will do it." His voice rose to a shout. "You will do it, and you'll do it right now!"

Bob looked back at him and gulped. Then he turned to Bernie for support. Bernie was equal to the moment.

"I guess me and Bob are finished here then, Bob. We'll clear out our office."

"Thank God!" interjected Stan. "We are finally getting rid of the know-nothing assholes."

Bernie sneered at him. Bob went white.

Bob, the president of the company, regained control of himself. "If you've got to go, you've got to go. But you will leave a full account of all your activities here. We have to be able to continue your work, Bernie."

He glanced at Donald, who was glowering. Bernie and Bob had also turned expectantly toward him. They addressed him mutely: *Here are your two faithful lieutenants being ruthlessly dispatched. Are you going to just sit there and let it happen?*

Outside, the sun was shining as usual, and the sky was a clear blue. A gentle, cool breeze wafted in from the nearby ocean inlet and played softly over the building in which the presentation was being made. People all around went about their business, happy and oblivious to the drama being played out in the nondescript building as they passed by. Inside the lecture theater, Donald said nothing. He just stared at Bernie and Bob along with the rest of Almost Infinity's employees. Stan and Bob watched him and knew they had won.

***

The aftermath was handled in a civilized manner. Bob came around to the office Bernie and Bob shared. It was their last day at work. They were clearing it out of all their personal possessions. "It's all in our lab books," Bernie told Bob, as they walked out to the parking lot. "The crew will fill you in."

But, of course, it wasn't in their lab books, and the crew couldn't fill anyone in. Nigel took possession of Bernie's lab book and stared fascinated at the pages describing the delta factor. It was set out in a series of bullet points as if a tidy, crisp presentation could somehow conceal the basic lunacy of the idea. Set fire to their cultures? Bernie didn't just appear crazy. He was crazy! Bernie couldn't see it, of course, and neither could any of the attractive young people who had belonged to Bernie's cult (as Al never tired of describing it).

One of the young people, Monica, who had a desk in the big office that accommodated Nigel and who decided she quite fancied him, mentioned a thought Bernie had expressed to her: They should just let the flames lick at the cultures, never actually allowing anything to burn.

"Maybe that's what he meant," she said helpfully.

Nigel went back to Bernie's lab book. It looked to Nigel as if Bernie had been trying to develop equations to express the delta factor. Nigel showed the lab book to Charlene, who freely admitted she couldn't understand a word of it. But Nigel had a PhD, didn't he? Surely, he understood it. He didn't. He could only conclude, he told Charlene, that Bernie was unbalanced. Charlene refused to accept this simple conclusion.

"How can you say he's unbalanced just because you can't understand him? Do you understand what Donald is on about? I know I don't. But he's the founder of the company we both work for."

"They are both unbalanced Charlene, just not in the same way."

And they left it at that.

***

Bernie and Bob went right to work after their departure from Almost Infinity. Bernie knew a venture capitalist who attended their church. He and Bob persuaded him to fund a start-up the three of them would run together. Bernie sold him on the notion that Jesus was guiding the company. They would always be kind and always tell the truth. At least, that's what they said. They decided to call the company Deltagene. The cult left Almost Infinity en masse and joined their former leaders at Deltagene, twenty miles down the road in Palo Alto.

Big Bob was glad to see the back of Bernie and Bob's human legacy. Now Bernie and Bob and all the young people were sent identical letters reminding them of their duties to their former employers. Bernie and Bob hired a lawyer who specialized in intellectual property issues. They and all the cult members met with him. To their great relief, he told them that in his opinion, the knowledge Almost Infinity appeared to be concerned about was simply tradecraft, and they could ignore the concerns. That was all they needed to hear. They collected all the letters and made a small bonfire on the grass in front of the building they were renting. Their time at Almost Infinity was consigned to flames and ash.

Deltagene began to pursue the same investors as Almost Infinity. Their venture capitalist founder contacted All Grains. Helmuth informed Bob of their approach.

"Ask him how many PhDs he's got on his books," was Bob's advice to Helmuth. "They are a pathetic joke."

Helmuth did as Bob advised, and Deltagene lost interest in All Grains. But Bob knew that Deltagene would have more luck with other investors, investors he didn't know.

All the scientists at Almost Infinity were glad to see the backs of the two born-again-ers. Only Emmanuel was sorry to see them go, but he'd already got his application in at Deltagene. He hoped to join them after Christmas. Bernie and Bob were already enjoying some success in attracting venture capital. *How,* the scientists at Almost Infinity wondered, *could this be?* It made them uncomfortable when they thought about the underpinnings of Almost Infinity. Bob found it ironic. Donald may or may not be able to create wormholes. But he and his acolytes could certainly conjure up venture capital.

CHAPTER 11

Donald the Time Traveler

BOB ASKED DONALD to present another demonstration of wormhole output for the senior management of the company. He thought it would be good for morale in the wake of their recent debacles. And timely, since Donald had been telling him how far the technology had advanced since his last demonstration. They were sitting in Bob's office at work, late in the afternoon, when Bob made this request. Donald asked for the usual two weeks to prepare the math for the event.

"Space-time is a fungible entity, Bob. But the breaches in its fabric are not all the same. Some of them, of course, are potentially dangerous. You and I always think of the peaceful uses of science. But what about weaponry? After all, one modern machine gun would have been enough to change the outcome of the Civil War. If it had been in the possession of the South, they would have defeated the North. And think about that enormous rent in the fabric of space-time."

"So that's what you mean by rents in the fabric of space-time, is it? Changing the course of history?" Bob looked at Donald with fresh respect. "Honestly, Donald, if you can really do something like this, there's no limit to your power."

Donald, from his new, lofty perch as the most significant mover and shaker in the history of mankind, looked down at Bob and smiled. It was the old, sly, slippery smile, and Bob knew immediately he was merely indulging his fantasies. He laughed at himself and patted Donald lightly on the upper arm.

"You had me going there for a moment, you son of a gun."

Donald, however, declined the invitation to join Bob in the real world, an invitation that, contrarily, his smile had extended. At this moment, as they sat looking at each other in quiet contemplation, with Bob's brain being tossed between sober realism and wild speculation, Donald's pseudologia fantastica burst into full bloom.

"I shouldn't really be telling you this, Bob," he began. The pseudologia sucked in the intimacy of the moment and the fantastica grew evermore irresistible; Donald felt an almost sexual excitement. "I'm from fifteen years in the future myself. I chose to come back to this time because it's a pivotal time in our intellectual development. I'm one of the early pioneers of time travel."

He stared at Bob's alarmed face for a moment. Then he shook his head.

"I could have come back sooner, but I couldn't bring myself to do it while my parents were still alive. But now they've passed … and, well, here I am."

Bob's alarm grew. He shifted his legs in protest.

"Oh, we're going to make a lot of money. Don't worry about that. But I don't have a clean slate, Bob. I can't go back to when my parents were still alive. So, you see, I am still constrained by the fabric of space-time. I can't just be as young as I'd like. My options are limited."

Bob continued to gawp at him. This man was telling him, in a calm and reasonable voice, that he was a time traveler.

He's much madder than I suspected, thought Bob. The voice in his head went on fearfully: *Whatever you do, don't argue with him.*

"You've made a tremendous sacrifice, Donald."

But, unable to contain his mounting curiosity, he went on: "So time-traveler Donald is fifteen years older than present-day Donald. What happened to present-day Donald when you arrived here?"

"Time-traveler Donald became one with present-day Donald. Present-day Donald just became time-traveler Donald."

"That's a hell of a price in years, Donald. So future Donald and present-day Donald have just merged? You shouldn't have done it. Wouldn't we have gotten rich anyway?"

Donald shook his head. "I needed to make a small tear in the space-time fabric. Otherwise, Almost Infinity was going to fail. Don't worry about the Donalds. There can only ever be one Donald." Bob looked him over appraisingly. Now he felt ashamed of himself for having momentarily panicked.

"I don't know what to say. Of course, I won't tell anyone about this. Your secret is safe with me."

"Thank you, Bob. You know, it's a relief to share my secret life with someone I trust, someone like you."

Bob reached out and shook his hand warmly, saying, "So we focus on salt and drought tolerance. Is that our clear path into the near future?"

"It is," Donald nodded. "We'll get there through genetic engineering. That's what we have to concentrate on. We will all become very rich."

Bob felt a quiver of excitement on hearing these words, but he still couldn't believe Donald was a time traveler. "So how does it work, Donald? Can you explain it to me without the math? In layman's language? I mean, where is present-day Donald now?"

"I'm still here," said Donald, smiling broadly. "I'm from a parallel universe. The universe where you and I are living now already had a Donald Plum in it. I came before I met you. Now I'm merely occupying my doppelgänger's body."

"Well, if you've come from fifteen years in the future, how old are you now?"

"The time traveler takes the current body's age," said Donald promptly. "The brain of the current doppelgänger ceases to exist at the moment he's occupied. Just as I ceased to exist in the future in which I was living. I'm completely forgotten in that future now. No, that's not right. I didn't just cease to exist—actually, I never existed."

"Well, Donald, if I might speak in layman's terms, this doesn't make any sense at all. How can you come from a future in which you didn't exist? The doppelgänger's brain is eliminated? And you, with your older brain, are now occupying his fifteen-year-younger body? That sounds like a real sweet deal for you. For him, not so much."

"Fuck him," said Donald irreverently. "He's in plenty of universes. That's what you've got to remember. That's the key to understanding all this. There is almost an infinity of universes. There is no sanctity to the life of any individual in any universe. We have an almost infinity of lives."

Now Bob began again to feel decidedly uncomfortable. "Come on, Donald, this isn't what I want to hear. People have to have significance, don't they?"

Donald opened his mouth, eager to pursue his fantasy to its logical endpoint, the endpoint of the ultimate atheist, where people are just interchangeable, ephemeral, soulless nothings. But then a wave of weariness suddenly passed over him, and the pseudologia fantastica faded. He closed his eyes and composed himself. He sought to unravel the knot in which he'd tied himself.

"Of course, you're right, Bob. There is no time travel. I made it all up." Then, seeing the horror gathering in Bob's face, he hurried on: "That's what you want me to say, isn't it? The truth is, you can't handle the truth."

Bob held up his hands in surrender. "I just can't understand you. How many times have you done this?"

"This is my fifth universe," said Donald unhesitatingly. "I've been both older and younger than I am right now."

"Do you remember each one?"

"Of course."

"And you're sure we are going to make a lot of money?"

"Of course. I've already lived it four times, Bob. You have too. You just don't know it. You haven't done any time traveling."

Despite his absolute certainty that Donald was deranged, Bob still felt a frisson of excitement on hearing these words. He clutched despairingly at his head.

"Why can't I understand this? I really want to get it."

"The wormhole is real. Don't you think I was surprised when it put in an appearance? The salt and the shade cloth are real things, aren't they? We've just got to stay calm." And he smiled his usual sly smile.

"Why were you surprised? Didn't you say this was your fifth universe? Surely, you'd seen it all before."

"The wormhole always surprises," said Donald dreamily. "It never gets old. It's meeting the universe face-to-face when you come into contact with a wormhole. You are contemplating the very mechanism of being. It's stark and God-like."

Bob waved his hand weakly. He could take no more.

"It's just too much for me to take in. I've got to go, Donald, if only to preserve my sanity. My wife's expecting me. But one last thing." His mind tossed out an ordinary, everyday question. "What is going to happen to Bernie and Bob?"

Donald put on his sunglasses in preparation for stepping outside with Bob. He flashed a brilliant, confident smile. "I've only met them in this universe. Your guess is as good as mine."

CHAPTER 12

Pork Chops on Trees

BOB WENT HOME with his mind reeling. Once out of Donald's presence, his skepticism came back with full force. There was no doubt now—he was teamed up with an absolute lunatic. How had he gotten himself into such a mess? His father had always told him he was too easygoing: "You'll get taken one day, young Robert. It's an absolute certainty."

The old man had been dead for ten years, but Bob heard his voice as clearly as if he were still alive. So what was the worst that could happen to him and Donald now? Well, they wouldn't lose any money. Neither he nor Donald had put a cent of their personal money into the company, and they had Real Excretions to thank for that. Donald would be exposed, people would laugh, and they would both be humiliated. He would never be able to raise venture capital again. So he should distance himself from Donald now before anything really bad happened. He was building a plant biotech company now, not a wormhole company, and Donald couldn't really expect to play the leading role.

Bob allowed himself to think about what Donald had just told him. He had come from another universe and was inhabiting the body of his doppelgänger living in the here and now. Bob's common sense reasserted itself. *Just think things through logically*, he told himself. Either Donald was one of humanity's first time travelers, or he was one of the many suffering from a mental illness. His prediction, and everyone else's, he thought, had to be one of the many. Time travel was simply too much. He was definitely going to push Donald further and further out of the picture. Almost Infinity's future, as well as his own, depended on it.

***

Donald breezed into the boardroom at seven thirty in the morning on the day he was to present his latest wormhole materialization. The math was all done—at least that's what he told Bob. But, of course, there was no math. The math had always been a façade erected by the pseudologia fantastica.

This time, already planted in the chamber beneath the scrap of dark gray cloth were the two items he'd selected to be delivered. A little piece of meat—a fragment from a pork chop he'd had for dinner the previous evening—and a sliver of bark from the apple tree that grew in the middle of the garden just outside his apartment. These items, he thought, would fit right in with the All Grains contract. Meat for food and trees for fuel. And not just any tree, a fruit bearer. He wondered if any of them would be able to identify the species of tree from the sliver of bark. He thought it unlikely. He also wondered if anybody would recognize the meat as a little piece of pork. The identification and significance of the two items he would leave to the scientists at Almost Infinity to determine.

At eight thirty, all the people and equipment were assembled in the boardroom. Present were the senior management group and, at Bob's urging, Stan. Marshall had excused himself, knowing the only reaction open to him was unqualified approval. The gathering looked expectantly at Donald. He wheeled forward the vacuum chamber and pump. Next, he plugged in and turned on the vacuum pump, and they watched as the needle on the gauge rose to almost minus 30 psi (pounds per square inch). The needle was at precisely minus 29.7 psi when he said: "Okay" and flipped on the colored light display.

"Can't we put a light on this?" asked Stan, peering suspiciously into the murky chamber.

"No use," said Donald. "As soon as the wormhole forms, any light will be sucked out through it. We would never see anything."

Stan nodded, still staring into the chamber. The colored light display provided enough of a distraction to make the interior of the chamber absolutely invisible to him. But he looked unconvinced by Donald's ready explanation. Donald flipped on the console. They were all startled as a strident voice ground out its countdown. This was repeated numerous times, enough for them to exchange glances of consternation at the racket, until quite suddenly, after five minutes, it stopped. Into the sudden silence there was the clear and perfect "ping" as the bell went off, signifying the closure of the wormhole.

"It's safe to open it now," Donald told them as he allowed air to rush into the chamber, opened the door, and looked inside.

He was pleased to note that the dark gray cloth had been sucked up into the inlet tube of the vacuum pump and had vanished from view.

Everyone crowded around the vacuum chamber and stared transfixed at the minute cube of pork chop and the sliver of bark. Nils spoke for them all.

"Holy moly," he murmured. "What is that?"

"That racket sounded like the start of a race. Like a kid's toy. The kind of crap you can buy in Radio Shack," said Stan pitilessly.

"It did, didn't it?" agreed Donald immediately. "And it was announcing the start of a race, wasn't it? Only this is not a race to compare speeds. This is a race with time."

And he flashed his sly, superior, and patronizing smile at them all, looking very pleased with himself.

Al moved to the vacuum chamber, carrying a forceps and a couple of empty Petri plates.

"What have we got here?" he asked thoughtfully, as he transferred the two items with the forceps, each to its own plate. "Looks like a piece of meat and a wood shaving of some sort, maybe tree bark."

Nils and Forrest both leaned over the plates, which Al had set down on the boardroom table, and studied their contents. Stan stood up and went to join them. He waited his turn at the plates, occupying himself while waiting by looking into the vacuum chamber.

"Hey!" he called out. "There's something else in here."

Donald hurried forward to crowd him away and take back control of his box. In a corner, under the port leading to the vacuum pump, the small piece of dark gray cloth had, once again, drifted back into the chamber.

"Shade cloth again," announced Donald. "What on earth could it mean?"

Stan looked him over appraisingly and with good humor.

"It happened at the first portal demonstration, didn't it? There's something funny about that, isn't there?" Stan smiled a suspicious, knowing smile. "Why does a piece of shade cloth keep appearing? What's it shading? There was nothing to hide in there, Donald, was there?"

Donald shrugged. "I wish I had more control over the wormhole. But the math is really difficult. Maybe it was because I used almost the same set of equations as before, and the product is reflecting that. If you'd like to go over the equations with me, I'd be more than willing."

"I'll pass on that, Donald. I'm no mathematician. Maybe you should get Marshall to go over them with you."

"He's already done that, Stan," Donald lied smoothly. He shook his head regretfully. "He didn't see this coming either. But we can't ask anyone else. No one outside the company, no cosmologist that is, can be allowed even a glimpse of our wormhole. We can't take the chance of sharing our work with anyone. We could completely lose our advantage. Bob will back me up on this."

"He's right, Stan. Until you come up with a few breakthroughs we can sell, Donald is our only ace in the hole."

"It's a hole all right, and we are all up it," said Stan insultingly.

Donald felt the hostility in Stan's remarks. He looked to Bob for admonition but was surprised to see instead a pleased look on his face.

What the hell? he thought. *They are all assholes, even Bob.*

In fact, the incomprehensible math, referred to but never displayed, the cheap gimmicks, and the mysterious reappearance of the shade cloth had merely caused all those present to doubt Donald's sanity. They all looked at Bob, who was wondering himself but concealing it well.

They thought: *He's a normal sort of a guy, and he backs Donald completely. Surely, if there were something funny about Donald, he would have spotted it.*

But now Stan, who was bolder than any of them, had spotted it, and his summary evaluation of their prospects was damning.

***

At O'Malley's that evening, Stan had everyone who showed up after work rolling around with laughter at his description of Donald's latest wormhole manifestation. Inevitably, though, the hilarity gave way to seriousness as they all moved on to consider their own situations. It was all very well to laugh about Donald, but the truth of the matter was they were all there because of him, albeit indirectly. Had any of them ever believed in the wormhole? Of course they hadn't. They had all believed in Al and Nils. These were the men with worldwide reputations, men who had published many groundbreaking papers. There was no questioning their suitability as mentors and leaders. It was only Stan—who had witnessed the behavior of these men in the presence of Bob and Donald, their fawning and obsequiousness, their abject surrender to the lure of money—who knew they were men with feet of clay. Dazzled by the money and the sunshine and trapped by their careless, lazy acquiescence of Donald's lunacy, these men had forgotten themselves. They had, as Stan put it brutally, simply sold out.

Increasingly, it was Al who ran the show now. Nils, quite unfairly, got blamed for the Bob and Bernie debacle. But Bob and Donald were still intent on using his reputation to draw in recruits. People arrived thinking they would be working with him only to find that Forrest, an old guy they had never heard of, was their boss. Al had assembled a team of promising young molecular biologists, the core of which was Oliver, Jeff, and Stan. These were the men to deliver for All Grains.

Jeff and Oliver went home that evening still thinking about Stan's description of the wormhole manifestation. They were wondering what kind of a future lay before them and how they had come to end up at such a company. They were going to be watching Al closely from now on.

***

A week later, Bob called Helmuth to tell him about the latest manifestations from the wormhole.

"As far as we can tell, it's meat. Probably pork, definitely not beef, but could be chicken. We'll know soon. The sliver of bark is more difficult, more a process of elimination than of positive identification. One of our botanists is guessing it could be from an apple tree, but he's not sure. We're going to sequence both DNAs, and that may take a week or two."

Helmuth was impressed. These Californians were live wires!

"Pork and an apple tree," he mused. "Are they related?"

"Well," lied Bob, "I don't eat pork myself, but isn't it often served with applesauce?"

There was a long pause at the other end of the line.

Finally, Helmuth said slowly: "Pork chops and apple trees. That's not such the unlikely pairing, is it? What if it's suggesting that both items—pork and apples—can be produced on the same tree? Maybe your guys, all those top molecular biologists, could actually produce an organism, say a tree, from which we could harvest apples and the pork chops. That would be a tremendous boost to the efficiency of the agriculture, wouldn't it? Maybe we could produce fewer pigs and get our pork chops off trees. Think of what that would mean."

"No more stick-thin, pious, finger-pointing, animal-loving vegetarians, for one thing," said Bob promptly. "How great would that be? And while I'm thinking about vegetarians, we would have fewer lagoons of shit. Hell, we'd be living in a much cleaner, healthier world, wouldn't we? So what are we saying here, Helmuth? Pork chops growing on apple trees. And you would like us to work on this?"

"No one can criticize that, Bob. That's definitely the worthy goal. If you guys want to try it, we would back you all the way. It would solve some of our biggest problems at the stroke."

"All right, Helmuth. You've identified a goal for us. I'm going to present it to our guys. There's no telling where it might lead us. Of course, this will certainly take us more than a year. How fast do apple trees grow? It might take all ten years of our contract. Who knows?"

He paused, wondering if Helmuth would be drawn into considering a longer, more substantial contract. Bob was acutely aware that Helmuth could pull the plug on them in six months by refusing to commit to another $20 million for the following year. Helmuth, however, let Bob's speculation hang. He liked the fact that Almost Infinity was heavily dependent on them. He wanted Bob to understand that he, Helmuth, was the boss of their collaborative enterprise. The All Grains board, he knew, considered they'd acquired a top-notch, state-of-the-art research group for a year, and they'd paid twenty million for it. The two hundred million figure stood off to one side, a chimera born out of wishful thinking and unrealistic optimism. Bob had never seen with such clarity, until this conversation with Helmuth, the pressing need for other large investors. He was going to have to get US Home Products back into the picture.

"Well, keep us informed, Bob," Helmuth said now. "Don't wait for the quarterly reports to give us the good news. The sooner we know about the progress, the sooner we can get those ducks in the row."

After this routine failure to employ colloquial English in his everyday speech, Helmuth hung up.

Bob was left thinking about Helmuth's parting words: "ducks in the row." But what did that mean? To grow all this new, clean, and wholesome food on apple trees bearing pork chops? Bob tried to imagine an orchard with all the trees loaded with apples and pork chops (boneless, of course!). There would undoubtedly be all kinds of bugs attracted to the trees, and with a diet of meat, who knew what the bugs would look like. Did bugs like meat? Well, he knew flies did. And flies produced maggots. Surely, All Grains would think of this. Maybe it wasn't so great after all. The trees would have to be doused with insecticides. He found himself liking the idea less and less. This could all turn into a nightmare. He was going to have to make sure it didn't become Almost Infinity's problem. Almost Infinity's role must finish with the production of the genetically modified trees.

Helmuth was pleased he'd had the conversation with Bob. He wanted Almost Infinity to continue to embrace the hope that All Grains would continue to fund them for ten years. And maybe they would! But it wasn't likely. He thought that so far, the research was going well. There were some very good scientists at Almost Infinity, scientists working in an environment conducive to progress. He thought the goal of growing pork chops on trees was, frankly, absurd. But he couldn't deny it was the desirable goal, the goal made irresistible to him by the fact he had thought of it himself. Would anyone at Almost Infinity have seen its agricultural significance? He didn't think so.

CHAPTER 13

Tune in, Turn on, Drop ... in

NIGEL HAD GROWN FRIENDLY with Ralph Pappo. Ralph had a desk in the same large office that also accommodated Nigel, Peter Blakely, Judy, and Monica. There were desks for six people in the office, and now five of them were filled. Ralph had lived his entire life in the Bay Area and treated the bright sunshine, blue skies, and cool air with indifference. Ralph was a chemist with a PhD from Berkeley. The fact he was living locally had been instrumental in him washing up at Almost Infinity, that and the fact that he knew Arthur Nanomura. Very few people knew exactly what he was doing at Almost Infinity, certainly not Bob or Donald. Something to do with renewable energy, solar energy, something pharmaceutical? No one was sure except Arthur, and he wasn't saying much.

One day Nigel came into the office and noticed Ralph carefully laying out tiny squares of paper in two large plastic Petri dishes. "What are you up to, Ralphie?" he asked casually.

"DNA samples in this one," said Ralph. "And a designer drug in this other one."

"A designer drug?" repeated Nigel, staring at Ralph. "Aren't you taking a chance there? You could go to jail for that, couldn't you?"

Ralph laughed. "Only if you turn me in, Nigel. And I'd deny it. Let's see them prove it. They'd never find the chemical because it's not a well-known entity. And how much of it is in one of these squares? I'll tell you: ten nanograms. Good luck finding that. It's practically impossible." He bent over the Petri plate and picked up one of the tiny squares of paper with a forceps. He dropped it into an Eppendorf tube and offered the tube to Nigel.

"Go on, give it a try. It won't do you any harm, and you might like it. Share it with Charlene. It's only ten nanograms."

Nigel stared at him, vacillating. "What's it supposed to do?"

He didn't take the offered tube.

"Go on, try it. The chemical is really innocuous, and it's present in such a small amount. Nanograms from Nanomura. Arthur is the designer here, not me."

"Arthur is the designer?" asked Nigel incredulously. "Really?"

"Of course," said Ralph. "Look Nigel, we chemists do this all the time. I don't know what it's like in the rest of the country, but here in California, designer drugs are all the rage. Chemists like Arthur are rock stars. And, as I was saying, it's completely invisible to the authorities. Plus, we don't usually sell our creations, at least the serious chemists don't, and we never allow anything that induces dependency to get established. I know you'll enjoy this one. It's a favorite of mine. It's a mood enhancer, one of Arthur's best, I think. Look, if you're worried, just cut the paper in half or even quarters. It'll still give you good feelings, even at such a low dose."

And he handed the Eppendorf tube again to Nigel.

This time, Nigel took possession of it.

"How quickly does it work?"

"You should feel something within the hour, if not sooner," said Ralph.

"And I just eat the paper?"

"Of course. It's rice paper, perfectly edible."

Nigel looked closely at the tube and then put it in his pocket. He decided to try the drug that evening when he was alone with Charlene.

"So what side effects should I expect, Ralphie?"

Ralph laughed and looked pleased with himself. "You'll see. I've had only satisfied customers so far."

"Has anybody at work tried it?"

"One or two, but I won't tell you who they are. They only get to try it if they are young and in a stable relationship. We are quite careful about who we give it out to. The fact I'm giving it to you means we think you are okay."

Nigel blushed his appreciation.

"Gosh, thanks Ralphie."

He went out into the lab to make up some media. As he lined up the chemicals to put together one of his media concoctions, his mind played over what had just happened. He'd been given a designer drug by one of the company's chemists. *Like a rock star!* He looked at the potassium nitrate and phosphate, ammonium sulfate, and magnesium chloride on the bench in front of him. These simple chemicals were his reality. What sophisticated chemical creation did he have in his pocket? Something organic, he thought. Potent in nanogram quantities. A mood enhancer, Ralph had said. He didn't dwell on potential dangers, but the drug was definitely going to affect his nerves. What if the potential changes were permanent? How likely was that? Come on, nanogram quantities!

There was no question of reporting Ralph to the authorities. He remembered how he'd thought about Ralph later, days later, when he was thinking more critically. He and Ralph both worked for a company that had a founder who believed he was producing wormholes. That put designer drugs into perspective, didn't it? He wondered if Ralph had supplied them to Donald.

***

Al was in his office with Stan and Jeff. They were deep in conversation about diseases in plants and about disease resistance genes. Al was on his soapbox, regaling the two younger men with the theory he thought of as his seminal contribution to the field.

"It's gene for gene, isn't it?"

"The challenge facing us is how to find plants that are resistant while, at the same time, maintaining the traits we prize, traits like yield," pointed out Jeff.

"We do it gene for gene. Anything else is just a pipe dream," said Al, heavily. "What do you think, Stan?"

Stan looked at Jeff and then turned to Al.

"So as I understand it, Jeff is concerned about maintaining yield, while you are more focused on disease. Maybe, for a company like ours, realism is the way to go. At least in the short term."

Al and Jeff warmed to him now, both pleased with his summation.

"Well, I do accept your gene-for-gene scenario, Al," said Jeff. "And it is the most reliable template to pursue in the short term. But the best we can hope for is a brief respite from disease. We've got to come up with something more if we want to improve productivity."

Al provided his own summary: "We've just got to work harder, cover all the bases."

Stan took his cue: "That's something Jeff and I can do. Definitely."

The discussion ended on this note, and Jeff and Stan repaired to O'Malley's.

***

Jeff sat back and took a drink of his beer. He enjoyed Stan's company when he was calm and sociable. Stan was, after all, a very successful research scientist. He already had several notable accomplishments to his name. He was probably going to go far, further perhaps than any of them. Sometimes though, the energy driving him boiled over, and he indulged in excesses of lust and ambition. Jeff, though, could see the clever and thoughtful man behind the outbursts of heat and bluster. And the clever and thoughtful man looked back and recognized a kindred spirit. They were united by their love for science. They left conflict and unpleasantness at the doors to the lab. Stan's relationship with Jeff and Oliver was as pure and free of complications as it could be. The young men simply loved science, and they liked each other.

"Donald might be a con artist, Stan, but we have to give him credit for originality," said Jeff. "I got a book out of the library the other day. Supposed to be for the layman, of course. The book's title was *The Universe is God*. There was a chapter in it on something called superstring theory. This covered the latest in our attempts to break down the atom into ever smaller units. The smallest parts of atoms are, apparently, something called strings. And get this—these strings are so small, we can never see them. And not just now, not ever. So not only is the universe too big to be comprehended, but, at its finest resolution, it's also too small. Most of us accept we won't be seeing God in our lifetimes, but I don't think people realize we can't really see anything at all at its most fundamental level. Hard to know if God and superstring theory are different, isn't it? Neither can be seen. And neither is testable."

"If it's not testable, it doesn't exist," said Stan. "That's my answer as a scientist. Physics is the real deal, though. Maybe we should give the benefit of the doubt to string theory. Maybe something cool will come out of it. Until it does though, I'm with you. They are all barking-mad assholes like Donald."

Jeff shook his head. "None of us knows about Donald. He might not be a serious scientist at all. He did go to Harvard, though. He's probably harmless."

"I don't think he's harmless," objected Stan. "I was ready to try for a faculty position at Berkeley before Bob and Donald came along and promised me great riches. Great riches and all the girls I could screw."

Jeff, who was quite a good-looking man, with fine features and kind eyes, looked Stan over. Stan's face superficially was that of a crude brawler. He had blunt features, flat cheekbones, and small eyes. His hair was a riot of untidy, wispy curls.

"What the hell do girls see in you?" Jeff blurted, momentarily forgetting himself and his natural courtesy. "You're just plug ugly."

He smiled winningly in apology.

Stan accepted Jeff's concise, brutal description of his lack of physical charms with equanimity. He didn't care what Jeff thought of his appearance. Jeff was his friend, and he didn't have many friends.

"It's simple, Jeff. Girls are interested in me because I'm single and available and have great prospects. They all want to share my passion for science. That's why I'm indulged."

Jeff looked at Stan reflectively. He might be crude, but at least he treated his women equally—there was no denying that. And he never affected a romantic interest in any of them. It was sexual gratification or nothing.

"You're a selfish bastard, though. You know that, don't you?"

Stan acknowledged this description of his personality with an indifferent shrug.

"Another beer?"

***

Bob had invited Donald to join him for a drink on his houseboat in Sausalito. Donald showed up wearing white pants and a blue shirt, open at the collar.

"I'm dressed for sailing, Bob!" he called out, as he clambered aboard.

Bob handed him a glass of sparkling white wine.

"Helmuth thinks the latest wormhole offering could be prompting us to create plant life that produces meat. He said he thought we should be genetically engineering plants to make them capable of synthesizing pieces of meat the size of an apple. Apples came up because I told him Niles Bennett—you know, our company botanist—thought the sliver of bark was probably from an apple tree. 'That's it, then,' Helmuth said. 'You've got to grow pork chops on apple trees. Pork and apples from the same orchard! What an advance!' I think he found it so exciting because he thought of it himself."

Donald shook his head in admiration at the audacity of the German's vision.

"How on earth did he manage to come up with that?" he asked, smiling broadly.

Bob looked at him closely. Why didn't he sound even slightly surprised? The thought crossed his mind that Donald had intended

Helmuth to be visited with this insight. It was a thought that affected him unpleasantly.

"Not surprised then?" asked Bob.

"It's the wildest thing I've ever heard of. But then I'm no farmer. I'm just a simple cosmologist."

"There's nothing simple about farmers, Donald," said Bob sternly.

"No, of course not," agreed Donald hastily. "That's what I was saying, wasn't it? These All Grains folks are a delight to work with."

Bob's eyes bulged threateningly in his fat face. He stared intently at Donald. Words, had they been uttered, would have been: "There is no wormhole; there's just you being an asshole."

Donald watched and waited, his eyebrows raised defiantly, daring Bob to speak. Then, suddenly, Bob relaxed and the moment passed.

Donald went on: "We get what we get. I can't call for specifics, you know that. Maybe if I brush up on superstring theory, who knows? With the marriage of superstring theory and gravity, anything is possible. Multiple universes could be everywhere, literally."

Bob waved a hand in recognition of his inadequacy to discuss the science with Donald.

"I'm going to get Stan, Jeff, and Oliver to come up with something. Those guys are our ace in the hole."

"I thought my wormhole was our ace in the hole."

Bob laughed and patted Donald on the shoulder.

"You're right, Donald. Your hole is beyond compare."

***

Nigel showed Charlene the Eppendorf tube that contained the impregnated rice paper. He took it out and placed it in the palm of his hand.

"We'll each take half," he told her. "Look at it. The amount of chemical is tiny. A couple of nanograms for each of us. I'll be amazed if we feel anything. He says it's a mood enhancer."

Charlene looked suspiciously at it.

"Why do we need that? We've got each other, haven't we? You are all I need."

"That's nice of you to say, Charlene. And I feel the same way about you. But we are both open-minded, and neither of us will dismiss something without at least first trying it, will we? And I like Ralph. He's a good guy. He wants us to be happy. He only gave this to me because I'm in a stable relationship with you. If I was on my own, I wouldn't have gotten it. That shows he's thinking about you too, doesn't it? We've really got to try it. Others already have, but he wouldn't tell me who."

"How long will it last?" asked Charlene, still hesitating.

"Just a couple of hours," lied Nigel easily. He had no idea how long it would last. "Let's take it now, before we eat. That's the safest time, isn't it? Lots of medications are taken like that aren't they?"

He cut the rice paper in half and popped one of the halves into his mouth. He swallowed and then smiled at her.

"Come on, you take yours. I'm feeling excited already."

She laughed and popped the remaining half into her mouth.

"I think it takes about an hour to start working," he told her, turning away.

Charlene went into the kitchen to begin preparing their dinner. Nigel sat down, watched television for a few minutes, and then went to help her. Somehow, he felt he just had to be near her. Neither of them spoke. Suddenly there didn't seem to be any need. About forty minutes later, after a meal consumed in preoccupied silence, Charlene looked at him as if coming to a conclusion reached after great deliberation.

"I'm so lucky to be with you here like this," she said softly. "What have I done to deserve this?"

"No!" protested Nigel. "I'm the lucky one. You are incredibly beautiful. And you've got such a perfect figure. Your legs are so long and thin and finely muscled. But gentle, not too sculpted—I've always loved legs like that."

They both stood up and looked each other over. They seemed slightly shocked at the transformation they'd undergone.

"There's only one place for us now, isn't there?" asked Nigel.

Charlene didn't answer. She just walked out of their kitchen and into their bedroom. She started to undress. Nigel followed, unbuttoning his shirt as he walked.

When he woke up the next morning, he was immediately filled with longing for Charlene. What a night! He'd lost track of how many times they'd made love. But, as he told his proud, laughing girlfriend, it couldn't be a record because it was wind-assisted. She appeared before him now having just taken a shower. She was toweling her naked body as she stood there looking down at him.

"You look just the same to me as you did last night," she told him, taking in his fine-featured face and lank blonde hair. "You're absolutely adorable."

He jumped out of bed and knelt before her. He embraced her knees.

"What knees! What perfection!" he exclaimed, kissing them.

She pulled him to his feet.

"Is it the drug?" she asked him seriously. "If it is, it hasn't worn off yet. At least not for me."

"Nor for me," he told her. "I don't know about a wormhole, but I feel as if I've gone through some kind of portal myself. A sense of constriction and then a sudden release into a wonderful new world. That's the best I can do. You know, I can't even remember what I thought about you before last night. A hazy memory of someone I liked and who had offered to marry me once—but now, well, we've just got to get married, Charlene, haven't we?"

"Of course, we have to get married," she confirmed softly. "We became one last night, didn't we? There's no going back now."

"No, there isn't," he said firmly. "Let's get engagement rings today. We've got to do things properly, haven't we?"

He hurried on: "Oh, let me just look at you! Oh, what a sight!"

And the talk of rings reached out and touched their families in Georgia and England. It gathered in their lives and bound them together. The purchase and wearing of the rings were the formality that attested to their new need for each other.

Of course, it was the drug. But when it did eventually wear off, it didn't matter. They remembered the transports of joy at the sight of each other, and the memory was enough to sustain their love. The mood enhancer wore off, but its memory was permanent. It had created a new reality for them. The rush to action it had precipitated was euphoric. They had seen each other at their very best, free from all the niggling reservations that populated their everyday world. They'd thought they might be made for each other. Now they knew it.

***

"Why can't you sell this?" Nigel asked Ralph. "This is not just some cheap thrill. This really is bringing a new objectivity to our perceptions of one another. That's the genius of it. It really does take you outside of yourself. You've got something here Ralph, you and Arthur, that is going to change the world for the better. Aren't you excited about it?"

"It's just too complicated, Nigel. And we've no idea about dosage."

"What? Of course, you do! It's five nanograms. That's what Charlene and I took. Just stick with that."

"Obviously, we were lucky with you and Charlene. But what if you'd gotten the wrong dose? Would you now despise each other?"

"Illogical, Ralph. If the dosage is too low, the chances are you'd notice nothing. There may be disappointment. But you could always go on and take a slightly higher dose. You could always work your way up to the magic threshold."

"Well, what about too high a dose? What does that do?"

"Nanograms from Nanomura," said Nigel. "As long as we're dealing with such trace amounts, and it's not a deadly poison, what harm could possibly come from it?"

"I'll tell Arthur about the experience you and Charlene enjoyed. He'll be pleased. Do you want some more?"

To his surprise Nigel turned down the offer.

"It was a wonderful experience, Ralph, and Charlene and I will be eternally grateful to you and Arthur. But we talked it over the next day when we got back from buying our engagement rings. We decided we wanted to love each other warts and all, if you have that expression here. Neither of us was comfortable at the thought of living life as an icon for the other. Just too much pressure and bound to end in disappointment. Particularly as we want to grow old together."

Ralph looked at Nigel with new respect.

"What a mature viewpoint. I don't think too many people would act in the same way. You two must really be in love."

CHAPTER 14

The Silver Trumpet Sounds

BOB WAS GENERALLY PLEASED with the state of his company. He could feel a sort of buzz in the air. People seemed eager to get to work. They had just started to keep statistics on attendance, and he noted with pleasure that the rate of short-term absenteeism was practically nil. *One of the advantages of a young workforce*, he thought. He also noted, as he took his casual strolls around the site, that there seemed to be a minimum of gossip. Everyone did seem to be working. Something good was bound to emerge from all this purposeful activity. He doubted the shops of their competitors were similarly engaged.

Donald wasn't happy. He thought the company had become a plant research institute when it could so easily have become something with much broader interests and activities. He did recognize, though, that this was the inevitable consequence of being funded, more or less entirely, by All Grains. Donald didn't try to exercise greater control over company direction by selection of wormhole product. He was grateful for the mysterious biology of plants, mystery proving surprisingly resilient in a world of increasingly sophisticated analytical tools. He knew, too, that he couldn't keep bringing mundane items like grains of salt out of the wormhole.

Forrest had assumed the administrative duties that had been withdrawn from Nils when his position changed from research director to research fellow. He was now the line manager of Nigel and all of his fellow senior cell biologists. This was a makeshift arrangement since Forrest knew nothing about cell biology. Susie, his personal assistant acquired from Marshall, was also, like Forrest, from a wealthy family. There would be no haggling over money with Susie. She was a chatty, friendly girl, and Forrest learned much from her about the department he was now heading.

One day she told Forrest that many people in the department were worried about the long-term stability of the company. They were worried that the money would soon run out. Forrest brought up the concern at a meeting of the departmental directors. Bob promised to ask Ben Benson, the company's CFO, to put out a memo detailing the current state of the company's finances.

"That," he said emphatically, "should shut up all the worriers."

He gave Ben the briefest of direction and then forgot about it.

Thus, it came to pass that one morning Nigel came into the office to find Peter Blakely at his desk staring at a sheet of paper with a look of fascinated dread on his face. He looked up and flashed Nigel a conspiratorial smile.

"What are you going to be doing come December?"

Nigel looked back, his curiosity piqued. Now, deeply in love, he found everybody, even Peter, interesting and likable.

"What do you mean?"

"Well," said Peter, "we've all gotten this memo from Ben Benson. It tells us how much we're spending each month, and it tells us how much cash we have in hand. If you divide the second number by the first, you come up with about four. This means we've got about four months left. Come December we'll all be looking for new jobs."

Nigel heard the words but didn't take them on board right away. This was Peter, after all.

"Surely not," he said now. "We would already have had plenty of warnings about this, wouldn't we?"

Nigel's experiences of workplaces, prior to Almost Infinity, had been confined to universities. You could get into trouble at a university and have your funding withdrawn. It had happened to him, hadn't it? *Thanks, Kutti!* But the idea of the very institution itself going under was unthinkable. And it would surely take years to come to pass, not a mere four months.

"Come on, Peter, there must be some rational explanation. This just can't be right." He picked up Peter's copy of the memo and read it standing next to the sitting Peter. "Oh, come on! This is just for year one of our All Grains contract. Ben Benson has limited the funds from All Grains to twenty million. But our contract is for two hundred million. That gives us ten years, doesn't it? My God, Pete, you had me worried there for a moment."

Peter, however, wasn't giving up his role as the messenger of doom. He reclaimed the memo from Nigel, laid it flat on the desk in front of him, and pointed to a line in it.

"It says right here, Nigel, that the All Grains contract is subject to yearly review. That means they can cancel it after the first twenty million. Come December we could all be out of work. Maybe they are compelled to warn us to prevent us suing them for breach of contract."

"Are you likely to sue them?" asked Nigel, smiling. "Charlene and I can barely make ends meet as it is."

Peter shook his head decisively. "No, they won't be worried about people like us. But what about the big shots, people like Al and Nils and Forrest? What kind of contracts have they got?"

Nigel stopped smiling. He had never heard Peter make so much sense. He looked again at the memo.

"You know," he said wonderingly and with a little fear in his voice, "you could just be right."

A pleased, self-satisfied smile spread over Peter's face.

"I am right," he said proudly. "Come on, let's go and see what everyone else is saying. At the very least it should be interesting."

But Nigel demurred.

"I'm telling Charlene," he said. "See you later."

Peter watched him leave and then walked out of the office himself. The first person he encountered was Oliver. Oliver might have word from Al on the memo. Oliver hadn't seen it. He'd only just arrived at work. He stared incredulously at it.

"Four months? That's what they're giving us? Christ, what can we do in four months?"

Peter was taken aback at Oliver's instant acceptance of his interpretation of the memo's message. He'd hoped for some reassurance that it really wasn't as bad as it seemed. But Oliver appeared as shaken as he'd been himself when he'd first read it. He'd looked for its lighthearted dismissal but had gotten, instead, a confirmation of his worst fears. Now he really was beginning to worry.

***

Bob was sitting in his office staring at Ben's memo. The stupid shit! Now he would have to call a company-wide meeting to calm everybody down. People needed to be focused on their research at this critical time in the company's existence, not on some hypothetical, looming catastrophe. Some people might even try to leave now. He let his thoughts play over the situation. What could he do? Well, he could get Donald to produce something from the wormhole, something reassuring, something that would allay fears of their imminent demise. But what could it be? He'd have to talk it over with Donald.

Al found himself facing Stan, who was enraged.

"Fucking hell, Al! I can't be out of work. Not even for a day! What kind of hellhole have you got me into here? Money running out in December? For God's sake, I thought you were a serious man."

"Well, I can't deny that's a possibility, Stan. But All Grains could also renew at the end of October, and then we'll be okay for another year. We'll have to get Bob's input," Al told him. "He might have all kinds of deals that are just not showing up in Ben's balance sheets. I'd say we've just got to trust in Bob and Donald."

Stan scowled and stormed out of Al's office. It was only nine o'clock in the morning, but Stan decided he was going to get drunk. He went looking for Jeff to take with him.

They were the only customers at O'Malley's.

"I didn't know the All Grains contract was good only for a year, did you? God, I was so mad I almost punched Al out."

"Two hundred million, I was told by Al," Jeff put in, curious to see just how mad Stan could get. "I guess it all depends on what comes out of Donald's hole next."

But the gust of rage had passed. Now Stan's little eyes sparkled with malice, and his thinking broadened beyond Bob and Donald. "He never said anything about yearly reviews. Should we be thinking of getting out?"

"What's Donald going to do now?" asked Jeff.

Stan ignored him. His thoughts had wandered involuntarily to his usual prey.

"What do you think of Judy? She's got to be desperate being married to a geriatric abomination like Jim."

"Not my type, Stan. Too Californian for me. Big mouth, lots of teeth. There is someone I do have my eye on, though."

And if Stan had shown any interest, Jeff would have gone on to tell him about a certain girl he fancied. But Stan was still fixated on himself.

"Fucking women! Such a distraction! What were we talking about?"

"Donald and wormhole product. I'd like to see something from next year come out of Donald's wormhole. Then at least we'd know we had another year. Or am I going crazy?"

"Well, let's tell Donald this is what we want. The whole thing is a crock of shit, isn't it? If he produces something on demand, he would be as good as admitting it, wouldn't he?"

"So," said Jeff, summing up. "If we tell him what we want and he produces it, it will definitely be a crock."

Stan shook his finger warningly.

"No, much as we'd like to, we can't say that. It is possible he got the math right."

And they both laughed.

***

In fact, at that very moment, Bob was demanding of Donald what Stan and Jeff had been joking about.

"Get us something unequivocal, Donald. Something that assures us of a future."

"The math is really hard. To achieve this kind of specificity is a great challenge, as I'm sure you can appreciate. It's hard enough to create a portal in the first place, but to go through it and secure something so, well, so particular—the equations are off the charts."

Bob followed through unrelentingly.

"No more goddamn math, Donald. This is just us. We want to let everyone know Almost Infinity has a future, that's all. And a bright one, at that."

"Three to five years, then?"

"That would be perfect," said Bob.

He stood up and moved around behind the sitting Donald. He put both his hands on Donald's shoulders.

"But let me see what you've come up with before we show it to everyone else."

"Okay, Bob. But this will be a one-off. I don't want it to jeopardize our genuine wormhole production."

"No fear of that." Bob squeezed his shoulders encouragingly. "I've still got absolute faith in you, Donald. You are the future of this company, you and your wormhole."

"Give me the morning, Bob. I'll come up with something convincing. I'll show it to you this afternoon, and then we can retrieve it from the vacuum chamber tomorrow morning."

"Good man!" cried Bob, continuing to massage his shoulders. "And we don't need to go through another wormhole demonstration, do we? You can just bring the item to a meeting of the senior managers that I'll call for tomorrow morning. I'll say I was with you when you got it. You're our savior."

Donald smiled weakly. His smile was no longer so sly and superior. Now it was faltering and uncertain. He realized he'd let Bob crash his way into his secret, furtive world. He still hadn't revealed all, though. But he knew Bob had glimpsed the truth about him.

That afternoon Donald came to Bob's office carrying a small piece of glass. It was actually a piece broken off a microscope slide. On the surface of the fragment, Donald had scratched two dates spanning three to five years in the future. He had also written "Almost Infinity" just below the dates.

"What do you think, Bob?" he asked shyly, handing the glass over carefully to him.

Bob looked closely at it.

"How did you write this?" he asked.

"With a diamond pencil," answered Donald, feeling himself continuing to unfold before Bob.

He felt a tightening in his throat. He stole a glance at Bob and wondered if Bob had any inkling of what he was going through. The pseudologia fantastica moved off to the periphery of his mind and hung there like a dark, threatening mass.

"A diamond pencil, eh?" Bob put his arm around Donald's shoulders and hugged him.

Donald allowed the older man the familiarity without demur. It was all part of his new status in Donald's life.

"Do you think the others will know about diamond pencils?" asked Bob.

"Al and Nils probably will."

"So why should we be using a diamond pencil in the future? Shouldn't we be using some future technology? After all, this piece of glass is from the future, isn't it?" queried Bob.

"That would be one way to look at it. But that's the beauty of wormhole product. People will try to construct a narrative out of the objects that materialize. Why would something so obviously archaic emerge from it? No, it'll get them thinking, Bob. It certainly won't be what they are expecting."

This Donald found wildly exciting. He was admitting to Bob that the wormhole was a fantasy.

"We'll say nothing more about this, Donald," Bob said now. "No one else needs to know what you go through to deliver from that wormhole. It'll be our secret."

Better and better. "Our secret!" No more veils of math to dance behind where Bob was concerned then. Donald looked at the fat, happy businessman with a keen, fresh interest. Bob was going to replace his parents as a helpmate in his struggle with pseudologia fantastica.

***

Al and Forrest sat and listened stone-faced to Bob's promise of further offerings from Donald's wormhole, offerings that Donald had assured him would bring them peace of mind.

"Tomorrow morning at nine o'clock!" cried Bob. "It will all be made clear to you. Look, I don't know what that stupid son of a bitch was thinking when he sent out that memo. He might just as well have sent you notices of dismissal. But I would never allow that. You are family to me—you know that don't you?"

They didn't. They stared back at him, disquieted by the strength of his reaction to Ben's memo, which seemed to them merely to confirm its veracity. He decided not to show them the piece of glass then. He would wait until tomorrow when more of the committee would be in attendance.

"Donald's going to answer all your questions," Bob went on. "You'll have nothing to worry about after tomorrow. What we want is for you to reassure the troops; let them know no one is in danger of losing a job."

"Well, once we are satisfied, we can certainly do that," said Al smoothly. "Ben definitely put the fear of God into me," he added, as cover for his obvious skepticism.

Bob turned to Forrest.

"What do you think, Forrest? I bet Harvard never treated you like this. But this is venture capitalism, and we don't have the safety net of an institution like Harvard. We are all out there on the high wire. It's what makes life exciting. But don't worry, there are going to be changes around here. You'll never get another memo like that."

Forrest inclined his head in gratitude for the reassurances.

"It would just be such a pity to see an exciting company like ours going under. None of us wants that."

CHAPTER 15

The Piece of Glass and the Troth

THE MEETING THE NEXT DAY with Donald was a strange one. He produced his almost square, jagged-edged fragment of glass, and everyone looked suspiciously at it. No one said anything. Bob attempted to rally them.

"Well, that's at least five years we've got then," he pointed out brightly.

But somehow the piece of glass depressed them all. It looked like a piece of trash rescued from the debris of an abandoned or destroyed facility.

"I wonder why we'd be scratching our name on a microscope slide," said Al. "No one does that anymore, do they?"

"Maybe for histological preps," put in Nils. "We used to use diamond pencils for those in Canada."

"Well, I don't see any histological prep on this bit of glass," said George Nipper. "I think it means we've run out of money and become a much smaller company."

"Oh, come on!" cried Bob angrily. "How could you possibly come to that conclusion?"

"It does look like trash, Bob," said George defensively, looking around for support from his colleagues.

Donald spoke up. "Look, the math wasn't straightforward here. It might not be representative of anything."

Donald, like Bob, was disappointed at the cool reception being given the prospect of five more years at Almost Infinity.

Marshall Hunt, who was stirring uneasily, finally spoke up.

"The math must be tremendously difficult. Maybe if Donald could just tell me exactly what he's done, I could try to turn it into layman's language for the rest of the company."

Donald could barely keep the contempt out of his voice as he responded: "Great! I'll just run it by Marshall and the rest of you can take your lead from him."

"The math should have gotten us something better," said Stan forcefully. "Something that would have far more significance to those of us in this room. You'll just have to do better, Donald. How can we explain this useless piece of trash when there are any number of objects of far greater significance which could have been transported?"

"Hey! Hey!" protested Bob. "Donald is bringing us items from the future, this last one from five years in the future. That was our prime requirement, and he's met it. It even has dates scratched on it. Someone from the future is sending us this message. Maybe it's even one of us!"

This novel idea arrested the attention of all of them. There was a moment of silence.

Then Nils spoke up: "Do we even know what this is? It looks like glass, but maybe it's some kind of super material. Maybe we should try and smash it."

He looked up and smiled around challengingly.

"We're not going to be doing that now," said Bob quickly. "I just want to show this to all our employees. I want them to see we have a future together of at least five years. You can do an awful lot of research in five years, can't you? We could have made all kinds of wonderful breakthroughs by then."

Stan decided he didn't want them all turning expectantly to him.

"It's obvious," he said loudly, loud enough to make them all turn to him. "There is something Donald can do, something that would answer all the questions. He can go to the future himself and bring back something convincing. He can save all our asses."

"The math is the problem, Stan. It's just so damned hard," said Donald, flashing his slippery smile at them all, pleased to be back again at the center of everyone's attention.

Stan disallowed the reservation. "Oh, you know what I mean," he expostulated. "It has to be you. And you'd probably only need to be there for a short time, hours rather than days. Just one little wormhole."

"But would he be safe?" asked Bob. "It wouldn't do us any good if he failed to survive the transport."

Stan, somewhat reluctantly, allowed this was an undesirable outcome.

"We don't have to take any big risks, Bob. We can always send Marshall first."

When everyone, with the exception of Marshall, had finished laughing at this outrageous suggestion, Stan went on seriously: "Of course, Donald has to be sure it's safe."

Stan's tone was now a rebuke—how could anyone even think he would be prepared to risk Donald's safety. "But if anyone else goes, they might never get back. What if understanding the math is a requirement for time travel? We need help in the here and now. It's of no use to us in the there and then, is it?"

No one, not even Donald, was quite sure what he was talking about. But they all understood, in general terms, he was proposing Donald travel to the future and return with information that would ensure the company's success. In the here and now, as Stan had said in the part of his comment that was understood.

"Is there any chance of this, Donald?" asked Nils gravely.

Under the circumstances, his manner suggested, the least Donald could do was offer to risk his life.

Donald shook his head decisively.

"No, I'm way off human time travel. Our wormholes are too small to allow a person passage. But I am trying to get there. You all saw the piece of pork. That was dead meat, but we don't know what it started as. Obviously, I would be no good to anyone as dead meat."

"This wormhole production is a bit of a crapshoot, isn't it?" asked Stan, ever belligerent. "It's almost as if someone is playing games with us. Who could that be, I wonder?"

Once again, Bob came to Donald's defense.

"Look, Donald is doing something remarkable here."

Stan remained on the offensive.

"So far, we've had a couple of bits of dirty gray cloth, some grains of salt, a piece of pork chop, a sliver of bark, and now a piece of broken glass with some scratchings on it. Hardly Nobel material, is it? As a matter of fact, all these items could be viewed as detritus from a post-apocalyptic environment. Like I said, it's almost as if someone is playing with us. Maybe the winner of the conflict. Who knows? Hell, we'd better check our bits of stuff for radioactivity. If they are radioactive, it's not just Almost Infinity's future that's bleak, it's the future of the entire world."

Everyone in the room stared at Stan. He had touched the imaginations of them all.

"By all means, check for radioactivity," said Donald now. "But even if they are radioactive, it wouldn't necessarily spell disaster for us. As I've already tried to explain to you, one of the central concepts at play here is the concept of multiverses. The artifacts we've recovered so far most probably come from a parallel universe. But right now, I don't know which universe this is."

Stan immediately attacked again.

"So how does any of this help us then? Another universe, even if it is parallel, whatever that means, may not be our future at all. It may not even be close."

"Mathematics helps us understand the concepts, Stan. That's all," Donald said kindly.

"In a parallel universe I might have no dick," replied Stan, unmoved.

Donald raised his eyebrows but otherwise allowed the crudity to pass unremarked upon. But to the others around the table, Stan had raised an interesting point.

"Well, how do we know these objects coming to us are coming from a universe like ours then, Donald?" asked Al.

"Of course, we can't know," began Donald evasively, "but in my judgment, it is what the math is calling for."

Bob rallied them all.

"Come on, people, we've got work to do. Check for radioactivity and then spread the good word among the troops. There's not a moment to lose. I think this has been one of our most productive meetings."

***

Nigel turned his head on the pillow to look at Charlene. God, she was beautiful. Did he deserve her? He wondered at all the admirable qualities he saw in her. It was no longer just a physical attraction, although that was burning as brightly as ever. Now he looked forward to sharing all his thoughts with her.

She recognized his greater forthrightness and repaid him with honesty of her own. They were setting the foundations for a long and happy partnership. She stirred slightly and opened her eyes. She turned to look at him. He was so unlike all the boys she'd known in high school and college. He was just so soft and vulnerable. She loved his lank hair and kind, thoughtful eyes. She'd opened herself up to him in the few days since they'd taken Arthur's tabs. And she'd felt accepted and welcomed.

"We are like each other, aren't we?" she asked him now.

"I wish," replied Nigel. "You are perfect. Me? Not so much. But I want to improve myself; I want to be what you deserve."

"Let's get married and have a baby," she said softly.

Nigel's eyes sparkled.

"I want that too," he said. "I just hope we don't both lose our jobs at the same time. If I couldn't find something quickly, I'd have to leave the country."

"Not if you're married to me," she told him. "I was going to marry you before, remember? And I only liked you, then."

"So is this the drug, still?" asked Nigel somewhat fearfully.

"No," she replied, with total conviction. "Not for me. It was how you reacted on finding out about me and Stan. I behaved badly with him. And you forgave me and helped me recover from my self-inflicted wounds. That was when I fell in love with you."

"We both need each other's protection, don't we? We should just surrender ourselves to the purity of love. No more weird talk and dwelling on recriminations. Let's just look to the future. From this moment on let's strive to always do the right thing. It'll be easy because it's what we want. It means never devaluing our love for one another."

"Or our love for ourselves," added Charlene, cheering up. "We have a vision of who we want to be, don't we? Let's try to live up to that."

"And we've got to be resilient," said Nigel. "There will be setbacks; that's a certainty. We've just got to rise above them."

"Oh, Nigel! You make me so happy!"

And outside their rented home, the sun shone brightly, leaves and grass glowed, the sky was clear and a brilliant blue, and a cool breeze wafted over it all. Oh, to be in love in California!

***

Helmuth got a call from Ned Crellin, who was a senior executive at Brown and Humphreys, one of the biggest tobacco companies in America. Crellin was based in Durham, North Carolina.

"There's only one man more despised by the American public than a tobacco man, Helmuth, and that's a Nazi. How are you, my old goose-stepping friend?"

At the other end of the line, Helmuth rolled his eyes.

"Keeping busy, Ned. You know, feeding the world, battling the disease, trying to cure the cancer. And speaking of the cancer, what are you up to these days? Still trying to buy the government?"

"Naw, we bought them a long time ago. Say, Helmuth, what's this I hear about you funding time travel? Tell me you haven't lost it, please. I've got to say though, it does sound interesting. Boy, would we like to turn the clock back."

"It's a company in California, Ned. Almost Infinity. You should consider investing in them. We have. Twenty mill so far."

"Heh, heh," laughed Ned mirthlessly. "What the hell are you guys smoking? We only sell tobacco ourselves. Marijuana is not legal yet in Minneapolis, is it?"

"It's science, Ned. This is a real deal. Almost Infinity's founder is a guy who studies the universe. For you that's the place up in the sky every night when you go to the bed. He's constructed this machine—a wormhole portal, he calls it—and he gets things from the future to appear in it. He showed it to us. It's just an empty box. First, he sucks the air out with a vacuum pump, and then he switches on his machine with the flashing lights and little bell, and *basta*! Objects appear in the box. It's like the magic trick, Ned. Something out of nothing. But there is no trick. He did it right in front of us all. There was no hiding place."

"Well, what kind of things did he produce?"

"Can't tell you that, I'm afraid. We all signed the confidentiality agreements. You'll just have to believe me when I tell you the objects were very interesting and relevant to our company. Odd, unexpected, no one could have dreamed them. If this was a trick—well, it was a very strange way of going about it. No, it was real, all right. And the objects were real as well."

"From the future, then?"

"No doubt about it. Then—the best thing—they took us to a circus in the evening."

"Took you to a circus," repeated Ned wonderingly. "What happened there?"

"Well, the damnedest thing. A girl fell off the high wire and crashed onto the floor right in front of us. There were no safety nets. But the show just carried right on. A couple of clowns ran out with the stretcher, loaded her onto it, and then ran off. The Almost Infinity guys told us it happens every show. Said if it was real, they would never have a couple of clowns like that attending to her. They would have called in the real emergency services. I don't know, Ned. It sure looked real to me. Anyway, it all impressed the hell out of me."

"So you think there could be something there for us, Helmuth? Boy, I'd really like to see that circus."

"I'll give you Bob Levy's number. He's the guy who runs things out there. You can set up the visit."

Bob got Ned's call later that day. He listened quietly as Ned introduced himself, exchanged a few pleasantries, and then moved on to describe Almost Infinity's business plan. In his description of the plan, he made time travel sound almost routine. In California and in the circles in which Bob moved, everyone, it seemed, was very comfortable with the new notion. Ned was left with the impression he had some catching up to do. Ned tried to inject incredulity into the conversation as the reaction of any right-minded American, but Bob wouldn't have it.

"No, it's really not so strange. There are countless books written about wormholes and time travel. I'll give you the titles of some of the best of them. Our claim to fame is that our founder has actually built a wormhole and gotten it to work. Of course, we're protecting it. I expect all the major companies will sign up with us eventually. I mean, how can they not? You could have the exclusive license for all tobacco-related production from the wormhole. In the longer term, we are looking to transfer the technology to our partners. To get them set up with their own wormholes."

Donald, of course, would have been startled to hear such a suggestion, and it certainly wasn't one he would have made. Bob made it recklessly, with no intention of following up on it. *All's fair in love and business*, he thought to himself.

Ned asked for a demonstration, and Bob said they could probably fit the tobacco company in in about a month. That would give Donald time to prepare the math. Ned listened, baffled, but didn't say anything. They agreed to talk again closer to the time of the proposed visit. Bob went off to talk with Donald. He wondered what kinds of things they could produce to interest a tobacco company.

CHAPTER 16

Shorty Cigarettes and the Beating

AFTER THEIR LAST CONVERSATION, Bob began to view Donald differently. Donald had let him into his secret world as a fantasist and dropped the veils of misdirection. Now Bob thought of him merely as a con man. He had known many such people in his life—heck, he was one himself, wasn't he? So now, when Bob and Donald talked, Bob was talking to a fellow practitioner of the con.

Donald found the conversations with Bob and planning the show for the tobacco company exciting. He saw his parents making an unlikely return to life in the large, slightly obese form of Bob. Sympathetic concern for his well-being that had died with them was flickering back into life through Bob. Bob, for his part, no longer bothered to maintain the fantasy of the wormhole. He discussed openly the fact that they needed special artifacts to convince the tobacco company of the reality of the wormhole. But what could they be?

"Any ideas, Bob?" asked Donald, getting a real charge from the conspiratorial question.

Bob grinned at him.

"Hey, you're the cosmologist. How am I supposed to come up with something? But I have been thinking about it, so I've got a start on you. What I might have come up with in an earlier life."

Donald waited, a slight, expectant smile on his lips.

"How about just cutting the ends off a few cigarettes to make them an inch shorter. We'll present them as the wave of the future. A shorter cigarette! They'll definitely buy it. Think of all the advantages from their point of view. Shorter, lighter, cheaper! And the unstated message: shorter cigarettes must cause less health problems. Of course, people will need to buy more to get the same fix. The tobacco company will use less tobacco per cigarette, and that will lower the cost of production. It could even present an opportunity to put up prices! And people can try to quit simply by smoking their usual number. They will continue their dance to death though, even if more slowly."

"You're a special man, Bob," said Donald sincerely. "I don't think many people could come up with such an idea, one that hits all the right buttons."

Each time Donald shared thoughts now with Bob, he felt a charge of excitement. There was hope for him! But his affliction was still there.

"I'd better get to work. There's a lot of math to do to achieve this result."

Bob looked at him, incredulous.

"What are you talking about? All you've got to do is chop an inch off a few cigarettes with a razor blade and put them in the vacuum chamber."

"How do you think they get in there, Bob? Magic?"

"You put them there, Donald. There is no wormhole and no math."

Donald looked back at him. The truth, so bluntly stated, made it all seem so tawdry and furtive and, at the same time, unbelievably exciting. He felt a lump form in his throat.

"Really, Bob. You shouldn't say such things. What do you think? That I've been lying all along?"

Now Bob felt a little thrill of anger. Why was Donald refusing to own up to his mendacity? They were friends now, weren't they?

"So what has this wormhole produced so far, Donald? Salt, a few pieces of dirty gray cloth, a piece of pork chop, a sliver of bark, and a fragment of a microscope slide with some scratchings on it. How can someone with my knowledge of you now take it seriously?"

"Doesn't Helmuth believe me, then? After all, he came up with pork chops on trees, didn't he? That was his idea. And what about Al and Forrest and Nils? Even Stan? Doesn't anyone believe me?"

"Helmuth and Stan, definitely not. The other three are daft enough to believe anything. They just can't conceive of a professor acting like you."

Bob looked him over fondly. He was thinking mawkishly that Donald could be the son he'd never had.

"No girls in your life, Donald?" he asked.

"There are a couple," lied Donald smoothly. "One's dark and the other's a blonde. I'm playing the field currently, Bob, sleeping with the both of them. It's quite exhausting."

"Atta boy!" shouted Bob. "Marry one and settle down, have kids."

"Yes, that's definitely the plan. When I go time traveling, I don't want to go alone."

Bob looked up quickly at this, mouth half open, ready to share the joke. But Donald was perfectly serious. He was still firmly in the grip of his disease.

**

George Nipper began to prepare for the visit of Brown and Humphreys. Ned Crellin definitely wanted a wormhole demonstration. He also wanted to go to the circus and see the fabulous falling girl for himself. He was disappointed to learn that the show had left town. In place of the circus, Bob suggested a trip to Marine World, Africa, USA.

"You can get your picture taken with a tiger," he told Ned. "A real one."

Ned said he was looking forward to it.

Bob warned him: "It's not in a cage. You'll be standing right next to it."

"I'll bring the chairman of our board. With a bit of luck, the tiger will be hungry that day."

"I'll see what can be arranged," promised Bob, laughing.

With at least five more years as a going concern now firmly in prospect, the level of tension surrounding the visit of Brown and Humphreys was much lower than it had been for that of US Home Products. It all went like clockwork. The tobacco executives had been deeply impressed by the wormhole demonstration and intrigued by the short cigarettes. All the subsequent discussion had been on the importance to Brown and Humphreys of exclusivity. It had been decided to leave it up to Bob and Ned to hammer out terms in the next few weeks.

Bob called a meeting of the senior managers to discuss what terms he should hold out for. Al thought the terms should be those of the All Grains contract with one modification.

"And this time, Bob, we won't make the payments subject to possible cancellation in a year. They have to see that's an untenable situation for us."

Heads nodded vigorously around the table. Bob took it as a rebuke.

"I couldn't do anything about that," he complained. "Brown may well demand the same limitation. These guys all talk to each other."

Forrest, who was beginning to grow into his role as an executive, said: "Well then, you could just tell them to take a hike."

He smiled around at them all with a mischievous glint in his eye.

"Or, what about this? Exclusivity was really important to those guys, wasn't it? Just tell them we're expecting a visit from Bull Tobacco. That should give them some incentive to make us happy."

"Okay," said Bob. "I'll try for this. Two hundred million over five years. Wormhole product four times a year. Funding to be reviewed once during the five-year contract, say after thirty months. That should net us a guaranteed one hundred million."

"That sounds fair," said Al. "And how much research do they expect us to do for them? These tobacco guys are pretty secretive, aren't they?"

"I think we limit our contribution to wormhole output. They can't get that from anyone else."

They all agreed with Bob's plan, and he went off to call Ned.

***

Initially, the call went surprisingly well. Ned made no comment on the two hundred million Bob asked for, which told Bob it was a number he'd been expecting. He did ask for a yearly review. So he had obviously been talking to Helmuth.

"It's not a deal breaker though, Bob," he said smoothly. "I'm sure we can work out a compromise. Maybe yearly, with the first one coming after eighteen months?"

"If nothing comes up in the meantime, I'm sure that will be okay," said Bob mysteriously.

"What do you mean?" snapped Ned immediately. "What can come up?"

"Well, we're going to be talking to Bull Tobacco," said Bob apologetically, taking up Forrest's suggestion. "Of course, we won't show them the shorty cigarettes. But who knows what will come out of the wormhole? And if you look at your confidentiality agreement with us, we don't promise exactly the same thing can't happen with someone else. We might find ourselves looking at shorty cigarettes again in the course of Bull Tobacco's visit, for all I know."

"Sonofabitch!" yelled Ned. "You promised us exclusive rights to tobacco products. If Bull Tobacco gets the shorty cigarettes, I'm going to sue your ass. I'm going to give you the mother and father of a beating, shithead."

Bob was taken aback by the sudden angry outburst. And he was afraid. He knew Almost Infinity couldn't survive a lawsuit launched by such a giant as Brown and Humphreys.

Ned's voice sank to a vicious whisper.

"Tell me we don't have to go down this road, Bob, you sneaky shit. Believe me, motherfucker, you don't want to be fighting with us."

The sneaky shit thought fast. He would have to cave, and he would have to do it with good grace and humor.

"We didn't know we were so important to you, Ned. Hell, forget about Bull Tobacco. They won't be coming out here, at least not to see us. We're part of the Brown and Humphreys family now, aren't we?"

"Damn right," growled Ned.

A long silence followed. Bob desperately wanted to make Ned laugh, but he couldn't think of anything remotely funny to say. Ned decided he wanted to hear more protestations of fealty.

"I think this has been a useful discussion, Bob," he said in a calm, thoughtful voice. "We needed to get to know each other better, didn't we?"

"Yes, we certainly did, Ned. I'm grateful for your honesty. We can go forward from here, can't we? We really want to work with you"

"Two hundred million over ten years with a yearly review for renewal of the contract," said Ned.

"Right," said Bob. "Sounds like a plan."

"Good talking to you, Bob," said Ned. "We'll be in touch." And he hung up.

**

Bob sat on, still holding the phone in his hand as he tried to absorb what had just happened. He definitely felt he'd been disciplined. Of course, the discipline had been administered over the phone, thank goodness. There had been no Ned sitting in his office calling him a sneaky shit and a motherfucker and daring him to do something about it. He was grateful for that. Thanks to that dithering old fart Forrest, he'd just run into the unacceptable face of capitalism. He realized Ned was a more serious man than him. To Ned this clearly wasn't a game. It was an elemental struggle in which he'd invested his entire life. Ned was the most serious man he'd ever met. And what was it that made him so serious? Well, obviously it was money, but Bob sensed it was more than that. Power, then? Yes, that had to be it. It was a lust for the exercise of naked power.

Bob doubted anyone at Almost Infinity was possessed by this lust. He thought about Donald and about all the senior managers. None of these. What about Stan? Stan was a nasty piece of work, wasn't he? He tried to imagine Stan and Ned negotiating with each other. There would be no quarter given on either side. Any argument that arose between them was bound to be short and brutal. But whatever the outcome, he knew Stan wouldn't cave. Stan, with the red mist before him, was always going to be formidable. *Stan's face*, thought Bob whimsically, *was their only face sufficiently unacceptable to gain entry into the capitalists' club.*

CHAPTER 17

The First Quarterly Report

ALL GRAINS SENT OUT A COUPLE of scientists to California to follow up on the quarterly report Almost Infinity had submitted. Billy Woodruff came with them. The All Grains scientists were now deep in discussion with Al.

"So you're saying that as well as salt and drought, disease is something we should be focusing on?"

"You know the theory, of course—my gene-for-gene hypothesis. It's a novel way of looking at disease. It means we can stay one step ahead of disease indefinitely. And no chemicals, just biology."

"But what about wormhole output? Isn't that your guiding light?"

"Well, it is," conceded Al. "But that's physics. I'm a biologist. Almost Infinity is more than just a wormhole company."

"Helmuth will expect you all to be working on wormhole output. I'm sure that was what was in the contract."

"Okay, okay, I'll check it out with Bob. Gene for gene can be used for drought and salinity, I'm sure. In fact, in those cases it will probably be easier."

But, of course, he hadn't thought it through.

Inside, Al was furious. He needed Donald to take a couple of diseased leaves and pass them through the wormhole.

The next day, he gave Bob the leaves and told him what he wanted.

Bob winked and said: "Let's see if Donald can find them in his wormhole. I'm betting they are in there somewhere."

And, once again, Al wondered what the hell he had gotten himself into. He knew now he was no longer going to be able to look Donald in the eye. *Lies upon lies,* he thought to himself. *Our company is floating on a sea of lies, and it's all flowing out of Donald.*

***

Nigel was talking with Charlene.

"We both know there's no such thing as time travel, which is what Donald is claiming he has engineered through his wormhole. To the future and back to the past! But, you know, I'm grateful to the company, to Nils and Bob. It gave me a place when I was desperate. And it allowed us to fall in love. Even an animal like Stan has played his part, hasn't he? So for us, it's a magical place, isn't it? And I know I want it to go on forever. Just as long as you are with me."

Charlene burst into tears. Nigel wasn't concerned. He understood her. He even felt like crying himself. He cradled her head in his arms.

"Nigel," she gasped. "I'm just so goddamn happy. I'll always love you, and I'll always love Almost Infinity. I know it's a crazy place, but then we're crazy too, aren't we?"

"We're a perfect match—crazy in California. But here we're normal, aren't we? We fit right in."

"Where will we live when Almost Infinity goes under?" she wanted to know now. "Georgia or England?"

"I've always wanted to live on the East Coast," said Nigel. "New York or Boston. Like England, but in America."

"I've never been to the East Coast," Charlene told him. "I don't think central Florida counts. Is Georgia still a possibility?"

"Of course," said Nigel. "As long as we're together."

More tears.

***

Donald was beginning to feel uncomfortable with the degree to which he was being exposed. He was happy enough being a liar—the *pseudologia fantastica* provided complete insulation from painful retrospection—but he didn't want it to be his defining trait. He knew he was different and thought it the inevitable consequence of brilliance. Bob, he thought, was the closest person he had to a friend. Bob! How wrong was that? What, really, did they have in common? His was basically a fractured personality. There was still a future for him, though, but someone would have to make him whole. He just couldn't do it on his own. Maybe a woman? Hope stirred faintly in his breast.

***

Later that evening, Billy called Helmuth to report on the events of the day. Helmuth listened quietly. He was pleased the All Grains scientists had called out Al for his lack of attention to the wormhole's demands.

"We didn't give them money for Al to pursue his academic interests. What about the pork chops on the apple trees? I was expecting the progress on that. That's what they should be working on, Billy. Did they talk about that?"

Billy told him no. It had never come up. He could tell from Helmuth's long silence after hearing this that he was angry.

"I'll make sure to ask them about it tomorrow, Helmuth," he promised.

Helmuth took a deep breath.

"Look, Billy," he began, "we are giving Almost Infinity twenty million dollars. We are giving them this money so they can do the research on the projects identified by the wormhole. This is not just some vague suggestion to be considered and then forgotten about. That should have been the first item on the agenda for the visit. Front on central. For us, it's a matter of the crucial importance that they take it seriously. I mean, Jesus Christ, the wormhole product is the very essence of their company, isn't it? The pork chops on the apple trees *is* the most significant and high profile of all our joint projects. If they aren't even working on it, they can expect no further support from us. I want to hear the detailed plans, with the milestones and the critical paths. I want it all laid out so we can evaluate it. Tell Bob to give me the call tomorrow."

He hung up without saying goodbye.

CHAPTER 18

The Bell Tolls

HELMUTH CALLED A MEETING of the scientists who were interfacing with Almost Infinity. From his demeanor, they could all tell this was an important meeting.

"In a couple of months," he began, "we have to decide whether or not we are going to renew our contract with Almost Infinity. That's a commitment of twenty million dollars. Now, I don't know who else they've signed up, if anyone. Their initial money, which wasn't very much, came from the Real Excretions. I think a couple of million at most. And then twenty from us."

"I don't like to think about what came out of the wormhole for Real Excretions," said Billy Woodruff, looking professorial. He summed up his reflections concisely.

"Scatology and eschatology," he went on, grinning around at them all. "Shit and the end of time. How appropriate for a wormhole."

"Seriously," Helmuth glanced disapprovingly at Billy and reclaimed leadership of the meeting, having no idea what he was talking about, "we have to make the decision here. Anyone want to speak up for all the good folks out in California?"

No one said anything. Everyone knew the form. This was corporate business. Merely by asking the question, Helmuth had signed Almost Infinity's death warrant.

"All right," he said, after a moment's silence. "Have we all gone off the heads? Pork chops on apple trees? How can a plant produce the meat? It just seems impossible to me."

Everyone knew it had been his idea. Almost Infinity had embraced it, and now they were going to pay the price.

"It is impossible," said one of the senior research fellows, a scientist not on the corporate ladder and therefore allowed to make sensible, commonsense remarks at the management meetings he was invited to attend. "Plant cells just don't have the right pathways. Think about what meat is. You could engineer plant cells to produce some of the constituent proteins of meat, but you could never get the texture. Almost Infinity will tell us they can engineer anything. But surely nothing discrete, hanging off the branches of a tree."

"Isn't this the big enough project for us?" Helmuth wanted to know. "What more do we need?"

He looked around. "And is there any intellectual property here? I very much doubt it. How can they get the patent on the wormhole? It's a fantasy, right? So, as you can probably tell gentlemen, I'm not in favor of renewing our contract with Almost Infinity. We've had a few good ideas off them, and we've got plenty to do. They've certainly been paid well for their ideas. And maybe now we could hire one or two of their best people. Other opinions?"

He looked around brightly. No one spoke.

"I'm giving them to the beginning of the December."

The attendees of the meeting imagined all the clever, engaged people at Almost Infinity, some with young families, being cut off from funding. What kind of Christmas would those folks have?

"I'm sorry, of course, but our sales have been flat this past quarter, and we are going to have to cut the research expenditure. If it makes you feel any better, it was them or you—and I chose you."

They all looked admiringly at Helmuth. What a job the man was doing!

***

Judy confided to Nigel she had had sex with Stan.

"We went to the boat last Friday, and we took Arthur's tabs. I'm not sure about them. I only took the one, and I can hardly remember any of it. Stan took a bunch. Jim even joined in. He's bi, you know. It was a frenzy. Stan definitely won't remember any of it, he was so far gone."

They were standing side by side at a bench in the main lab when she told him this. Nigel looked at the bright-eyed, diminutive young woman standing next to him and felt sorry for her.

"Stan's an animal, isn't he?" he ventured, not sure of how Judy was regarding her most recent sexual adventure.

Maybe she'd enjoyed it and, for the moment, liked Stan. But if she did, it wouldn't last. There was a Zen-like justice in Stan's fate. He'd launched into the sex with a wild, reckless abandon, and now, if Judy was to be believed, he could remember none of it. Nigel was quite certain, though, that Stan had had no desire to be a participant in sex with Judy and Jim together. In the cold light of sobriety, he would have violently rejected such a role.

***

There was nothing said, nothing concrete to point to, but Bob sensed a change in the air. Communications with All Grains dried up. He thought about his recent contacts with Helmuth and realized they had all been initiated by him. In October, All Grains was expected to renew their contract with Almost Infinity and commit to another twenty million. Bob had been fairly confident they would do that. Now he was not so sure. He looked at Almost Infinity's burn rate and realized that with no further infusion of cash, they had just under three months left. He decided to talk it over with Donald.

Donald rarely appeared in the lab these days. His appearances had become ever rarer with the departure of the charismatic duo Bernie and Bob. Now he had no one to talk to in the middle of the night. Bob invited Donald to his boat, and the two men shared a glass of wine in the sunshine.

"Tough times could be ahead, Donald," Bob began cheerfully. "If those bastards at All Grains cut us off, we'll be in big trouble. And soon! Three months at the most."

"Do you think it will happen, then?"

"I can't really tell. I do know it's gone quiet between us. But who knows what that means?"

Donald smiled his smile. Still as slippery as ever, but now tinged with sadness.

"I've ruined it for everyone, haven't I? My wormhole. I mean, how could all our young people believe in that? Do you think they are even still employable?"

"What do you mean?" asked Bob, squinting at him suspiciously. "What are you talking about?"

"My credibility is shot, isn't it? I mean, they believed in my wormhole once. They put their futures on the line. It was the glass slide, wasn't it? I knew that was feeble. And, of course, it wasn't real."

"What are you saying, Donald? You're the inventor of the wormhole. You are producing out of it. You've convinced me, Nils and Al, Forrest, even Marshall."

Donald waved a hand resignedly.

"You know me, Bob. The others? No. They all think I'm crazy. I think my life is essentially over. If All Grains pull out, there's nothing left."

Bob goggled at him.

"Goddamn it, Donald, I don't think *my* life is over. I'm going to fight like hell for the survival of this company. And so are you. We're in this together, remember? We've got to back each other up. Look, we've talked about the wormhole, haven't we? I'm quite okay with it."

Donald felt strange. He was coming as close as he'd ever come to seeing himself clearly. Wormholes were nothing but a big lie, and he was the biggest liar. He was held for a moment in this shaft of insight. His face grew serious and the slippery smile faded. The inner, uncorrupted Donald looked out hopefully at Bob. Bob noticed the change in his expression and was shocked. What the hell was going on here? Donald was a normal human being, after all? It couldn't be!

"Look, Donald, everyone knows you're really bright. A genius, in fact. But you didn't invent wormholes—other people did, and they've written about them. I would say the majority of the scientific world believes in them. Have you ever heard one of your colleagues say they are a joke? I don't think so. They don't want to look stupid. Of course, very few people can do the math. But you can, and you went one step further and actually built one. I've read about people contemplating building wormholes, but they always end up saying it's impossible, at least for now. Well, you didn't. You actually built a wormhole and retrieved objects from the future through it. We all saw you do it, Donald. There's no shame or loss of credibility in believing in you. None whatsoever. You convinced me, and I don't think I'm incredibly dumb."

Bob's words rallied the pseudologia fantastica. Donald slipped out of the in-between state he'd found himself in and banged the door shut on his uncorrupted inner self. The flat reality of life independent of the disease flickered and then faded away. He was left staring at Bob. Bob believed in him! His slippery smile reappeared and Bob was reassured.

"Attaboy, Donald!" he cried. "We all need you. We're not done yet, not by any means."

* * *

Nils had never met anyone suffering from pseudologia fantastica; very few people had. It was a barely discernible but distinctive pathology. The lies came unprompted, and they were always plausible. Overall, Nils had formed a favorable impression of Donald. He admired his learning in cosmology, appreciated his efforts to come to grips with the technology behind biotech, and most of all, appreciated his great success at raising money. The doubts raised by the slippery smile melted away in the face of the millions Donald had raised. This was a skill that all senior scientists valued. Money meant security and a bright future working away at the science they all loved. If you could get money, you were bound to be successful, weren't you? And then more money would come. Donald, as founder, attained mythic proportions in Nils's imagination.

Al's first reaction to Donald had been similar to Nils's. Only, unlike Nils who'd professed a broad interest in all things plant biotechnology, Al had chosen to focus on his gene-for-gene hypothesis.

"This is a major new concept," he'd told Donald. "If you allow me to focus on this, I'll be pleased to join you in California."

Almost Infinity's concentration on plants had been assured by Nils's appointment as its first research director. Bob hadn't really wanted this. His background was the pharmaceutical industry, and medical doctors his primary customers. But all the best scientists in the health care field were already in excellent positions, and many were living in California. Bob and Donald really had nothing to offer them. They also tended to be disbelieving on the topic of the wormhole.

"Find a cure for cancer in the future," one of them had said. "Make it a pill, and then you can rule the world. If you can't get something like that through your wormhole, the future will depress everybody."

Bob and Donald had laughed, albeit uncomfortably, but they had to admit he had a point. It wasn't easy to see how they could get the wormhole to produce a cure for cancer. One public failure and the company would be finished.

So, reluctantly, Bob had given up on pharmaceuticals and settled for plants. The future of food was vaguer, more influenced by fashion. Food and how to get it was no longer one of life's imperatives—unless, of course, you were poor. And even poor people never starved these days, at least not in California. No, food was now a lifestyle choice. Many people could eat whatever they liked, within reason. Affluent, clever people sought out food that was going to give them an advantage. There was, however, very little in the way of science behind this. No one was really sure what the best food was. Diets came and went. People wrote books on the food that was the healthiest, food that prevented or at least delayed cancer, food that could be produced without killing the birds and the bees, the butterflies and the earthworms. The hope for near immortality shone faintly behind all this scholarship. But even the most banal and noncontroversial recommendations proved amazingly immune to statistical proof.

***

The more Stan thought about his situation, the angrier he became. He knew he was an outstanding scientist. He should be in some universally admired institution like Stanford or Berkeley. He'd chosen the diversion of Almost Infinity because it offered him the chance to work with Al and was also more money than a postdoc's stipend. There were some potential mentors at Almost Infinity: Al, Nils, and Forrest. But after taking the measure of these men, he decided only Al could offer him anything. Nils, he concluded, had never worked in a university and was not really top-class. And at his present age, he wasn't particularly energetic any more. In Stan's mind, he was definitely a has-been. However, he would continue to be courteous around him. He could know someone important, and there was no point in taking needless chances. Forrest was a plant breeder. These were strange people, enthralled by the phenotypes of crop plants and by their possible association with yield. But this wasn't science as Stan understood it.

So that left Al. Al he could respect. Al had an idea. He may or may not be right about plant disease, but at least he was pursuing his belief in a rational and scientific manner. And if he was right, it would be a big deal. So Stan was happy about that. He had his own ideas, of course, but he realized that success and recognition would be his sooner if he aligned himself with someone who had already made it. And that was Al. Stan was a man in a hurry. He wanted success and the acclaim that followed, and he wanted sex—lots of it. His greed for satiation cut him off from the finer things in life like love and kindness.

Donald and Stan were lonely men—Donald obsessed with his self-image, and Stan with his greedy ambition and lust. Honesty and altruism were alien concepts to them both. Donald was just a liar, but that was his illness. Beneath it all, he was a kind man. Bob had seen this kindness and also seen its lack in Stan. Superficially, he got on with the both of them, but while he liked Donald, he was a little afraid of Stan.

CHAPTER 19

The End

THE GOVERNMENT OF NIGERIA contacted Bob. Their consulate in San Francisco called him and told him Almost Infinity was going to receive a proposal from the government of Nigeria, and the consulate advised Bob to take it seriously and treat it in confidence. The next day, he received a fax from the Nigerian Secretary of Science and Industry, based in Lagos. It read:

Dear Bob,

We have learned about your fine enterprise. We will put in two hundred. We are looking forward to learning about our future.

With great respect and felicitations,

Obi Mikel
Secretary of Science and Industry

P.S. The two hundred is coming to your bank. Kindly place ten in our bank—account number given below—to begin transfer of funds. Thanks again.

There followed the address of a bank in New York and an account number. Bob stared at the missive. He was completely baffled. Two hundred what? And why did they need ten of this mysterious amount to begin transferring funds to Almost Infinity? The Nigerian government contacted Bob again a few days later, a much more formal and correct letter. Curiously, though, there was the same ambiguity about money in its text. Once again it talked about putting in two hundred, but it didn't say two hundred what. And, once again, it asked for ten to be put into a bank in New York. Bob wrote back inviting representatives of the government to visit Almost Infinity.

"It will," he wrote, "definitely be worth your while."

This was October, and the Nigerians proposed sending a delegation to visit in January of next year. Bob filed away this response and forgot about it. There would be plenty of time before Christmas to make preparations for the visit.

***

Bernie and Bob were going great guns down in Palo Alto. They'd received five million in start-up money from a venture capital fund based in Boston and had now rented and equipped a smallish building and hired about twenty people. A local venture capitalist, David Hallauer, who was also a born-again Christian and who attended the same church as Bernie and Bob, was helping them with the fundraising. A number of former Almost Infinity employees, including most of the cult members, were among their hires. Bernie and Bob welcomed all their new employees with prayers and exhortations to join them in feeding the hungry of the world. They weren't in it just for the money, unlike those bastards up in San Carlos. The business plan was essentially a copy of Almost Infinity's without the wormhole.

Bob, up in San Carlos, noted their progress with a jaundiced eye. The proximity of Stanford and the beautiful suburbs of Palo Alto made Deltagene an even more attractive place to work than Almost Infinity. At last, Bob bestirred himself. He instructed the law firm representing Almost Infinity to send a letter to Bob and Bernie reminding them of their obligations to their former employer. Bob knew they hadn't signed no-compete agreements. No Almost Infinity employee had. But they had signed confidentiality agreements, and they were obliged to honor those. Bernie handed his letter to Bob. He'd gotten his first.

"The bastards are still after us," he said cheerfully. "I don't know why they are so concerned about us."

"I'll read it in the crapper," said Bob.

A little later, when Bernie next saw Bob, he asked him what he thought of the letter. Did he find it threatening?

"No," said Bob. "Not threatening, disappointing. I flushed it down the toilet."

The born-again-ers both roared with laughter at that.

"It's great being our own bosses, isn't it, Bob?" asked Bernie when they'd both laughed themselves out. "No more stupid office politics, no need to hide things from anybody."

"All those dipshit, thick PhDs," said Bob. "Thank God we're done with them."

"Hallelujah!" cried Bernie, with gusto.

And they both hurried off to continue their experiments on the delta factor.

In the lab, Bob looked at Bernie. "So you think fire is the answer, Bernie?"

"Not *the* answer, Bob, obviously. Our Lord and Savior is *the* answer. But if we ignore such an elemental force, we're being close-minded, aren't we? I've run two experiments here. Kevin has helped with the both of them."

"He's a good boy, isn't he, Bernie?"

"The best. The first group of tissues I just let the flames lick over. And these tissues all grew better than the controls. One hundred percent, Bob! They grew more rapidly and were more vigorous. The second group I let the flames actually singe the tissues. I knew that wasn't going to work. The equations told me that. But I wanted to be thorough, and Kevin was keen to do it. Well, that little taste of hell was enough. They all turned black and died. It was quite dramatic. So what is it about that little touch of fire? Callus can't have a soul, can it?"

***

Bernie, Bob, big Bob, and, to a lesser extent, Donald, were throwbacks. They were present-day shamans dancing at the altar of the new power: Science. They were appealing to the half-forgotten, atavistic yearnings that floated just below the surface of modern consciousness. What motivated the ancient shamans is difficult to make out at this distant remove. Probably sex and power. But who really knows? They certainly had a belief in the value of their knowledge if not in the knowledge itself. And now shamans have moved up in the world! They are more a force in their own right. They no longer need the patronage of rulers to flourish. They can accumulate money, and themselves become rulers. The new god is money, and in today's society, shamans are protected by rules that allow them, once successful, to keep their money. There has never been a better time to be a shaman.

Big Bob dimly recognized this profound truth as he joined the dances around the new god. He thought hard about how he and Donald fitted in. Though not one himself, he had spent his lifetime around scientists. Unconsciously, he was following the path of his ancient forbears. In bygone times, the shamans had cultivated warriors; today they cultivated scientists. And there are far more shamans around today than there were in ancient times. There is even a career path one can follow. You can become a venture capitalist! Oh, it is all dressed up in business jargon to conceal its true nature, but it is still dancing for money. Bob Levy had achieved recognition as a venture capitalist. Bernie and Bob had set their hearts on achieving the same goal. Donald, however, remained a scientist, a man whose residual integrity prevented him from pursuing shamanhood exclusively. Big Bob recognized his bedrock beliefs and felt protective of him. To get to the money, he knew he needed Donald.

***

Nigel told Charlene what Judy had told him about the tryst with Stan. Charlene was, predictably, appalled.

"Good God, Nigel, how could they? Even if they don't remember it all."

"Arthur Nanomura and his tricky tabs have a lot to answer for," Nigel told her. "Mood enhancers, indeed! But I suppose the poison's in the dose. Funny Stan didn't realize that."

Charlene was glad she and Nigel hadn't taken any more of them. Half of one had been almost too much, and who knows how many the greedy Stan had scoffed.

Nigel told her Stan had been in a deep sleep for a long time before waking, apparently with no memory of what he'd done or of what had been done to him.

"We've got to get away from California, Charlene. It's making lechers of us. Don't you feel it? The sunshine and the pleasant air? Exposing your body to these gentle elements? It's just so seductive, isn't it? A constant invitation to Californicate. I don't want to spend my life in thrall to my body."

"Thank God I've got you," she told him fervently. "You are definitely the one for me."

She looked at him closely, noting again his kind brown eyes and lank blonde hair. She reached for him, putting an end to the conversation.

***

Helmuth had had a sleepless night. Well, not actually, but it felt like it. He'd lain there at three thirty in the morning, wide awake. He'd finally come to a decision. Almost Infinity was a crock.

But Helmuth had been the one to believe that the wormhole could lead to a marvelous future. The wormhole was going to bring everlasting life and perfect happiness. And all this was going to happen—where else?—in sunny California! It was truly the wormhole to heaven. What he finally realized on that sleepless night was that Bob Levy and Donald Plum were hucksters, and he had fallen for their improbable scheme. He couldn't believe he'd been taken in.

All Grains was paying for direction. They didn't expect to have to provide it themselves. In the heat of the moment, that was what

Helmuth had done. They had embraced it and flattered him, and he was pleased at first. But as he gave it further thought, he decided he didn't like it. It had all been so easy, and he began to feel like a mark. But he couldn't be a mark. Who among his colleagues could? He settled on a likely candidate. Wormhole product was the stuff of fantasy, and it was Billy Woodruff who had fallen for it. After all, he claimed to have seen the girl fall at the circus, and he'd been the one to lead the most recent visit to Almost Infinity. He'd been taken in by their bogus reporting. Poor old Billy. Well, he couldn't let it go on any longer. Now he had to bring it to an end. If it hurt Billy's feelings, so be it.

He announced his decision at work that morning, when he turned up red-eyed and worn out. They would, of course, have to inform Almost Infinity of the decision not to renew their contract. This was dictated by the terms of the contract, which called for a three-month disengagement period, and it was already early October. Helmuth was afraid the light would go out of Almost Infinity on hearing the news, and that would mean the waste of about five million. He was going to break the bad news to Bob Levy immediately and then suggest to Bob he delay passing it on until the end of November. That way, their employees would get one month's notice of the termination of their employment.

He was quite sure Almost Infinity would not be able to survive without All Grains. He allowed himself to imagine that busy warehouse, now full of bright young men and women, standing empty in December. That would be a sad day. All Grains, of course, would make offers to the best of them. But he wasn't sure how easy it was going to be to persuade people to leave the land of year-round sunshine and pleasant, balmy air for the frozen wastes of Minnesota. Maybe one or two of them would take it on for the novelty of the experience, but he wasn't really confident.

"I'm sorry," he'd told the bemused Billy at the end of the meeting, "but there's nothing more I can do for you and Almost Infinity."

***

Bob had become more and more conscious of the winds of change blowing over All Grains. The drop-off in daily contact between the two companies, the lack of curiosity about Almost Infinity's dealings with other potential partners, the coolness of the reception of their recent quarterly report—all pointed to disengagement for Bob. Helmuth, however, was as congenial as ever. A little too light-hearted, thought Bob, as he reflected on a recent conversation with the German in which Helmuth had shown no interest in their dealings with US Home Products.

Bob had nothing to tell him about US Home Products, anyway. After their abortive visit to California, Bob hadn't heard anything further from Ernie Sikorsky. George Nipper had talked to Ernie once or twice on the phone but reported that he seemed vague and uncomfortable.

"We shouldn't have dragged that British aristocrat through the muck," said Bob, laughing.

"No," agreed George. "But it was a lot of fun, wasn't it? U-S-A! U-S-A!" he chanted, pumping his fist in the air.

"Well, we've got to lay that one at Don's door, I'm afraid."

"Not Jim?" queried George. "After all, Jim is Don's boss, isn't he?"

"No, not Jim, George. Definitely Don. He got quite worked up about the whole thing. Someone asked him why he hadn't put up Wet Floor notices. That sent him right over the top, apparently."

"The rage of the guilty, I suppose," mused George.

"Better not let him hear you say that," warned Bob. "There's no telling what he might do."

"It was a good laugh, though, wasn't it?" asked George, his eyes gleaming with pleasure at the reminiscence. "I know we aren't supposed to laugh at the misfortune of others, but really, he was transformed from an elegant, superior prick to a dirty ape in less than a second. I'd never seen anything like it. Funnier than all the clowns in the circus, wasn't it?"

Bob grinned back at him, nodding in agreement.

But, amusing memories notwithstanding, much more worrying for Bob was the complete silence from Ned Crellin. Remembering how vitriolic the tobacco man had been in the course of their last conversation, Bob—the sneaky shit—had to steel himself to call him up.

"Just wondering if you were thinking of us," he began.

Ned Crellin, with a light, mocking laugh, assured him he hadn't been. Ned knew what Bob only suspected. Helmuth had told him All Grains was pulling out of their relationship with Almost Infinity.

"They're dead, Ned," he'd been told.

"Thought any more about investing in us?" Bob asked now.

Ned rolled his eyes. This guy just didn't know when to quit.

"Not really," he answered and then, unable to prevent himself, went on: "Why should we invest in a couple of con artists? Wormholes, for God's sake. How did you come up with that one?"

Bob raised his eyebrows at Ned's words but said nothing. He allowed himself a conspiratorial chuckle.

"How are our shorty cigarettes working out?"

Ned heard the word "our" in the question and flared up.

"They are not working out, Bob. Our people trashed the idea. Unworkable, I think, was the kindest thing they said. Our people weren't very complimentary about your people, Bob."

"Well, you won't mind then if we go ahead and offer it to others. After all, no money has changed hands yet, has it?"

"And it's never going to, Bob. Go right ahead, be our guest. See what our competitors think about it. God, I hope someone takes it on; they'll be the laughingstock of the entire industry."

"Why the sudden change of heart, Ned? You were hot for it a couple of weeks ago."

"We're a conservative company, Bob. Cigarette size is just not an easy thing to change. For a start we'd have the regulators all over us. And you know how much we love them. We can't give them any chance to further restrict our product. No, it was never on. And we don't believe it came from the future either. Kind of threw the whole thing into question. Quite frankly, Bob, none of us believes in that wormhole."

"Well, you've only seen it in action once, Ned, haven't you? Come and see what else we can pull out of it. You might sing a different tune then."

"Same one Helmuth is singing?" asked Ned nastily.

Bob said nothing. He hung up without saying anything else. Ned, enraged at what he thought was Bob's incivility, called right back. But Bob wouldn't take the call. He sat on alone at his desk. It was all up with Almost Infinity, and now he knew it.

CHAPTER 20

Bob Keeps the Faith

THE END SEEMED TO HAVE come with shocking speed. Bob thought about all the people they'd attracted to their enterprise. They were overwhelmingly young and so would easily be able to start again. Almost Infinity would just be an interesting blip on their résumés. The older, more senior staff might have more difficulties, but for those people, any financial embarrassment would be a minor matter.

So why was he sad? The young people from out of state could think of their time at Almost Infinity as an extended vacation. The older ones had enough resources to hang on in California if they wished. He, Nils, Al, and Forrest could work to place the younger employees in good positions, and that task shouldn't be too difficult. No, nothing to be sad about there. But Almost Infinity was coming to an end.

He thought about Donald for a moment. Well, of course, he still had his position at San Francisco State. He doubted if anyone there even knew about Almost Infinity. He was quite certain Donald hadn't told anyone, although he probably should have. Maybe Donald would get a talking to, but because the company had failed, he doubted anything more serious would ensue. Donald would go on teaching cosmology and mathematics to the students entrusted to his care.

And if he ever did decide to talk about his experience as a founder of Almost Infinity, no one there would believe him. He was still living with his pseudologia fantastica and was, Bob knew, still recognized as a liar.

Finally, he came to think of himself. Finding places for people to work wasn't exactly what he wanted to be doing with his life at this late stage in it. And he, personally, might even lose a little money. But it wouldn't be catastrophic. No, he would go on, backslapping, shoulder-hugging, hale-fellow-well-metting. Big Bob.

***

Donald, to Bob's amazement, didn't seem at all downcast by the news of Helmuth's and Ned's epiphanies. As usual, with Donald it was all old hat. He'd had the same epiphany himself some time ago. But he didn't tell Bob about it because he knew Bob would find it difficult to understand. The wormhole Donald was a phantom, an insubstantial presence flickering at the edge of the real Donald's consciousness. The phantom had acquired corporeity driven on by the pseudologia. Pseudologia fantastica was a real and very serious mental illness, but it didn't attract the attention of health care professionals. It was, of course, quite rare and almost never gave rise to violent or criminal behavior, at least on the part of the sufferer. No, where a sinister illness like schizophrenia had its occasional rape and murder victims, pseudologia fantastica had only its deluded and self-anointed heroes. Once Donald had revealed his wormhole, it took on a life of its own. Now, as Donald thought about it, he realized he was offering a religious experience. He was actually offering a gateway to heaven.

***

Bob called together the senior management of Almost Infinity. He told them of his fears about the All Grains contract. He wasn't absolutely sure yet, but he was beginning to think the contract was coming to an end. There would be no $20 million next year. Nils, Al, and Forrest didn't appreciate the gravity of the situation. Yes, it was serious, but they had a lot of other irons in the fire, didn't they? Brown and Humphreys—not ideal, it was a tobacco company, after all, but something good could still come out of the wormhole, couldn't it? They could save lives and help Brown and Humphreys reinvent itself. And they were still waiting to hear from US Home Products, weren't they? Maybe they would step up.

Bob, to his credit, didn't try to sugarcoat the perilous situation they were in. He told them frankly about his telephone calls with Ernie Sikorsky and Ned Crellin. The latter had been so unpleasant he'd hung up on him. It seemed to Bob now that there was a general air of disbelief surrounding the wormhole.

"All Grains," he told them, "is the leader. Where All Grains goes, others follow."

There were one or two bright prospects on the horizon, but he didn't know how to feel about them just yet. He was talking here principally about the Nigerian government.

"Can we take two hundred million from them?" he asked hopefully.

Nils, Al, George Nipper, and Ben Benson all very definitely could. Forrest said nothing and looked grave. Then he told them if the company became dependent on the Nigerian government, he was going to resign. This was really the first time that ethical considerations, of a sort, had intruded on the inner workings of Almost Infinity. Bob was definitely not welcoming. He shut it down now, intending to return to it later, if necessary. He definitely didn't want some lame-brained concerns from Forrest influencing any decisions he might have to make.

"Well," he said now, "we don't want you quitting. We'll just have to drum up the money from somewhere else. Anybody got any ideas? George? Ben?"

Ben didn't have anything to offer. Yes, he dealt with money, but he dealt exclusively with its dispensation. He was no venture capitalist, and he wasn't paid like one. None of his business contacts were in a position to commit large sums of money to risky ventures. He could get a loan, but it would only be for a small amount, and it would be tied to the value of their assets, which meant their equipment and anything else of value that they owned. It just wouldn't be worthwhile.

George was more bullish. He'd been talking up the wormhole with his business contacts, and several of them had expressed wonder and interest in it. He would give them a call just as soon as this meeting was over. Bob looked him over fondly. George was the most like him of all the senior executives. He could look at George and imagine himself thirty years ago. How would a young Bob conduct himself in these circumstances? Well, he wouldn't get depressed. He knew himself well enough to know that. No, he would throw himself into the task of raising money. He would just keep trying until he got a nibble.

"See what you can do, George. We all appreciate your efforts."

George wondered if Donald couldn't do something to silence the doubters—arrange some dramatic demonstration of the wormhole's potential.

"It's all been kind of vague, hasn't it?" he asked Bob.

"The product has been vague, certainly. But there's been no doubt about the reality of the demonstrations, has there? I mean these things really did come out of nowhere, didn't they? Are we saying we think Donald is nothing more than a magician?"

"Yes, we are," said George promptly. "Only a real one."

Bob smiled approvingly.

"I'll ask him if he can come up with something spectacular," he promised. "But he tells me he is right at the limits of his abilities with the math. I'm not sure what more he can do. Still, it can't do any harm to let him know how desperate we all are."

"We're making great progress with the drought resistance," put in Nils. "I'm going to have drought-resistant soybeans very soon. We can definitely sell those. And Al is on the point of banishing disease as a problem for crop production. That's got to be worth billions."

Al couldn't let that pass. He wasn't prepared to let Nils give them all the false impression that this major agricultural problem had been overcome. It would destroy their credibility and severely hamper any chances their employees had for a life after the wormhole.

"We're making progress, Nils. Let's just say that. I don't think we can say any more at present."

Nils looked back at him, accepting, even welcoming his caution but at the same time retaining a look of baffled hopefulness on his face.

"Of course, Al," he said with a smile, a smile that invited the others around the table to share his hopes for Al's success. "You don't have to say anything now. We all understand."

"All right, gentlemen," said Bob, beginning his summing up. "We've got three months as it stands. And then the money runs out and we have to shut up shop. Of course, I'm hoping it won't come to that. I want all of you to keep confidential what we've talked about today—and that means from everyone, Marshall and Arthur included. I can see no point in worrying them. Don't tell another soul outside this room what we are up against."

Then, looking at Al, he added, "And that means Stan too."

Al nodded gravely. He was pleased to be asked to keep Stan in the dark. He would tell him all about it when the crisis was over, and then Stan would realize he wasn't upper management yet. The put-down would do him good. They dispersed with the weight of Bob's confidence on all their shoulders. With the exception of Ben, they went their respective ways, empowered by the need for action. There wasn't a moment to lose. All Ben could do was watch and wait and look for unobtrusive ways to cut back on their spending. Bob took himself off to find Donald.

* * *

He tracked him down in a nearby coffee shop they'd taken to frequenting. Donald was just sitting there looking out of the window, lost in his thoughts.

"Penny for them," announced Bob cheerfully, coming up and catching him unawares.

There were only a couple of other customers in the shop. It was the middle of the morning and a weekday. Bob glanced carefully at Donald as he sat down with his coffee. He thought Donald looked strained.

"What's up?" he asked lightly.

"I've been thinking, Bob, thinking about what Stan said about me going through the wormhole. And I am the only one who can go through and get back. We have to do this to convince Helmuth and

Ned. I've been working on the math, and I think now I can make it as big as a man."

Bob stared hard at Donald. He wasn't smiling. He looked perfectly serious. What was he suggesting now? He knew there was no wormhole, didn't he? He had as good as told Bob that the last time they'd talked. Not for the first time, Bob entertained the likelihood that Donald was deranged. It was hard for Bob to think like this because they had come such a long way together.

"You know, Donald, it's okay," he said kindly. "You've done all you can. You don't need to run any risks for those nasty pieces of work."

"No, Bob, I'm serious. We can do it between us."

"What do you mean?" asked Bob. "What can I do?"

"I'm going to need an assistant. I've thought it all out. I will enter a box, or a cubicle, if you like, with a front door and a trapdoor. This will be the site of our wormhole portal. I will close the front door after me, and I will enter the wormhole portal through the trapdoor. When I leave, I will close the trapdoor after me. You have to be there to choreograph my departure."

"Where are you going?"

"Into the wormhole and on into the future. I've had an idea, Bob. I think we can pull it off."

"Is it dangerous?" asked Bob, hating himself for beginning to play the role of accomplice in Donald's fantasy.

"Not dangerous at all. There's absolutely nothing to worry about. I'm just wondering what I can bring back with me."

"What you can bring back with you," repeated Bob softly. "Come on, Donald, I thought we had this out last time we talked. There's no such thing as a wormhole. At least, that's what I thought you told me."

"I don't think I actually said that. You may have inferred it, but I'm pretty sure I didn't say it. Hell, you're beginning to sound like Helmuth and Ned. When did you start to lose faith in me? How did I fail you? And here I'm thinking I've solved the analysis of the particle vibrations. Now, for the first time, I can find or identify a precise wormhole location, essential for the formation of one above a certain size, one big enough for a man to pass through. All we need to do is to set up the vacuum pump and wormhole facilitator at the exact site, but I won't know where this site is until I do the calculations. Once I do know, I'll be able to go through it, and I'll be able to come back. The key to the breakthrough was letting the site choose itself. Choosing a site a priori restricts the size and availability of wormholes, but I only realized this the other day. Maybe I can bring something back with me, something good. Any ideas?"

Bob rubbed a hand slowly across his face. Any ideas? What on earth was Donald talking about now? Wasn't he the one preparing to travel to the future?

"The only way I can have any ideas, Donald, is if you take me with you."

Donald laughed but then grew serious. He gazed at Bob with a fond look on his face. "It is a thought. We could go together. But I'm not really comfortable with the idea. There is a certain amount of risk, you know. To be perfectly honest, I don't even know if I'm going to come through unscathed. And the math would definitely be more difficult. Maybe next time I'll be able to take you with me. It's quite a thought, isn't it, sharing something like that?"

He found the thought of Bob being right there with him when he worked his magic quite stimulating. He and Bob would share the physical experience. It would be help from another person for the first time since his parents had helped him when he was a young man.

"No, we can't go through together, Bob, not this first time, anyway. But we will definitely do it together in the future—you have my word on it."

Once again concerns about Donald's mental health surfaced in Bob's mind. At this point in time, Donald definitely sounded like a believer in time travel. He was even concerned about safety—his own and Bob's, for goodness' sake! Bob tried to relax. He was just going to have to go along with it.

Donald continued: "We've just got to come up with something good. It doesn't even have to be a physical object. My disappearance and reappearance will provide the reality of the event. But I must come back with at least one mind-blowing idea."

"An idea, then," repeated Bob. "Let me think about it. Maybe I can come up with something from the business world."

"I'm going to need a month to get ready for the trip. And, of course, I've got quite a lot of math to get through. But I'm pretty sure I can do it. Set it up for a month from today, Bob, and get Helmuth and Ned and maybe Ernie here to see it. We'll also invite all our employees to witness the event. We need to keep up morale, don't we?"

"You're quite sure you can do this, Donald? If something goes wrong here, we're finished."

"Absolutely. All you need to do is open the door to the portal and show everyone I'm gone. It'll be a great success, don't worry. I know what I'm doing. Our business friends may even change their minds about investing in us. Who knows?"

Bob looked closely at Donald. He appeared a little excited but was otherwise entirely normal. He looked back at Bob with sparkling eyes and a slight smile curving his lips. He seemed aware of the closeness of Bob's inspection and appeared to welcome it. Bob looked away. He glanced around the coffee shop at the few other customers. Donald really didn't stand out in any way. Yet here he was, this slightly rumpled, middle-aged man, calmly stating his intention to become the world's first time traveler. And he was going to do it in a month.

"November the fifth, then, Donald?"

"Okay."

"That's a day over four weeks away, if that's important."

"It isn't," said Donald decisively. "Important, I mean. The vibrating particle field is quite stable once I've established its parameters. And I've already got a pretty good idea where it is. This kind of analysis is what I do all the time. I just need a couple of weeks to refine it, that's all. So set it up for November the fifth, Bob. I'll tell you all where to assemble the day before I go through the portal. We'll make a day or an evening out of it."

"There's no going back once I announce this event, you know that, don't you? The disappointment would be terminal."

"Keep the faith, Bob."

CHAPTER 21

Donald is the New Jesus

"I THINK IT'S EXCITING," said Nigel. "Our fearless leader is going through a portal to the future. And doing it in front of us all. He's really got balls, hasn't he?"

Nigel was sitting on the patio at the back of their house watching Charlene as she monitored the grilling of some hamburger patties. He had just pulled the cork out of a bottle of red wine. Charlene looked beautiful in the sunshine. Tall and slim, she moved about with an easy grace. Cascades of soft brown hair framed her serious, attentive face. She was wearing white slacks and a blue-and-white polka-dot top.

"You look really pretty, Charlene," he told her now.

She flashed a small smile at him.

"You look pretty nice yourself," she replied.

"November the fifth," Nigel said musingly. "That's Guy Fawkes Night in England. That's the night we light bonfires and set off fireworks. We make an effigy of the poor man and burn him. All done very cheerfully, though. I should bring fireworks to Donald's departure. Give him a proper November-the-fifth send-off."

"Who's this guy, Fawkes?"

"He wasn't just any guy," said Nigel, enjoying the wordplay. "He was a man who tried to blow up the Houses of Parliament. The man behind the gunpowder plot."

"What happened to him, then?"

"He was executed."

"Hardly a favorable omen, Nigel, is it? We don't want to encourage the thought that Donald is about to be executed, do we?"

"Oh, it wouldn't do that. No one except British people would have the faintest idea of what it all meant. This is California, after all. It could be a late Fourth of July. Whatever, man."

Now Charlene grinned at him.

"Whatever, man? You're turning into a native, Nigel. Next thing, you'll be talking about dudes and chicks and being far out."

"Okay, okay, Guy Fawkes was a cool dude and his ambitions were far out. Then he got topped."

"Speak American, Nigel. None of us can understand this English slang."

"We've all got to become bilingual," declared Nigel. "Then the language can meld into one again. The two of us already communicate in a kind of hybrid lingo, don't we? What will our kids speak?"

"Well, if they grow up here, they'll speak Californian."

"No, I can't have that. I'm going to take them to England at regular intervals so they can learn to speak wot's proper."

"You know what kids are like. Ours will be no different. They'll want to speak what's cool. We will literally have no say in the matter."

"You're an educated and clever girl, Charlene. Good with language. Not a typical American at all, really."

"What!"

She came at him with the tongs she was holding. He ducked away, laughing.

***

Stan was quizzing Al about Donald's planned journey into the future.

"What's going on, Al? All this sounds a bit desperate to me. He's going to do what I suggested as a joke the other day? I thought he told us the wormhole was too small to allow a person to pass through. Has he shrunk himself?"

Al looked at him pityingly.

"Of course not. He's done the math. He must have made a breakthrough. None of us can understand the math anyway, can we? Not even Marshall. I'm only telling you what Bob told me."

"It's Helmuth, isn't it? He's doing it to convince Helmuth. All Grains is not going to renew our contract, is it?"

Al had no intention of admitting Stan into the inner circle of Almost Infinity's senior management even if he was knocking loudly on the door.

"All Grains hasn't told us their intentions yet. And we have a number of other irons in the fire. We are definitely not done. Have you thought about the full implications of what Donald is proposing to do? If Donald can really travel to and from the future, the future for all of us is very bright, isn't it? Science and religion will fuse in the person of Donald Plum. He will literally be a modern-day Jesus."

"What a prick," said Stan. "Does he really expect us to believe this? Why should we believe him? It'll be some kind of trick, and this time I'm going to do my damnedest to expose it."

"I'm going to suspend judgment, Stan. If he pulls it off, we'll have to believe him. Aren't you even prepared to believe the evidence of your own eyes?"

"He hasn't done it yet. I'll believe it when I see it. When are you going to tell us that the money's run out?"

"We are not going to tell you because it hasn't happened," said Al emphatically. "Look, do you really think All Grains would let us crash and burn after putting so much into us? It's not likely, is it? Come on, Stan, we're all trying to do our best here, aren't we? And you're very important to us. We need you to produce disease-resistant crop plants. Anyway, think about what Donald is doing. He's making us all look small, isn't he?"

This last remark was exactly what Stan didn't need to hear. He marched off furious at Al. He immediately told Jeff and Oliver that

Donald was the new Jesus. The three of them sat in the conference room, looking at each other as Jeff and Oliver digested Stan's words.

"We'd better tell Emmanuel," said Jeff. "He should know a new Messiah is here on Earth. He and his congregation can worship Donald now at their meetings. And what about Bob and Bernie? They are born-again-ers, aren't they? Someone should tell them Jesus has been born again, whatever that means."

"Well," said Oliver, "I'm a doubting Thomas. I'm going to have to see Donald disappear and reappear before I can believe any of this. I just can't imagine what he's going to do."

"He's a prick," insisted Stan. "He could do anything. We've really got to watch him carefully and catch him at whatever slippery trick he's going to pull on us all." He stood up. "Come on, let's get back into the lab and find some sanity. At least there we know what's what."

**

Donald's plans didn't boost morale. In fact, they upset almost everybody. Donald was encroaching on private beliefs, and it was resented. Stan was going around telling everyone with great relish that Donald was the new Jesus. Suddenly the activities of the company were sacrilegious. The believers among them had their own views, and Donald, with his sly, slippery smile, didn't meet their notion of a savior. The non-believers resented Stan's flippancy. They thought he was simply trashing the company. Which, of course, he was.

In fact, Stan had put in an application for the position of assistant professor in the Department of Plant and Microbial Science at Berkeley. He hadn't told anyone at Almost Infinity he'd applied for the job. And neither had he used Al as a reference. It was, he told the dean of the college, a company thing. The dean had understood completely. Berkeley was being very accommodating, and Stan thought a job offer was a formality. He'd be paid about as much as he was making now, and he'd acquire all the security the institution offered to its employees. Oh, he'd have to prove himself, of course, but he had no doubt he could do that.

***

George Nipper called up Ernie Sikorsky.

"Ernie! George Nipper here!"

"Huh?"

"George Nipper of Almost infinity."

"Oh, hello George. How's it hanging?"

"It's all happening here, Ernie. Donald is going to go through the wormhole in person on November the fifth. He's going to be the first person in the history of the world to time travel. He doesn't know yet when he'll be coming back, but he told Bob he definitely won't be in the future for longer than two weeks. He's aiming for 2175."

Ernie was predictably incredulous.

"He's going to do what? I thought the wormhole was too small to accommodate a person."

"He's made it bigger, much bigger. He's done the math. Why don't you come and see for yourself? It'll be a historic occasion."

"Well—is the circus in town, now?"

"What?"

"The circus. I really wanted to see that. If it is in town then we'll come. Okay, Georgie?"

"All right, Ernie. I'll look into it and get back to you."

"Attaboy!"

George Nipper put the phone down slowly and sat at his desk thinking. It was much worse than they'd thought. Ernie Sikorsky would come out to Almost Infinity to witness Donald time traveling only if the circus was in town. Donald's heroics alone weren't enough.

He called up Helmuth, and his worst fears were confirmed. Helmuth also asked about the circus. George wearily consulted a copy of a free local newspaper that was brought into Almost Infinity each week by Emmanuel. The "coming events" section showed no circus listing. No circus, no Ernie and Helmuth. He didn't even bother calling Ned Crellin. Maybe they should just put the whole thing off until the industrial magnates could be persuaded to attend.

He took the bad news around to Bob's office. Bob was disappointed and frankly puzzled at the responses of Ernie and Helmuth—but only for a moment.

"We don't need those bastards!" he shouted. "We'll turn this into a media event. We'll get a local TV station and, maybe, the major networks' local affiliates out here and show Donald to the world. Helmuth and Ernie can watch it on TV. They'll be sorry they missed it, and they'll look ridiculous. We're going to make Donald's departure into a big celebration."

"Will Donald want other cosmologists to see it?" asked George doubtfully. "He might not want the exposure."

But Bob, once he'd articulated his idea, fell in love with his own daring.

"We believe in Donald, George. He's why we're here. Donald is doing groundbreaking work. We've got nothing to hide. Let's promote him like the star he is."

"I don't know. Does Donald want all the publicity? His life will never be the same again. I know I wouldn't want it."

This thought gave Bob pause.

"Yes, you're right. He might not want it. We have to find a way to establish his credibility, though. This is ridiculous! Won't come unless the circus is in town? How old are these people?"

***

The day after this conversation, Bob called the Almost Infinity senior management group together to review their situation. They were all annoyed with Stan for spreading the notion that Donald was the new Jesus.

"He's destroying our company," complained Arthur Nanomura. "People feel strongly about this. They don't want their lives trivialized."

George was too upset even to discuss it. He'd told his wife what Stan was saying, and she'd been scandalized. People couldn't go around comparing themselves to Jesus, even in California, and not incur opprobrium. *Stan should be fired*, he thought. George didn't tell the management group this, but he did convey his own keen displeasure at Stan's behavior.

Nils, Al, and Forrest were not themselves particularly religious. They were all fairly typical scientists—easygoing and agnostic. But they had respect for the opinions and beliefs of others and realized that Stan had crossed a line. Al, forgetting he'd been the one who'd coined the "modern-day Jesus" appellation in the first place, said he would talk sternly to Stan.

Bob floated his idea of broad media coverage for Donald's journey through time. He still wasn't sure if it was the right thing to do. The thought of Stan telling national TV reporters that Donald was the new Jesus, however remote a possibility, was enough to kill the idea off. They settled for a single local TV station where they could control the release of information. They all wondered at the lack of enthusiasm on the parts of Ernie and Helmuth. Now Bob told them of earlier conversations with Helmuth in which the German had expressed reservations about their long-term relationship.

Finally, Al put it succinctly: "So it really looks like it's all up with All Grains, Bob?"

"Looks that way to me," said Bob, in a resigned tone. "But we all knew that anyway, didn't we?"

They didn't, of course. They had all been living in hope. Now the end of the company hovered into sight, and it looked close and real and desperate. A flicker of fear ran around the room.

"Anyone else out there, George?" asked Nils.

"Nobody here at home," said George mournfully. "There's still the Nigerian government," he added.

"They're still interested? How much could they be in for?" Bob wanted to know.

"I talked to their consulate the other day. They were still talking about two hundred million."

"Don't let them know All Grains is pulling out," said Bob promptly. "We've got to keep that quiet. All our jobs are depending on what we do now."

"Will they be supplying the money in dollars?" asked Ben Benson.

"For God's sake, Ben, you'll jinx it before it even gets started!" Bob yelled at him.

They all fell silent

"So," said Bob at last. "It's come to this."

He didn't say, "All our futures are now in the hands of the government of Nigeria," but they knew what he was thinking.

"Thank God for Donald," said Nils.

CHAPTER 22

The Countdown Begins

OCTOBER ROLLED AROUND, and All Grains duly passed on the opportunity to renew funding Almost Infinity. Ben Benson went to Bob, highly agitated by this turn of events.

"We've got to tell everybody, Bob!" he yelled. "Everyone should know exactly where we stand. It's the only decent thing to do."

Bob didn't agree.

"Look, Ben," he said soothingly. "Donald is going to go through the wormhole on November the fifth, remember? If we tell everyone we're in trouble now, we'll lose the chance of attracting new investors. No one will care about Donald then. Let's keep our nerve at least until he makes his departure. Hold off for another month before you go public with the All Grains news."

But Ben was adamant.

"We have a duty, Bob," he insisted.

Reluctantly, Bob gave way.

"Okay. But we can't let it come as a shock. At least give people the impression we are in control. And let me read it first."

And that was what Ben did.

Nigel, like practically all the employees, read the memo and decided that, come Christmas, they would be out of money. Peter Blakely found it all wildly exciting.

"We are for the chop!" he declared. "There's no money left. I was never appreciated anyway."

Nigel didn't want to believe the memo's simple message.

"It can't end so lamely, surely? I thought All Grains was in for two hundred million."

"That's not what the memo says," said Peter. "Is it?"

Nigel had to admit he was right. But, in the absence of signs of panic from any of the senior managers, he simply put the memo to one side and forgot about it. And that's what almost all the employees did.

Stan, however, was offered and accepted a faculty position at Berkeley. He didn't tell anyone at the company, but in January he would be in a new job. He was going to hold on at Almost Infinity for as long as he could. Two weeks' notice was his legal obligation. He didn't want to miss out on any big settlement if they got bought out. Stan possessed the largest number of stock options of any employee outside of the senior management group. If Almost Infinity got bought out for a large sum, say five hundred million, he would become an instant millionaire. He knew if he resigned now, he would forfeit that money. Bob had inserted that clause into the contracts of all employees who had been given stock options so that while there was a chance of anyone buying the company, none of the senior executives would leave.

Bob scoured his contacts for new investors. Many people professed interest, particularly when they learned that Almost Infinity was supported by All Grains. But, of course, Bob had eventually to come clean, and when he did, all these promising new leads faded away. He found a company in Los Angeles called Ingene. Ingene expressed interest, particularly in all the genetic engineering. They talked about a partnership. Ingene announced that they would send a couple of executives to visit Almost Infinity.

They were going to come on a Friday afternoon, expecting to meet with Bob and one or two of his colleagues. Bob, in turn, told George Nipper and the other members of the management committee about the visit. Word spread fast, and an air of excitement momentarily gripped everyone. Could this be salvation? Ingene was quite a small company, Stan told everyone, much smaller than Almost Infinity—just fifteen employees.

"Small, maybe," countered Bob, "but they do have money."

Quite how much no one was really sure. Very likely more than enough for Almost Infinity, Bob told anyone who'd listen. He began to speculate, knowingly, on their behalf, and he talked freely before the senior management committee. Maybe there wasn't enough money to save all the employees, but certainly the vast majority of them. It even sounded as if he had some leverage over them. Good old Bob!

The Ingene executives didn't want a demonstration of the wormhole, but Bob wasn't discouraged. He decided that the entire company should turn out to welcome the small Ingene deputation. He wanted these Angelinos to know how important they were to their San Franciscan cousins. A memo was sent out informing everybody of the visit. The schedule was still a little hazy, but Ingene would probably arrive sometime late on Friday afternoon. Everyone was encouraged to stay after work to meet the visitors. These people could be the new owners of the company—and, as Bob said, it's never too early to start making a good impression, is it?

At around three thirty, Bob took himself off to the airport to meet the visitors. The Angelinos were flying in to save the day! This was an American company, a company with money, almost a neighbor, and they were all going to be fine. Bob called to say they were on their way. The plane had landed safely. Thank God! He told Maria to assemble everyone in the main lecture hall to meet and welcome their LA guests. Everyone dutifully repaired to the lecture hall to wait. They sat around and tried to stay calm. There were one or two outbursts of hysterical laughter, which brought disapproving frowns from everyone. Rumors were exchanged breathlessly. The whole room settled into a state of high excitement.

Nigel looked around. Almost everyone was there, but there were one or two no-shows, of course. He couldn't see Ben Benson, for example, or Arthur Nanomura. He wasn't surprised at Arthur's absence. Perhaps it was curtains for him; maybe Bob had told him to stay away. After all, he'd always been on the periphery of the company, hadn't he? The Ingene presence began to be felt more strongly the closer their arrival approached. He tried to consider the situation calmly. He wondered if there wasn't to be an injection of realism into the company as well as cash. Realism and cash, both cold. The plant breeders were all there, and Nigel considered that a good sign. They were people with their feet firmly on the ground. There was, of course, no sign of Donald, but that was only right, wasn't it? There could be no place for Donald in this businesslike atmosphere suddenly sweeping the company. Time travel, indeed! Ridiculous! They had all thought so, hadn't they?

The office staff were assembled, all except Ben Benson, and this underscored the gravity of the moment. They would switch allegiance from Almost Infinity to new owners in a heartbeat. The office staff were serious people who did serious work. They were the glue that held the company together. They saw to it that bills were paid, that equipment and chemicals were ordered and delivered, that coffee and snacks were always available. They interacted with the custodial staff, protected the premises from thieves, and made sure everyone's salary got paid. They arranged all company-wide functions. They didn't understand the research work, but they didn't need to. The comings and goings, hiring and firings, purchases and sales (none yet!) were all executed by them.

It got to be five thirty. Where before, everyone had sat around chatting idly, enjoying being at work without having anything to do, now they were on their own time. People began to look about anxiously, and in some parts of the room the talk faded away. The employees paid by the hour continued gossiping cheerfully. They were still on company time. Bob was still coming, no word to the contrary. At a quarter to six, one or two people faded away. But not Nigel. He knew how important this was. He'd begun to think of it as a kind of test, a winnowing out of the chaff.

At ten to six, Bob arrived at the back of the hall, ushering in a thin, bespectacled, serious-looking man of about thirty, accompanied by a fresh-faced, younger individual. They both looked taken aback at the size of the group awaiting them. They were, however, despite their relative youth, both senior executives at Ingene. Bob led them to the front of the lecture hall, and the bespectacled individual introduced himself. He told them he and his colleague were from Los Angeles. He went on to say that his company was very careful with its money. They wasted very little. They were presently a small company that had hopes of growing. They saw an opportunity in Almost Infinity. He was glad to meet them all. Then he moved to the side, indicating the conclusion of his remarks. Bob took over, telling them all that he was going to be holding talks with Ingene later that evening. Then they all left together.

The entire presentation had taken four minutes. The Almost Infinity employees sat on, dazed. Nils got up and said a few words. He attempted to rally their spirits. He didn't know what would come out of Bob's discussions with Ingene, but he, at least, was hopeful. He gave them all a big thumbs-up at the conclusion of his brief remarks. Then, in the near silence that greeted his words, Lynne, once Nils's assistant and now secretary for the cell biology group, spoke up. She wanted them all to bow their heads and join her in a prayer of thanks for their rescue. She invited them all to marvel at the mercy of God, who works in mysterious ways. Nigel was wondering what would happen next. He certainly didn't feel like praying. But perhaps Lynne had some inside information; perhaps she knew something no one else did. Nigel thought about the Ingene presentation and decided it, on its own, certainly didn't merit any prayers of thanks. Lynne was clearing her throat, about to lead the prayers, when one of the molecular biologists, a clever, serious woman, spoke up.

"Well, just a minute, Lynne. Why don't we wait until we've got more information? Nothing was promised us today. I'm all for giving thanks, but we have to have something to give thanks for."

Her words punctured Lynne's brittle, desperate optimism. People began to get to their feet all around the lecture hall. The meeting was finished. Nigel walked back to the office with Peter. Peter hadn't been impressed.

"He didn't say much, did he? They are very careful with their money? They are a small company? Not much there for us, was there?"

Nigel had to agree. He couldn't see it either.

"Maybe it will be salvation for a few of us," he ventured.

"Maybe so," agreed Peter. "But that won't be me. I've got to start looking."

"Surely not," Nigel objected. "People here think very highly of you."

He didn't really know this and suspected that, in any case, it wasn't true. He said it simply to try and cheer Peter up.

"We must have a couple of years left, surely."

Peter smiled at him. Nigel was bullshitting him and he knew it.

"Burn rate and capital on hand. That's math I can do. We're going to be finished in December, if not sooner."

They went into their office and sat down in their respective chairs. They faced each other across the surfaces of their two desks. Nigel was finding Peter more likable by the day. Adversity seemed to bring out the best in him. He no longer talked so much and seemed more interested in other people. He was just sitting there, looking quizzically at Nigel, when Nils put his head around their office door. He didn't say anything, but he looked first at Nigel and then at Peter and gave them both a big thumbs-up. He withdrew as suddenly as he'd appeared.

"Thank God," said Nigel fervently. "He must know something to have done that."

"Let's hope," said Peter.

**

The next Monday, everyone came to work eager to learn the upshot of Bob's dealings with Ingene. They were all hoping to be given good news. Their positions had all been secured for the foreseeable future! It was going to be great. Everyone thought warmly of Los Angeles and the bespectacled man who'd spoken to them briefly on Friday evening. Slowly, the news trickled down from Bob to them all. Ingene wanted to buy two of their large refrigerators. And they proposed changing the locks throughout Almost Infinity's facility to prevent anyone from filching other equipment they may want to buy in the future. Two refrigerators!

Peter told Nigel he'd heard that the extent of Ingene's generosity was to pay fifty cents on the dollar for the two nearly new items, rather than the twenty-five cents that was standard for used equipment. Nigel doubted that Bob's standing in the company would survive such a disappointment. To have whipped them all into such a frenzy of expectation and then to let them down so cruelly, it was a serious black eye. And really, what could they expect from Angelinos, anyway? He thought back to Friday and told Peter he was thankful they had not offered up any prayers of thanks. Peter agreed with him, shouting his incredulity at Lynne's suggestion with boisterous enthusiasm. The more he witnessed the dickheadedness of Almost Infinity's management team, the better he felt about himself.

Nigel was thinking he could really get to like Peter when another memo arrived. This was brought to them personally by Maria, looking as beautiful as ever. She didn't seem to mind this lowly task; in fact, she seemed pleased to have something to do. Nigel and Peter were both distracted by the brief appearance of the gorgeous Maria. Happy smiles still lingered on their faces as the door closed behind her. This, of course, was by Bob's design. Maria was Bob's personal assistant, and he sent her out now because he knew her appearance would give all the men a lift and divert attention away from him. And he didn't want his name, with the associated shame of the recent Ingene debacle hanging over it, to distract from the good news that Donald was bringing them all.

The memo announced the departure of Donald through the wormhole on November 5. It was to be at 5:00 p.m. from a field on the outskirts of Half Moon Bay. They were all invited to attend and wish him "bon voyage."

"This means it's going to take place after work," Nigel pointed out peevishly. "They've got a nerve, haven't they?"

Surprisingly, Peter was more forgiving.

"Come on, Nigel, give them a break. And they are still paying us. No, we really will have to go. And anyway, it'll be interesting, won't it? I mean, how is he going to do this? He's going to disappear from the middle of a field. You have to admit you're interested."

"I just hope he doesn't embarrass himself. All of us will suffer then."

***

Research went on unhindered. They flung themselves into it. They would get the results that would save the day. All Grains would see the progress and reconsider. Nigel's work began to get interesting. *Spartina townsendii* turned out to be a treasure trove of interesting phenomena in the field of salt tolerance. Even Nils began to show interest in his progress. And Nils himself, with his two young research assistants, began to generate a head of steam. Six more months and they could save themselves. Stan, Jeff, and Oliver had laid the foundations for a first-class molecular biology effort. Everyone took pride in the fact that, despite the craziness all around them, they were at least competitive with other research groups in the field of crop improvement. Then the pride burst forth. Hell, they were more than competitive; they were leaders!

They began to receive visits from competing scientists, both in private industry and academia. Everyone was interested in looking over this young, vibrant initiative that could be for sale. As always, Nils and Bob tried to recruit everyone who came through. And one or two did agree to join. It was, after all, such a beautiful environment, and people didn't seem hard-pressed for funds. In fact, they seemed to have everything they needed. They had even been the subject of a recent article in the *New York Times*! They had to be on the up and up. It was a very confusing time for those already at the company. In the face of all the promising research and the ongoing hiring spree, the specter of financial collapse receded. Now it seemed like a distant, barely remembered nightmare. Bob and his fellow businessmen couldn't let such a thing happen, could they? They must have arranged alternative financing. It all went very quiet. No news is, after all, good news.

Now talk of the Nigerian government resurfaced. Yes, it was the Nigerians; they were going to save the day. And then, in a few months, when all their groundbreaking research had begun to attract the attention of the scientific world, new investment streams would open up or buyers would appear. It would all quickly swell into a flood of opportunity.

Bob continued working away imperturbably. Ben Benson kept making payroll every two weeks. George Nipper kept chasing leads and had one or two nibbles. But Bob was more cautious now, after the fiasco with Ingene. There were no more company visits, at least none that Bob publicized. He often came around with small groups of strange men, but he never introduced his guests to anyone. Life ran along gaily under the bright sunshine and the clear blue sky. Days passed, indistinguishable one from the other. Gentle, cool, dry breezes passed over all the people in the Bay Area as they sat in their mostly tiny yards, surrounded by gorgeous flowering bushes and small trees. It was truly life in paradise.

And in Minneapolis, Helmuth watched and waited.

CHAPTER 23

Davis, Nigeria, and a Sewer

A LARGE INTERNATIONAL scientific meeting to review progress in crop improvement was held in October at the university in Davis, just up the road from San Francisco. A large number of Almost Infinity employees attended. Most of the leading academics were there, among them Ben Storey-Moore, a world-renowned professor of plant physiology at Yale. Ben Storey-Moore was an Englishman who had lived in America for almost thirty years. He was in his middle fifties and was tanned and spare, appearing to be very fit. He looked like he belonged in California. The academic scientists and their students cast envious eyes over their Californian colleagues, particularly those in apparently well-funded smaller companies like Almost Infinity. They gossiped among themselves about these young bucks, who were really rather undistinguished as scientists, making oodles of money. Often, in the course of these conversations, they lamented their comparative poverty.

Nigel found this particularly galling. He knew most of the academics held permanent, secure, well-paying jobs with great benefits and that if anybody had the right to be envious, it was the employees of Almost Infinity whose futures were all hanging by a thread.

"These bastards," he said now to Peter, "they've crawled out of their cushy ratholes and come to California. They see the sunshine and the beautiful, untroubled people and are envious. Everyone has it so much better than them. The lousy hypocrites, they make me sick."

He said this in an undertone because he was sitting at the same table as Ben Storey-Moore. They were at lunch on the first day of the conference. Along with Ben were a couple of his female graduate students and several young industrial scientists like him and Peter. Nigel would have been an academic just like Ben if it hadn't been for Kutti. Ben was holding forth on the merits of long-distance running, a recreation he now pursued fanatically. In fact, he'd just returned from a 20K run that very morning. He accepted the exclamations of surprise and wonder from his acolytes and young friends with a small self-satisfied smile.

"Now I know you're all wondering why I'm eating salad for breakfast, why I'm not tucking into the donuts like the rest of you. Well, it's because I'm living my life like the Tarahumara of Mexico. This is how they eat. And I'm running like them also. See my shoes? These are merely coverings for my feet. Barefoot is best, but I can't do that yet."

And then, as Nigel was thinking what a prat he was, Ben suddenly and unexpectedly pitched face forward into his salad bowl. He lay there, draped across the table, his arms and legs twitching gently away. They all stared at him in horror, frozen in indecision. He slid slowly off the table and fell onto the floor on his back. Nigel was first to his side. He noted he was still breathing. He felt at his neck for a pulse. It was there and beating slowly but quite strongly.

"Call an ambulance!" he shouted up to the onlooking young men and women.

One of Ben's girls hurriedly did so. The other diners at breakfast tore their gaze away from his prostrate body and resumed eating, all the while glancing over to check on him with kind, concerned eyes. The ambulance arrived quickly, and the paramedics loaded their patient onto a gurney. Lettuce leaves were still stuck to his face, and one of his burly handlers gently removed most of the greenery.

Ben Storey-Moore was pushed out through the watching diners, unconscious.

"He's probably had a stroke," said Nigel. "All that running, I expect."

And he bit thankfully into his donut.

**

Ben Storey-Moore had not had a stroke. He had merely fainted. They kept him in the hospital overnight for observation, but the next morning found him once again at the conference breakfast. He was sitting there enjoying the undivided attention of his two female graduate students when Nils joined him.

"You feeling better, Ben?" the Dane wanted to know.

"All good now," Ben assured him. "I guess you can overdo it."

Nils looked him over appraisingly. Nils was still the biggest dog at meetings like these; everyone knew who he was, and he reveled in his primacy.

"How about becoming a consultant for us?" he asked now. "You won't have to do much. Just give us your opinion from time to time. And, of course, Almost Infinity will pay you handsomely."

Ben glanced sideways at his female companions. *See?* his look said, *I've still got it. Still potent, still wanted. I might have fainted yesterday, but there's life in the old boy yet. How many of these other tossers could have run 20K before breakfast?*

The dark-haired nymph, watching him closely, read his thoughts.

"What about you, big boy?" she asked, turning to Nils. "Who do you want to boff?"

Nils wasn't known as the doofus at Almost Infinity for nothing. He stared back at her, uncomprehending, a slight smile on his otherwise expressionless, craggy face.

"Never mind," the girl said, after a moment's contemplation of the Danish mask in front of her.

Nils turned expectantly to Ben.

"Well, what do you say?"

The blonde girl, Amanda, said quickly: "Almost Infinity's broke, Ben. Everybody is talking about it. You'd never get paid."

"Forward these girls, aren't they, Ben?" said Nils. "They should learn some manners."

He sounded slightly accusatory, as if Ben had somehow failed as a supervisor.

"Oh, they're just taking advantage of my weakness for them. You know what pretty young girls can be like."

"As a matter of fact, I don't," said Nils huffily.

He stood up, nodded to his acquaintance, and walked off.

"You shouldn't have said that about Almost Infinity, Amanda. Nils Jensen is a very proud man."

***

The next Monday, all the conferees from Almost Infinity were back at work. Many of them had taken the opportunity to put out feelers for other jobs while at the conference. The lucky few whose interest had been encouraged were bright and hopeful at the start of the new week. Overall, however, the mood at the company was somber. As word of their financial difficulties had spread in Davis, there had been a general sympathetic interest that was impossible to ignore. It had reawakened the feeling of dread that had been temporarily placed in abeyance by all the recent busy activity in the warehouse. The rate of progress in research was once again assessed and once again recognized as simply being too slow. Even Bob accepted this. And so they all squirmed under the grip of these temporal restraints.

Bob decided to follow up on the Nigerian interest. He contacted the Nigerian consulate in San Francisco. He referenced their previous communications and asked for clarification on the two hundred and confirmation of the seriousness of their intentions. Two hundred what? He asked this as diplomatically as he could. He proposed putting ten thousand dollars in the account in the bank in New York that the Nigerians had designated. The Nigerians replied that this was a small amount, but it would do to get things started. Bob wired the money and asked for further instructions. None came. He waited a week and then went into town to visit the consulate in person. He took his correspondence with him.

The consulate turned out to be a large building in its own grounds in a quiet suburb of the city. He showed the large young man seated just inside the front door the name written at the foot of the letter he'd received from the consulate. Then he found himself in front of a young lady, a receptionist he thought, who affected an air of importance. She seemed genuinely amazed at his letter, almost angry that he'd allowed himself to receive such a missive. She read the letter closely and then hurried off without saying anything to him, taking the letter with her. He watched her go, teetering on heels that were too high. Then a large Nigerian man with a dignified air appeared before him. They shook hands, and the man ushered Bob into a nearby room.

They sat down on either side of a bare desk. The man put the letter down in front of him, smoothed it flat, and shook his head sadly at Bob.

"These rascals," he began.

Bob then heard about people ("probably Nigerians," admitted the man grudgingly) who were operating scams and bilking money out of people here in America.

"They rely on shame, Mr. …" He looked again at the letter. "Mr. Levy, is it? They think rich people here will be ashamed when their friends find out that they were considering making money out of a poor country like Nigeria, with all its millions of undernourished souls. And it's a safe bet, Mr. Levy. People here don't want everyone looking at them as if they are greedy and cruel and, because they fell for it, stupid. It's not pleasant, Mr. Levy, is it?"

Bob stood up. He was outraged.

"We thought we were doing your country a favor," he said bitterly. "We were going to bring prosperity to your shores."

"Really," said the Nigerian coolly, looking up at him. He waved a hand at the letter Bob had brought with him. "And you were going to do this how? By bringing the future to my people?"

"It sounds fantastic to the common man, I know. But we have about two hundred people working on this. We really can see into the future. Our founder has constructed a wormhole."

The Nigerian's lips curved in a disbelieving smile. This Levy certainly had a nerve! First, he'd tried to con money out of Nigeria and now, here he was, calling them all common.

"A wormhole," he repeated caustically. "And this is where? In the ground? With the worm? Has he dug the hole himself?"

"It's not literally a hole," said Bob unhappily, realizing that without Donald he sounded very foolish. "It's all about the math. I can't do the math, but our founder can."

"I see. I think…," said the Nigerian slowly. He reflected for a moment and then went on: "That might be the best we can do for today. We are a simple, common people, after all. You want us to invest in an imaginary hole that has been created by math you can't do or understand. We want to be able to feed our people. Not a lot of concordance there, I think. Once again, of course, that's just common old me talking."

He smiled broadly at Bob.

"Look," said Bob, anxious now to leave with at least a shred of his dignity intact, "I know it's a difficult concept. Very few people can understand it. But if you contact my secretary the week before November the fifth, she will tell you where to go to witness a demonstration of the wormhole in action. You would be very welcome to join us. You'll see—we are not stupid, greedy, or cruel."

"I'm sure you are not, Mr. Levy," the Nigerian said, standing up and extending his hand. "I'm looking forward to the demonstration. And, for the moment, no more money need change hands."

Bob shook his hand and left. It was only later, when he thought over his visit, that he realized the man, whose name he'd never learned, had probably been worried about bad publicity and had wanted to make sure that no lawsuit would materialize. He needn't have worried. Big Bob was entirely deflated.

***

Nigel found himself once more growing irritated with Peter Blakely. Now that he and Nigel were friends, he had resumed his incessant chatter. He was telling Nigel about an Amanda Watkins from Yale, who was looking for a job. She'd sent her résumé to Nils, and he'd passed it on to Peter.

"She can come immediately," he told Nigel, his eyes bulging incredulously.

"I met her at the conference," said Nigel. "Pretty girl, doing a PhD with Ben Storey-Moore. She's a Tartar, Pete. Better watch out."

"What does that mean?" beamed Peter. "A Tartar! Sounds exciting."

"Oh, it'll be exciting, all right. She's a handful now. When she gets to California, look out!"

"She's really strong on paper," Peter went on. "Better universities than me."

"Are you going to have her in for an interview?"

Peter shook his head.

"I think I'll just offer her the job," he said laughingly.

Nigel looked hard at him.

"Is that fair? What about the state of the company? You said yourself we are all going to be out of work come December."

"That's just it, Nigel. If I don't get her now, I may never get her."

"It's your call, Pete. But like I said, watch out!"

* * *

Nigel talked it over later with Charlene. They were at home.

"He's desperate, Charlene. He really wants a girlfriend."

"Sleeps around, does she?" asked Charlene. "What chance will Peter have with a girl like that? Got all the old men at the university chasing after her? I could have been like that. But I took pity on them, left them with their dignity intact despite their best efforts to lose it."

"You're a saint," said Nigel, running his hands down her back. He took her in his arms. "So when are we getting married? Let's make it next spring."

"All right," she said, twisting away from him. "I'll alert my mother."

* * *

Donald had found the manhole of his dreams. It was in the middle of an enormous field next to a wastewater plant just on the outskirts of the town of Half Moon Bay. The manhole cover itself, Donald was pleased to note, was not made of metal. It was some kind of polymer. Fiberlite was its name. It would be invisible to a metal detector. The manhole cover was situated about four inches below the surface of the grass. The shaft below the manhole cover led down a ladder into an enormous pipe about six feet in diameter that was running along about ten feet under the surface of the field. He shone a flashlight into the black interior of the pipe. The pipe was mostly dry with just a trickle of water running along its bottom. He would return tomorrow night to complete the necessary excavations.

***

Bob tried to call Helmuth. Helmuth, however, would never return his calls. Bob left him messages. He hoped Helmuth would come to witness Donald's journey through the wormhole. Bob's messages grew more desperate: the circus was going to be in town. This caused Helmuth to check the circus's schedule. He found out it was going to be in New York on November 5. Helmuth told his secretary he didn't want her to pass on any more of Bob's messages. He was officially persona non grata. Bob didn't pursue Ned Crellin. Ned Crellin he would leave to George Nipper.

George tried all the people he knew. One or two said they would come to witness Donald's departure to the future, but he didn't believe them. The majority of his contacts expressed mild interest but were generally disbelieving. The typical response George heard was: "He's a charlatan, of course, your boss. Travel to and from the future is impossible in this day and age."

George would try to argue: "No, really, he's a famous cosmologist. He's done the math."

"I don't care if he's won the Nobel Prize. Don't you know what it would mean if we could travel back and forth in time? We would literally never die. We would have transformed Earth into heaven. So that's all he's promising, is it?"

Ned Crellin fully justified Bob's aversion to further contact with him by the vitriol of his response to George's gentle inquiry.

"That sneaky, slick bastard! What pile of horseshit is he selling now? Travel to the future? I wish he'd travel to the bottom of the crapper where he belongs."

"So that's a no, then?" George got in before Ned slammed down the phone. "You only had to say 'no, thank you,'" George said out loud to his empty office.

CHAPTER 24

Warm, Pink, Quiet

TOWARD THE END OF OCTOBER, Ben Benson came to see Bob in his office. "We'll just have to tell everybody, Bob," he said. "There are new employees showing up every day. What about them? We don't want the legal liability."

"Hope springs eternal," said Bob trying, but not quite succeeding, to direct a broad, confident smile at Ben. "We've got a couple of irons in the fire. And I'm going to go back to US Home Products. I heard that the Britisher who headed up their party while they were visiting has since left their company."

"You mean the guy you dumped on the floor and dragged through the slime in the new wing?"

"That's the one. He's gone now, and I think they'll be much more favorably disposed toward us. He went to a direct competitor, for God's sake. I'll call up Ernie Sikorsky, and we can have a good laugh about his misfortune here."

"Yeah, I have to admit that was funny. But only in retrospect. At the time it seemed like an absolute disaster."

"Can't we carry on until Donald has done his party trick?" implored Bob. "I'm just so nervous about breaking our momentum. If we can just keep going for six more months, we'll have enough in the way of progress to attract new investors, I'm certain of that."

"All right," said Ben. "We both know we don't have money for another six months, but you are our leader, Bob. We just have to have faith in you. Otherwise, there's no point in our being here, is there? But after the party trick, and not six months after, we'll have to pull the plug. We'll have no money left, and you will be on the end of obligations that could ruin you within a week."

"I won't let that happen, Ben. We may have to survive a brief down period, but I'm sure I can get new investors. It might take all of six months, though. I expect most of the senior guys will be able to see it through."

"I don't know, Bob. Life is really unforgiving in the Bay Area. They might all leave."

"As long as we've got Donald, we'll be okay. No other company will have a time traveler on their books. Just Almost Infinity."

"Just almost bankrupt, I'm afraid," echoed Ben unhelpfully.

***

Bob and Donald talked over Donald's planned trip to the future.

"You're really going to be gone, Donald? I mean, we won't find you crouching under the platform contraption pretending not to be there?"

Donald laughed.

"Why would I be crouching, Bob? Surely, you've got more faith in me than that?"

"I've got faith in you, Donald. It's just that I don't know what to expect. We're playing for awfully big stakes here, aren't we? If anything goes wrong, we're finished. And not just for now—forever."

"Okay Bob, first I will enter the cabinet. Once the door is closed, there will be no more verbal communication with me. But everyone will know exactly where I am. Now I'm actually in the wormhole zone, not standing outside it. I can talk or I can go through the wormhole, but I can't do both."

Bob looked at him admiringly. He was fearless. And he sounded so serious. He looked carefully into Donald's eyes, looking for the glassy indifference of mental illness. But there was no sign. Donald looked back at him, eyes sparkling, brimming with happiness and confidence. He was the very picture of mental health.

"There will be no verbal communication, Bob, but there will be communication. And you're going to play a central role here. You have to have your laptop or smartphone with you. I'm going to send you a series of GPS coordinates, and you're going to arrange to have the platform wheeled to each location specified by the coordinates, each one in turn. When you reach the first location, you will wait exactly two minutes, and then I'll send you another location. I could be sending you as many as five locations in all. I'll tell you when we've reached the final location, and then you can bring up the vacuum pump and wormhole facilitator. You can read GPS coordinates, Bob?"

It turned out Bob couldn't. Donald explained them to him.

"I'm going to put this program on your laptop and smartphone so you'll be able to use either. On the evening of the day of my journey, I'm going to send you enough numbers to allow you to get to within a ten-foot radius of any designated spot. And you have to get this right, Bob, otherwise I can't go."

"Why can't you tell me the coordinates now?" asked Bob. "Wouldn't that be the easiest?"

"It would, but it can't be done. I don't know them currently."

He closed his laptop and looked encouragingly at Bob.

Then he smiled and went on: "The gravity and the vibrations are always changing and shifting with time. At this moment I can only say approximately where a wormhole will open up. I can get within a hundred yards of it today, but no closer. I can be precise only at exactly the right time. The time for this particular portal to open up is at fifteen minutes past 5:00 p.m. on November the fifth. I will get a series of close readings just before that time. Then, I'll get it exactly and can go through. Generally, there are three or four or even five false starts. And listen, this is very important: When we arrive at the final location, you have to delete all the previous locations. You must remember to do this. If you don't, I may be killed. We are dealing with tremendous energy surges here."

Bob, listening closely and empowered by his new understanding of GPS coordinates, briefly imagined himself an equal partner with Donald in the adventure of time travel.

"What do you mean, 'generally'? Have you already been through the wormhole? You have, haven't you. You've already told me you are a time traveler, haven't you?"

Donald, enjoying his rapt attention, looked knowingly at him.

"Do you really think I'd take such a risk as doing this for the first time in front of hundreds of people? Of course I've been through a wormhole before. You already knew that. But those little trips were different. For one thing, now I'm going to a distant future. I'm covering much greater spans of time."

Now Bob was agog with expectation.

"Well, come on, Donald, what were the little trips like?"

Bob's near-certainty that Donald was making the whole thing up was thrown into fresh doubt. He'd never really admitted he was lying, had he? And now, all this information about precise times and GPS coordinates had tipped the balance. For the moment, Bob was once again a believer.

"What's it like?"

Donald looked back at him, seeming genuinely puzzled.

"Well, it's the damnedest thing Bob. On these little trips, when I get back to this time, I can't remember what the future was like."

These words stopped Bob's wild and hopeful imaginings dead in their tracks.

"What do you mean you can't remember? You can't just say that."

"It's the strangest thing. It's as if my mind has been wiped clean. Maybe I'm just not staying there long enough."

Now Bob looked angry. "So you can't remember. What's the point of going, then? You can already get artifacts sent back to you. What the hell is the point of going?"

Donald nodded and smiled resignedly at Bob's outburst.

"I'm going to about 2175. That's what the math is calling for. The exact year is still to be worked out. It's like GPS coordinates for time. I've just learned to travel in time as well as space, that's all."

"But you can't remember, Donald. You can't remember. No one is going to believe you, not even me."

Donald shook his head sadly.

"Too hasty, Bob. You should have waited for me to tell you the rest of the story."

"The rest of the story?" Bob repeated incredulously.

Was it a story all along? And he, fool that he was, had actually started to believe.

"I've sent a message back from my laptop. Nothing detailed. Want to see?"

"You bet your sweet ass I do!"

Now Bob was wildly excited again. He jumped up and stared down at Donald.

"You're going to show me something you wrote in the future?"

"In 2125," put in Donald.

"Something you wrote in 2125 and sent back to the present day?"

"Well, it's only a brief message, Bob. Here it is."

He flipped his laptop back open, tapped out a few keystrokes, and invited Bob back to his side to view the screen. There it was, in his inbox. The subject was "me." It was dated July 4, 2125.

"Thought I'd go on Independence Day, make a historic event of it, so to speak."

Bob's eyes greedily drank in the first private information Donald had ever shown him on his laptop. The message consisted of just three words: "Warm, pink, quiet."

"What does it mean?" whispered Bob, staring at the date. "Your computer says the date you sent it was 2125. 'Warm, pink, quiet.' Sounds post-apocalyptic, doesn't it?"

"Oh, the date is accurate. I reconfigured the time so now it's showing the actual date the message was sent. Of course, your computer won't show this. Yours will show today's date, even for a message I send from the future. Computers can't handle time deviations. This one I've modified."

He closed his laptop again and smiled at Bob.

"I hope you'll believe me now."

"Warm, pink, quiet," said Bob slowly. "Seriously, what does it mean. For some reason it sounds to me as if you were underwater. Warm, quiet, but why pink?"

"Maybe it's more straightforward. Maybe it was the end of the day, and I was looking at a sunset. It was a warm evening, and I was somewhere quiet. Anyway, don't worry; there's going to be nothing ambiguous about my next messages. I'm going to send you a much fuller account of life this time."

"So are you still alive in 2125, Donald?"

"There is a Donald there. In a universe without time travel, I am, of course, very definitely dead."

"God," said Bob fervently, clutching his head. "It's just so goddamn confusing."

"Not really, Bob," Donald said soothingly. "The first thing you have to keep in mind is that there is almost an infinity of parallel universes. In some of these universes, time travel is possible, while in others, it isn't. There is no way I can travel in time to a universe in which time travel is impossible."

"But it was impossible in this one before you came along."

"Was it? That's not true, Bob. There were others before me. But they are in our future. Some universes are doomed to expire without ever experiencing time distortion. Time in these universes remains in orderly sequence. And there's nothing anyone can do about it. I shouldn't say 'nothing' really because there are parallel universes within parallel universes, and, of course, anything is possible there. You see, Bob, in this universe there's no such thing as the first time traveler. That's precluded by the very nature of time. Anyway, I just sent that first message to satisfy myself it could be done," he went on. "I remember thinking, I'll just make it short and sweet."

Out of all the confusion, Bob pounced. "You remember thinking? I thought you said your mind was wiped clean."

Donald never missed a beat: "Well, that's right. But, with the prompting of something tangible like this message, things come back. It's the strangest thing, like a kind of bridge, really."

Bob thought over what Donald was saying. It didn't make total sense to him, but somehow it sounded credible.

"I'm believing you now, Donald. No one could make up such a complicated story. I feel so honored. I'm in the presence of a man who is going to change the world, at least our world."

Donald smiled his familiar slippery smile.

"This is only the very beginning for us. Time travel is going to be ubiquitous and free. The fabric of the space-time continuum will change."

Bob smiled at him, dewy-eyed.

"If I can't make money out of this, I deserve to be shot."

He imagined again being at the heart of the white-hot excitement generated by Donald's amazing technological advance. It had been coming, hadn't it? And now here it was—a time machine.

So Bob had completed his journey with Donald and come full circle. He'd started out as a believer in Donald's wormhole, if an uncertain one. Then, as he got to know Donald better, he went from being a believer to having doubts, not the least of which were raised by Donald's own mixed messages. The doubts grew to outright skepticism and finally to not believing at all. Then Donald had allowed him to see his own uncertainty, and this, paradoxically, had turned the corner for Bob. All that remained now was for Donald to demonstrate time travel in front of the world on November 5 and Bob's belief would be total. If Donald could really vanish, there would be no room for doubt.

***

Charlene's mother came out from Georgia to visit them. She and Charlene's father had been divorced for almost twenty years. Nigel remembered something he'd read in a novel when he was a teenager, when he was really too young to understand what he was reading. One of the characters had declared: "Always take a good look at the mother, son. That's what your soul mate is going to look like in twenty or thirty years' time."

Nigel did so now, but, of course, he couldn't imagine what the passage of time would do to them both. His dad was an old man. In his mind's eye he, Nigel, remained remarkably well preserved. Charlene's mother was shorter than Charlene and a little on the heavy side. But she was blessed with a kind, attractive face and a very personable manner. She was, in fact, a joy to talk to. Nigel briefly reviewed his impression of her.

"Good enough," he concluded. "In twenty-five years' time, I'll be married to a very similar woman, except she'll be taller and slimmer and we will have brought up a couple of kids. Not too bad a prospect. I just hope she doesn't have a hidden nasty streak, but really what are the chances of that? This, after all, is Charlene I'm thinking about."

Charlene was delighted to have her mother with her and delighted that she seemed to get on so well with Nigel. She took her shopping, and they went out to eat together. Sometimes Nigel came with them. When he didn't, she never stopped telling her mother how lucky she was to have found Nigel.

"I'm sure he loves me, Mom. We are going to be very happy."

"Like me and your father," said her mother. "I thought like you once, but now I know better. Look who I ended up with. A know-it-all, useless shit."

"No, Mom, Nigel's not like Dad. You'll see. Just give him a chance."

"All right, Charlene," said her mother, now. "I can see how he looks at you. You've definitely got him. And he is quite nice-looking, isn't he? I'll hang around with you for a little while and get to know Nigel better. If that's okay with you, of course. Maybe yours won't turn out to be a useless shit."

And on this breezy note of hope, mother and prospective son-in-law began their relationship with wariness and Charlene's best interests at heart. The three of them decided that Charlene's mother, whose name was Mary, should stay for a month. She would still be with them on November 5. Charlene and Nigel were going to take her to Donald's wormhole demonstration.

"You'll get to meet our co-workers, Mom. And our founder, Donald Plum, is going to disappear into the future before our very eyes. It should be an exciting evening all round. Especially if he pulls it off."

CHAPTER 25

Donald Travels to the Future

EMMANUEL CAME TO SEE JIM. Jim, who had a very small office in the administration building, rarely received visitors there. Don was the only other person who regularly put in an appearance. Jim was pleased to see Emmanuel and greeted him effusively.

"Looking forward to Christmas, Manny? I imagine that's a busy time of year for you."

"It is, Jim," he answered.

Jim grinned at him now and said, "What can I do you for?"

"We've run out of hand towels."

Jim looked at him wonderingly. "So?"

"All John won't supply us with any more until we've paid our bill."

Jim sat back and relaxed. He could deal with this. This was his job. "Leave it with me, Manny. I'll have a word with Ben Benson."

He took fifty dollars out of his wallet.

"Here, take this and go to Sam's Club to get some temporary towels. Bring me the receipt and the change, and I'll get the money you spent out of petty cash."

Emmanuel nodded and left. He wasn't pleased to have to go to Sam's Club. It would be an interruption to his well-ordered day. The paper towels he bought were a little bit larger than the ones All John supplied, and he had to cram them into the dispensers back at Almost Infinity. Now they were difficult to get out without tearing them, and the torn pieces began to litter the floors of all the restrooms at Almost Infinity. After a couple of days of this, Bob noticed and mentioned it to Jim.

Jim then remembered he had to talk to Ben Benson.

"I guess we haven't paid All John this month," Jim began, as he stood in the doorway to Ben's office.

"Haven't we?" asked Ben disingenuously. "Let me check that and get back to you."

Jim went off, job done.

Ben sat at his desk and pondered the developing situation. He might have guessed it would be the local vendors who would start squealing first. The bigger companies, the chemicals and equipment suppliers, generally had longer billing cycles. If you didn't pay them, they just sent out another bill with a reminder. Then, after continued failure to pay, they cut you off from further purchases and pressed for redress. But with failure to pay the first major vendor, there came the spreading of the word that you were in trouble. All the other major vendors would be alerted, and consumables would quickly become impossible to obtain. Maybe you could get some supplies from abroad, but you couldn't rely on that. Ben reckoned they would have to shut up shop by the third week in November. He would have to tell Bob the jig was up.

Ben entered Bob's office exuding despair. He looked at the happy, chubby face of Almost Infinity's chief executive and felt a pang of sorrow at having to deliver such dire news to his boss. Bob caught his expression and immediately adopted a look of kind concern.

"At the middle of next month, Bob, we won't be able to make payroll. We've come to the end of the road."

To his amazement, Bob seemed buoyant.

"This is why we're called Almost Infinity, Ben," he chuckled.

"I don't understand," said Ben weakly.

"*Almost*, Ben, *almost*. *Almost* implies 'just before the end,' doesn't it? And this is almost our end. But" —he waggishly raised a finger— "not quite. Donald has still to go through the wormhole. He will save us. It's going to be great."

"But where will we get money from, Bob? Without money, we can't exist. We just don't have any time left."

He looked imploringly at Bob, willing him to offer some solution to their predicament.

Bob stood up and offered his hand. Ben took it uncertainly.

"Do your best, Ben. Win us an extra week if you can. That's all we'll need."

"The coffee machines are being taken off the premises on Friday. We'll have to buy toilet paper, paper towels, and soap from petty cash. The bathrooms will continue to look a mess. And at some point, we'll have to announce that we can't make our next payroll."

"Put together a memo, Ben. Donald and I will sign it and then get all the senior managers to sign. Address it to all employees at Almost Infinity. Say that we, the senior managers, aren't ready to throw in the towel. We are going to continue without salary while we look for new investors. We are very confident we will be able to find them after Donald's first demonstration of time travel. This is going to revolutionize our world. Yes, Ben," he went on, ignoring Ben's quizzical look, "I really believe we are on the threshold of a revolution. Prepare the memo for next Tuesday, the day after Donald's departure, and I'll proof it. Call a company-wide meeting for Friday to distribute the memo and to tell all our employees that we can't make payroll. We'll ask them to join us, the senior managers, in our sacrifice."

Ben, imagining next week, thought first about Donald's planned demonstration. He would probably bungle it, and that would be the final nail in Almost Infinity's coffin.

He asked Bob now: "What if nobody joins us? That, I think, is very likely. And we will have left it to the very end to tell them all, won't we?"

"We'll fire their asses!" shouted Bob, grinning hugely. "We'll fire them for lack of spunk. God, after all we've been through, and they can't take even one week without pay, the greedy rats."

Bob's irrepressible good humor, brimming over from his corpulent body, began to wear on Ben. He suspected Bob's high spirits were edged with hysteria, although this was quite invisible. He regarded the big man's beaming face with a weary resignation.

"Is that what your employees are to you, Bob? Greedy rats?"

Bob roared laughing.

"Of course not, Ben! I love all our employees. I think of them as family. Don't you?"

Now Ben was hopelessly confused. He'd come to Bob's office with what he knew was dire news. He had expected sadness, even tears. The money was all gone. There was no tomorrow for Almost Infinity. How ironic was that for a company based on the notion of travel into the future? But Bob seemed oblivious. And here he was telling him he loved all his employees like family. He shook his head.

"I can't understand you, Bob. Why are you so happy?"

"It's Donald, Ben. Donald. He's going to save us. This is by far the most exciting thing that has ever happened to me. I know he's going to be gone on November the fifth, and I know he's going to be sending us messages from the future. I've accepted this. He's my new reality. People are going to be fighting for the privilege of investing in us. And Donald is going to travel to the future repeatedly. He'll have to, won't he? Next Monday will just be his first trip." He paused for a moment and collected himself. "I'm sorry, Ben. I get carried away when I think about what is happening to us. I've got to keep calm. You've got to think outside the box, Ben."

Ben managed a small smile.

"I'm afraid we'll all be thinking inside a box, Bob—a prison cell."

Once again, Bob howled with laughter.

"Come on, Ben. You are right on the brink of the most exciting time of your life. Surely, you can see that."

Bob laid his meaty hand on Ben's neck and gave it a squeeze.

"Be happy. Don't worry, baby. Everything's going to be all right."

***

The day for Donald's trip to 2175 arrived. Work finished early at Almost Infinity, and a significant number of the employees made the short trip to Half Moon Bay and assembled at the field selected by Donald and the imaginary math. There was a television crew from a local station in attendance. The question of media coverage had been mulled over again, and it had been decided to restrict it to one station. The risk of Stan telling reporters that Donald was the new Jesus and then of everything getting out of hand was too great to entertain. So they'd decided on one local station where they could control access to the reporter. Al would make sure to limit Stan's access to whomever the station sent.

Charlene and her mother and Nigel, with a box of fireworks, were sitting on a rug spread out over the grass. Many people were sitting around similarly situated. "Through the wormhole on Guy Fawkes Night," announced Nigel. "I'll bet I'm the first person ever to have uttered that sentence," he added proudly.

"That wasn't a sentence, Nigel," pointed out Charlene's mother. "There was no verb."

They were all sitting together looking up at the cart and platform that Donald had designed. It was quite an arresting sight, with its oversized wheels and with the platform supporting a tall, relatively narrow, rectangular box. Nigel, ignoring this box, thought of a tumbril and, by association, a guillotine, although he'd never seen these except in illustrations of the French Revolution. He consigned Mary to the contraption now as punishment for her nitpicking.

Stan, Jeff, and Oliver were standing together, watching suspiciously as Bob fussed around, conspicuously brandishing an oversize smartphone. The senior management group, accompanied by the Nigerian chargé d'affaires, all stood near Bob, watching him anxiously. Bob commandeered Peter and Emmanuel to help him move the platform. They stood by his side, waiting. Donald appeared. He had been there earlier positioning the cart, and now he'd come back. He was wearing a blue suit and a white shirt, open at the neck. He waved vaguely at all the employees and went over to Bob. The two men stood close together exchanging a few last-minute words. The exchange was mostly Donald giving Bob his final instructions.

Amanda Watkins had arrived from New Haven that afternoon. She had taken a fond farewell of Ben Storey-Moore and was now standing in the field with Judy and Jim, her new fellow employees. Judy pointed out Donald to her. She grinned incredulously on being told that he was about to go through a wormhole.

"Where is it?" she asked. "Where's this wormhole?"

Judy drew her attention to the platform. "It's going to form in the vicinity of that cart," she said.

"Wow! Compared to this, Yale is just so dull."

***

Nigel lay on his rug idly watching the three of them as the conversation unfolded out of earshot. He wondered why she'd shown up. She must know that Almost Infinity was in trouble. He remembered his fireworks. He'd brought along a few rockets, a couple of Catherine wheels, and a bag of sparklers. He took himself off to the edge of the field to find a couple of trees to use as vertical surfaces on which to present the Catherine wheels.

Stan turned to Jeff.

"Who's that chick with Judy and the captain?" he asked.

"Amanda Watkins, out of Yale. She's only just arrived. Al introduced me to her. All of her things are in a truck that's still in transit."

The sun had set, and it was almost dark. Nigel set up one of his rockets in a long, thin, glass receptacle he'd borrowed from the lab.

Donald mounted the platform. Nigel was still thinking of it as a tumbril. Donald waved weakly into the gathering gloom. Most of Almost Infinity's employees weren't even looking up at him. Nigel noted his tie-less, open-necked white shirt. The condemned man had been given no chance to take his own life and cheat execution, he thought, whimsically. Nigel laughed. He was about to draw Charlene's attention to Donald's appearance when Donald suddenly entered the cabinet and closed the door after himself. There was nothing but the blank face of the door left up there now. Donald was gone. Bob called over Peter and Emmanuel and assigned them to the cart's handles. Bob then remained motionless, staring at the screen of his smartphone.

It seemed he was never going to move again when suddenly his head snapped up and he said: "Let's go," pointing to the edge of the field nearest to Nigel.

Peter and Emmanuel leaned into their task and got the cart moving. It seemed to be quite heavy from the amount of effort it was taking to move it. They pulled it about fifty yards, coming quite close to Nigel's rug before passing by. Then Bob, who was walking along beside the platform, held up his hand.

"Stop here. This is it."

The three of them stopped and again all just stood there, waiting for further instructions. A couple of minutes passed before Bob, all the while studying his phone, stirred into action again. This time they headed off in a different direction. This stopping and starting was repeated a few more times, and then they came to a final stop. Now Bob deleted all the previous GPS locations and called everyone over to the cart. He called for the vacuum pump and the wormhole facilitator. Jim brought them and the emergency generator to the designated spot in his pickup truck. People gathered around and watched as first the emergency generator and then the vacuum pump sprang into life. The display on the wormhole facilitator began to wink on and off. The engine of the emergency generator provided a background throb while the vacuum pump supplied a deep rattle and the occasional muffled belch. Everyone took an involuntary step backward when the wormhole facilitator suddenly blared out its countdown.

Bob allowed the vacuum pump to run for exactly five minutes before shutting it and the wormhole facilitator off, but not before the facilitator had produced its final, definitive "ping." Then, in the sudden silence and with the crisp sound still echoing in their ears, he held up his hand and looked around at them all.

"Shall I see if he's gone?" he asked.

"Where could he have gone?" asked Stan disbelievingly. "He's up there in that cabinet. He couldn't have gotten out of that."

Bob clambered up onto the platform and opened the cabinet door. He looked inside and then turned and looked down at the waiting people.

"He's gone."

A ripple of surprise ran through the little crowd. Stan was up alongside Bob in a flash. He stared into the empty cabinet. Then he looked down at the floor and noticed the latches. He knelt down and raised the trapdoor up on its hinges.

"It's obvious where he's gone," he announced in a loud voice. "He's gone through the bottom of this box, and now he's hiding under the platform. This is definitely going to be embarrassing."

Amanda clapped her hands and laughed delightedly.

"Such a trusting lot, our fellow employees, aren't they? Hiding under the platform? Time travel? Oh, it's just so delicious!"

Stan scrambled off the platform and flung himself down to look under it. There was nothing there but grass and air. He got back to his feet looking slightly sheepish.

"Okay. So he's planned it a bit better than I gave him credit for. Move this cart a few yards, you two."

Peter and Emmanuel did as he asked, both looking slightly resentful at being ordered about by Stan. Stan put his hands on his hips and looked around challengingly at them all.

"All right, who's got a shovel?"

It turned out that someone who worked in the greenhouse had one in the back of his pickup. Stan grabbed it off him and plunged the blade savagely into the ground, ground that had been beneath the platform moments before. He succeeded in prising up a clump of sod with lumps of dry soil hanging off it. He stopped as suddenly as he'd begun and stared at the violated, wholly unsuspicious ground he'd attacked. There was obviously no hiding place concealed in its earthy anonymity.

"Where the fuck has he gone?" he asked, in a whisper.

Bob, who'd been watching with his heart in his mouth, sprang to life. He was suddenly deliriously happy.

"He's done it!" he yelled. "You all saw it. He's gone through his wormhole!"

Everyone gathered around the cart, with the cabinet sitting up on its platform, high and unquestionably empty.

"This is impossible!" yelled Stan, startling all the quiet, watching people. "Where did he go?"

"He went to 2175," said Bob. "That's what the math was calling for."

"You stupid fuck!" Stan continued to yell, causing Bob to take a step backward in the face of the onslaught. "This is impossible. None of us believes in this wormhole crap."

"Well," said Bob, privately noting how out of control Stan appeared, "why don't you tell us where he is?"

"It's a trick. It's got to be. I don't know how he did it, but there's no doubt in my mind that somehow he's fooled us all."

"How many of the rest of you are doubting Thomases?" asked Bob, turning in appeal to the watchers.

His gaze settled on the murky countenance of Nigel, and he addressed himself to the familiar face.

"You saw him enter the cabinet up there. Look at it. How could he have gotten out of that without anyone seeing him? It's just impossible. You saw the vacuum pump and the wormhole facilitator, and you can see now that he's gone. What you or I can't understand, of course, is the math. And that is the essential difference between Donald and the rest of us. We, like him, can talk about time travel. Talk is cheap." Bob suddenly became grave. "Look, he's gone into the unknown. We can only hope he's okay. He's laid his life on the line for us."

Stan turned away, cleared his throat, and spat in disgust on the ground. He began to walk away. Bob, now deeply serious—a man's life was at stake!—looked at his retreating back with contempt on his face.

"He told me he was going to send us messages from the future. Let's wait and see what these messages say, shall we? The man can do nothing more to prove himself to us."

Nigel, who'd been paying close attention to all that Bob and Stan were saying, decided it was time to cheer things up. He set off his rocket. All heads snapped back to watch its ascent. There was a collective "aaahhh" as it reached its apex and burst into a shower of multicolored stars. Nigel began handing out sparklers. People accepted them dully, as if beaten down by all the assaults on their sensibilities. He set off a Catherine wheel, and it spun around furiously, spraying sparks everywhere. The flashing lights, the vacuum pump, the roaring countdown, the "ping," Donald vanishing, Nigel's rocket, the sparks flying about everywhere from the Catherine wheel, the sputtering sparklers—it was simply overwhelming.

Nigel's own mind was racing. Somehow Donald had vanished. Clearly, the vacuum pump had to be the answer. Without that, it would simply have been a miracle. But the vacuum pump had effected a change, a necessary change that had allowed Donald to vanish. This was the change that had catalyzed wormhole formation. He had seen it with his own eyes. Peter came over to him, grinning furiously.

"Well, Nigel, what did you make of that? As one of the cart pullers, I'm bound to be famous. Will we get the investors we need now?"

"It had to have been the vacuum pump," said Nigel. "That was the only believable mechanical contrivance in the whole show."

"So what did the little lights do? And that big tube from the vacuum pump. Not big enough for Donald to pass through though, was it? What on earth was its purpose?" asked Peter. "I'm no physicist, but really, how could he generate any kind of vacuum through such a large aperture? The tube wasn't attached to anything, was it? It can't do anything can it? Donald just brought up the vacuum pump to make us all look like mugs."

Nigel was indignant.

"Well, where did he go? He is gone, isn't he? Or do you think he's hiding somewhere?"

"I do," said Peter. "I don't know how he did it, but somehow he got out of that cabinet without anyone seeing."

"Well, where is he? You've got no answer to that question. Where is he? You're just a doubting Thomas, like Lippowitz. And did you see him? How ridiculous did he look with that shovel?"

"We're not doubting Thomases, Nigel. Belief has never been an option. We are unbelievers, despite the evidence of our own eyes."

"What makes people so skeptical?" asked Nigel, turning to Charlene and her mother. "It's the modern thing, isn't it? The skepticism is selective. Science is the new religion. But science turns out not to be a belief in anything in particular. You believe in Jesus, Mary, don't you?"

Charlene's mother nodded. She was still dazed by what she had just witnessed. She looked open-mouthed at Nigel.

"You believe in Jesus, but you don't understand him, do you?"

"She can understand the message, Nigel. And that's all we've got in this day and age, isn't it? Jesus was with us two thousand years ago. Does Donald have a message?"

Charlene spoke slowly, with deliberation. Nigel appreciated the weight of her words, but almost immediately the shock of Donald's disappearance reclaimed him.

"But where is he, Charlene? Do you have any ideas?"

"There'll be an explanation," she said. "I don't think he's gone to 2175, do you?"

"I don't know what to think. All I know is he's gone and he didn't appear to travel through space. Doesn't that leave time as the only medium in which he could have traveled?"

Similar conversations were taking place all over the field in which the crowd who'd witnessed Donald's departure was sitting and standing.

Stan, like Nigel, kept repeating: "Where is he?" Again, like Nigel, he kept returning to the role of the vacuum pump. "That must have significance. But what the hell is it?"

Jeff and Oliver, who were standing with him, were shell-shocked. Neither of them said very much at all. In the senior management group there was shock, but also jubilation.

"He did it," said George. "He didn't let us down. You've got to admit that. He is actually traveling in time at this very moment. We've got some exciting calls to make tomorrow," he said, turning to Bob. Forrest stood by in silence as did Al and Nils. The three of them, all of whom had dismissed Donald as a kook, were abashed at the success of his demonstration.

Nils, speaking for the three of them, said softly: "I just hope he's still alive. He's taken a tremendous risk, hasn't he? I've read a little bit about wormholes. Apparently, there's tremendous pressure on the walls of the wormhole, and it can collapse. There would be no coming back from that."

Bob refused to be brought down by Nils's bleak remarks.

"We're not going to be gloomy here, Nils. We all saw him go, and I don't doubt we will all see him when he comes back. In the meantime, he said he was going to send me emails from 2175. When we receive one, we can all stop worrying."

"Anything yet?" Al asked immediately.

Bob took out his smartphone and looked through his messages.

"No, nothing yet," he reported cheerfully. "We wouldn't expect one so soon anyway, would we? What's the first thing you'd do on arriving in 2175. Send an email? And do they still have email in 2175? Who knows?"

They all laughed.

"But I've got complete faith in him. If he can send us messages, he will."

The Nigerian chargé d'affaires was looking around the field with an expression of wonder on his face.

"He's gone," he breathed. "There is really no doubt about that. But where?"

"The year 2175," said Bob promptly. "Listen, this is your big chance. You're the only serious investor here. If you come in for twenty million, I'll cut you in on the action, and I'll tell you what he says in his messages."

The Nigerian shook his head and laughed.

"Twenty million, Bob. That's a lot of money for a few messages."

And with these simple words Bob got the first hint of the difficulties that still lay before him. This man had, after all, witnessed Donald's departure. He had been as shocked as anyone. Yet he was still reluctant to commit any money to their cause. Suddenly, Bob felt the confidence draining out of him. At this exact moment he now felt, thanks to the caution of the Nigerian, a lot less confident of enthusiastic and unqualified approval from Helmuth, Ned, and Ernie. But this unwelcome caress of doubt passed quickly, and soon he was once again beaming proudly at them all.

"Well, at the very least we've got a rejuvenated workforce," he declared. "All of our employees will have renewed faith in Donald now and in the direction the company is taking. You can't overestimate the value of that. It's huge."

Ben Benson, standing nearby, cleared his throat but said nothing. He was thinking of the coming Friday when he was going to announce they couldn't make payroll this week. A major new deal now, if it could be put together over the next few days, might just save them. A delay in payroll of a few days might be tolerated; however, if there were nothing to set against that blow, he was absolutely certain all those who could would leave and would do so quickly. Still, even the most sought-after employees needed a week to find and nail down another job—and then there would be the practicalities of making a move, for those who had to, out of the Bay Area. So that was the time frame for their lingering death: about ten days. Not really so lingering.

CHAPTER 26

The Shit Hits the Fan

NIGEL WATCHED AMANDA Watkins leaving with Judy and Jim. The three of them piled into Judy's car, laughing. He looked around for Peter, but there was no sign of him. On their way home in the car, Nigel asked Mary if she had really taken in what they had all just witnessed.

"He disappeared, Mary, vanished. You saw it. He was there one minute, stepping into that cabinet, a man in a blue suit and open-necked white shirt. We all watched the door close behind him. Then, about twenty minutes later and after five minutes of the vacuum pump, we opened the door and he was gone. We checked everywhere for him, didn't we? There was no sign of him above or below ground. He was simply gone."

Nigel was reciting these facts as much for his own benefit as Mary's. He still hadn't come to terms with the events of the evening.

Charlene shook her head. "It had to have been a trick, Nigel. Don't you feel just a little bit exploited?"

Mary spoke up.

"I'm with Charlene," she said. "I think it was a trick, a very clever one, and we can all admire that. But still a trick."

"That is a possibility," allowed Nigel, inwardly marveling at how alike Charlene and her mother were. "You have to admit, though, that time travel is also a possibility."

Mary proved obdurate.

"Well, I don't really," she said doggedly. "Human history is littered with good tricks and brilliant illusionists. But I've never heard of anyone traveling in time. That's because no one has done it."

"There has to be a first time, Mary."

"Why?" she asked disconcertingly.

Nigel frowned. He hadn't expected such resistance from Charlene's mother. He turned and glanced at her pleasant face, noting the slightest of smiles that animated her features. The smile nettled him.

"The fireworks were good," put in Charlene consolingly.

Suddenly, Nigel boiled over.

"Really, Charlene, what the hell are you talking about? We've just witnessed the first unequivocal demonstration of time travel in the history of mankind, and all you can say is 'the fireworks were good.'"

"Well, you brought them," retorted Charlene. "I was just paying you a compliment."

***

Donald's disappearance had had a profound effect on Amanda. And it came against the backdrop of the sunshine and the brilliant blue sky of California, with the wind soughing through the trees and the air, cool and pleasant, on her face. She knew what she'd just seen, and she couldn't understand it. This was a new experience for a clever girl like Amanda. She brought all her considerable brainpower to bear upon the mystery, but the mundane explanations for Donald's disappearance, which immediately presented themselves, depressed her and made her question the wisdom of her move to California. Why *had* she come here, anyway? She'd acted on a whim. It had been a moment of madness. Set against this tumultuous start to her new job, the fact that the moving company that had shipped all her belongings had yet to be paid was a trivial and unimportant detail. In the event of default by Almost Infinity, she would be personally responsible for a bill of $5,000 dollars.

***

Ben Benson called a meeting of all company employees for the coming Friday morning. Attendance was mandatory. The volume of chatter within the company about its now-probable impending doom was deafening. Motivation sagged, and people essentially stopped working and sat around talking all day.

On Thursday afternoon, Peter and Nigel were sitting in their office alone, trying to guess what tomorrow would bring. Nigel was telling Peter he thought they'd be told they had three months left with the current contracts they had in place. Really, he was just thinking about All Grains since the others were too small to be significant. Also, Nigel had heard about a French cement company that was looking to expand its interests beyond its core business. And then there was a British company that wanted to get into the propagation of oil palms. Maybe Ben was going to tell them that if these two companies came through, they would be saved for the foreseeable future.

Peter had heard these rumors too, but he wasn't sure how solid they were. He and Nigel were sitting at their desks staring at each other when Nils's head suddenly appeared around the office door. He beamed at them and extended a big thumbs-up. He left just as suddenly as he'd appeared without saying anything.

"Thank God," breathed Nigel, as relief flooded over him. "He must know something positive to have done that, surely?"

Peter wasn't so sure.

"Either that or he's an idiot," he said acerbically.

***

Stan, Jeff, and Oliver had repaired to O'Malley's to talk over the crisis. Stan was holding court. "Al has been talking to David Hallauer. He's a guy who's clued in to the venture capital community. David wants to take a meeting with me and Al on Monday. Maybe we'll be able to put something together. There'll be jobs for you guys, of course, and your teams. But I'm not sure about the rest of the shower—Nigel, for instance. I don't think so. And Arthur Nanomura? It'll be Nonomora for him."

Jeff and Oliver looked blankly at him. The thought of working under Stan was not an appealing one. He was okay as a colleague, of course. And he was bright. But as a boss?

"Still no word from Donald?" asked Oliver. "I really hope we get to the bottom of that mystery."

Jeff agreed with him.

"It's left me feeling a bit unbalanced. And I don't like feeling like that. It was truly fantastic, wasn't it? Should we go back to the field and just dig it all up?"

If Stan was disappointed at the lack of enthusiasm shown by Jeff and Oliver at the prospect of working in a start-up run by him and Al, he gave no sign.

"A waste of time," he said now to Jeff. "Didn't you see how big that field was?"

"He's right," said Oliver to Jeff. "And you'd have no idea where to dig. How could you narrow it down?"

"If we knew where the platform started from—but I wasn't paying attention to that. Once it was moved, there was no finding it. And it was dark. Anyway," Jeff went on, "that has to be the answer whether we can find it or not. The alternative is that Donald has become a time traveler, and *that* I can't believe."

The three of them shook their heads in unison. Stan grinned wolfishly at his two colleagues.

"I'm going to make him rue the day he made fools of us."

***

On Friday morning, before the company-wide meeting, Bob made a pro forma attempt to contact Helmuth. He didn't get past his secretary. He left a message with her. Helmuth's secretary didn't pass it on. She thought he sounded demented. What was he talking about? The year 2175? Helmuth had more important matters to occupy his time. Bob did manage to talk to Ernie Sikorsky of US Home Products. Ernie couldn't keep the disbelief out of his voice.

"He did what? He went into the future to 2175, and he did this last Monday evening? Where is he now, then? No ... impossible, surely. And no one has seen him since?"

"No one, Ernie. He's simply vanished. We looked everywhere for him, even dug up the ground under the platform. He's done it, I tell you, gone to 2175. It was covered by our local TV station. You and your buddies Helmuth and Ned are going to look awfully shortsighted when word gets around you turned down the chance to work with the world's first time traveler. How are you going to explain it to your boards?" He paused, considering what to say next.

Then he went on: "Think of it, Ernie. US Home Products will be forever associated with this history-shaping event if you make an investment in us now. People will be proud to buy your products, even more proud than they already are."

Ernie's skepticism was further shaken when Bob went on to tell him that the piece on Donald had been picked up by the national networks and would be shown on television across the country that evening.

"Really, Bob? ABC, NBC, and CBS? All the big boys?"

"Yes, that's tonight, Ernie."

"Okay, I can come on Monday," said Ernie at last. "I'm not like Helmuth or Ned, but really, the way you treated our former CEO wasn't very respectful, was it? Dragging him through all that muck."

"None of us wanted that, Ernie. But even your own people were laughing at the end."

"But not me, Bob. It's not US Home Product's way to laugh at other people's misfortunes."

"They weren't really laughing at Sir David, Ernie; they were more laughing at themselves. That's what we all liked about you guys—you didn't take yourselves too seriously."

"Good of you to say so, Bob."

The conversation was going better than Bob had dared to hope. Now Almost Infinity and US Home Products were almost back to their positions of mutual respect before the disastrous visit. In a flush of gratitude for Ernie's understanding, Bob decided to tell him the truth about Almost Infinity's predicament.

"We've got no money left, Ernie. None at all. We can't make payroll, and it's due today."

The wild hope that Ernie might wire him a half million to avert this disaster clutched at his heart.

"You can't make payroll?" Ernie queried softly. "And it's due today? That's more serious than I thought."

There was a long silence—Bob waiting hopefully, Ernie re-evaluating his position.

At last, Ernie said: "I'm looking at my diary here. I've just realized I've got a commitment for next Monday that I can't get out of. Leave it with us and we'll reschedule."

"For next week, though?" asked Bob, with a sinking heart. Why hadn't he kept his big trap shut?

"Very probably," said Ernie kindly. "I'm looking forward to seeing you guys on TV tonight."

Ernie took his leave of Bob politely and then sat on at his desk. He thought about the desperation he'd heard in Bob's voice. He puffed out his cheeks. Couldn't make payroll! What kind of rinky-dink organization was that? Ernie couldn't conceive of a situation getting so out of control. At US Home Products, they would have taken all the necessary steps to avoid this situation months, if not years, in advance. He definitely wouldn't be going to California next week.

***

Nigel and Charlene came to work on Friday in a state of trepidation. The big meeting was at ten o'clock that morning. Nigel had convinced himself they were all about to be given three months' notice. Rumors flew about in the short time before the meeting. Stan's research was more important than anyone else's, and his entire group was going to be spared. No, it was Al; he was setting up a new research division in a slimmed-down company with Stan, Jeff, and Oliver taking leading roles. All their people would be spared. No one held out any hope for those working for Forrest, and Nils and his small team were bound to be gone. Those who had convinced themselves of their irreplaceability bestowed looks of kind concern on their less fortunate colleagues.

They assembled in the large meeting room. Nerves got the better of some people, and there were frequent eruptions of loud laughter around the room. There was definitely fear in the air. Some people, like Peter for example, were afraid but didn't recognize the emotion. Peter just couldn't stop smiling, although he would have been hard pressed to say what it was he was smiling about. Nils kept giving people who caught his eye the thumbs-up sign.

"He really is an idiot," grinned Peter at Nigel.

Amanda Watkins was now seriously concerned. Everyone was expecting to be laid off?

"We're going to get three months," Nigel told her now. "And I do think that's a worst-case scenario.

She, a clever, sharp-witted, freethinking young woman, who'd always been on the right side of adversity, finding herself now in one hell of a mess with no one to blame but herself, looked at him.

"I don't have any money," she told him miserably.

Peter, who was standing next to Nigel, grinned at her and said: "You can always go on the game."

This was Peter, in his own fraught state, being cool for Amanda. He was astonished to see her eyes fill with tears before she turned away. He turned to Nigel, mouth agape, traces of the grin still lingering on his lips.

"What did I say?" he appealed helplessly.

"You told her that she could always get money by becoming a prostitute," Nigel told him wearily. "Not exactly what she wants to hear on a morning like this."

He watched as Peter wandered off. Peter was an odd bird, wasn't he? So self-absorbed and insensitive. And he wondered why he couldn't find a girlfriend! He made a final, quick scan of the room and noted the absence of Kevin, his technician. He pointed out his absence to Judy.

"Oh, he's joined Deltagene," she told him, with a bright, knowing smile. "He's been gone for a while."

Nigel nodded seriously, but didn't have time to digest the information. He just felt a vague sense of loss and wondered at the wisdom of Kevin's decision and why he hadn't noticed the defection earlier.

Ten o'clock arrived and they all began looking around, wondering what was going to happen. They could all see Bob at the back of the room, deep in conversation with the senior management group who were gathered around him. For a moment, everyone watched him. Ben Benson appeared and strode to the front of the room. He raised a hand for attention.

"I'll keep it short," he began. "No one is being paid today. We can't make payroll. There are no exceptions from Bob on down. The company is in serious financial distress. Maria will be handing out memos to you all, explaining the actions taken by senior management. Please make sure you get one before you leave this morning. What it says is that those of us who have signed the memo have committed to continue working in the absence of pay. Our commitment is total. I know some of you were at Donald's departure from Half Moon Bay the other night. There, we witnessed our founder becoming the first time traveler in history. We are expecting a communication from him in the next few days. Obviously, our company is going places. We don't know how long we will be without money, but we are doing all we can to rectify matters. These kinds of things happen when you're trying to get a groundbreaking business started. The management team thanks you all for your services up to now. Thank you again for your attention."

And he strode out, walking purposefully, as if proceeding at that very moment to a meeting with a potential investor. Everyone just watched him leave. No one attempted to ask a question. A stunned silence hung over the room. They were all still lost in contemplation of Ben's first substantive sentence. *No one is being paid today. No one*, they were all thinking, *and that definitely means me!* After a minute or two, a few people began to stand up and leave. There was very little talking. Peter, of course, made a few sallies, but Nigel just ignored him. He stood up himself and looked around for Charlene.

Now everyone started to move. People were anxious to get home to let their loved ones know of their changed circumstances. After all the excitement and fear, the actual announcement had been peculiarly anticlimactic.

***

Nigel and Charlene sat in their car in the driveway in front of their house and studied the memo that Maria had passed out. They scanned the names of the senior managers, checking for any omissions. No Arthur Nanomura and no Jim. But did Jim really count as a senior manager? Nigel didn't think so.

"What are we going to do?" asked Charlene tearily. "No money, but we've still got jobs?"

Nigel shook his head. "No money, no jobs. We are not senior management. We don't have extra resources. And what does it mean for my visa status? No money but still with a job? Surely that undermines the purpose of the visa. We've just got to go in on Monday and start to get our résumés out there. I was sure they'd give us at least a month, though. Hell, for people like me, that has to be a legal requirement."

"What about the rent?" asked Charlene. "That's a thousand dollars. We don't have enough now to pay it."

Nigel frowned. "We'll just have to hope we can persuade our landlords to take our deposit in lieu of next month's rent. We've only got five hundred in the bank between us."

"Two weeks then," said Charlene. "Two weeks from today. Maybe my mother can help us."

"Absolutely not," said Nigel heavily. "That's definitely not happening."

"And we can't get married now, Nigel, can we?"

Nigel twisted toward her and suddenly sat up very straight.

"It's strangely liberating to have absolutely nothing. And we've got each other, haven't we? What's the worst that can happen to us?"

"No health care and we can starve to death," said Charlene promptly. "And you won't love me when I've got no teeth."

"No, that's true," admitted Nigel, sobering up.

Similar conversations were taking place in practically every Almost Infinity household. Generally speaking, the more generic the job, the more confident the jobholder was they could get something else quickly. For people like Nigel and Charlene, Peter and Amanda, Jeff and Oliver, it was more problematic. They were specialists, and job opportunities were rarer.

And when Monday rolled around, it was disproportionally the specialists who were left. The secretaries, the maintenance crew including Don Klingel, the custodians including Emmanuel, assorted office staff including the entire HR department (Connie and two others), and the personal assistants all had left.

The place had a hollowed out look to it when Nigel came in that morning. Peter was already in the office and was busy working on his résumé.

"Better get this done while we still have access to the company's computers," Peter said, grinning. "I'm expecting them to shut the power off to the buildings at any moment."

Nigel promptly set to work on his and Charlene's résumés. Bob strolled through the labs noting who had shown up. No one paid any attention to him, not that there were many people there in any case. He still retained some power and influence, but it was greatly reduced. Nigel nodded respectfully at him.

Bob smiled. "Keep up the good work, Nigel. We know who the important people are now, don't we?"

Nigel nodded again but made no reply.

"I'm expecting a communication from Donald any day. Haven't forgotten about him, have you? And we're receiving visits from potential investors tomorrow. Will you be around?"

Again Nigel nodded but remained silent. He walked into the main lab. It looked like a Sunday out there to him. There was almost nobody around. He stood for a moment, sadly surveying the emptiness. The craziness had come to an end. Nigel went back to the office and watched Peter busily stacking papers on his desk.

Nils created the mold, and the scientists had filled it with enthusiasm, following him into Donald's world of crackpottery.

Now, all had collapsed, and no one in the wider world would be at all surprised. Nigel exempted himself from this. He, after all, had been forced into it by the execrable Kutti. He would never have chosen to come to Almost Infinity of his own free will.

No, his choice had been different, hadn't it? He had chosen Almost Infinity and America over no job and a humiliating return to England. He refined his choice. California and Almost Infinity—the blue skies and bright sunshine—over the dreary land of drizzle watched over by people who would bolt to California instantly if they ever got the chance. So, in fact, his choice had been easy. He was wondering if native Californians ever dreamed about the sunshine when a thought suddenly struck him.

"Are the phones still working?"

Peter shrugged indifferently. At that moment, almost on cue, the phone rang. Nigel picked up the receiver. It was for him. He recognized the voice. It was an old friend from England, a contemporary who had done a PhD in the same lab as him. This friend, he knew, was also in America now, working for a large pharmaceutical company on the East Coast. This company was looking for someone with Nigel's experience and qualifications. He asked Nigel to submit a résumé. They fell easily into conversation. His friend's boss had heard of Almost Infinity's difficulties from Helmuth. Nigel told him what had happened last Friday. His friend sounded sympathetic, but Nigel could tell he didn't feel the desperation.

Later that morning, he got another call, this time from a start-up in Davis, the site of the conference they had all just attended. Someone, probably Nils he thought, had suggested his name to the research director there as a potential employee. Once again, he was asked to submit his résumé.

He went home for the day at lunch time, eager to tell Charlene the exciting and hopeful news. Two companies had contacted him! Already! On the first working day after the announcement and before he'd made any applications! That had to be good news, didn't it? Better than good, it was fantastic!

The next day there were a few more people at work. Judy and Jim were there, just passing through as Judy said. Jeff, Oliver, and Stan all put in an appearance. Nigel received two more phone calls from companies interested in employing him. He was astonished at the level of interest in his services. This had never happened to him before. He realized these companies thought of themselves as competitors of Almost Infinity and that Almost Infinity was regarded as a trendsetter. Somehow, Donald's fantasy had taken hold and nurtured a proliferation of copycat research groups all around the country.

It was Nigel's first introduction to how sheep-like companies large and small were in his research field. They didn't really know what to do, so they simply did what everyone else was doing. Almost Infinity and All Grains had simply set off this latest explosion of ass-covering. They had headed down one path, and everyone had charged right after them. Nigel had been in the job market a year earlier, courtesy of Kutti. Opportunities then had been few and far between. But now, after his year at Almost Infinity, he was suddenly desirable. He had direct experience of the work they all wanted to do. Fears about starving to death and he and Charlene losing their teeth receded. Charlene made a fuss of him at home and made him feel important.

They were going to drive up to Davis together at the end of the week for an afternoon interview at the start-up, and then they were going to fly out to Connecticut early the next week for his interview at the pharmaceutical facility where his friend worked. He and Charlene were probably going to be okay.

On Wednesday, Nils stopped by to ask how he was coping. Nigel told him about his upcoming interviews, and Nils seemed pleased. He urged Nigel to wait before committing to another company. He wanted him to hear what Donald was going to tell them about the future. Bob, apparently, had received a communication from him and was going to read it out to everyone on Friday. He was also going to report on the progress he was making in attracting new investors. Nigel told Nils that he and Charlene would be there. And on the domestic front, their landlord had agreed to accept their deposit in lieu of rent for the next month, and so they had a little breathing space.

CHAPTER 27

This is the Future

FRIDAY ROLLED AROUND, and Nigel and Charlene showed up at the large meeting room in the admin building. There were about twenty other people in attendance. Bob had tried to get the local TV station to cover Donald's communiqué from the future, but they hadn't shown up. Stan, Jeff, and Oliver were there along with the entire senior management team with the exception of Arthur Nanomura. Judy, Jim, Amanda, Peter, Nils's two research assistants, and a smattering of young people attached to Al and Forrest were also there. Bob looked around at the little gathering and gave a slight shrug of his shoulders. He was clearly disappointed at the low turnout.

"Don't know what you have to do these days to draw a crowd," he muttered to himself dejectedly. Then he straightened up and, in a firm voice, began: "This is a message from year 2175 from the founder of our company, Dr. Donald Plum. I'm going to start reading it now. There are hard copies of Donald's remarks for you all here."

He indicated a stack of papers to his right. "All right, this is Donald now:

> Greetings to all my fellow employees at Almost Infinity. The temperature here seems a bit warmer than it is in our present.

It could be the result of global warming, but I don't really know. Anyway, it is warm today. First of all, the big news: there are no longer any cities or cars. So there's not a lot our environmental activist friends can complain about. Dwelling places are spread evenly across the landscape. I guess food is now all produced offshore, although I haven't seen the farms. Keep working on those salt-tolerant crops. They are definitely the wave of the future. All communication is now digital. For those of you wondering about romance in the future, selection of partners is now all done online. In fact, there is no longer any significant presence off-line. And that means for everyone. There are one or two isolated communities that maintain the old ways, but they are not allowed to farm. Farming, as we know it, is finished.

Food is plentiful; hunger, poverty, and crime are consigned to history. Surprisingly, life expectancy has not increased by more than a few years, but, of course, with the availability of time travel, it's irrelevant anyway. The 2130s are a popular destination for a lot of the older folk. Time travel, of course, means people can essentially live forever if they so choose, and that seems to be the unanimous choice. People can avoid living a repetitive life by simply moving to a parallel universe. As I've told you repeatedly, there are very many parallel universes to choose from. There are still accidents, and one or two people die each year. There are very few babies born now. The replacement rate is vanishingly low, and societal development has more or less ground to a halt. Passing on one's genes no longer has any meaning in a society where one can live forever.

Sexual pleasure is still sought after. People still find one another attractive particularly when they are young, but since it's no longer an existential matter, the edge has gone out of sex and a lot of anxiety has gone out of first meetings. It's a much softer, gentler society these days. And vanity about appearance has just about vanished. You can't imagine how much better people look because of that. People still take pleasure in beautiful things, and religion survives principally as art. There always was a strong connection between the two, wasn't there? Even in the earliest of times? It's going to take another hundred years from your present time for nationalism, patriotism, and capitalism to wither.

Nobody, of course, will be able to imagine this. But love of power alone is not enough to keep these things in place. When you can have everything without depriving others of anything, the exercise of power to deprive others merely seems absurd. Well, that's all I've got for you for the moment. Don't know exactly when I'm coming back, but probably soon. Anyway, the most important thing for us is the salt-tolerant crops. We can assure ourselves of fame and fortune and, more importantly, of relevance as long as we are pursuing this objective. My immediate goal is to find out specifics if I'm allowed, but that will have to wait for another trip. We need to set up demonstration plots on the surface of the ocean. I'll see you all soon, Donald."

Bob reverently laid down Donald's printed email.

"It's humbling, isn't it? What does this mean for us? I think in the first instance, it means we are going to live forever. Donald has brought us all eternal life. He's conquered death. Doesn't that excite you? I know it does me. Donald really is the new Jesus, Stan. You were right! He's the new reality that is the basis for all our lives in the future. There is no off-line! No more hunger, crime, poverty, nationalism. No cars, traffic, cities, and no farms, at least on the land. And God lives on through art! How neatly Donald's report from our future takes care of all our concerns."

He stared around at them all, bug-eyed. He was overcome with the emotion of the moment.

Nigel shakily raised his hand. "It's all too much, Bob," he said weakly. "We are not ready for this."

Stan glared at them all and shouted: "You want to live in a place like that? I'm happy here. At least I can shag who I want. And no commitments."

Just for a moment, Stan stood at the center of their thoughts. They were all thinking of him as a throwback, a curious misfit who didn't belong in any future world. They regarded him with a patient tolerance. Poor Stan. He and people like him had to be allowed to die out. Not for them the wonders of time travel. He and his ilk would go out railing impotently against the coming light of peace and tranquility.

Nils crinkled his eyes kindly. He shrugged.

"I'm not a young man anymore. It sounds pretty good to me."

A silence fell on the room. No one could think of anything else to say. They were all overwhelmed. It was Donald's greatest triumph. At last, Al put their reverence into words.

"All of us knew science was the way forward, didn't we? Well, now Donald has proved it. Thank God," he went on perversely, "we chose science and not religion as the path to eternal life. We can never be the same people again."

Nigel, along with everyone else, listened to Al's paean of praise to science in silence. His own thoughts were chaotic. He was wondering about his first impressions of Donald—the shifty eyes and the slippery smile, the unconvincing voice with its slight whine. The overall impression was that there was something not quite right about him. But how trustworthy were first impressions anyway? People, including Nigel and Charlene, began to wander out of the room. Very little more was said. It was as if they were afraid to break the spell Donald had cast over them all.

Finally, Bob and the senior managers were the only people remaining. George Nipper puffed out his cheeks and exhaled slowly.

"I just feel inadequate, Bob."

"You're not the only one," put in Ben. "None of us can even begin to understand this."

"So," began Forrest, who, being older, was less deeply impressed, "what, in practical terms, are we supposed to do now? We still need money if we're to save the company."

Bob looked around at them all, bright-eyed and alert.

"I still have to tell you. We've had some preliminary interest from French and British businesses. And I'm going to go back to US Home Products. If Donald can send us back some specifics of direct commercial relevance, maybe we can hook them."

"But are they right for us, Bob?" asked Al anxiously. "After all, Donald is telling us that capitalism is dead. That's not what US Home Products wants to hear, is it?"

"They don't need to know," said Bob promptly. "We'll get them to pay us to work for their extinction. There'll be some satisfaction in that, won't there?"

"I never had you down for a socialist, Bob," said Ben, sniffing disapprovingly.

"Oh, come on!" cried Bob, in a rare public show of annoyance. "Socialism, capitalism, who cares now? All these labels belong to the past. Embrace the future! Be a trendsetter. Who wants to live in the past?"

"But we don't live in the future, Bob. We live in the present," put in George Nipper. "What you're talking about might still be a hundred years off. What does it mean to us now? It's simply too early for this kind of talk, isn't it?"

Bob looked at him, momentarily distracted from his worship of what was to come. A frown of annoyance briefly reformed on his face. Then he gathered himself, preparing to launch a fresh onslaught of optimism and enthusiasm on his team, some of whom clearly still hadn't gotten it. Into this brief silence, they all heard a familiar voice speaking out.

"He's right, Bob."

They all turned to look at the open doorway at the back of the room. Standing there, in his blue suit and slightly grubby open-necked white shirt was Donald. They all gawped. Bob was the first to react.

"You're back!" he cried incredulously.

He covered the ground separating him from Donald in an instant and shook him warmly by the hand. The others followed with alacrity. Everyone shook Donald's hand. There was a moment of respectful silence, and then Donald spoke.

"I was delivered to my home. The technology is much better in 2275. You can actually target the exact time and place in your original world."

"The year 2275?" croaked Bob. "I thought you said you were going to 2175."

"That's what I thought," admitted Donald. "But, obviously with me, it's not an exact science. I made a mistake in the math and ended up a hundred years farther on. I still thought I was in 2175 when I sent you the communication."

"Everyone appreciates your honesty, Donald. It's why we all believe in you," said Al.

Donald smiled shyly.

"The pace of change slows in the future. We reach a plateau and then settle into a long period of stability."

"What about the expansion of the sun and the Earth burning up?" Nils wanted to know. He had been doing some reading on the ultimate fate of the Earth. "How are we going to escape that?"

"Two billion years away," said Donald. "No one cares. Why should we? We can always travel back in time, can't we? It's a hell of a lot easier than trying to find another residence out in the universe, which can only ever be temporary. And that's one thing about the universe—this universe and all universes—nowhere is safe forever. Everything is permanently changing. Remember Herodotus. 'There is nothing permanent except change.' That was true then, but now we know time is the only place in which we can find permanence, and it never stands still and it never changes. Time travel changes the nature of our existence forever. History itself is a meaningless concept in a world with time travel. We are going to accomplish great things, gentlemen. At least in this particular universe."

"So we are going to get funding then, Donald?" asked Bob quickly, seeking refuge from Donald's mind-bending commentary on permanence and time.

"Of course," answered Donald. "US Home Products is going to come to our rescue next week. Give them a call tomorrow to get the ball rolling."

The senior management team looked to their founder with heartfelt gratitude. Donald suddenly appeared to be enormously charismatic. The mysterious aura of 2275 hung about him, a miasma of glamour and fantasy. George Nipper spoke for them all, as well as for his own little crew at home.

"Donald, you've restored my faith in the incorruptible goodness of humanity. Mrs. Nipper and the little nippers will always have a place in their hearts for you."

***

Nigel and Charlene were on their way to Davis. They would get there in time to have a late lunch with the research director of DNACal, the company looking to recruit Nigel. They'd left Almost Infinity just before Donald had shown up.

"No cars and no cities," said Nigel wonderingly.

"No hunger, no poverty," answered Charlene.

"Food produced on farms that exist on the surface of the oceans," continued Nigel.

"There is no off-line," remembered Charlene.

Nigel glanced at her. "None of this is going to happen in our lifetimes, Charlene. We are still going to grow old and die."

"Why?" she asked. "Why should we? Thanks to Donald we can go through the wormhole too, can't we?"

"I'm sure we can, Charlene. But can we get back? After all, we can't do the math. And do we want to come back?"

"I do," she said firmly. "I'll miss my mom. I want to be there for her when she grows old."

"How is this going to work, then?" asked Nigel. He looked at her from the driver's seat with a touch of irritation on his face.

"This is all very confusing," Charlene complained. "Won't most people choose to remain at a young age? I'm not very old, but I know I was a lot fitter when I was younger."

"Me too," agreed Nigel. "Fitter and stupider. Time travel is a crock from every aspect, isn't it? I thought I'd be all for it. But now, facing its reality, I'm not so sure. And can everyone make his or her decisions independently? How many separate lives can each of us lead? I mean, if I go back to be with an eighteen-year-old Charlene, will I be eighteen, also?"

"You would have to be eighteen as well. Otherwise, you'd just be a dirty old man to the eighteen-year-old Charlene."

"I say, Charlene, is that how you think of me? And what about you?"

"Two dirty old people together," laughed Charlene. "Romantic bliss."

"Donald seems to have gone into the future, though, hasn't he? What if he can't get back? What if we never see him again?"

"It'll be all right just as long as he keeps sending us emails."

They both laughed. Charlene grew serious.

"I think we have to get away from here, Nigel. If only to preserve our sanity."

"Emails from the future. It's the hipster life in California."

***

Donald went home. He was, he told Bob, quite tired. He had to admit, he confessed to his partner before he went, that he'd found the future overwhelming. The truth, however, was that he'd been uncomfortable in the sewer pipe and had managed only a couple of hours' sleep at a time. The air smelled bad down there, and he hadn't eaten very much. He was going to take air fresheners down to his lair over the next few days and try to improve the atmosphere of the sewer. He'd had a headache for a lot of the time he'd been underground.

He'd told Bob he'd be going back to 2275 in a couple of days. Then he'd try to send back detailed information about the technology of the future, information they could use to build their business in the twenty-first century. He was quite confident in his ability to make up something plausible and equally confident in the ability of Almost Infinity's scientists to produce something inspired by his fantasy.

When he was alone with Donald and before Donald went home to sleep, Bob asked him about his memories.

"You said you couldn't remember anything Donald, remember?" He smiled broadly. "What happened this time?"

Donald waved a tired hand. "I just had to change the math, that's all. Now I remember everything. But I still need to go back. I need to see if I can find something that will make money right away. And that's not really so easy, Bob."

"So I was right about ocean agriculture, Donald? That was something, wasn't it?"

Donald, who'd forgotten it had been Bob who'd planted this idea in his brain, looked mystified.

"Well, who have you met there?" went on Bob.

"That's the thing," Donald grimaced. "I haven't met anybody. Everything is virtual. People have no need for actual physical contact. It's really a different world."

"How do you eat?"

Again, Donald waved his hand dismissively.

"Oh, there's always food available. Don't ask me about its preparation. Everything, of course, is automated. Just think of living at its easiest and most comfortable, and that's what it's like there. I'll try to be more observant next time. It's just too much to take in at first blush, Bob."

Bob grabbed him by both his shoulders. He looked admiringly into his face.

"You've exceeded everyone's expectations, Donald. We are all so proud to know you. Even now I can hardly believe you've traveled in time. It just seems so incredible. You're going to be a historical figure, aren't you? No, excuse me, you are going to be *the* historical figure."

"It's very nice of you to say that, Bob. But as I was saying before, history's not such a big deal in the future."

Bob laughed.

"Everyone loves you. You're a hero now to all the employees of Almost Infinity. In a little while you're going to be a hero to everyone on Earth."

"Same field as before on Tuesday evening, 5:30 p.m. Have the wormhole platform, the facilitator, and the vacuum pump taken there. I'm going home to get some sleep now."

***

A couple of days later, Stan, Jeff, and Oliver were drinking in O'Malley's. Stan told them about his new job at Berkeley. Jeff and Oliver weren't surprised, but they were both impressed that he had found such a good position so quickly. Jeff had sent job applications out to a number of universities. He'd decided he was finished with industry. All Grains had contacted him, but he had put them off. Oliver was holding out for a recovery at Almost Infinity. He hadn't applied for any jobs yet. Stan was chastising him for his complacency.

"You've got to get something out, Oliver. You'll want a university position, and that takes time. I've already lost a month of wages thanks to that incompetent prick Bob. So have you. But in another month, I'll be at Berkeley, and they'll be taking care of me."

Oliver glanced at him. He realized Stan must have been preparing to leave Almost Infinity for at least a month. He wondered at his dissembling and his affectation of concern for Almost Infinity's future. Why should he care now that he was leaving? Strangely enough, Oliver didn't feel envious. He didn't want to work at a university. He wanted to be in the thick of things developing new products, products that would make a difference to people. That, he thought, was real achievement. He had no interest in writing grants, and he didn't think he'd make a particularly good teacher.

Stan told him again: "You'll want a university position, Oliver, and that takes time."

"Some company will hire me, Stan. But I'm not sure I need to move yet."

"You'll need to move. Just ask Jeff."

They both turned to face Jeff, who was following the conversation closely.

"I think he's right, Oliver. Management at Almost Infinity has lost the plot. I admit Donald gave us hope today, but I'm convinced it was only that. Can you see Bob finding the kind of investment we need to carry on? I just don't think he can do it."

Oliver looked at them both and wondered at himself. Was he a loyal employee or someone simply caught in a net of inertia? These were his two contemporaries, closest to him in age, ability, and interests, and they had both decided to leave. Had they made a bad decision? After all, Almost Infinity had failed to make payroll, and that was inexcusable. On the other hand, he had been deeply impressed by Donald's communication. Neither Stan nor Jeff had been able to explain it. Donald had said he was going time traveling, and in the absence of another explanation, Oliver was inclined to believe him. Oliver could still see a glorious future for the company.

"Bob asked me and Nigel to help with Donald's next voyage on Tuesday evening. You knew he was back from the future, didn't you?"

They did, and despite themselves, they both felt a pang of disappointment at having been passed over by Bob for the honor of assisting Donald.

"Why you?" asked Stan peevishly. "And why Nigel? That prissy British shit. You two guys have been brown-nosing together?"

Oliver looked back at him steadily.

"Maybe it's because he and I showed Donald a bit of respect. I'm not going to apologize for it."

Jeff looked at them both and then said to Oliver, in a voice that managed to sound consoling, appeasing, and humorous all at the same time: "Stan and I will come with you. We can't leave you alone with Bob and Donald."

"Too right," said Stan vigorously. "God knows what they would have you doing."

Oliver laughed.

"Really, I'm a big boy. I can look after myself. I'm not going to go traveling to the twenty-third century, at least not knowingly."

"We've got to really watch him this time," averred Stan. "If we can catch him at his tricks, it will bring you to your senses. This time I want to uncover the deception. And make no mistake, it's definitely deception. No cars, no cities, farming at sea, religion is sustained in art—you've got to hand it to Donald, he's certainly got imagination."

"I wish I'd been there when he walked in on the senior managers," said Jeff. "I would love to have seen their faces."

Stan summed it up: "Somehow, he tricked us, evaded our attempts to find him, and slunk off to hide somewhere. He hasn't been to the future at all. This time, for everyone's sake, we just have to catch the fucker. God, I'm so looking forward to it."

***

Bob was on the phone with Ernie Sikorsky.

"Ernie, I know Helmuth and Ned have told you our company is finished. Hell, I told you myself! And I have to admit, it's not in the best of health at this moment. Still, now Donald has traveled to the future and done it before many witnesses. He's come back with a very interesting view of life in 2275. You'll have to make up your own mind, but he's either been to the future or he's got a tremendous imagination. I don't believe anyone could have imagined the place he's describing. He's decided to go back there next Tuesday. Please come and see for yourself this time. We've decided to offer you exclusive rights to the fruits of Donald's travels. Basically, you can have everything. It's going to cost a billion dollars, spread over ten years. And we want five percent of all the business that his travels generate. But really, we're talking trillions of dollars here—this is just a drop in the ocean. US Home Products will be the biggest company in the history of mankind. I want our partner to be you, Ernie, not Helmuth or Ned. There are no obligations. Just come and see for yourself."

There was a long silence, and then to Bob's amazement and delight, he heard Ernie say: "Okay, Bob. I've always had a soft spot for you and Donald. I'll be there next Tuesday."

Bob was beside himself with joy. It was all coming true! Just as Donald had told them it would.

"You won't regret this, Ernie. I'll pick you up at the airport. Just let me know the time of your flight when you're ready."

Ernie reflected. He hadn't promised anything he couldn't get out of, and now his daily supply of bonhomie was exhausted. He exchanged a few banal pleasantries with Bob and hung up. In business dealings, he felt he could trust Bob. And he liked Bob better than he liked Helmuth or Ned. These were dull, conservative men who would never do anything exciting; men who would cast a pall on any new idea, certain it would fail; men who could laugh comfortably at trendsetters like Bob and wait for them to burn out. But maybe, this time, the trendsetter wouldn't burn out.

Ernie knew he was different. He wasn't like Helmuth or Ned. He was prepared to go out of his way for the chance of engaging in something new and exciting. And Almost Infinity's claim to time travel was certainly that. If it turned out to be true, how stupid would those two dinosaurs look then? And now Bob was offering it to him on an exclusive basis. He would be able to sell it on to Helmuth and Ned. It was this thought that made it irresistible. Ernie imagined himself receiving the grudging and envious congratulations from his fellow captains of industry:

"You're a crafty one, Ernie, waiting until you could get it exclusively."

"You must have had great insight to see the promise in this technology. You've certainly proved that, Ernie.

"Cut us in on the pharmaceuticals, Ernie; you know it's our specialty. Let's go fifty-fifty."

He closed his eyes and looked inside himself for a respite from all the clamor seething in his mind. He told his secretary that he was going to California on Tuesday afternoon. He would take the company plane, and he would go alone.

CHAPTER 28

Ernie and Al

NIGEL AND CHARLENE drove home from DNACal, feeling optimistic about their professional futures for the first time in months. On Monday, Nigel met Peter, who listened enviously to the account of his interview and his job offer.

"But it was very hot, you say?" Peter confirmed now.

"Brutal," said Nigel. "Much hotter than the week of the conference. It was almost like a different place. Still, you can't have everything. You should apply, Peter. They are sure to want someone with your skills."

"I've got an application in. I just haven't heard anything yet."

"Just a matter of time," promised Nigel.

Peter's background, though, wasn't as strong as Nigel's, and his time at Almost Infinity hadn't been so successful. Somehow his oddness popped out of his CV and put off prospective employers. Nigel wondered if he was really suited to research. He could see him flourishing in production or quality control, something that provided an outlet for his fussiness. They were sitting there looking at each other when Bob came bustling into their office.

"We need you on Tuesday night," he said without preamble, to Nigel. "Donald came back from 2275 on Friday, and he's going back there tomorrow. We need you to pull the platform. I've got you and Oliver down for the job."

"Can I come?" asked Peter promptly. "It was such fun last time, and historic too."

"Of course," said Bob, beaming at him. "You are always very welcome, Peter."

Peter shot a pleased look at Nigel. *See?* it seemed to say, *they want me as well as you.*

Nigel was pleased for him.

"How is Dr. Plum?" he asked Bob now.

"Oh, he's tired, of course. He covered about two hundred and seventy years in a few days. I don't know; I can't get my head around thinking about time like this. But Donald can, thank goodness. Anyway, he says he's going back to get some specifics to help us in the here and now. And guess what? I've got Ernie Sikorsky coming out."

***

The small number of Almost Infinity's employees who were still hanging around uncertainly at work began to assemble at the large field near Half Moon Bay. It was early Tuesday evening. There had been about a hundred on hand to witness Donald's first journey into the future. For this second trip, thanks to "No one is getting paid today," there were fewer than thirty. Jim and Judy showed up with the platform complete with its attached high cabinet, the emergency generator, the vacuum pump, and the wormhole facilitator, all neatly stored in the bed of the company pickup. Nigel and Charlene were there again with Mary accompanying them. Peter and Oliver (with Stan and Jeff tagging along) were also there. At four fifty-five, Bob turned up with Ernie Sikorsky. Al and Nils arrived immediately after them, suggesting they were all coming from a meeting. In fact, they had been out for a light meal together, with Bob footing the bill.

Bob took Ernie around to meet the employees who had turned up.

"These," he told him, "are our key guys."

Stan had met Ernie before, and they shook hands warmly. Oliver looked him over as a potential employer. Jeff, Nigel, Charlene, and Peter all regarded him with the reverence appropriate for a man who controlled vast sums of money. Ernie seemed excited to be there. He had managed to snatch a couple of hours of sleep at his hotel in San Mateo immediately after arriving from New Jersey. He looked at them all, bright-eyed and bursting with energy.

"I saw Donald's last departure on the news," he told them. "I was kicking myself for not being here. This is a world-changing event, isn't it?"

Bob spoke up: "There aren't going to be any fireworks this time, Ernie. That was a British thing Nigel was celebrating. Some guy the British burned hundreds of years ago."

"I'm sure he deserved all he got," said Ernie absently.

He looked around for Donald, whom he had met once before and who had shocked him with static electricity.

Bob, who was watching Ernie closely, guessed the object of his quick, searching glances.

"He's always punctual, Ernie. He'll be here in about twenty minutes."

Ernie nodded and then turned away from him and began to talk to Stan. Bob wondered what they were talking about. He considered sidling around and joining them, just to act as a moderator in case Stan's discourse became too offensive. Then he decided he just didn't care. Stan could say what he liked. After what Donald had done, Stan couldn't touch him. Donald's actions were above criticism, and Ernie was surely going to see that.

***

Earlier that day, Al had met with David Hallauer in Palo Alto. David had shown up late but had looked cool and self-possessed.

"Sorry, Al," he apologized, as he finished entering something into his handheld. "Can't do without this these days. Don't know how I managed in the past. So," David said, putting his device away, "Bob and Bernie tell me Almost Infinity didn't make payroll this week."

Al nodded.

"It's a mess, David, and Bob is still pushing Donald as the world's first time traveler. I think that's a mistake. We have some of the brightest young minds in the country at Almost Infinity. We can take agriculture by storm."

"So what do you want to sell specifically?" asked David, again taking out his handheld and studying it.

"Gene four gene," said Al, promptly. "That's gene, numeral four, gene." He wrote it down on the pad he'd laid in front of himself: Gene-4-Gene. "Cute, don't you think?"

David looked at him admiringly.

"That is cute. You know, I really think I can sell that. Gene-4-Gene—it works on so many levels, doesn't it?"

Al didn't understand what he was talking about and so said nothing.

"I really like working with you biology guys," said David expansively. "Take Bob and Bernie, for example. What a hoot! And investors love them. Bernie gets up in front of them and starts talking about his delta factor. He talks about things that everyone can understand. About fire and salt."

"He stole the salt from Almost Infinity, David."

"Well, that doesn't matter now. In a week or two, there'll be no one left to argue about it. Bernie can then take full advantage of all he learned at Almost Infinity. Salt will belong exclusively to Deltagene."

"Bernie's a bit strange—you know that, don't you? It's not science with Bob and Bernie. Neither of them has a PhD. No, you're bankrolling a cult with Deltagene. They'll never make you any money."

David looked at Al's serious, concerned face and laughed out loud.

"But Bob and Bernie get it, Al. They know it's not about science. It's about appearance. And they are both really good talkers. They make the investors feel intelligent. Do you think you could do that?"

"I thought investors were supposed to be hardheaded businessmen."

"Well, of course, some of them are. But what they all have in common is the ability to recognize schemes that can make money. I'll take your word for it that Bob and Bernie aren't great scientists, but with money behind them, they can hire the best. So, you see, real success for them is not inconceivable. At some level all this is a game. In order to play it, you can't take yourself too seriously."

Al smiled. He made a creditable effort to absorb and reflect back some of Hallauer's confident buoyancy. He was ready to take part in this new game.

"Gene-4-Gene. That's not so difficult to understand, is it? I've just got to get them on board."

Hallauer looked kindly at him. "All right, Al. I'll set up a meeting with a couple of people who've got more money than they know what to do with. I think you've got a chance. You might want to bring along a couple of your younger colleagues, a couple of personable guys. Youth always impresses."

He and Al stood up and shook hands. Al thought to himself: *This venture capital crap is easy after all. I can certainly do this.*

CHAPTER 29

Back Again to the Future

DONALD ARRIVED AT THE FIELD at twenty-five minutes past five. He glanced around at the small crowd waiting for him and felt himself relax. This was going to be a much lower-key event than last time. It was practically dark already. No one could really see him, and he liked that. He and Jim had moved the cart to the starting GPS coordinates above the manhole an hour earlier. Then he had deleted the coordinates. He went over to Bob and asked if everything was set. Bob assured him it was. Bob introduced him to Ernie Sikorsky. Donald shook his hand and smiled his slippery smile.

"No lightning bolts this time, Donald." Ernie said cheerfully.

Donald had completely forgotten he'd met Ernie before. He hadn't expected ever to see him again after the debacle of US Home Products' visit. His eyes glazed over, and he just looked through the businessman. Ernie was not impressed. Donald didn't linger with them.

He glanced at his watch and then mounted the platform. People could just make out his shape moving around in the dark. He gave a small wave to the nearly invisible crowd and then vanished into the cabinet and shut the door. His shadowy figure was gone. There was simply no more Donald.

"What was he carrying?" Ernie asked Bob.

"A laptop," said Bob. "He's going to send me a series of GPS coordinates and then, when the ionic vibrations are correctly configured, we bring up the vacuum pump and the facilitator, and he creates the wormhole. You won't see him again until he comes back from the future."

Ernie goggled at Bob.

"When did you become a scientist, Bob? I didn't understand a word of what you just said. What are ionic vibrations? I feel as if I'm in a movie."

Inside the cabinet, Donald was having trouble with his laptop. Now it was frozen, and it was too dark for him to see the keys. The last time, he had sent Bob a couple of messages before entering the sewer. He had known before he'd left the cabinet it was all systems go, and he was loath to deviate from a successful protocol. But now he had no choice. Once down in the sewer, he found the flashlight he'd left down there and finally got his laptop started again. He prepared to send the first coordinates. When he was finished tapping them out, he pressed the "send" command and then watched, incredulous, as all the entries in his mail app, which was standing open, began to roll rapidly off the bottom of the screen.

He knew immediately what the problem was: his computer had picked up a virus. These annoyances were always being loosed on the virtual world, usually by kids. For someone like Donald, removing the infection was a trivial matter, but he knew it would take him a little time. He would have to reboot his computer, maybe more than once. It could take up to half an hour. Now he thought about getting out of the sewer and going back up into the cabinet.

He imagined himself explaining to the people waiting up there in the dark that his laptop was infected with a bug. What kind of impression would that make? Here he was, purporting to be a time traveler, telling them all that something trivial like a computer virus was holding him up. It was altogether too banal. What would Bob's Home Products guest think? Maybe he'd blow up and just leave. That was certainly something he might do in such circumstances. It would be another disaster for them all.

What to do? Then, he thought, *What if I don't do anything?* Bob would open the cabinet and he'd be gone. What would happen then? Would they tear into the ground as Bob told him they had done the last time he'd made this trip? He thought some more. It would be completely dark up there now. How energized would they be in total darkness? Not very, he thought. And would any of them have brought shovels? Very unlikely. His fears were illogical.

They would wheel away the platform at Bob's command and return it to the bed of the pickup. Once again, the site of the manhole would disappear into the invisibility of the night. He knew he was taking a risk, but not, he thought, a big one. He looked at his watch. He had been in the sewer for almost ten minutes. He realized that the decision had been made for him. Returning to the cabinet now was no longer an option.

Up above ground, Bob was staring at his laptop. There was the message from Donald sent a few minutes ago. The message was not GPS coordinates. It was just three words. "I love you."

Nigel and Oliver had taken up the handles of the cart bearing the cabinet and were waiting for Bob's instructions on the direction to take. They watched as he studied Donald's baffling message. Now Bob was embarrassed. The message was bizarre, wasn't it? Did Donald really love him? And why tell him now, like this? Maybe Donald thought of him as a surrogate father. Surely that was all the message could mean?

Bob looked at Nigel and Oliver.

"I guess we won't need you guys this time. It doesn't look as if we're going anywhere. Maybe Donald can cause the portal to form now at a site of his choosing. Maybe this is it. I'm going to assume that that's the case. Let's get the vacuum pump and facilitator going and have at it."

Jim clambered into his truck and backed it up close to the platform. He started up the emergency generator and then the vacuum pump. He switched on the facilitator. People stared at him from out of the darkness, silently admiring his mastery of all the equipment. Jim knew what to do! The colored lights sparkled into orderly action and the countdown rang out stridently over the dark field.

Standing by the side of the platform, Stan grinned knowingly at Jeff and Oliver. He looked excited, eager for action. As before, Bob waited precisely five minutes before telling Jim to shut everything off. The racket ceased and was followed by a clear "ping." Jim shut off the vacuum pump and the emergency generator. All was silent. Bob climbed up onto the platform and then, moving cautiously in the murk, opened the cabinet door. Once again, the cabinet was empty.

"He's gone," he called out, an announcement greeted by a slight, barely audible gasp from the shadowy figures standing around.

"I guess the vibrations were exactly centered on this site. Donald must have refined his protocol," Bob said knowledgeably. "I suggest we all go to O'Malley's for a celebratory drink."

Ernie was up on the platform staring into the empty cabinet.

"Where the hell did he go?" he asked wonderingly. "He can only be under the ground."

"He's in the future, Ernie. He's gone from this place now. He really is a time traveler. Humanity's first one." Bob delivered this declaration with relish. He went on: "He's gone into the future, and he's going to come back with information for US Home Products. We are all going to make a lot of money."

Ernie remained staring into the empty cabinet. Then he knelt down and started to feel around the base of the tall wooden box. His fingers found the latch of the trapdoor. He pulled it up and looked down into the hole and at the surface of the field below.

"He's got to be under there," he said softly, but loud enough for Bob to hear.

"We'll check it out," said Bob confidently. "This is exactly what happened the last time. We tore up the ground and found nothing."

Unexpectedly, Nigel appeared on the platform beside them. Ernie and Bob looked queryingly at him.

"I know something about underground pipes, Bob. I worked on the sewer systems of Liverpool, in England, one summer when I was an undergraduate student. The way to look for manholes beneath the surface of the ground is to use a metal detector. I've got one in the boot of my car. I checked where we'd finished up the last time Donald went time traveling, but there was nothing there."

"See?" said Bob triumphantly, to Ernie. "Checked and nothing. I told you. He's really gone."

"Go and get that detector, son. Satisfy a skeptical old man," said Ernie.

Nigel promptly jumped to the ground, a jump which provided a little excitement since he couldn't see the ground in the dark and it arrived sooner than he was expecting. He staggered under the sudden jolt but managed to keep his feet.

"Don't move the platform," he called out as he headed for his car.

Jeff, Stan, and Oliver, their interest piqued by the unfolding developments on the platform, wandered over to join Bob and Ernie. Jim stood by with Judy, watching Bob for the word to load the cart onto the bed of the pickup. Forrest, Nils, Peter, Charlene, and her mother joined Jim and Judy. Nigel, now the center of everyone's attention, hurried back clutching the metal detector and a bunch of long, thin, metal rods. Crouching on the floor of the platform, he pushed a rod through each corner of the opened trapdoor deep into the ground, and then he and Peter wheeled the platform out of the way. Jim took possession of it and extended a ramp from the bed of his truck in preparation for rolling the cart up onto it.

"All right," Nigel announced to the avid onlookers, "now we'll check this square for a manhole. This time we know exactly where he's gone."

In the heat of the moment, Nigel acted without thought, the possible consequences of his actions remaining unexplored. Now he was sure he had never, even for a moment, considered it possible that Donald was traveling in time. He forgot about Donald the man, and in the thrill of the chase, Nigel lost sight of compassion. He joined Stan in seeing Donald as the enemy of reason who needed to be squashed. And what was all this about the loss of personal vanity in the future? If anyone was vain it was Donald. So Nigel pressed ahead in pursuit of his quarry, unmindful of any consequences that might result.

He ran the metal detector carefully over the area inside the rods, listening for the telltale change of pitch that would signify the presence of metal beneath the surface of the ground. The whine from the detector continued to squeak out unchanged.

"It doesn't look like there's anything here," he called out cheerfully.

Bob looked Ernie over with a kind expression on his face.

"I told you, Ernie, there's nothing there. It was just like this last time. Of course, we didn't have the metal detector then; we just dug the ground up. Stan did it. He only succeeded in making himself look foolish."

Ernie shook his head admiringly.

"I would never have believed it if I hadn't seen it for myself," he said softly.

"Of course," called out Nigel, ever the scientist, "it's possible that the manhole cover isn't metal. Sometimes they use polymer covers. I'll just press a few of these rods into the ground to check. A bit more scientific than tearing into the ground with a shovel, I should think." He glanced disparagingly in Stan's direction as he said this.

The rods were about three feet long. He pressed home the first one, and it passed by the plywood board with the manhole cover beneath it.

"Nothing yet," he called out to Bob and Ernie.

Bob watched him and, for the first time, felt serious intimations of misgiving. What was Nigel expecting to find? And why was he being so thorough? Donald was time traveling, wasn't he? They hadn't found anything suspicious that first time, had they? But as he thought about it, he realized this time was different. For one thing it hadn't all gone smoothly. There was the strange email message—"I love you"—and then no GPS coordinates. Perhaps he should have waited for those before bringing up the vacuum pump. Donald had said nothing about not sending GPS coordinates. It had been his, Bob's, decision to go ahead anyway. Perhaps he should have sent Donald a message asking for further instructions or at least asking if it was okay to open the cabinet. Maybe he should just have made up coordinates and moved the cabinet away from its starting point. But it was dark, and he'd been in a hurry to impress Ernie Sikorsky. It was too late now anyway.

Nigel had already marked out the spot. Suddenly he felt afraid. He was seized with a presentiment of catastrophe.

At that very same instant, Nigel called out: "Hello, what have we got here?"

***

Donald, crouching in the sewer directly underneath the manhole, heard the tip of the rod impact the plywood base and realized instantly what it was. He felt the blood first draining from his face in fear and then rushing back to burn his cheeks. The gravity of his situation came crashing down on him. He was going to be discovered! The shame was unimaginable. Here he was, fresh from the triumph of his first journey in time, about to be exposed as a phony. He would never live it down. He would be permanently ostracized from what little of society he had gained access to in his brief sojourn on Earth. He would have to explain himself at the university, and there was a chance he might even lose his job. If that happened, he would never get another one. Almost Infinity, of course, would vanish without a trace. It would just be a big joke, and all the people who'd joined the company were going to look like fools, their reputations permanently tainted. None of the scientists would ever forgive him.

Of course, in a life spent under the spell of pseudologia fantastica, many of his lies had been publicly exposed, and he'd often been called to account. His parents had helped him then. They knew him inside and out and treated him with kindness and understanding, his mother especially. After all, she was his mom. His parents had offered explanations to offended parties, asking for tolerance. Always it had been given. Pathological lying as an illness was unknown, and people were just glad they didn't have it. This time, though, he was going to have to face the music alone. He didn't think he could do it, and he'd never let his lying get so out of hand after his parents had died. His loneliness was going to be unbearable. Not even Bob would like him.

He scrambled around, frantically collecting the items he'd brought down to the sewer to see him through his brief visits. His one hope was that he could get away. He hadn't explored the sewer last time.

Most of the time he'd been down there, he'd been asleep. And he'd slept deeply. But for some reason, it hadn't been refreshing sleep. Now he shone his flashlight up the tunnel. He hoped to find another manhole cover he could escape through. Time travel was over, but at least he could escape humiliation. He just couldn't allow himself to be discovered down here in the sewer. All the cans of food he'd brought down were in a large cardboard box, as were his little stove, dishes, cutlery, water, soap, air freshener, and towel. He stuffed his sleeping bag on top of these items and then threw in his few books, his transistor radio, and the battery-operated lamp, all of which were still here from the previous stay. He placed the box on top of the folding chair he'd used both to sit on and as the base for his bed. He emptied the water onto the floor of the sewer.

He looked around frantically one last time with his flashlight and then wedged it between the box and the folding chair. Yes, he thought, he had everything. His burden was heavy, but he could just about walk with it. Noting that there were one or two puddles of filth to pass through in order to make his escape, he staggered off up the sewer pipe. He assumed an upright posture, even leaning back slightly to balance the weight of the box and chair he was carrying. It made it difficult to see where he was going since the box blocked his view of what was in front of him. He forced himself forward, taking one step at a time. It was precarious progress.

***

"Al talked to me yesterday," George said to his wife. "He's been talking with David Hallauer, a VC guy, about starting up another company. Al's looking for a business partner. And that would be me. The new company's going to be called Gene-4-Gene with the number and not the preposition in its name. He wants me to be a founder of the new company along with him. He says I could be its president."

"George!" cried his wife. "That would be perfect. And we could keep the sunshine and the blue skies."

"Of course," said George, "Bob won't like it. But unless he gets lucky with US Home Products today, I don't think we'll have much of a choice."

"No choice," his wife agreed firmly. "Simply no choice."

"I've got a lunch meeting with the both of them tomorrow."

"Go for it, George," urged his wife. "Or should I call you Mr. President?"

***

Nigel slid in another rod about six inches from the one that had encountered resistance. Again, he encountered obstruction. He shone a flashlight on the two rods sticking out of the ground and noted that they were at identical heights. He chose a position equidistant from the two protruding rods and slid in another. Again, obstruction at exactly the same depth.

"I think we've got a manhole here, after all," he announced. "It's definitely not a rock."

"How deep is it?" asked Bob.

"About a foot," Nigel told him, looking at the two feet of rod still above the ground.

"Well," said Bob, "Donald would have had quite a challenge to dig up that amount of soil and replace it perfectly on top of himself in under ten minutes. I would go as far as to say it's impossible."

But Nigel knew now what Donald had done. He could barely contain himself. He examined the ground around the rods carefully with a flashlight and discovered the seams in the rough grass. He called to Jim for a shovel, and Jim promptly supplied it from the back of his pickup. Nigel eased its blade into a seam and levered the square of sod up out of the ground. It was really heavy, but it came up easily as one piece, plywood board and all, under which he had managed to get the blade of the shovel before lifting. Nigel lifted it out, set it to one side, and then looked into the shallow hole at the manhole cover.

"Very possible, Bob," he said softly. "Clever too. He would just have to set this square of sod on the edge of the opening and on top of the manhole cover. When he replaced the manhole cover, the sod would fit seamlessly with the surrounding earth. He'd have to align the square of sod with the square he'd cut around the manhole, but, for someone like Donald, that would be a trivial problem. Probably just a couple of marks on the underside of the cover and the opening to line up. Once we moved the platform from this exact spot, we would never be able to find it again."

"What happens now?" asked Jeff, who was following this exchange closely. He looked first at Bob and then at Nigel.

"I can go down," volunteered Nigel. "I did this all the time when I was working in Liverpool, checking for obstructions. We just have to hope Donald isn't down there and that he really is time traveling."

Stan snorted in derision.

"What the fuck are you talking about? Of course, he's going to be down there, the skulking rat."

Ernie glanced at Bob. This kind of talk definitely wouldn't be tolerated at US Home Products. But Ernie blamed Bob rather than Stan. Bob really should run a tighter ship.

"He's not going to be there, Ernie, you'll see," reassured Bob. "He definitely wasn't there last time."

"But we're starting from the right place this time, Bob," put in Nigel quietly.

"Agreed," said Bob, cursing himself again for having skipped the GPS involvement and opening the cabinet so hastily. "But we have also run the vacuum pump. That's what allows the wormhole to form, isn't it?"

"Well, yes. But now we've found a manhole."

"It's an asshole down a manhole!" shouted Stan, laughing. "And fuck the wormhole!"

He grinned wolfishly at Jeff and Oliver and then said: "Look, Bob, he got us good last time. None of us could figure it out. But now this guy," he gestured dismissively at Nigel, "with his intimate knowledge of life in the sewers, has solved it for us."

Nigel heard the inevitable mocking tone in Stan's sneering voice and was ashamed. Of course, he'd wanted the mystery resolved, but not like this.

"What about the facilitator and the vacuum pump? He had to have them, surely?" Bob asked pleadingly.

"You really believe that crap, Bob? Start up the vacuum pump and the Radio Shack gizmo right next to the magic wooden cabinet, and it will miraculously create a wormhole? Which parallel universe are *you* from?"

And he grinned again at the smiling Jeff and Oliver.

Bob was beginning to feel horribly exposed. He turned in supplication to Nigel. Nigel, for his part, was feeling sorry for Bob and was already dreading meeting Donald in the sewer pipe below. But before he could muster up the courage to announce that he wouldn't be going down the manhole after all, Stan, shepherding Jeff and Oliver before him, appeared at his side.

"We'll be right behind you, Nigel," he promised brightly.

With one last apologetic look at Bob's stricken face, Nigel lowered himself into the hole and began to clamber down the underground vertical ladder. Stan ushered first Jeff and then Oliver after him. He made his own descent after taking one last triumphant look around at all the bystanders. The horizontal pipe at the foot of the ladder had a diameter of about seventy inches, and so Nigel, who was about six feet tall, had to bend his neck slightly while standing, waiting for his three accomplices to join him. He looked around with his flashlight and discovered what had eluded Donald on his previous trips. There was a light switch about halfway up one side of the pipe. He flipped it on, and the entire interior of the sewer was lit up with a ghostly yellow glow. He looked down along the sewer's length to the right and left and noticed dark pools of liquid, interspersed at intervals along its length in both directions. He wasn't looking forward to wading through those disgusting pools when it became necessary to do so in the pursuit of Donald.

CHAPTER 30

The Conquering Hero Comes

THERE WAS NO SIGN of Donald in either direction, but then Nigel noticed the footprints leading off to his left. He looked up at his three colleagues from under his brow, all of whom were bending their necks to avoid the ceiling of the pipe—even Stan and Jeff, who weren't quite tall enough to need to.

"I'm guessing he went this way," said Nigel, and he began moving away from the shaft they had all climbed down.

"No," said Stan promptly. "How do you know that's right? If I were him, I would have gone that way."

He pointed in the opposite direction and began to walk on what was the drier floor. Jeff and Oliver obediently shuffled after him. Nigel ignored the three of them.

"Well," he said over his shoulder, "the footprints are going this way."

Stan ignored him, but Jeff and Oliver stopped and turned around. Stan walked on a few yards and then glanced back over his shoulder. Realizing he was on his own, he cursed and turned around himself.

Nigel gingerly led the way, picking a path around the pools wherever he could and, where he couldn't, reluctantly splashing through them. They had traveled about a hundred yards when Nigel, who was continually scanning the ground about fifty yards in front of them with a flashlight, suddenly stopped.

"Look," he said in a whisper.

At the very edge of the beam cast by the flashlight, they could just make out the body of a man sprawled in front of what looked like a large cardboard box.

"I think it's him," said Nigel softly. He hesitated, then called out: "Donald?"

Stan barged roughly past him.

"The bastard's asleep," he snarled. "I'm going to welcome him back from his journey into time."

He turned and showed his teeth to Jeff and Oliver in an atrocious smile.

"I'm going to piss on the fucker's head."

Nigel registered Stan's insane intent with distaste. The man truly was an animal. Stan strode and then ran angrily toward Donald, fumbling with his zipper in preparation to urinate. When he was within twenty yards of Donald, they heard him snort in disgust. He got a few yards farther, and then suddenly all his actions were in slow motion. He sank to his knees and then pitched slowly forward onto his face.

Nigel knew immediately what had happened.

"It's a pocket of toxic gas!" he shouted and without hesitating for a second, raced after Stan.

The two molecular biologists watched as he came to a halt about ten yards short of Stan. He was preparing himself for the final dash into the gas by taking several deep lungfuls of air in preparation for holding his breath. Oliver moved forward himself, thinking Nigel was having second thoughts about going to Stan's aid. Stan's last words were still ringing in his ears. But then Nigel dashed forward again. He reached Stan, slid his hands under his armpits, and heaved him back to a sitting position. Then he began dragging Stan backward. Stan was heavy, and it was quite slow going. Nigel made it to within thirty yards of Jeff and Oliver before he was forced to take a breath.

They watched, horrified, as the strength just seeped out of him. He staggered and then leaned against the wall of the sewer, unable to take another step. Now they dashed forward, grabbed their two stricken colleagues, and backed away rapidly up the sewer pipe.

They had gone about ten yards when Nigel recovered. "Keep moving away," he gasped. "It's hydrogen sulfide. It's a common hazard in pipes like these. Stan isn't out of the woods yet, and Donald may well be dead."

Jeff and Oliver goggled at him. Donald may be dead! Oliver took his arm and put it around his own neck in preparation to assist him in walking. Nigel shook him off.

"I can walk now. Help Jeff with Stan. We've got to get him to a hospital just as soon as we can."

Jeff and Oliver each took one of Stan's arms and staggered away. Nigel watched them go and then returned his attention to Donald. He played the flashlight over his prone figure. Then his eyes widened as he noticed Donald's foot give a little twitch. He was still alive! Now there wasn't a second to waste.

He immediately dashed toward Donald, pausing once again to fill his lungs with as much relatively clean air as he could force into them before covering the last twenty yards or so to Donald. He was praying Donald wouldn't be as heavy as Stan, and thankfully, he wasn't. But Nigel had to go farther this time. He made it back with Donald almost to where he'd reached with Stan before being forced once more to take a breath. This time he passed out.

Jeff and Oliver labored with Stan back to the vertical pipe where they were greeted by Peter's astonished face staring down at them.

"What's happened?" he shouted down. "Where's Nigel?"

"Call 911," Oliver shouted back. "Exposure to toxic gas. One possible fatality. Stan's injured. Do it right away!" he yelled as he heard Peter relaying the information to someone nearby—probably Bob, guessed Oliver.

Ten minutes later the paramedics arrived. Four burly men took over the scene. First, with several of them showing great strength, they managed to winch the still unconscious Stan up and out of the vertical pipe. He was placed in the ambulance, and various monitors were attached to him. In the meantime, Jeff and Oliver had gone back down into the sewer in search of Nigel. Much to their amazement, they discovered his and Donald's unconscious bodies out of the main cloud of toxic gas. The paramedics reprised their muscular virtuosity twice more and popped both men out of the vertical pipe.

As they were being brought out into the night air, Nigel regained consciousness.

"How's Donald?" he croaked at Oliver.

Oliver just patted his arm and said nothing. En route to the hospital, the paramedics connected Stan, Nigel, and Donald to a range of monitors. The paramedics could see that, of the three of them, Donald was in the most serious condition.

Charlene and Mary followed the ambulance to the hospital in their car. Oliver had told Charlene about Nigel's heroics—how Stan and Donald would probably be dead now if it hadn't been for his selfless and courageous acts. She was bursting with pride at how Nigel had conducted himself and was so happy her mother had been on hand to witness it. She realized, along with all the other employees, that Almost Infinity wasn't almost anything anymore. It was completely finished.

Two of the paramedics had gone back down into the sewer to check that there were no other bodies down there. They reappeared, brandishing their respirators.

"These beauties saved our lives," they proclaimed. "Too bad those three guys didn't have these. What were they doing down there, anyway?"

No one answered them. No one could bring themselves to say that Donald was pretending to be a time traveler and that Nigel, Oliver, Jeff, and Stan had gone down to catch him in his charade. It was just too humiliating. The paramedics, to everyone's great relief, decided they didn't need the immediate presence of the police.

Bob's status had passed unnoticed by the paramedics. They had all assumed that Jeff and Oliver were the organizers of the gathering. Bob was now sitting on the grass, looking ahead blankly. Ernie stood before him, grave and expectant.

"This is the end of the road, isn't it, Bob? There's no coming back from this. Helmuth and Ned were right, weren't they?"

Bob looked up at him, and a lone tear coursed slowly down his cheek.

"I'm his only friend, Ernie. This is all my fault really. I should never have allowed myself to believe all that time travel shit."

Ernie looked closely at Bob and felt sorry for him. The large, fat man sitting on the grass with his short legs stretched straight out in front of him just looked so sad.

"It's not your fault, Bob. You didn't know about this sewer, did you?"

Bob shook his head. "I believed in him, and I believed in Almost Infinity. How stupid does that make me?"

He looked up at the few people who hadn't left and who were still hanging around.

"It's all over for everybody."

***

The next morning, Bob woke up and immediately began to weep. His wife fussed around in front of him, attending to his every need, real and imaginary.

"This didn't have to happen," sobbed Bob. "Maybe time travel is more dangerous than anyone realized."

"Sshh," his wife said, cradling his head in her arms. "There is no such thing as time travel, Bobby. Donald just hid in a sewer and pretended. At least he was unconscious when they found him and was spared the shame and humiliation of discovery."

"No one is going to invest in us now," moaned Bob, mopping his eyes with a tissue.

"Well, I'm glad it's finished," his wife told him. "Had any of you thought about what it all meant? All this traveling to and fro between now and the future? I don't think Donald was a well man. Somehow, he convinced himself it was true."

Bob passed his hand wearily over his face.

"He almost admitted it to me once, you know. I was thinking we'd agreed that wormholes were just a silly fantasy and he should marry, settle down and have kids, when he says: 'That's my plan, Bob. When I go time traveling, I don't want to go alone.' And he was perfectly serious. So what was it with him? Can you explain it? And then there was that first time. He definitely went somewhere then."

Bob's wife got him to recount exactly how it had happened. She pointed out that he could have gone underground before they'd begun to move the platform. Bob looked at her, incredulous.

"But the vacuum pump! What about it?"

"It doesn't do anything, Bobby. It's just part of the trick."

"What?" He stared at her and then grabbed his head in his hands. "Oh God, I've been so incredibly stupid, haven't I? Why didn't I realize this myself?"

"Calm down, Bobby. Donald obviously has an illness. I don't think he knows himself what's true and what's fantasy. I just hope people realize that and give the poor man a break."

***

There was someone else who recognized Donald's illness, and that was Mary, Charlene's mother. She was overcome with pity for the unconscious, bedraggled figure the paramedics had rescued from the sewer. While she was at the hospital with Charlene, worrying about Nigel, she had looked in a few times on Donald. She thought he had an interesting, sensitive face. Of course, she'd never seen the smile. She noted the complete lack of visitors to his bedside. He was still unconscious and clearly very sick. She bought a bunch of flowers and left them in his room. She hoped he'd see them when he woke up and know someone had had a kind thought for him. She asked Charlene if he was married. Charlene didn't know, but she didn't think so. Mary promised herself she'd keep an eye on Donald and would try to protect him from the scorn bound to be directed at him if and when he recovered. Poor Donald! She was sure he was a kind man.

At the hospital, Stan and Donald were fighting for their lives. Nigel had made a full recovery as far as anyone could tell and had been allowed to go home the next morning. Hydrogen sulfide exposure is extremely damaging to all the major organs of the body, with the brain being a particular concern. Stan and Donald would carry the scars of their encounter with the gas for the rest of their lives. The paramedics decided Stan was the true hero of the incident. He was the real first responder. He'd been the one who had put his life on the line for Donald and Nigel, without a second's hesitation. He was definitely one of them.

Nigel, they were cooler toward. For one thing he wasn't an American, and he'd been more calculating, only getting in on the action when there was less danger. He hadn't suffered the same exposure to the toxic gas and thus had recovered very quickly. They were completely satisfied with this confabulation. Nigel wasn't truly one of them; he was a wannabe. One or two of the paramedics were around at the time of his release from hospital and thought they detected shame in his demeanor. Also, he didn't seem willing to share in their admiration for Stan, and that, they decided, was odd and suspicious. Maybe Nigel's involvement hadn't been entirely innocent. They bade him a formal and correct farewell. There would most likely be an inquiry, particularly if someone died, and the truth would come out. It might not be good to be too close to Nigel.

In fact, Nigel was ashamed. He felt directly responsible for the perilous situations of Donald and Stan. After all, he had been the leader of the small mob that had pursued Donald. Why hadn't he been more thoughtful? What had he expected to happen when they confronted Donald in the sewer? And Stan was right there with him, intent on humiliating and destroying the founder of their company. If Donald had been conscious, it would have been an unbearable scene. Nigel tried to think of what else he could have done. Well, he could have gone after Donald alone, when there was no one else around. Of course, it would have been a tremendous shock for Donald to see Nigel suddenly materializing in his hiding place, and he would've known in that instant the game was up.

Then what would have happened? They would share the knowledge that Donald was, at best, a fantasist and at worst, a simple liar. But that would just be the two of them. The key difference between this and their present reality was now everyone knew Donald was a scheming and manipulative liar. And Nigel worried about Donald's future. What had he done to the man? How could he go on after such a public humiliation? He hated himself for thinking it, but maybe it would be better for everyone if Donald just died. This was a thought he wouldn't be sharing with Charlene.

***

He was thinking it now as he sat next to Charlene on the drive home from the hospital. Charlene noticed his quietness and wondered if he was fully recovered. When they got into their house, Nigel went and sat quietly on the sofa in the living room. Charlene came and sat down next to him, and they remained there silently, side by side. This was something they never did. After a moment, she glanced sideways at him and was shocked to see the tears on his cheeks.

"Nigel," she said softly, "what's the matter?"

He leaned his head against her shoulder and rolled slowly into her embrace as she put her arms around him.

"Don't cry," she whispered. "My brave, wonderful boy."

"I'm such a prat," moaned Nigel. "I nearly killed Donald."

"Donald nearly killed himself, Nigel. Accidentally, of course. You didn't make him go down that sewer."

"But I could have handled it so much better. He could have escaped the hydrogen sulfide entirely."

"However it had come about, he would still have been humiliated. And you would have had to tell us all he was a fraud. There was no escaping that."

Nigel sat up and looked at her. She looked so beautiful. He looked closely at her eyes and noticed the kind little wrinkles at their edges. He was suddenly put in mind of Mary.

"Where's your mother?"

"Well, you know her a little bit now. She's got a sentimental streak. She wanted to hang around at the hospital and be a friendly face when Donald wakes up. She bought him a bunch of flowers, you know."

"I don't deserve you, Charlene. Nor my prospective mother-in-law. You're both so much better than me."

"Well," she said, "who do I deserve? Stan? That's how great I am."

He clutched her fiercely to his chest.

"You're my sunshine, Charlene, not California."

"Tell me exactly what happened in that sewer then, Nigel," his sunshine commanded him.

Nigel gulped and turned away, then said, "Stan really is a first-class arsehole."

"Why? What did he do?"

"I don't know if I should tell you," Nigel said quietly. "It's really gross."

"The paramedics think he's a hero."

Nigel snorted contemptuously.

"I taught a course in England for those guys once," he said, with some animation. "They are all the same—all brawn, zeal, and good intentions, but not too bright."

"My mother's brother is a paramedic."

"Well, what's he like?"

"Brawny, zealous, and a nice guy." They both laughed. "So come on, Nigel, what happened?"

He recounted the underground events of the previous evening, leaving out nothing.

Charlene framed his face between her hands and looked deeply into his eyes. Her own eyes were sparkling with pride.

"So you're the hero, Nigel, not Stan?"

"Definitely not Stan. We both know what he is. But not me either, I'm afraid. Without me none of this would have happened."

She wiped the tears off his cheeks and hugged his head to her chest. He lay there, passively, in her arms.

He felt exhausted, probably the lingering effects of the hydrogen sulfide he'd inhaled. And, of course, the hospital had made quite sure he didn't sleep last night, nurses waking him every hour to take vital signs. If there were any curative powers in sleep, and, of course, there were, the hospital made quite sure they were denied to patients in its care. Now, he wondered if Stan and Donald would make it. Well, he was fairly certain Stan would, but Donald had had more exposure to the gas, and he might have some long-term deficits. He thought about Mary and about how Charlene thought there was nothing remarkable about her behavior. Why did Mary feel such empathy for Donald? After all, he was a complete stranger. She couldn't really fancy him because she'd hardly set eyes on him, at least not close up. And anyway, who could fancy Donald now? He wondered if she would still feel so warmly toward him once she'd gotten a good look at him, after he had smiled at her once or twice. Donald the time traveler.

Well, the joke was on all of them. He and all his scientific colleagues had come to work at Almost Infinity certain time travel was impossible, or at least as certain as they could be as scientists. And that meant not *absolutely* sure, because as a scientist, one could never be so sure. That tiny residue of uncertainty had been enough to allow Donald to operate as a shaman and to get away with it. He couldn't think of a single person who had really believed in Donald. Maybe Bob? He would be the only one, but then Bob wasn't a scientist. Nigel wished he could travel in time now. He'd only want to go back to yesterday. He'd keep his rods in the car and wouldn't find the manhole. Maybe he'd use them later, in private, just to satisfy himself that Donald was a charlatan. Then, he would share this knowledge only with Charlene. He'd let Donald continue telling his stories and would pretend to be convinced.

The truth was bound to emerge eventually, though. If greedy folk came around before it emerged, looking for miracles and a quick buck, well, he would have let them. That, of course, wouldn't have been ideal, especially if large sums of money were involved, but at least Donald and Stan wouldn't be in the hospital now. As he thought about the two men and how their lives had impacted his, he decided neither of them was particularly evil. Donald had never hurt anybody physically, and you could look at Almost Infinity as a pleasant learning experience. And Stan, once you'd experienced his monstrous selfishness, was just sad. He only made you sad if you embraced it with him. Stan, if he survived, was sure to lead a lonely life. Finally, Nigel realized, for better or worse, he was connected to all the people he knew. Interconnectedness was what made life fascinating. He had a touch of Donald and a dash of Stan in him now after making their acquaintance, and yesterday he had come close to losing those parts of him. The deaths of Donald and Stan would have definitely diminished him.

"I don't want to sound like a hipster," he said now, smiling up at Charlene, "but we're all part of each other, aren't we? None of us is truly alone, not Donald, not Stan, none of us. And when one of us dies, we all die a little with the deceased, don't we? It's why we feel sad when someone famous dies, someone we've never met or even seen in the flesh. We feel sad because we've lost a tiny part of ourselves. And sometimes that might not be such a tiny part either."

Charlene looked at him and summed up his ruminations concisely like the clever person she was.

"So we grow when we meet new people and develop new interests in life?"

"We do!" cried Nigel. "You know, I'd never thought about it quite like that, I mean quite so simply, until you just said it. Of course, we do. That's why it's been so great at Almost Infinity, all the new people we've met. We've grown so much bigger because of the shared experience. It's a place we'll never forget."

Charlene drew back and stared at him. Her face was intense, an intensity centered in her eyes that were now deep pools of introspection.

"It's been a wonderful experience, Nigel. It's been the turning point of my life. I love you, I really do. I've never been more sure of anything. I love everything about you. We've been through some odd experiences here, haven't we? Done things we've regretted, at least I have. But now I know what it means to grow together."

He looked back at her, a little intimidated by the topography of the turn taken by the conversation. He wanted her back with him on the more mundane plateau where they usually dwelt. He couldn't think of what to say next.

"What's Mary up to with Donald?" he asked her now, mainly just to say something.

Charlene looked at him kindly, recognizing the awkwardness her sincerity had imposed on him.

"My mom feels sorry for him. She heard the unkind way people were talking about him, and so she decided to take his side. Absolutely typical of my mom."

"I hope Donald gets better and can forgive me," said Nigel. "And I hope Mary can forgive me as well."

"She'll forgive you, Nigel. My mom's a very kind, simple person. I wonder if Donald has ever met anyone like her before."

He raised his head from her chest and caressed her cheek.

"We're going to continue to grow together," he told her gently. "But I'm me and you're you. We are lovers, lovers transformed by love's purity, and together we are immune from the evil in the world."

"Transformed lovers," she repeated. "Well, I think that's all I'm going to remember from this conversation. You see, unlike you, I don't have a PhD. I can't remember the rest of it."

They both laughed.

"You know, Charlene, I'm also thinking now about Kutti. In my present frame of mind, I think I can forgive even him. Do you think he can forgive me for being so rude and ungrateful to him? For looking down on him because he's Indian?"

"Don't be turning into a saint, Nigel. I won't be good enough for you then. You'll have to turn your attention to my mother. But I think she's thinking seriously about Donald at the moment."

"Come on, Charlene, what do you think Kutti would say if I were nice to him, if I showed him that I wasn't bearing any grudges?"

Charlene looked him over fondly.

"Maybe that gas in the sewer affected you as well as Donald and Stan. And who knows? Maybe the two of them have been turned into decent human beings."

"It's an unexpected side effect of being gassed by hydrogen sulfide. Nasty pieces of work are turned into gentlemen and scholars. We'll have to start a company. This is the way real scientific progress is made, isn't it? Having good luck and recognizing it."

Charlene kissed him and looked proudly at him.

"Fortune favors the prepared mind."

CHAPTER 31

Sound the Trumpets

AMANDA WATKINS COULDN'T BELIEVE what was happening to her. In her one-bedroom apartment in Palo Alto, she was staring at a letter from US Van Lines. And what a letter! US Van Lines had not received payment from Almost Infinity for her move to California. So now, US Van Lines was expecting her to reimburse them for the full cost of the move. The full cost was $5,000. Amanda looked through tears at the number. Five thousand dollars! She didn't even have five hundred. And the rent for her apartment was due in two weeks, and that was another seven hundred. Now the moving company was threatening her with a collection agency. She could expect to have any wages she might receive garnished until their bill was paid in full. Amanda knew there were legal remedies available to her. But she also knew she would need a lawyer and that wouldn't be cheap. One way or the other, she was going to be on the hook for a large sum of money, and her life was going to be a mess for the foreseeable future.

So here she was, alone in sunny California where suddenly it didn't seem so sunny any more, facing the rapacious, unforgiving monster always lurking just beneath the surface of everyday life in the country of her birth. A monster with the capacity to turn heaven into hell in an instant, or so it seemed. She looked out of the window of her little apartment and noticed the magnolia trees standing proudly in a line along the side of the street. They were, as always, bathed with joyful sunshine. No, this couldn't be happening to her; the sunshine wouldn't allow it. But, for one of the few times in her life, she was in trouble truly through no fault of her own. What was she going to do? Who would help her? This, she decided, was a problem only old friends could help her with. And really, she meant friends who were old. After all, these were the people with money. She thought about writing to Ben Storey-Moore to ask him for a loan. But five thousand! That was simply too much, wasn't it? Was their friendship that close? Well, she would just ask him for advice. She was sure he wouldn't let anything bad happen to her.

If she was going to write, she would have to do it soon—otherwise he'd have no time to come to her aid. She wondered if he would expect her to sleep with him again. Well, she would. He wasn't too bad—old, of course, but not too bad. She dashed off a note to her old boss explaining what had happened to her since arriving in California. She was going to go on the game after all. She collected herself and went into work to look for Bob or Donald.

***

The first person she met there was Peter. He sat behind his desk in the shared office grinning at her. She decided that he was intensely irritating.

"Have you heard the news?" he asked her, his grin getting ever broader.

"Why don't you tell me?" she replied calmly, affecting to be sorting out papers on her desk.

"Well, Donald went time traveling again last night and—"

"Fooled you all again, did he?" she snapped derisively. "Had you all running around in circles shouting 'Where is he? Where is he?'"

"He didn't, as a matter of fact." He leaned forward, and his eyes glittered with excitement. "He didn't because he's in the hospital, fighting for his life."

"What?" Amanda gazed incredulously at him. "What do you mean? Did you attack him? He's not in the hospital; he's time traveling."

"Not this time," said Peter, shaking his head. "He's actually in the hospital. I saw them taking him away in an ambulance. And why should we attack him? What kind of people do you think we are?"

Amanda sat down and stared at Peter. Why the hell was he smiling? Why did he always have to try to come across as such a know-it-all?

"I don't believe you," she said at last. "It's some kind of sick joke."

"No, really Amanda, he's actually in the hospital. He was poisoned by toxic gas in a sewer."

"What was he doing in a sewer?"

"It was where he escaped to from the wormhole cabinet. He let himself out of the bottom of the cabinet and then went down a manhole that was under the platform. We didn't find it the first time, but this time Nigel got it."

"Nigel?"

Peter nodded confirmation.

"Bob asked us both to help with locating the wormhole for Donald's return trip to the future. He wanted us to pull the platform supporting the cabinet. Then something went wrong with Donald's computer. At least that was what we all assumed. He sent Bob an email from the cabinet telling him he loved him. The message simply said: 'I love you.'"

"The 'I love you' virus," said Amanda. "It was all over the East Coast just before I came out here. I may have infected Donald's computer. I sent him a couple of emails yesterday about my moving expenses."

"Anyway, this time we didn't have to move the platform. There were no GPS coordinates sent from the cabinet. There was no communication with Donald at all, really. Bob just brought up the vacuum pump and the facilitator, ran them for five minutes, and then opened the cabinet. And Donald was gone once again."

Peter then told her about Nigel working in the sewers of Liverpool, England.

"He knew how to find buried manholes, Amanda. He had those rods."

Amanda found herself wishing she'd attended last night's display of time travel. Nigel had shown them his rods!

"Well, he found the manhole cover with his rods. Donald had tried to camouflage it, and we would never have found it if the platform had been moved around like it was last time. But this time it wasn't, and we did."

"So he went down there the first time too, then?"

"It looks like it," said Peter mildly.

"You know, I really wanted to believe in time travel. It all sounded so exciting. He'd done the math. He could travel to the future, easy-peasy. But he could also come back. He was actually living with us in our quantum universe, and it of course, is deterministic. Free will is an illusion here. You can't change the unknowable. But now, with time travel, he could. Suddenly the future is knowable. He did it by changing universes. He was literally boggling the mind."

Peter looked admiringly at her.

"I hadn't realized you were so well informed about time travel, Amanda."

"That's what was so great about Yale," she smiled. "I attended a course there given by a big-shot cosmologist. He took pity on us and didn't burden us with any math, thank God. I could almost understand some of it."

Peter continued to stare at her, his mouth hanging slightly open. He was dazzled.

"Tell me more, Amanda. I've always wanted to know what Donald was on about. But I was afraid to ask, afraid he'd smile at me. Wow! Just one flash and I'd be toast."

"Well, I'm good at remembering things, Pete, things I don't necessarily fully understand. I remember this one guy's view that every potential outcome embodied in a quantum wave function is realized in its own separate parallel universe. This universe we're in is only one of an infinite number being realized. So here's what I thought. I thought when Donald was time traveling, he was going from one parallel universe to another. And, not to put it too indelicately, he was making that journey through his wormhole. So there would be no self-contradicting circumstances at play."

"I don't know what you're talking about Amanda, but I can tell you now, categorically, Donald never went time traveling. All he did was hide in a sewer while we all thought he was living in 2175. Unless, of course, you're saying he really did go to 2175 and then came back and found himself in a sewer in this universe."

Amanda smiled winningly at him. "You've lost me there, I'm afraid, Pete. You know, if you didn't talk so much, you wouldn't be bad-looking."

Peter blushed. Amanda was amused at his bashfulness.

"Are you rich, Pete? Do you want to sleep with me?"

Peter recovered his nerve.

"In this universe, the answer is no and yes. But in another one it might be yes and yes."

"Well, I'm holding out for that one. Gödel says if we were in a spaceship and if our universe were spinning—and, of course, like all these cosmology dickheads, he tells us it 'might' be spinning"—she held up her hands and framed the word "might" with finger quotes as she continued—"then the trajectory of our spaceship traveling in a spinning universe could return us to our place of origin before the time of our departure. Our rotating universe, if it existed, could then be viewed as one all-encompassing time machine. Now, of course, they've spoiled all this by telling us they've decided our universe isn't spinning."

"Who's Gödel?" asked Peter, feasting his eyes on this clever, pretty girl.

"Some old cosmologist dude," said Amanda. "He's probably dead now, but with these cosmologist dudes you can never really be sure. Anyway, microscopic wormholes can apparently be continually produced by quantum fluctuations of the gravitational field, although, of course, no one has ever seen one. But that's what's called for by the math. Macroscopic wormholes remain a fantasy. So, you see, Donald's claims weren't too outrageous, really."

"Donald had the perfect qualifications for this, didn't he?" asked Peter. "He was a fantasist as well as a cosmologist. And he had the math. There was no holding him."

"What I concluded from my course at Yale was that the entire field is a fraud."

She went and stood next to him and put her hand on his shoulder.

"Are you sure you're not rich, Pete? No rich members of your family?"

Blushing furiously, he shook his head. He didn't trust himself to say anything. She gave his shoulder a friendly squeeze and moved away. Out of her scent, his head cleared and he recovered himself.

"Well, never mind," she said. "You know, some of these guys do doubt time travel is possible. The doubters always ask the same question. If time travel is possible, why haven't we received any visitors from the future? That's a pretty simple question, isn't it? And impossible to answer for all the believers. The simple and obvious answer is that there are no visitors because it's impossible. But no one wants to hear that, and so it's ignored. As a matter of fact, this is exactly the same question Enrico Fermi asked about visitors from outer space. Where are they? Maybe we just can't recognize our limits."

Peter was rendered speechless for a moment, which didn't happen very often. Amanda was beautiful—well, at least very good-looking—and here she was talking knowledgeably about time travel and knowing our limits. This was what his life was supposed to be like.

"He was found hiding in a sewer, passed out. It's sad, isn't it?" he managed at last.

***

Jim presented himself to Bob in Bob's office. There was a certain formality in his demeanor, and Bob wondered what was coming.

"The conclusion is inescapable, Bob. Donald is a lying sack of shit."

Bob held up his hands in admonition.

"Easy Jim. The man nearly died. We've got to show some respect."

"He hasn't shown us any respect. He's put us all in a pretty bind, hasn't he? You know me, I'm never the mugg-ee. But, I've got to say, I'm feeling pretty close to it here."

Bob was sitting at his desk. Immediately before Jim's arrival, he'd been lost in thought, allowing the new reality to settle on him. Donald and time travel were finished, but maybe not Almost Infinity in its entirety. Earlier that morning he'd been looking through his mail. There had been one or two interesting items.

"You know what, Jim? Even at this stage of the game, all may not be lost. I've received a couple of letters this morning from potential investors. One from a cement company in France interested in expanding into agriculture. They think we might be the ideal vehicle for such an expansion. And one from a British company running plantations in Malaysia. They think we might be able to help them clone oil palm trees. Of course, they aren't talking All Grains money, but we might be able to save half the company out of the ashes."

"Not with me and Judy. We're leaving early next week. We're sailing out of here. We're going to take the boat down to Mexico first and then on to the Gulf Coast. Judy has some ideas about a business she wants to set up. Holistic living and organic plants to accompany a contemplative life. She's set her sights on Louisiana. I don't think we'll be making much money, but we won't need much, and life will be a lot less expensive there than here."

Bob was shocked. He'd always thought Jim would be one of the last people to leave Almost Infinity. He was old, and his opportunities were limited. Jim was one of the first people he'd worried about on learning All Grains was withdrawing its support. Yet here he was, calmly and cheerfully telling him he'd made plans for a life after Almost Infinity, that he was going to be okay. Bob reflected and was relieved. He smiled at Jim now, professional and businesslike. "We've certainly appreciated the help, Jim. You'll be missed."

Jim, who hadn't sat down, looked back at him and held out his hand.

"I guess we won't be seeing each other again."

Bob stood up and shook his hand. Jim walked out.

Alone in his office, with Jim's parting words lingering in his mind, Bob was overcome with melancholy. *Guess we won't be seeing each other again.* How many more times would he be hearing that over the next few days? Would he be seeing Donald again? Maybe once or twice for business reasons—the signing of documents, the tying up of loose ends—but not, he thought, for socializing or planning other business ventures. They were finished with each other.

A lot of Almost Infinity's employees had already left, but they were mostly locals, people he could expect to see around town once in a while. The people who were going to make a clean break were those with special skills, mainly the PhDs. These folks, he would, in all probability, never see again. He thought about Stan, Jeff, and Oliver, Nigel and Peter, Arthur Nanomura, and Marshall. The senior men—Al, Nils, and Forrest—he was going to try and keep. News from the hospital was that Stan was making good progress, while Donald was still in and out of consciousness. He was told of a woman who'd taken to sitting by Donald's bedside and who brought flowers from time to time. No one seemed to know who she was. A relative, perhaps? But she said she wasn't. She said she was the mother of one his employees. Bob just shrugged it off. It would all explain itself in time.

***

Jeff and Oliver had been to see Stan. They told him Nigel had saved his life. Stan was unimpressed.

"That British shit! It was him that got us all into that mess in the first place, wasn't it? If it hadn't been for him, none of us would have gotten poisoned."

"But Stan," Oliver pointed out reasonably, "you were going to piss on Donald's head when you thought he was sleeping. Don't you remember?"

Stan did remember, but he wasn't going to admit it. He glared at Oliver for bringing it up. "Well, if I said that, I meant it just as a bit of well-meaning fun. We could all have had a laugh about it afterwards."

"How would you have felt about yourself if you'd actually done it? He was close to death, after all. You might have killed him," Jeff pointed out.

"All right, I know. It wouldn't have looked good. I know that, and I'm sorry if I said it. I never would have done it, of course. But Nigel is still an annoying shit."

"Nigel saved your life, Stan. If he hadn't acted so promptly, you would have succumbed to the hydrogen sulfide. He really is a hero. He put his own life in danger to save you and Donald."

Stan scowled back at Oliver but didn't say anything.

They talked a little about Almost Infinity and admitted they were ashamed of themselves for ever having entertained the notion of time travel. Stan let Jeff and Oliver include him in their soul-searching without protest. But he knew he had never believed it. It was a stilted, unsatisfying conversation. Jeff and Oliver left the hospital and went to find Nigel to thank him for his courageous actions. He wasn't at work, and so they got his home address from Bob.

Charlene let them in. They took one look at her and decided Nigel was a lucky man.

"He's sitting on the deck out back," she told them. "Go through."

Nigel was pleased to see them. He was feeling down. The more he thought about his actions on that pivotal night, the more convinced he became that he'd been the prime instigator of the poisonings—his own as well, of course, but he didn't think of that.

"I nearly killed them both," he told his visitors, without preamble. "I nearly killed them showing off. I'm a prat."

Jeff wouldn't let him blame himself.

"It was Donald, Nigel. He did everything he could to fool us. You were mad, that's all. We all were."

"How's Stan?" asked Nigel, when he was told where they'd just been.

"Back to normal, unfortunately," answered Oliver.

"He's an animal. He proved that, didn't he? Didn't leave much room for doubt," said Nigel, with a tired smile. "He won't change."

Before the recent dramatic events, Jeff and Oliver would have bristled on hearing Stan thus described. He, after all, was a molecular biologist like them, one of the cognoscenti. Nigel, by contrast, was a know-nothing cell biologist. He just didn't have the standing to talk like this about Stan. But now, Jeff and Oliver had glimpsed death together with Nigel, death in all its frightening starkness, and that bond was stronger than the one they shared with Stan in their work lives. They welcomed Nigel into their inner circle, welcomed him as an honored guest.

"He is an animal," Oliver agreed. "I've got to admit it. I'm ashamed of him. And he's really got it in for you."

"Well, we probably won't be seeing each other again," said Nigel. "Charlene and I are going out to Connecticut in a couple of days. I've got the chance of a job there. Believe it or not, Almost Infinity has turned out to be good for me."

"I wish I could say the same," said Oliver. "But hey, more power to you!"

"Anyway," put in Jeff, "we really came around to thank you for being so courageous. To allow us to draw a line under Almost Infinity. We just had to see him in the sewer. And despite what Stan says, he knows you saved his life. We won't let him forget it."

He shook Nigel's hand warmly, and Oliver did the same.

"You're a cool guy, Nigel," said Oliver, as he and Jeff took their leave of him.

"They said I was a cool guy," Nigel told Charlene later. "That's good, isn't it?"

"Like I told you, Nigel, you're a hero."

CHAPTER 32

Beat the Drums

MARY CONTINUED TO GO to the hospital to visit Donald. She'd been there once or twice when he'd briefly regained consciousness. She'd smiled at him and squeezed his hand. Donald, of course, didn't know who she was, but she had a nice face, and so he'd smiled back. Eventually, Donald was out of danger. Stan, in the meantime, had gone home. Donald's recovery was slower, but he made steady progress. One day he asked Mary who she was. He thought she might be a relative, someone he'd known and then forgotten.

"I'm the mother of one of your employees," she told him. "Charlene." Donald was none the wiser.

"Well, Charlene, thank you for coming to see me. It seems no one else has."

"No, I'm not Charlene. Charlene is my daughter. My name is Mary."

Donald frowned at her, confused. Mary smiled back and squeezed his hand.

"Well, you're not very popular right now, Dr. Plum. A lot of people are very upset with you."

"Why?" he wanted to know. "What did I do?"

Mary wondered at the question. It raised a number of questions for her. Had he really forgotten, or was he just dissembling? Had his feelings been hurt?

She answered carefully: "You convinced everyone you were a time traveler, when, really, you were just hiding underground."

She didn't add "in a sewer." She thought that sounded too hurtful. Donald looked amazed.

"I did that? Why?"

"To raise money for your company, Almost Infinity."

"Never heard of it," he said shortly. "What kind of a name is that? There is no such thing as almost infinity. The very name is bogus."

Mary looked at him, wide-eyed. "Don't you remember anything?"

"Of course," he said, still sounding annoyed. "I'm a professor of cosmology at San Francisco State University. I've been there for almost twenty years. I did my undergraduate degree at Harvard and my PhD at San Francisco State. Do my parents know I'm in the hospital?"

Mary didn't know anything about his parents.

"I … I don't know," she faltered.

"Let them know for me, will you?" he asked her seriously. "They'll be worried that I haven't talked to them for a while. How long have I been in here, by the way?"

"Two weeks," said Mary promptly. "Maybe they'll let you out soon. You do feel well enough, don't you?"

"Yes, I do," said Donald. "I'm ready to get on with my life."

***

Mary went home and reported her conversation to Charlene and Nigel. Nigel mentioned to Bob that Donald was asking for his parents.

"He must have forgotten," said Bob, frowning. "What did that gas do to him? Both his parents are dead. I wonder if he really is all right." But Bob still didn't want to see him, and so Mary took it upon herself to break the news to him about his parents.

"They've been dead for fifteen years," she told the stricken Donald.

"How could I have forgotten this?" he asked piteously.

Mary put her arms around him and gave him a hug. Donald peered up gratefully at her through tear-filled eyes.

"I don't even remember you," he whispered. "How could I have forgotten about you?"

Mary held him and said nothing.

Finally, she prevailed upon Charlene and Nigel to go with her to the hospital to visit Donald.

"He's getting out in a couple of days," she told them. "I'm sure he'll want to thank you for saving his life, Nigel."

Nigel wasn't so sure. What if the sight of him brought back the terror-filled moment when he knew he was about to be discovered in the sewer? But neither Nigel nor Charlene had ever spoken to Donald, and it was quite likely he wouldn't know who they were.

And so, it proved. With Mary talking away and filling in all the little awkward moments, they got through their visit unscathed. So did Donald. He told Mary her daughter was very pretty and polite and he was glad she and that nice young British man who had saved him were getting married. He was sure they'd both be happy.

"Have you ever been married, Donald?" Mary asked him.

"I don't think so. Never met anyone who would have me, I suppose."

Driving back from the hospital, Nigel was very quiet. Charlene concentrated on chatting with her mother. Finally, she could stand Nigel's silence no longer. She turned to him.

"Well, what is it?"

Nigel shook his head. He seemed bewildered. "He's like a different man, isn't he, Charlene? So normal and straightforward. I think he even looks a bit different. And you know what? The biggest surprise?"

"What is it?" she asked again.

"His smile has gone. His tricky, superior, condescending smile, it's gone! Vanished without a trace! Is it possible?"

"Then you've done it, Nigel. You've simply wiped the smile off his face. It has gone, hasn't it?"

"Yes!" yelled Nigel. "Yes and yes! Wiped it off. Now I know what that expression really means," he went on conversationally.

"Well, I think that sounds harsh," said Mary. "Makes me think of you holding him down and slapping him until he stopped smiling."

"I did that, Mary. I made him stop smiling. Only I did it with poison gas, not slaps."

"Poor man, he doesn't remember any of it. But I do really like him. I feel as if I've made a new friend. It's such a shame his company failed, isn't it? And I can't believe it was his fault."

Nigel and Charlene said nothing.

***

Bob and Bernie, the born-again Christians, thought it hilarious that Donald had nearly been gassed to death in a sewer underneath the wormhole cabinet.

"Nearer my God to thee," laughed Bernie. "Only at the end of Donald's ladder, there was a sewer."

"Fitting for a dirty rat," laughed back Bob.

They both forgot now that Donald had been their greatest supporter in their time at Almost Infinity. They only remembered they'd left and he'd stayed. They thought him weak and were contemptuous of him.

"Time travel and wormholes," sneered Bernie. "See where that's gotten them. Let us thank our Lord and Master we are out of that nuthouse. And they were demanding we tell them about mermaid's milk! David was telling me Al had been to see him about setting up a company called Gene-4-Gene. That's gene, numeral four, gene. Cute, isn't it? He's just stringing Al along, of course. If he can get anything good out of him, he'll pass it along to us. I'm frankly amazed Al doesn't realize David is bankrolling us. The ignorance is just staggering!"

Bob shook his head sadly.

"We don't have PhDs, Bernie. That's all Al ever thinks about. But we do have funding though, don't we?"

"We most certainly do," agreed Bernie. "And soon we'll take on more people who've been laid off at Almost Infinity. Not the PhDs, of course, but if someone like Stan or Jeff begs, who knows? There are plenty of clever people up there, people who haven't been brainwashed."

"We'll show them," said Bob. "Fire and ice, that's Deltagene. Fire and ice."

This had become their new mantra since Bob had had the idea of complementing Bernie's fire treatment with a spell on ice. Believing in the concept of what doesn't kill you makes you stronger, they were using these two forces from the physical world to select for super plant cells. They would show everyone. PhDs could never think of this!

***

Nigel and Charlene flew out to Connecticut. Nigel was interviewed for two whole days. His old school chum gave him the impression his hire was a formality, but the big boss gave off more equivocal vibes. He had a PhD from Yale, and his field of study had been insect physiology and genetics. Now he was leading the pharmaceutical company's foray into plant breeding. He reminded Nigel of the old Donald. He had the same superior smile and treated his subordinates with the slightly pained demeanor of one having to deal with inferior intellects. But he was always perfectly polite, personable, and not as shy as Donald.

"It's quite nice here, isn't it?" asked Charlene. "By the seaside and with all these beautiful trees. It's quite dazzling. It rains a lot compared to California, but I'd have thought you would like it. We are, after all, in New England. Not as good as old England for you, but not bad."

"And this is a big company. Substantial, like a university. They'll look after us. The big boss seemed genuinely astonished when I told him we had no money. He thought we would want to buy a house out here if I was offered a job. Apparently, everyone in the department has their own home—I mean *owns* it. No renters here. I told him we couldn't afford that. He said that if I was hired, they would arrange something."

"Our own home." Charlene was enchanted. "That's a thought, Nigel, isn't it?"

"Steady on, old girl. You're talking as if we are going to get married, that we're going to have kids."

"You deserve it," she told him. "You're still a hero in my eyes, don't forget."

A formal offer letter arrived one week after they'd arrived back in California. Nigel and Charlene thought it over for a few days. Now, with offers from the pharmaceutical company and DNACal, the world was their oyster, as Nigel told his lover.

"What the hell are you talking about?" she asked, genuinely puzzled. "The world is our oyster? That sounds deranged. Are you sure you're really all right? Are you quite over your poisoning?"

"You decide. DNACal or Connecticut?"

"My hero," she answered. "I fancy the house in Connecticut."

"Done!" he yelled. "Done and done!"

And from that moment, they didn't think about it any more and began to prepare for the move without fuss.

***

Bob had followed up on the interest of the French cement company. Thankfully, they weren't interested at all in time travel. They only wanted to pursue agriculture. Bob even persuaded them to sign a short-term interim agreement, as part of which the French company was granted the right of first refusal on the purchase of Almost Infinity. They had also provided four hundred thousand dollars to Almost Infinity to preserve its integrity as a going concern. The British Oil Palm company had expressed an interest in time travel, but Bob thought this was a reflexive interest triggered by the company's desire to be seen as faithfully carrying out its due diligence. They were talking now about a collaboration focused on cloning the oil palm tree. They were prepared to invest $3 million in the project.

Now Bob did the right thing. He paid off Almost Infinity's creditors, including all the employees who hadn't been paid and who were still on the books. He paid off Amanda's moving expenses and the first two months of her rent. He formed a new company and offered jobs to all those who were still jobless. He cast about for new investors looking to expand the scope of his new company beyond French cement and British oil palm trees. He talked to David Hallauer, who told him Al had been to see him and was seeking to set up his own company. Gene-4-Gene, it was going to be called. Bob was outraged, but since Almost Infinity hadn't been making payroll, there wasn't much he could do about it. What he did do was formally fire Al. Al told him he was taking Jeff and Oliver with him, and so he formally fired them as well. Shortly after this, Al found out David was ending his interest in Gene-4-Gene. It was, he told Al, in conflict with his interest in Deltagene. Bernie and Bob didn't want him to have any dealings with ex-Almost Infinity folk. He was sure Al would understand. So Al, Jeff, and Oliver were left with nothing but the boot from an angry and resentful Bob.

Nils and Marshall were still hanging around, but Forrest had left. As had Ben Benson. He'd joined a light engineering company a couple of blocks down the street from Almost Infinity, working as a financial manager in charge of payroll. George Nipper was in discussions with Ernie Sikorsky about taking a position at US Home Products in business development. George told Bob he preferred to set himself up as a consultant. Bob wished him luck. If George could get something else, more power to him. Bob decided he was too expensive to take on at the new company anyway. He could offer George a job, but not at the same salary he'd been making at Almost Infinity. It was a conversation Bob didn't want to have.

Peter hadn't had any interest from any position he'd applied for. Bob told him he could work for his new company and that he would be paid soon in addition to the arrears he'd already received. Nigel told Bob he and Charlene were going out to Connecticut to work for a pharmaceutical company. Bob wanted to keep Nigel. The French company was interested in salt tolerance and saw Nigel as an asset. Bob talked to Nigel about the wonders of California, about the sunshine and the pleasant, cool evenings.

"Nowhere is like this," he told him. "You'll never be as happy anywhere else."

"We've got no money, Bob. They are going to help us buy a house. Charlene is pretty happy. Can you match that?"

Bob couldn't. He acquiesced with reluctance to Nigel's intention to leave. He knew Nigel was in the once bitten, twice shy frame of mind. He asked Nils to try his luck.

Nils dutifully turned up on Nigel's doorstep. When Nigel opened the front door to him, he was confronted with a beaming Nils presenting him with a big thumbs-up sign. "Hello, Nigel."

"Hello Nils. What's the good news?"

"What?"

"The thumbs-up sign."

"Oh, I just want you to be happy. That's all that means."

"Really? All this time we were thinking you must know something. But you were just wanting us to be happy?

"Afraid so."

Nigel found himself thinking of Lynne, Nils's former secretary. He realized she'd taken her lead from Nils in her response to bad news. Good news, however, even if it wasn't really that, had brought out exhortations to prayer, and that was Lynne being herself.

Nils followed him through the house and then out onto the patio. They both sat down. Nils smiled at Nigel. Nigel waited for him to speak, but he said nothing. Nigel was thinking of how Stan, Jeff, and Oliver always referred to the great Dane—he was always "the big doofus."

"Well," said Nigel, at last, "what's the good word?"

"Bob tells me you're moving to Connecticut."

"That's right," Nigel nodded. "We're leaving the first of the year."

"It'll be cold there, maybe even snowing. Have you thought about what you'll be missing here? The sunshine and the blue skies, the lovely cool evenings? Isn't this just too beautiful? Life's too short for snow."

"It is beautiful," agreed Nigel. "But Charlene and I weren't paid for three weeks. We still have no money. We can't afford to stay here."

"Bob told me to tell you the both of you are going to get a check to address salary concerns. And he's going to cut you both new checks as an advance on your jobs in his new company. So money won't be a problem for you at all."

"They are going to help us buy a house in Connecticut."

Nils grinned foolishly at him. He was thinking he knew any number of plant scientists as good or better than Nigel. But would any of them be daring enough to come out to join Bob's new company after what had happened to the old one? He doubted he could persuade anyone credible to take such a chance.

Nigel wanted to know more about Nils's perspective on the debacle.

"And what about the name, Nils? Why was it called Almost Infinity? Why not just Infinity?"

"Donald did explain it to me. It was the first question I asked him when he and Bob recruited me. He said he just liked the name and it would allow him to judge people's understanding of the company's goals. Well, I don't know how true that was in practice. It's a paradox, you see. You can't have almost infinity. Either there is infinity, or it doesn't exist. There is no 'almost.' It was, he said, the same with time travel. This wasn't airplane flight where you could get the wheels off the ground for a few seconds and then gradually extend it. Time travel was all or nothing."

"Did he say he could do it, then? That he could travel in time?"

"Oh yes, of course. He was quite definite about that. You heard him, didn't you? You have to remember that."

"Yes, Nils, I do remember, but then I found him in the sewer. Once I saw him in there, there was no time travel. And then there was no Almost Infinity."

"Just stick around, Nigel. You're going to regret running out on us. This is a once in a lifetime opportunity for you."

"Can't do it, Nils. Got to think about Charlene, you see. We want kids. So I'm looking for something safe, now."

Nils realized it was pointless to pursue the matter further.

"Well, I hope you two aren't making a mistake. If, when you get out there, you have second thoughts, don't hesitate to call me. We can always work something out."

Nigel walked back with him through the house to the front door. Nils grinned at him as he prepared to get into his car.

"Stan thinks you nearly murdered him and Donald."

"Stan's an animal," said Nigel reflexively. "But I have to admit, that is a thought that's occurred to me. They could both have died, and it would have been my fault. If only I hadn't been such a show-off."

"Almost Infinity," said Nils, returning to the topic of the company's name, "can, as I understand it, also refer to a very, very large number. Just not an infinite one. Donald said the concept was needed for the math to work. Told me that cosmologists and mathematicians would understand it."

"There is no math, Nils. Donald just made everything up." Nigel held out his hand. "Well, goodbye, Nils. I'm sure we'll see each other at conferences and suchlike."

Nils shook his hand and smiled his goofy smile. He got into his car and drove away. Nigel never saw him again.

***

"What's Mary up to?" Nigel asked Charlene as they started another meal without her.

"She seems to be spending all her time with Donald these days. She goes over to his house practically every day. I've told her everything I know about him, which really isn't all that much. She just listens and smiles."

"What did you say about him?"

Charlene shrugged. "Oh, you know, about him always seeming so superior, always telling us about math only he could understand, about his smirking, self-congratulatory smile, about him producing items from the future, and finally, about claiming to go there himself. Of course, she was here for that part of the story and saw it for herself. She seems puzzled. She told me the other day it was almost as if Donald was two different people. She told me the Donald she is getting to know is just nothing like the person I'm describing. She says he is modest and rarely smiles at all. I think she is getting serious about him. She is so softhearted and just feels sorry for him. She only ever hears unkind remarks about him from our friends at work. Remember that barbeque we were at the other night, where everybody was laughing about Donald's famous smile? She couldn't understand it. She said she'd never seen him smile like that. And she took offense at being told he was a liar. 'He's never told me any lies,' she said to me later. How is it that she sees him so differently than everyone else?"

Nigel sat and stared at her. She'd spoken facts as they were known to her. She hadn't given him an account of her feelings or impressions. She'd told him her mother had said Donald didn't smile a lot, that he was modest and didn't tell lies. The Donald Nigel knew could never be described like this. Of course he told lies! They'd found him in a sewer, hadn't they? There was no getting out of that. There was only one possible conclusion.

"Maybe he has changed. We both noticed how oddly he was behaving when we went to see him in the hospital, didn't we? I even thought he looked different. The superiority and smugness seemed to have vanished. His smile was gone. What has happened to him?"

Charlene was, as usual, attentive to detail.

"Did we know him well enough before his poisoning to even have an opinion? Maybe nothing happened to him. Maybe he's just ashamed."

CHAPTER 33

The End Again ... Really

DONALD WASN'T ASHAMED. Mary had told him he'd been pretending to be a time traveler. And that made him smile. Donald didn't doubt Mary was telling him the truth but was unable to recognize himself.

"I can't believe I did that, Mary. And everyone believed me? Why?"

"Well, Nigel tells me they all believed you because you had done the math."

"What math? I'd really like to see it."

One day, when Mary was visiting him at his apartment, Bob stopped by with some papers for Donald to sign, papers documenting the formal end of Almost Infinity. The two men said very little to each other, and Donald had signed everything without comment. Mary accompanied Bob to the front door.

"Have you known Donald long?" he asked her as he paused to say goodbye before getting into his car.

"Only a few weeks," Mary told him. "I'm Charlene's mother."

And then, when it became clear Bob had no idea who Charlene was, Mary added: "Nigel and Charlene."

"Nigel," repeated Bob, apprehension dawning in his face. "Of course, Charlene is Nigel's girlfriend, right?"

"Fiancée," said Mary. "They'll be getting married soon."

Bob shook Mary's hand.

"Well, it was very nice to meet you." He waved a hand at Donald's domicile. "He's changed, hasn't he? He doesn't even look like the Donald of old."

Mary smiled at him. "That's the only Donald I've ever known," she said apologetically. Then: "Oh, and ... er, Bob. Do you know where the math is? Donald is asking for it. Everyone says he has done the math but he can't remember it. And now there doesn't seem to be any."

Bob stared at her. Her words brought it all back to him. The math is calling for it, it's required by the math, pieces of pork, grains of salt, slivers of bark, chopped up cigarettes—it was as if they had all been suffering from a shared insanity. And now it had passed. There was only this pleasant, cheerful, middle-aged woman left with an extinct Donald. A Donald freed from the eruptions of pseudologia fantastica, a disease which no one knew he'd had or recovered from. They were the eruptions that had passed over them all, like bursts of a furious wind blowing away life's doubts and uncertainties.

***

Amanda went to work to see Bob. She wanted to know what was happening. She noted the return of paper towels and toilet tissue to the bathrooms. She also noted the return of operational coffee machines. Bob put the phone down and looked at her as she came into his office.

"We're back, baby!" he called out exuberantly.

The smart, slim blonde looked appraisingly at him.

"Really, Bob? That's good to hear. But you mean you're back. Everyone else seems to have left."

Bob waved his hand good-humoredly.

"How would you like to be Director of Molecular Biology? The position is open, and you've got a PhD, haven't you? You'd be perfect for it."

"Do I get a raise?" she asked immediately.

"Sure, why not?"

"Let's say I'm interested then and that I'll probably take you up on your offer. But first I'm going to have to see a check. You can't blame me for being cautious, can you? After that business with my moving expenses and then not being paid for three weeks."

Bob slapped his big paw onto the desk in front of him.

"We've got money again now. And I'm going to want you to come out to dinner with me and the French delegation, when it arrives. We have to put our best foot forward there. You were at Yale, weren't you? You'll do very nicely."

Amanda laughed, a bright tinkle of sound.

"You're incorrigible, Bob. You're fat and old but you do have a certain charm."

Bob's eyes widened in wonder at the young woman's brutal frankness. He laughed and waved a meaty hand at her.

"I'm going to have to keep my eye on you," he said jovially.

"So no more time travel, Bob?"

"It's a thing of the past," he quipped. "I've forgotten about it already."

"What's our new company called, then?"

"You think of a name and tell me this afternoon. And think of some clever device to go along with the name. We can get envelopes and writing paper made up right away. And business cards."

"Yes, sir!"

Bob leaned back in his executive armchair and commanded: "Sit down. I want to talk to you."

She did as he bid. He looked her over, noting her bare knees and thin muscular legs. He was really going to enjoy being around such a bright, desirable young woman. He would have to make sure he kept her away from his wife. His face grew reflective.

"You know, I'm going to miss Donald."

"Almost Infinity," said Amanda. "That's a paradox, Bob. You knew that, didn't you."

Until she'd said it, the name had passed from his mind completely. In any case, he wanted to forget it. He looked back at her with his mouth hanging slightly open. "What do you mean—a paradox?"

"Well, we can't imagine infinity. No one can. We can only imagine a very large number or a very large amount of something. Oh, all the clever dicks talk about rooms in hotels and God knows what else, but none of that can ever be infinity. We can always imagine adding a little more to any huge entity we can come up with. This means that something can never be infinity. And, conversely, infinity can never be something. So there is no such thing as almost infinity or, indeed, infinity itself. It's like us trying to imagine nothing. We just can't do it. Infinity and nothing are the same in that regard. We can't imagine either of them. They are outside our limits, Bob. The first thing for us to recognize is that humans have limits."

"I can imagine nothing," protested Bob. "It's not difficult at all. I'm thinking about it right now. It's a space with absolutely nothing in it. No atoms, no particles, no gravity—simply empty space. I really can see it now."

Amanda looked fondly at the fat, sharp-eyed man sitting in front of her. She was just so much cleverer than him it almost hurt her to think about it.

"And does your space have boundaries, Bob?"

"Of course! It has to have, doesn't it?"

"Well, if it's got boundaries, it's not nothing. The somethingness of your nothing is established by its boundaries. We can't think of nothing because we happen to be something. Infinity is something with no end. Unimaginable for us. We, after all, are mortal. You see, we tell ourselves we can imagine these things. But we can't. It's physically impossible. All or nothing. Both unimaginable. I really like the people who tell me we will be able to imagine infinity in heaven. But you know what that means, don't you?"

"What?" croaked Bob, overwhelmed by Amanda's flinty intellect.

"All we are saying there, Bob, is that we can't imagine heaven. And that, everyone agrees, is outside our limits. We accept that. We welcome it, in fact. I know I do. You see, I'm not an atheist, Bob.

No, I believe in the reality that exists between all or nothing. And in that reality, we have religion. Believe it or not, I actually believe in Jesus. He performed a miracle I can understand. And what was this miracle, I hear you ask? He introduced into our lives the notion of us living selflessly and helping each other out. Of loving each other. I can imagine a world like that, and some people even try to live their lives according to his teachings. Not many, I accept, but if only everyone would give it a shot. Isn't that a much more attractive world than the world of multiverses and wormholes, of eleven dimensions and black holes? Of course, it is! And best of all, it's something everyone can understand. It's not something restricted to an elite. And that's important, Bob."

"But what about your tits?" blurted out Bob desperately, sounding positively deranged in his eagerness to gain a measure of control over the conversation. "Everyone, every man that is, can imagine lavishing attention on them."

"Not everyone, Bob. But you, certainly. I can't help that. You have to control you." She smiled at him. "You're not a bad man, Bob. You're trying your best. You wanted to believe in Donald, didn't you? I think we all did. After that first demonstration, he had me hopelessly confused. I kind of lost my bearings then. I could have spent years in the grip of Sodom. Like a lot of Californians, I expect. Money and sex. That would have been enough for me until I got old. Thoughts of Jesus were forgotten. But look what happens. Donald turns up in a sewer and Jesus comes roaring back. The scales fell from my eyes. So yes, I'll be your director. But know who you've got. Donald's poisoning has sobered me up. Are you sure you still want me?"

Bob continued to goggle at her. He looked as if he were contemplating a life-form from another planet.

"Oh yes," he whispered, at last. "I still want you."

"Hope springs eternal," said Amanda, with a light laugh.

***

Peter wandered about sadly in the deserted lab. Nigel never came in now. He was leaving with Charlene for Connecticut in the very near future. Peter had seen Stan once, but Stan had ignored him. He'd seen Bob a few times and Nils once. No one seemed very keen to talk to him. He came into the office and sat down at his desk. He was sitting there when Amanda suddenly breezed in.

"Hiya, Pete! How are you doing?"

His eyes leapt to her. He was ecstatic to see her.

"Amanda! Where have you been? I've been all on my own."

"The frogs are on the march, Pete. They'll be here next week, and I'm looking to you to blind them with science. Have you been paid in full?"

Peter shook his head.

"I got one check, but that was all. Have you?"

"I'm going to take care of it for you, Pete. You'll get all the money that's owed to you tomorrow. And now you're working for a new company."

Peter registered that, for some reason, Amanda was in the know and he wasn't. But he was too excited to see her to think much about it.

"A new company?" he echoed. "What's it called?"

"I'm calling it Plum."

"But what's its name?"

"I told you—Plum."

"That's what you are calling it, Amanda. What's everyone else calling it?"

"Plum. Bob asked me to name it, and that's what I decided. In honor of our former founder, of course."

Peter began to look irritated. Amanda might be pretty, but she could certainly get on his nerves.

"He's not the founder of the new company, Amanda. He was the founder of Almost Infinity. He was a 'time traveler,' remember?" He held up his hands and curled his fingers to frame the words with air quotes as he said this. "Everyone wants to forget him. You can't call it Plum."

"Why not? It's trendy, and it has significance for Bob, our new founder. If you can call a company Apple, I don't see why you can't call one Plum. And I've thought of a great logo too."

Peter held his head in his hands. Suddenly, he felt very tired. "What is it?"

She placed a blank sheet of paper in front of him.

"It's what you're going to come up with, Pete. I've thought about you quite a lot recently. You've got a streak of artistic flair, haven't you? Go on, tell me I'm wrong. And now that I'm your boss, I can tell you to do anything. If you do a good job, I might order you to kiss me."

Peter's tiredness was instantly forgotten. Kiss her! He'd never kissed anyone unless you counted his mother and the little girl they'd made him kiss at his eighth birthday party. Kiss Amanda! He looked up at her face and noted the adorable nose and lips. She smiled slightly. He took in her eyebrows and cheeks and then moved on to look into her eyes.

"I'll give it my best shot," he whispered fervently.

Men really are idiots, thought Amanda. She ruffled his hair and stroked his cheek. He looked up at her, ready now to pledge himself to her eternally.

"Be a good boy then, Pete, and go and get the logo worked up, ready to print and copy. Come and show it to me before you copy."

She went out, leaving him staring at the blank paper. His mind was in turmoil. He'd felt the first stirrings of jealousy when she'd come into the office, but now that was forgotten. She'd said she was his boss. What did that mean? Was she serious? But she'd also said she might order him to kiss her. Oh, he would definitely raise no objections to that! The thought transported him. He just couldn't think clearly at a time like this. She had stroked his cheek! It was simply impossible!

***

Nigel and Charlene were sitting in the departure lounge at San Francisco Airport. They were about to board their flight to the East Coast. They had taken their leave of Mary and Donald a few moments earlier, but otherwise there had been no farewells. They had both felt themselves delivered into the care of their new company the moment the movers had shown up. They hadn't been required to lift a finger to help with the move. The movers hadn't wanted any help. Their treatment of the young couple had made Nigel feel like royalty, or at least how he imagined royalty felt, as they moved around the world.

"Please be so good as to load up our collection of sticks and rags, my good man," Nigel had announced to the bemused foreman of the moving crew as he opened the front door to him, an opening command that had created an immediate and unbreachable barrier to any further meaningful communication with the movers.

Nigel and Charlene had hung around watching as their belongings were bundled up, boxed, and carried out to the waiting truck. Their possessions were to go into storage until they had found a house to buy. They had spent the previous night in a hotel room, and they both felt somehow disengaged from the Bay Area now. It was no longer their home. Now they were merely visitors, passing through. Their thoughts had already moved on to Connecticut. And, wonder of wonders, for the last three days it had been pouring down with rain. This had taken Nigel completely by surprise. A curtain was being drawn on their time in the Bay Area. This Nigel knew. He just hadn't expected it to be a curtain of rain.

Nigel looked around the departure lounge. There were the usual business types, families with small and some not-so-small children. To his left, he noticed two young women sitting too close together to be mere acquaintances. Family, perhaps? Then he watched as they allowed their lips to brush together in an unmistakable display of intimacy. He turned his head away from the private moment only to find himself staring at two men engaged in the identical behavior to his right.

"Only in San Francisco," he whispered to the grinning Charlene. "It's the sunshine. No one can resist its warm but not-too-warm invitation. But even that seems to have come to an end for us, doesn't it? What's love got to do with it?"

* * *

Mary and Donald walked hand-in-hand out of the airport. Donald couldn't believe his luck in having found Mary. She wasn't a young head turner, but she was nice to look at and pleasant to be around. She was so optimistic. Donald felt as if something good had come into his life at the very moment something bad had departed. That good was, of course, Mary. The bad he wasn't sure about. The bad was only vaguely perceived; it was nothing clear, it wasn't even a memory. It was, of course, the pseudologia fantastica, mysteriously driven out of him by the lungfuls of hydrogen sulfide he'd inhaled. It was, like all mental illness, insidious and almost completely invisible to the sufferer.

Donald had been enjoying conversations with Mary without realizing they were the first conversations he'd had in the last twenty years when he hadn't felt the need to boast and tell stories. A couple of nights ago, Mary had kissed him on the lips and told him she really liked him. Donald had been floored. No one had ever spoken to him like that before, and of course, he'd never been kissed. He asked her to move in with him, and she agreed. She was still sleeping in his spare room, but he knew it was only a matter of time before they shared a bed.

He hadn't told her yet he was still a virgin. But he was definitely going to. Charlene had been completely supportive of her mother as she embarked upon the relationship with Donald. She and Nigel both realized Donald had undergone some kind of transformation. It was as if a new human being had been born, fully formed, and had taken the place of the old Donald. If there were such a thing as time travel, this was it. They certainly didn't hold his past against him.

"Maybe he is a time traveler after all. Where did this Donald come from? He was lucky you poisoned him and wiped that smile off his face," Charlene had told Nigel. "Who would have thought there was such a nice man hidden behind such an ugly mask?"

***

Oliver was standing at his desk, wondering what he wanted to take with him. He'd just begun sorting through a stack of reprints when he caught a glimpse of Al standing at his desk in his office. He walked over to the open door.

"Just getting ready to take off, Al. Bob fired me this morning. I've got to be out by the end of the day. Is there anything you can do for me? Get him to change his mind?"

Al looked at him and smiled grimly. "He fired me too, Oliver. Word got to him I'd been talking to David Hallauer about starting up my own shop. He got quite prickly, told me he couldn't let anything jeopardize his deal with that French cement company. So he was letting me go. I don't have the stomach for any more of this business, Oliver. I'm going back to the Midwest. Heading first to Madison for an interview. There are several universities that have shown interest in having me on their faculty. Have to start writing grants again, I guess."

Oliver looked at Al and noted a touch of despair in his manner. He was quite a big man, slow of speech and action. Oliver wondered how often in his life he had faced such ignominy. He thought perhaps never. Al was moving about deliberately, loading up a couple of cardboard boxes that were standing on his desk. He looked as if he was taking comfort in the fact that he had something to do.

"I don't have anything yet. He must have found out about my involvement with Gene-4-Gene, but he didn't tell me that. Jeff got fired today, as well. Seems he's pretty ruthless if he thinks you're a competitor. Anyway, he doesn't have to worry about us. Jeff and I have no contacts in the VC world. I guess we are just not as charismatic as Bob and Bernie."

Al's face had darkened as he realized he'd been the one who had gotten Jeff and Oliver fired. Why hadn't he kept his mouth shut about taking them with him? He focused his anger on Bob and Bernie.

"Bob and Bernie aren't scientists, Oliver. They are cult leaders, snake oil salesmen. They are not like Donald. Donald really believed in what he was selling even though it was quite mad. Bob and Bernie know what they are selling is pure horseshit. They've got energy though, and they'll flourish in the sunshine. They'll get money, but of course, nothing will ever come out of their outfit. I don't want to be part of this bizarre world any longer and neither, I think, do you. You're a bright guy, Oliver. Your time will come. Me? I'm too old now. I don't have the energy to waste talking to all these know-nothings. Life's too short."

Oliver agreed, and on this note they parted.

***

Bob sat at his desk and looked sadly at Nils. The big Dane had on his usual goofy smile. Bob wondered what he and Donald had ever seen in him. He wore his smart sports jacket and fashionable narrow pants. And he was definitely handsome in a rugged sort of way. But boy, was he naïve. Bob wasn't sure where to start. He roused himself and smiled across at him.

"Well, Nils, that was Almost Infinity. Quite a ride, wasn't it?"

Nils flashed a broader smile back at him, and Bob was put in mind of the powerful Kennedy family with its toothy charm.

"What are you going to do now?"

Nils still didn't say anything. He raised a hand and gave Bob his trademark thumbs-up sign.

"So you've got something lined up, then?" asked Bob, surprised. "That's great. Well, this will have to be the last week with us, Nils. We're moving on, and we've got nothing for a man with your skills and experience."

The truth was the French didn't want him. Bob had saddled him with Almost Infinity's failure, but Bob wasn't going to tell him that.

Nils's smile took on a slightly fixed look.

"There's no one else left to observe the formalities, Nils. Ben Benson has moved on, and George Nipper left to become a consultant. He and his family moved to Milwaukee. Forrest has retired, and Marshall has gone back to teaching. Al has left by mutual consent. I don't know where Arthur is, and I'm not sure what direction my own life is going to go in at the moment. So you've got something, then? That's good."

Nils continued to watch him silently. Bob waved a hand and stood up. It was early afternoon. Outside it was, once again, warm and sunny. A gentle breeze wafted over San Carlos. The sky was, as usual, a brilliant blue. In gardens all around, the plants shone a vibrant green. Blossoms were everywhere, eye-catching and colorful. Roads wound up and down in the hills that overlooked the bay. Everyone lived a private life in this glorious paradise. Lovers of all ages and affiliations hurried to and from midday trysts. Marriages flourished and creaked, little kids were oblivious, the older ones wondered. Up in Belmont, a wind soughed through the trees and briefly burdened their branches with its gentle caress. The wind headed out languidly to the coast, carrying with it dreams of time travel and heaven on earth. It passed almost silently over the invisible sewers of Half Moon Bay.

But it was all okay. No one, especially not Nils, could resist the weather for very long. It was always going to be the good life in sunny California.

ACKNOWLEDGMENTS

The author would like to thank the team at Warren publishing (Karli Jackson, Monika Dziamka, Melissa Long, Amy Ashby, and Mindy Kuhn) for their unfailing good taste and humor throughout the editorial process. They made the book better, and it was a pleasure working with them.